To Allan,
Best wishes 79.

Willie

KU-287-579

THE BOOK OF SECRETS

Fiona Kidman was born in 1940 and spent her early years in northern New Zealand. After working as a librarian and later as a columnist, critic and writer for television and radio, she committed herself to serious fiction writing in the late 1970s. She now has eleven books in print. Her first novel, *A Breed of Women* was published in 1979. She has held a number of major writing appointments and has been twice awarded the New Zealand Literary Fund Scholarship in Letters. She is well-known as a teacher of creative writing and has recently received an OBE. Her novel, *The Book of Secrets,* won the 1988 New Zealand Book Award for fiction.

Fiona Kidman lives in Wellington.

Books by Fiona Kidman

THE BOOK OF SECRETS

FIONA KIDMAN

PUBLISHED BY PAN BOOKS
Auckland, Sydney and London

A Pan/Heinemann Book

First published 1987 by Heinemann Publishers (N.Z.) Ltd
This Picador edition published 1988 by
Pan Books (New Zealand) Ltd
29 Pearn Crescent, Northcote, Auckland 9
in association with Heinemann Publishers (N.Z.) Ltd

9 8 7 6 5 4 3 2

© Fiona Kidman

ISBN 0 330 27140 7

This book is sold subject to the condition that it
shall not, by way of trade or otherwise, be lent, re-sold,
hired out or otherwise circulated without the publisher's prior
consent in any form of binding or cover other than that in which
it is published and without a similar condition including this
condition being imposed on the subsequent purchaser.

Printed and bound in Australia by
The Book Printer, Victoria

For Amelia Herrero-Kidman

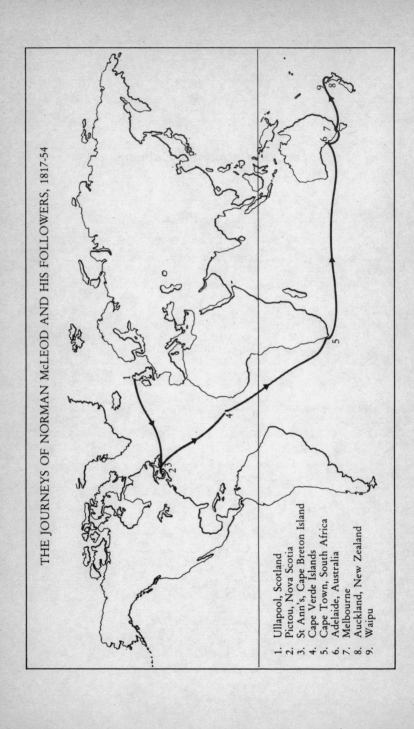

THE JOURNEYS OF NORMAN McLEOD AND HIS FOLLOWERS, 1817-54

1. Ullapool, Scotland
2. Pictou, Nova Scotia
3. St Ann's, Cape Breton Island
4. Cape Verde Islands
5. Cape Town, South Africa
6. Adelaide, Australia
7. Melbourne
8. Auckland, New Zealand
9. Waipu

CONTENTS

PREFACE

Norman McLeod was a real person, as were many of the people described as having accompanied him on his journeys. They really did undertake the migrations in the circumstances of the book. Beyond this, the work is fiction. All of the people on the Ramsey family tree are fictitious, and so are the family members of Eoghann MacKenzie. Any names or likenesses to people, living or dead, in those contexts, are coincidental.

I thank my many informants who spent valuable hours with me; and several more who offered help but whom I was prevented from meeting because of time or distance. For very practical help, I am especially grateful to Warwick Flaus and his wife Janet Cameron, Wellington; John and Sherry McPherson, Halifax, N.S., and Clinton and Jean McPherson, Port Morien, N.S.

The people of Waipu set me on the book's path many years ago, and during their lifetimes the late Misses Lang gave invaluable advice. All of them are remembered with affection and respect.

Thanks are due, too, to Marvin Wodinsky and other staff at the Canadian High Commission in Wellington; to very kind staff at both Public Archives in Halifax, N.S., and at the Beaton Institute, University College of Cape Breton; and also at the Gaelic College, St Ann's, N.S., and the Alexander Turnbull Library in Wellington.

In 1985 I held the New Zealand Scholarship in Letters; it was essential to the writing of this book.

PART ONE

THE HOUSE

1

MARIA WAS OLD and the stairs were steep. There was a wind that evening, not a high one, but a persistent singing across the sea. The old timber creaked, the iron on the roof was almost rusted through; another winter or so and it would be through all over. Already she kept a large china bowl under the leak in the corner of her room.

The state of the roof did not unduly worry her. It would hold for another year or so and that would be long enough. Maria did not intend to live forever. But tonight she was tired, although she didn't know why, for she had done little except walk to the gate to collect her deliveries after the grocer had left them. They had not spoken to each other, nor had they done so for more than fifty years. It was not the same grocer of course, they had come and gone. The gate was too far away for her to get a good look at them when they stopped, but she always knew when there was a new one. Sooner or later he would have to write a note in response to hers. This was how they did business, she and the men at the store. Each week she wrote a list of the things she needed, and the next week the goods were delivered.

But things had changed as the years passed. They no longer supplied calico, molasses was not always available, there was a shortage of wheat meal, or worse, they did not always know what her orders meant. Once she sent for a stone jar; they sent her back a curious flat bag called a hot water bottle. It took several weeks of notes to establish what this was all about. She nearly went to see the man at the gate but this seemed to be tempting fate.

Doing things this way had worked for so many years that it seemed unwise to alter the pattern. Besides, Maria did not know for sure whether they would allow her to speak with the grocer. Perhaps it no longer mattered what she did, or to whom she spoke, but there were other times when she could not be sure. The edges of the past blurred and fused with the present.

It actually frightened her to think that she might be able to walk through the grass and across the paddock, to open the gate and keep on walking along the dusty path that ran to the village, and into the shop itself, and that no one would stop her. Maybe they wouldn't even notice.

When she was half way up the ladder-like stairs, holding onto the slight rail as she went, one thickened hand after another, there was a smash below, the glass in a window breaking downstairs.

After that, there was a silence for a moment. But then a sound both delicate and biting followed, as if some of the glass had caught on the window ledge, hovered and balanced, then tinkled to the floor.

Voices called. *Ma-ri-a . . . Ma-ri-aa.* Young voices distilled on the night breeze.

Another window smashed.

Maria? It was a question on the wind now. Would she answer them? *Mari-aa.* Laughter.

Yes, they would notice if she walked down the road. They had not forgotten she was here.

The voices moved away.

Maria was panting with exertion as she reached the top of the stairs. She was not afraid. Fear had flown out the window long before the rocks came through. But if she was honest with herself, there was still anger. It was not just the climb which made her breath rasp.

Three. Three panes now. There were three gaping holes at the front of the house and there was no paper or sacking left to block them up. Why did they do it to her? Would they like to see her ride out of the window onto the old macrocarpa tree on a broomstick? Eh? Was that what they would like? Ah, that she could have flown.

She knew little about flight. But she knew there were aeroplanes. She did not keep in touch with the world and time passed without her always knowing what month, or even year it was, and for the most part she had shunned the newspapers which could have been brought to her house in the delivery van if she chose. But she had avoided seeking them out since the last ones had been used to reline the walls of her bedroom. They were still on her bedroom walls, yellow and brittle with age, the year 1897, the year the world had stopped. Or she had stopped being in the world. It was neither here nor there.

But every now and then one would arrive wrapped around her orders, and then secretly, as if in some perverse rite at which someone might catch her, she would scan each word, reading and re-reading the page and storing it under her bed to look at again some day.

So she had come to know one or two things that went on in the world.

And she had seen the plane overhead, she knew what they were.

Would she have flown if she could? Maria did not know for sure any more, and only vaguely recollected that once, of her own accord, she had made a decision to remain here.

Perhaps fate, and the Man, had decreed that she should be here. Though they were one and the same. Her kinsfolk would say it was God, but she knew better. She thought it was the devil, and to be afraid was pointless for she was committed to darkness and the devil. They were part of a logical process that would never end. There was no heaven.

Something brushed her face, and she almost dropped her candle. Ah— now she was frightened.

But it was a tiny trapped sparrow, more frightened than she was, that had flown in through one of the broken panes.

Ah, her voice soothed—there, there, hush little bird. Don't be afraid— quiet now, quiet, you'll beat yourself to death on the rafters. Poor little bird, what were you doing out so late? There now, don't break yourself.

The sparrow clung to the ceiling beam, tottering as if stunned. She thought it would fall but it recovered itself, staring at her with tiny terrified eyes, its breast rising and falling, the feathers fluffed and trembling.

Well well. Nobody ever asks if they can come in here. Nothing comes for years and then sooner or later there's always something comes crashing through without asking.

—That being the case I suppose there's no point in telling you to go. No doubt you'll stay here as long as it's convenient to you—

She put the candle on the dresser and climbed into bed, then remembered that her hot water bottle was still downstairs. She shivered. It was a long way to go down again. It would be cold by now anyway, lying on the kitchen table, and she had banked the fire up for the night so that it would take a long time to heat more water. She would have to go cold. The blankets were so thin you could see the light through them when they hung on the line for their summer wash. They scratched against her chin.

The bird stirred on the rafter, stretched its wings and cheeped.

In spite of the wind, she slept. She dreamed.

PART TWO

MARIA:
TELLING IT
1953

2

I HAVE LIVED alone in this house for a long time. I have not kept records. I do not have marks on the wall, or diaries, though I am the keeper of certain books which do not belong to me but have fallen into my hands. I have a suspicion that these things never happen entirely by chance, for among them is what I call the book of secrets. This was my grandmother's way of telling it, the secrets of her life. They are secrets to which I am linked through being her kin, and we are bound by the common thread of my mother's life. Once I would have dismissed this as being of no importance but now I can no longer ignore it, the binding together which it made. We all had a voice, a way of telling it.

I will come back to the secrets, for they haunt me always, but now it is time for me to tell it, for myself. I tell it aloud as I go, here in this house, though no one can hear me while my hands move across the page.

I am Maria McClure. I was born at Waipu, a coastal village in the northern part of New Zealand, in 1878, twelve years after the Man died. The birth took place in this same old house that I live in now, a board house of two storeys, near the river arm that comes in from the sea.

The house stands alone in a paddock. At the back are macrocarpa trees, and alongside of it a single stark, skeletal giant that has been stripped of its leaves by lightning. The great tree just died. It is not entirely safe, so close to the house, but no one would think to remove it. It stands there bleached white now as the years pass and sometimes in high winds I imagine that it will fall over but it never does.

I think it is about fifty-five years that I have been on my own. I live away from the society of people in the world.

I say in the world, though it is difficult to say much about what the world is like, or what it means to the people who have joined it. I doubt if there are many still alive of those whom I knew when I was forced to abandon their company.

There is only one, whom I dream of seeing, and she came later.

Is she alive out there in the world?

I have come a long way by snow and ice to this land of sunlight.

I? Maybe not I, but those I spoke of, the ones who came before.

I spoke of a Man. His name was Norman McLeod, whom the people also called Tormod. He led a group of men and women across the wide world from the Highlands of Scotland to Pictou in Nova Scotia to St Ann's on Cape Breton Island to Australia to New Zealand. The journeying took thirty-five years, and longer for some. It was like Moses in the wilderness. It was done in the name of God.

He was born near Stoer Point in rugged Assynt, Sutherland County, Scotland, in 1780.

His parents lived by the parted rocks at Clachtoll in a house of stone and turf. His mother gave birth to him at harvest time when the barley was being gathered, by the light of a fire fuelled with bog fir. The slate grey Atlantic bore a rim of silver on its horizon, but close at hand the wild green sea pounded on the headland of streaming rocks. The machair grass tossed in the wind and a violence was on the land.

McLeod grew tall, and his eyes turned also to cool slate. He had black hair when the journeys began and a lean hard mouth in a thin face. My grandmother said it was a cruel mouth. Others, when they spoke of him, said that he was a caring man who did what he believed was right for the people who followed him. But across the breadth of the world they could not decide whether he really knew what was right for them or not. Now he has lain in the cemetery by the sea for close to ninety years and still, I'll wager, there will be some who cannot agree. There is no doubt in my mind that he was proud, and that his pride led him to harsh ways. He thought that he knew better than all the Church of Scotland, believed that he had discovered a better path for his people to follow (indeed, you would think he had invented it) and that they were like children who would not know what was in their own best interests. I call that pride. I have been accused of the sin of pride myself, and look where it has landed me. I will shortly tell you.

One thing is sure, that when the people in the community spoke of the Man, there was only one person to whom they were referring. Around these parts there are many strange names given to men—they are called the 'Bear' and 'Prince', 'Captain', 'Red', 'the Black', 'the Strong One' and other names to identify one from the other, but if anyone said 'the Man', then there was only one and it was him. Though he did call himself Norman, like the Apostle Paul of old. He thought of himself as one with Paul.

His people, who were also mine, were driven out of the north-west Highlands of Scotland by the terrible clearances of the crofters a hundred and fifty years back. The crofting people had occupied cottages and land owned by the lairds, since time immemorial. The lairds were like fathers to them, they would do pretty much anything that a laird wanted, including defend him and fight for him. They never thought that they would be evicted from their homes, but things changed after Culloden and Bonnie Prince Charlie. The lairds said they had been betrayed; they were hungry devils who wanted some reason to put the people off the land. That is how it has been told to me. They wanted to run sheep on the land, blackfaces they called them, and there was no room for men and women and children alongside of sheep. They wanted also to make money from the kelp industry. This was a cruel affair, for the people who worked it got killed in the freezing waters of the Atlantic. Oh, but it was very profitable though.

I know about these things because my grandmother told me of them, my grandmother Isabella MacQuarrie, the one they did say that I took after, a wild one, yes, they said it was her I might thank for my wild and wicked ways that have put me away inside this old house far from the sight of decent men and women and certainly of children for fifty-five years. Thanks to her, they say, I am called the witch of Waipu. They may think I do not know of this, but I know more than they think. I know things because I hear them come through the ground in the night, I press my ear to the ground and the word travels; the damp smell of the earth is a revelation. Thank God, I say, for one day I will be put in it for good and it is a fine thing to know I will go on hearing things down there. I am not afraid of being locked in that fastness, the earth is a warm blanket full of hum and carry on. And I can hear stories on the breeze at morning, in the crackle of crickets in the midday sun, and in the birdsong at evening. Ah the old woman is truly mad, she hears voices, they do well to shun me. No, I tell you it is them that are mad and do not know what is all around them, for I have learned many things, here in my board house by the sea, and I have been told things. For I have not always been alone.

I was banished to this house for the sin of fornication. I was a girl of just twenty years when I met Branco the road mender. At that time the north was full of dark men from Dalmatia, which from my random newspapers I now know as part of Yugoslavia. All the good British people (with whom the Scots were for better or worse lumped in) did not like the Dalmatians in their midst. They were great gum gatherers. That is, they dug out of the ground lumps of a clear hard substance called kauri gum, bright gold in colour though it was translucent. It was used for making varnishes and polishes and it was valuable. They called it poor man's gold, although a man who was prepared to dig in mud and filth, and not give up on it too easily, could get rich with greater certainty than those who sought gold. That was what the Scots and English would do, not take it seriously, just go on digging for a bit when it suited them and not stick with it. But the Dalmatian, well, he would dig and dig, and take his pickings to the trading post and get his money and go back to the fields and go at it again and again, and after a while he'd accumulate enough money to buy a farm and the others would have nothing, like as not drank it away. They got to believing that the Dallies were stealing from them; they certainly felt superior. And some of the Dallies looked round and saw that it was nothing but land hunger and greed, and nobody to service the landscape or do any of the dirty work, so they decided to do that as well, and get richer in the process. Branco was a workman but he planned to get rich, make no mistake about that.

I wonder sometimes if he ever did.

My dark and curly-headed foreigner had come in off the gumfields when first I met him. I saw him that first time one morning when I was shaking the crumbs off the tablecloth outside the house.

Only then I was still a girl, and I lived here with my mother who was a widow. My grandmother was not long dead and we often grieved for her. Well, that is partly true, for I was beside myself with sorrow for the old lady. I cannot tell you, even now, how much I loved the old woman. But I think my mother was weary of her. She needed her, but I do not think she ever liked her much. There were stories about my grandmother, about her early years. As I have said, there was much blamed on my grandmother for the way that I was when younger. I never saw any sign of impropriety about her, but piecing together here and there things that were told to me and things that I have found out since, here in this house, there was a kind of truth in it all.

She had spirit, she had a way of telling tales that made ordinary things shine, that I do know. She was nearly a hundred when she died, and that was another thing about her, that her life went on and on, which is not necessarily a good thing for the children. You can go at it, this business of living, for too long. That is what has happened to me, I suppose. When they decided that I should stay here in this house, they never imagined it carrying on like this year after year, they believed it would all be over soon—I don't know how they thought it would be resolved, but you just know about people, they don't conceive of a situation going on forever and outliving them. In their secret heart of hearts they would see this as outwitting them, and that is what people do not care for.

The night before I met Branco I had seen my grandmother in a dream. She was propped up in bed with her long white hair straggling against the pillows, both so white you could hardly tell one from the other, just the way she had been in the last days of her life. Only in those days her eyes had been half shut, a slit of colour in the seams of skin that covered the place where her eyes should have been, and her voice was a half whisper. She made little sense, only some days she would take my hand and raise it to the window and then I would know that I must open it when there was no one around, and let the wind touch her face. She would lift her face, her once beautiful, fine-boned profile, matted with thick flesh now like a giant pale curd, covered in whiskers, to feel the brush of the air. In the dim light that was kept on in the room I would see only the outline of her face, but the breeze would take away the fetid odours of her dying body, and I would touch her hand, still cool and dry, and remember her as she had been. Her hand would return my pressure and then I would quickly close the window so that we were not discovered. It was the nearest to a rebellion, and a communication, that I had experienced with her in a long time, and I would often think that the next day she would speak to me, say something special that she had saved for me and only me, but the days passed and what she had to say never came, and then she died and I was alone with my widow mother who was strict and harsh in her views of the world and observed the Sabbath with the intensity of the old people.

No one can know, who has not experienced it, how strict and fierce the Sabbath was. Back in Cape Breton, come Saturday nights, the sap trays which caught the maple syrup were overturned so that no syrup could collect on Sunday, no pleasure was observed and if accidental pleasure was taken in performing the Lord's work, like skating across the ice to church, the Man would take the skates and hurl them in the waters beneath the ice. There was no preparation of food allowed, no exchanging of money no matter how great the need for goods, no admiration of the handiwork of children, no singing, no whistling, no dancing, no playing of musical instruments, nothing at all. There was, though, a great deal of praying and reading of Scriptures and sitting around with a face like a green raspberry, oh yes.

I'm not saying it was quite as bad as that when we came out here but it wasn't much better. My mother, who took very much to heart her responsibilities to her fatherless child and unluckier even than most with the cross of a witch in the house, made sure it was as much like the old days as possible.

Except that in my grandmother's time, if she were around she managed to cast me a mocking smile that stopped it from being so bad, and I think my mother must have known. Yes, I think that among other things, she did not like my grandmother for not being as attentive to the Sabbath as she might have been, and this stemmed from somewhere back in time, to the place whence they both had come, and beyond that to my grandmother's homeland. She was afraid I would be corrupted; directly, you might say, as if the bad blood which ran in my veins was not enough. Not that she was untouched herself, of course, but the way my mother acted you would think she had put a cleansing rinse through her own veins.

I speak harshly of my mother. Yet in truth, she loved me. That remains my dilemma. I did not, could not, hate her. I did not like her much, but surely that is a different matter.

In the end it was a life for a life. That is not easy to accept. But she chose to live her life in the mould of the old people. I did not choose that my life should be the same, however she tried to make it as hers. She paid with her life, but she left the old people to nest in my dreams.

And it has gone on for so long. So long, I tell you, whoever can hear me, whoever is listening.

This night, the one that I spoke of, when I was young and before it had all come to pass, I had seen my grandmother in my dream and her hair hung and her breath laboured and her flesh stank; her skin was the colour of scone dough but her eyes were wide open. Yes, that is what I am coming to, those wide shining eyes. They were twinkling and shining in the gloom of that deathbed room. They were as big as saucers and dark as the centre of a Black-eyed Susan. I leaned towards her and I knew that she was about to tell me the secret I had been waiting to hear and then I woke.

Standing outside in the morning light, I hurled the tablecloth at the sky to blot out the sun. I would have called out aloud in my frustration, except that I was afraid my mother would hear me and come running.

I tried to recapture my grandmother's face. I would have called if I could, 'Isabella, oh, Isabella,' her lovely name like an ornament on the bright winter air.

Such a clear morning with only a hint of frost, and that would probably be the extent of the winter here in the north, in this climate of honey bees in winter and spring flowers on the vine even before the season has turned. We do not suffer cold or hardship as did our forebears, there are none of the frozen waters of the northern hemisphere, we do not get bays closed in by ice, nor the long and dangerous spring when the thaw begins and the drift ice moves and churns agains the land. No, the sea warms us, we are cosseted by the Pacific. For those who come from the south by Brynderwyn Hill and look down to the flat plains of the Braigh, they will see the shining blue floor of the world, the bay that stretches from Bream Tail to Bream Head, and the small islands they call the Hen and Chickens perched on the sea, and near to the ocean there is the village where my people live.

Isabella.

I listened to her name on the air, over oceans.

Isabella.

I dared only whisper it.

And then, as the cloth settled and I drew its corners together, I saw Branco walking towards me.

He was a swarthy man not more than five feet six inches measured roughly by my own height, and muscular. I remember particularly his eyes which were narrow and deep-set. His hair was crinkly. At first sight I would have said that it was wiry although later I found that it was not. It was just the tightness of the curls which gave it this appearance.

A closed brooding face, I thought, as he advanced towards me. I stepped back, afraid.

He saw my fear and hesitated. In his hand he carried a tin pitcher. He stood quite still as my own hand sprang to my mouth to cover a scream. He held the pitcher out and then he smiled.

I never saw such white teeth in a human face. They were large and glowing and strong. His eyes narrowed even more as he smiled, so that I could hardly see them at all. He looked as if he had worn his clothes for a long time without changing them, for they were rumpled and his boots were muddy. I could not take my eyes off this twinkling rough gypsy. For that is what I thought, that this man was a gypsy.

'Good morning,' I said, and I heard my voice like a little wisp in the air.

He inclined his head, still smiling. His shoulders lifted in a little self-deprecating gesture, yet at the same time I knew that he was mocking me. I could not speak his language and he didn't care. He would get what he wanted with or without language.

'Water? Milk?' I said foolishly.

It could not be water for there was a clear stream nearby. I held out my hands, opening and shutting them as if I was squeezing a cow's teats. He watched this performance with tolerant amusement, seeming about to laugh out loud.

'Milk, iff you pleez.'

I guessed that he had known the right words all along, and I was ashamed that he had made me go through the silly charade I had just done for him.

'I'll ask my mother. Wait here on the step,' I said, making my voice as haughty as I could as I swept inside.

Oh I make it sound as if I was a grand lady in a crinoline but I wasn't anything like that. My dress was a plain woollen cloth of a dark colour. It was narrower than I would have liked, for my mother would have thought a full skirt to be an extravagance. There should never be too much of anything, only enough, she would always say. In this I knew she was echoing the sentiments of McLeod. One of his favourite ploys to humiliate the women of the parish had been to upbraid them on Sundays from the pulpit about their unseemly dress and in particular about their bonnets. Not a feather, even one they had gathered from the hedgerows themselves, or a tiny bow or a piece of lace, would be tolerated on their headgear. He would make such dreadful fools of them. He even did this to his wife, a poor tender creature who had borne him ten children in not so very many years and spent most of her life seemingly half off her head. Her apparent feebleness of mind and body had kept her more out of the church than in it. But at least she missed his ranting and I wondered if she might not have been a truly canny woman in spite of what they said.

My grandmother thought very well of Mary McLeod. She was a kind woman with Christian charity, she told me, not like some of the mealy-mouthed fools who believed they ran the world with their own brand of fine moral superiority. It was talk like that that upset my mother.

'Don't you know, the Man had our best interests at heart?' she would cry. 'Have you no idea how he suffered? Would you have us all pickled in rum, and selling our bodies on the harbour front at Pictou? That's what happened to women who went against him, you know. Death and destruction, death and destruction.' Then my grandmother's face would close with some secret private thought, some agony, some conflict, and she would fall silent before my mother's reproaches. Sometimes it was as if my mother had acquired a tough upper hand which she enjoyed as my grandmother got older. But as they had both thought well of Mary McLeod on this subject quarrels between mother and daughter quickly ran out.

No, it was the matter of dress that held sway. Certainly the way we dressed was dictated from the old days; you would have been hard put to find fancy clothing in my wardrobe. Though I did have little ways of getting round the problem. I was one of the best knitters in the district, a gift that was highly prized. By the time I was fifteen I could knit a sleeve while walking to and from the store for supplies with my bag slung over my shoulder. I could do diamond rope, the shape of fishing net mesh (for our patterns have names and are often called after the objects of the sea), worked in plain, purl, moss, and double moss rows, and net masks, and print o' the hoof, and ups and downs, or marriage lines as my mother called them, and oh, pretty well any you could name. It was a sinful exhibition of course, for there was no doubt that I was proud and enjoyed the attention I drew to myself, but it was one of those things about which my mother was strangely silent.

No. Wait.

That is a lie.

Silent, maybe, but not so strange, for in my secret heart of hearts I knew the truth of which I have already hinted. Though she might not exhibit her pride, and though she exhorted me to modest thoughts, I was the darling of her whole life; when others praised me, she glowed as if it was she who had received approval.

In short, my mother idolised the ground that I walked on. When the sleeves of my pullovers were a little fancier than she might have expected, when there was a touch of tantalising colour where all should have been grey and drab, she would manage to turn a blind eye. By devious ways I could do a little primping. I relished these vanities. I have to say that it was not least because they represented a victory of sorts.

For the most part, though, my sensible dresses swept to the floor and covered my ankles, suggesting all modesty and propriety, and when I turned that morning and stepped high into my mother's kitchen, I cannot imagine that Branco would have thrilled greatly to what he saw.

And yet he came again.

Branco, the Dalmatian. Like his countrymen, he had come to the kauri gumfields and dug and dug, turning up mountains of gum. I try to imagine the stuff in my dreams as it coagulates from a gleaming lava-like flow into hard bright shapes.

When the men arrived off the boats and were despatched north they had nothing except the clothes they stood up in. At the trading posts the storekeepers equipped them with a billy and some tea, a spade and some boots, and a rough kind of tent for shelter. Then they made their own way. With the first of their gum they paid off their debt for the gear. After that, they made profit.

Branco dug in the mud and the rain, he dug when the sun was beating down like fire on his back and the earth was like bricks. Sometimes he dug alone, but he also dug with the Maoris. A few of the Dalmatians got rich. Often their health failed. That was what happened to Branco. Come the last winter he had had first a cold then pleurisy. He nearly died out there on the gumfields.

The Maoris nursed him and healed him with their medicines.

He worked on in the gumfields through the summer, over at Dargaville on the west coast where the weather was not so hot, but his breathing had been affected. After a couple of hours doubled over he would begin gasping and his lungs would labour and then he would have to rest for an hour before he could go on. As the winter closed in again the Maoris told him he would die if he kept going. So he took to the roads, building new ones and mending old ones. That was hard too but at least he wasn't doubled over in the pits like an animal.

I didn't know any of these things the morning he came to my mother's house. And it is hard to explain how I came to know them later, for our language never did bridge as many gaps as it might, and yet there were things we learned about each other.

When he went away I did not think much of him. I sat in the kitchen of this house and I knitted and I sewed, and I milked the cow in the morning and set the cream and made butter. My mother and I grew a small garden at the side of the house and late in the mild winter we planted a row of beans and one of peas, and another of carrots, and a line of tomatoes against the house.

The winter turned to early spring. The apple tree and the plum trees which had been planted by my parents when the house was built were illuminated with blossom. Flowers enchanted me, and because I had been low in spirits—still thinking of Isabella each spring, though it was the third year since her passing—my mother capitulated and let me sow a

27

line of marigolds down the edge of the path and a handful of sunflowers next to the tomatoes. She considered flowers to be a decoration that required labour better spent on other things, but then I reminded her that we could provide flowers for the church and she agreed to me planting night stock as well, for the rich perfume. It was to the glory of God, I told her, but I did not go too far for fear she should think of incense. Still, the flowers grew and were plentiful.

In those days our kitchen shone, the stove was like dark obsidian where I polished it, there was a simple dresser in the corner and on it stood a row of blue and white plates and another of hard white bone china dishes, tureens and the like, which had been carried with great care from Nova Scotia. There was little that had been brought in the migration because the ships were full to bursting with people, but some things were too precious to leave behind; items which had been laboured for and skimped over as the people, once crofters from mean huts, had erected their proud solid houses. The reminders of their first prosperity could not easily be abandoned.

There were some things in my mother's house even finer than the china. These were household items that Isabella had brought to the family as part of her dowry; Isabella, the London girl who married a crofter and finished up fleeing the persecutions with him. The goods were few but they were precious. Here and there in the kitchen, then, a hint of shining brass, and two silver candle-sticks, and some very fine white linen, so old now that it looked as if it would break after it had been starched and pressed, but simon-pure in its whiteness.

As well there were old heavy iron pots and the tripod where a great stew pot could hang across the open fire, and rough furniture which had been fashioned from planks by my father. I did try to remember my father, and in the work of those seats arranged around the long kauri table, and in the house which he had built with his own hands, I could almost see a picture of him, a plain, decent, sober hard-working man who had nonetheless been prepared to take a risk and follow the Man.

Of course I know now that family pictures can lie.

My father had not done so well by his wife, although later no one would speak of that for it would have been, as they said, to speak ill of the dead. But when I think of my mother now, I wonder if her pictures had already dimmed before the hour of my birth, or even by the time I was conceived. I think she may have gained a kind of strength from excluding the truth while acknowledging that it existed. The tragedy is not so much what is, but what we believe. Or exhibit as belief. Myself, I do not believe there is any truth which can be avoided.

Look at me. Look at my life. What sort of recommendation am I for the truth? I do not blame my mother now. Ah, not now. But then.

So I felt my father as a vague presence who had provided for us and then vanished to his rest before his time was due. Now and then he was conjured up as a force to be reckoned with, when other measures of restraint had failed. When I was wilful or unkind, I was asked, 'What would your father have said?' To which I had no answer. I did not know. I did know that he had built the cradle in which I slept. That might have been rich information had I not also known that I was not the boy intended for the cradle.

My mother had been waiting and hoping for a child for the better part of thirty years. She was growing old, in terms of the years of child bearing, when at last I was born. She had this in common with her own mother, for Isabella was nearly forty when mother was born, only she had other living children before her. Still, she knew what it was to have hard labour and old bones parting for the onslaught of childbirth.

My mother, whose name was Ann, had also given birth to other children but they had not lived. There had been one which came to half term and she had taken his tiny body still curled in foetal form and planted him in Cape Breton soil without a burial service, and another one which the midwife had looked at and said that God was good in taking his life; that was in Australia, and then there had been here in New Zealand a child who survived and gave my mother the consolation of a funeral service. They were all boys. Then there was me. McLeod had foretold my birth to my mother from his deathbed, and she had never given up believing it would happen although twelve years were to pass before it did. And of course she was sure I would be another son, that was what she waited for, a son who would survive and whom she would call Ishmael. Then I came, a girl who lived, even though in the beginning I was a pitiful ragged piece of flesh that cried and moaned night after night.

Through me, my grandmother found a new meaning to her own undone life, and what with my father dead and my mother seeming as if she too would perish in fevers and night sweats and vales of terrible tears, it was Isabella who stroked me to life and had me wet-nursed, so that slowly my survival was established, my eyes focused, the crying abated, and suddenly I was thriving and, they said of me, I was a beautiful bonny child.

My mother reached the turning point of her illness, the moment of crisis, in the hours before dawn when I was two months. Afterwards she had no memory of my birth, or what had followed. She saw me only as a healthy child of whom she was mightily proud. I became her special weakness. And she called me Maria, a name that floats well on the breeze, whispers backwards and forwards from the macrocarpa trees in the night, climbs in and out of chimney stacks, roars up in flames from the fire on dark nights, maria maria marisabella mariann annisabellamaria yesyes. Our names blending, mothers and daughters all of us.

To this house, then, haunted already by the past yet shining and more grand than many of the settlers' houses, Branco returned, wishing to see me again.

He knocked on the door one day in summer, just after Christmas. The brown-top grass that the settlers had brought in the hay in their mattresses was flowering. How that grass had taken hold. Nova Scotia had transplanted itself to the New Zealand soil so easily you wouldn't believe it.

When I heard the knock something turned over in my chest. I do not know why I was so suddenly unnerved, yet I had a strange premonition. I remember, as if it were yesterday, that I glanced around the kitchen in a desperate, scared kind of way, as if to imprint it upon my memory as it was; as if somehow I was about to lose it.

My mother opened the door and Branco was standing there. He was holding out the tin pitcher in one hand. In the other he held a shilling.

'Who are you?' my mother asked, her voice peremptory. I had a quick vision of how she must appear to Branco. She was a plain woman with heavy jutting eyelids, a high red complexion and a receding chin. Yet she was imposing in the way she stood, above average in height and of a full-busted stoutness that went well with her stature. For a moment it looked as if she was towering over Branco.

'It is the roadman, mother,' I said, before he could speak. 'No doubt he wants milk'.

'And what do you know of him?'

'Nothing,' I said, and shivered. 'He has been here before. I told you mother, that I gave milk to a roadman. I do not think he speaks English or Gaelic,' I added quickly, to establish that I had had no conversation with him.

'How do you know that he is the roadman?'

'We've passed him many times,' I said, in such a reasonable way that she was calmed.

But this too was a lie. I was guessing. I do not know why I had said this. I do not know how I knew. Even now.

In the late autumn I saw him often.

I took to walking. In the long evenings I would throw my cloak around my shoulders and leave the house. Across the paddocks lay a tributary of the sea we called the River, where the ferryboats plied their way backwards and forwards. I would walk to the River in order to watch them. My mother asked me where I was going and I would tell her to the ferryboats, mother, to the ferryboats.

'Do you see a man there?'

I laughed openly in her face. 'A man? Mother, ask anyone, ask my Uncle Hector, he will tell you no, that I wave to the boats passing by, then turn and walk the other way.'

Perhaps she did ask Black Hector, because for a time she left me in peace. Then she started asking again, 'What takes you to the boats, Maria? It isn't natural.'

'Walk with me, mother,' I would say, and one evening she did. But she had become so stout, addicted to butter and to cream mixed in her potatoes, that it proved too much for her and she had to rest a long while before she could return. We sat on the banks of the river as a boat laden with timber passed. The men aboard waved to us. I sat with modest downcast eyes, only raising my hand for a small acknowledgement. 'Good evening, ma'am, a nice night for a walk,' they called to my mother, and did not give me second glances.

We made our way home as the shadows slid towards the edges of the earth. I bade her goodnight, took my candle, and climbed the stairs, a steep sharp incline up to my room under the roof.

As I had expected, she did not ask to come again, and appeared to accept my nightly 'taking of the air', as she called it. She said that I looked well, and sometimes when I sat by the fire she would pause as she passed me and place a reflective hand upon my head. I had a good head of hair in those days, a light gold-brown and very thick. It was something else she was proud of, though she never said so for fear of making me vain.

Branco liked my hair too. When I speak of shadows on the land I speak also of him. Branco merged with the trees and the fallen logs where the bush had been cleared, he slid in and out of that landscape as if he were one of the wild creatures that inhabited it. At first neither my uncle nor my mother, nor the ferryboat men, nor any of the people whom I met on my rambles were aware of his presence. And because I was able to turn aside each enquiry about my solitary walks, no one ever thought to ask how long it took me from the house to the riverbank, or back again. I understood guile without ever having been taught it. Perhaps Branco and I taught it to each other.

I don't know why I went with him. I wanted someone different from all the others, that's the only thing I can tell you now. My mother believed in bad blood; that is an explanation I cannot accept. I think it went outside of us: the old people were breaking up, the changes had already begun.

Though not for girls like me. We were expected to stay inside the community.

I don't know why it had to be me that broke away. They thought I was crazy. They think, still, that I am a witch too, and that is where the bad blood comes into it.

But it began simply enough, with a man and a woman in a kind of innocence which turned to power over each other, and knowledge.

I didn't know much about men, but I felt I had been waiting to find out for a long time. I was very impatient. I think he was shocked. At

31

first he thought I was mocking him, but as I insisted he grew bolder. He seemed to circle me, touching me as if I was fragile, but to every touch I responded with such vigour that he could do nothing but return my passion. So one thing led to another and it will come as no great surprise to say that I became, before long, what is known as a fallen woman. The nights of prowling around each other came to an end, my desire knew no bounds; I would walk to the riverbank and underneath my skirt I would wear no garments, the quicker to allow him into me when we snatched each other into the shadows. We didn't say much and made no great noise of passion, for I had not thrown all caution to the winds, if only to protect myself for more meetings with him.

And yet in a way we exchanged some feeling, something which I still think of as loving words and endearments. Sometimes I would catch a glimpse of his face in the evening light, looking at me in a curious kind of way, as if I was a strange creature whom he did not understand.

Why should he have understood me?

For I did not understand myself.

At nights when I had returned to the house and was safely in bed I would try to think of the future. Up on the Braigh, the young men from Nova Scotia had cleared land. Now their sons were taking it over; already a whole generation of people had passed over the land since the migration. There were clear green fields where once there had been timber. The timber had made the newcomers rich already, as the logs were turned into ships (of which there were no finer builders in the country than the men from Nova Scotia) or shipped to Auckland and Wellington for the building of the new houses in the mushrooming towns. It would be a fine thing for my mother if I were to wed one of these young men, and no bad thing for me, if I were to admit it to myself. There had been one or two of them I had eyed in church when I was half grown. Unashamed, I mentioned them once to my grandmother.

'Ah, the young Bear,' she said. 'You think you would like him? He's got fine shoulders and a nice straight back. You could do worse. If you must consort with men.' And there was a sudden bitterness which I did not recognise, around her eyes.

'Mother.' My own mother's voice was as quick and sharp as a razor on a strop. 'How dare you talk to the child like that?'

Yet it was true, there were some handsome men in the congregation, and they were mostly such brawny big men, you could not help but notice them. In the years that followed, I did look at them, in spite of my seemingly downcast eyes. There was young Donald MacKenzie, and John Lachie John McGrath (meaning that he was John son of Lachie son of old John McGrath) and a whole crowd of the McKay boys, all of whom I'd been to school with, or at least their younger brothers and sisters, and all of them like family. I would have nothing to lose by joining up with any of them, and I was no bad catch myself. It wouldn't be difficult. I was easy to look at, I baked bread, milked a cow with a quick wrist and firm fingers, and my mother could entertain without ever raising a hand to make a scone, for I did it all. As well, I would inherit a house and land of my own. Altogether I was considered a fine and quite remarkable young woman. I could have nearly anyone I chose. It seemed, those nights when I lay under the eaves and the stars glinted at me through the window and a skylight which I could almost touch, that all my destiny had been aimed towards such a marriage.

And now I did not want it.

As simple as that. As simple and as terrible. I loved the roadmender. I could think of nothing else and the rest of the world had ceased to exist.

A kind of madness. When I was not with him I was exhausted, and ill with anxiety as well that I might be thwarted from seeing him. My mother no longer said that I looked well. Instead, she wore a strained and hunted look too.

The winter closed in and passed. The nights were cool and that year a sea wind keened in across the land towards us, and the dark fell early. I had to arrange to take my walks before night; the ground was harder and less accommodating, but still I went to him.

The roadmender moved during the winter from a tent to a little hut deserted by timber workers long before. I met him there sometimes, but in order to reach this place I had to cross open ground. I would wait in the deepening shadows until night was closing in upon us, so that I was less likely to be seen. Then it would be dark when I left him.

One night he was not waiting for me. Nor was he the following night.

I was beside myself, not knowing what to do. On the third evening my mother said, as if carelessly, 'Why bother to go out tonight? The weather's still cool and you might catch a chill.'

I said I would be quick. She watched me with troubled eyes as I pulled my cloak around me. The cloak was worn and ragged round the edges. It had been used too often as a blanket beneath my lover and me. I looked like a wild creature.

The night, too, was wild as I hurried towards our meeting place. The wind that had fretted round for months was rising. I called Branco's name, softly at first, then greatly daring, louder and louder.

There was no reply, and I drew close to the shack where he had taken shelter. Throwing caution to the winds I gathered myself together and ran.

In the evening light, the door hung open on its rusting hinges, banging forlornly backwards and forwards. The room was empty. There was no sign that I could detect at first of his few possessions. The straw mattress that we had lain upon had been ripped open and its contents were strewn over the floor. My foot caught in the pitcher he used, crumpled as if a boot had been placed on it.

I looked around in disbelief, as if somehow I could make him materialise from the draughty corners of the room. There was a box on its side where he had kept a picture, a little daguerrotype of a woman with shining wings of black hair and a close and secret look on her narrow face, the woman I knew to be his mother. She was gone.

I knelt on the floor and began to cry. I don't know how long I stayed there but it was quite dark when I got to my feet. As I walked home the shadows were menacing and I was afraid; I felt I was being watched from behind every tree and log.

When I entered the house my mother was sitting by the fire rocking, backwards and forwards, not looking up as I came in.

'There is broth made. Sit down and eat some.'

'I don't want anything.'

'You may not, but you'll have it. You look like a scarecrow.'

'That's my business.'

She had lumbered to her feet, and her voice was raised. She had never shouted at me before.

'Pull yourself together, girl. Stop all of this.'

'Stop what, mother?' I knew she meant my tears which had started again, but there was nothing I could do now about that.

'Everything. This unseemly crying and noise, this perversity, this ...this man, this roadmender. You hear me?'

'Oh aye, I hear you all right, mother.'

'Or I tell you, the wrath of God will strike you dead.'

Like a voice from some other place, I heard myself answer her. 'He's already killed me. I'm dead now.'

'That's enough. You'll not take the name of the Lord in vain. No more of this wild talk.'

I looked at her, trying to unravel what she was saying. I felt so tired. The fire cast its flickering light on her. I thought she looked crazy, but then I knew that I was seeing myself reflected in her.

'I cannot stop, mother, I cannot.' I could hear myself again, bleak and piteous.

She picked up the poker. I thought she was going to strike me. 'You've heard of the five foolish virgins?'

'What have they to do with me?'

'Who knows? When the hour comes it might be too late.'

'Mother, it is already too late.'

There was a silence in the room. At last she said in a whisper, 'Too late? You do not mean a word you say, lass. You don't *know* what you mean.'

I did not reply, steadfastly watching the fire. It is the heat in the room, I thought, the rising wind outside, the sound of a defiant heart beating, and hers, plodding its way towards eternity; we are locked into this room with madness and no way of escape. Her voice had become pleading. 'Tell me you do not mean it, Maria, my beautiful girl. Tell me.'

And to ease her pain which was overwhelming me, I said, 'I do not mean it, mother.'

'Aye.' She rocked backwards and forwards, not just the chair but her whole body. 'Aye, that's better. You, you've been touched by the hand of the Man, by Norman McLeod himself.'

'He died before I was born,' I said, sick of the old notions that were in conflict with anything that seemed important to me now, yet too weary to contradict her any more.

'Yes, but don't you remember all that I told you of it when you were a bairn?'

'Tell me again,' I said, already letting her words wash over me, and beginning to hope for hot milk when I went to bed.

'We went to the window of his house and he lay there dying, Maria, and all the people were crying out and weeping. He spoke to us, though his strength was failing, and he scarce had voice enough left to say the words, and we who were younger remembered how we had followed him from St Ann's across the sea, while our parents, the older ones, recalled the land before that, whence they had come with him.'

'From Assynt in Sutherlandshire,' I murmured.

'Lochalsh and Harris,' the rejoinder.

'Applecross and Skye.'

The names like a litany in the room. Almost shutting out the night. And her chanting on.

'Then on to Nova Scotia, and from there to Australia, and the sicknesses, and the mad gold-diggers, and yet still we came, following him to the ends of the earth, forty years or near enough in the wilderness, like the men of old, but he had led us to a safe haven—well, we stood there remembering all of this, and he looked at me, and he said, "Annie McClure, you're a good woman and bonnie, you must have patience in your sorrow, you won't be without a child forever." '

'And you were patient, mother.'

'Aye, I was. We must all learn patience.'

'And what happened?' I said, turning away this new reproach.

'When I was sure it was too late I found myself with child again, and I said to your father, "I know this time it will go well." '

'And I was the child?'

'You were. And you had golden down on your head the day you were born.'

'You remember that?' I said cruelly, for her recollection was not quite as my grandmother had described the events of that day.

She lifted her chin. 'I was near to death on account of my age, you

35

understand, and grieving for your father, dead and gone before the birth. I looked at your bonnie head, and it gave me the will to live.'

I thought she had finished, but she looked at me and said, her voice now matter-of-fact: 'So you see, Maria McClure, you are a child blessed by the Man, and you will not bring shame on this house consorting with vagabonds, and a Papist to boot.'

Up, under the roof. The brief rain had stopped and the wind dropped, quickly, as it does here in the north. The stars shone out of a clean black sky, and the names, the names of the old places stalked through my dreams, the ghosts chanting from afar, Assynt, Stoer, Lochalsh, Applecross and Skye, Achiltibuie, Skye, Lochalsh, repeating and going on and on. Voices in my head, mother, it is a new world we have come to make but the old places going on and on...

In the morning I thought what a daft way she had of talking me round.

For nothing had changed from the night before. Branco was not there.

I stood outside, emptying the crumbs, flicking the table-cloth at the sky. The same place, the same sky, the same cloth. For a moment there was darkness, followed by white light. I had a strong temptation to eye the sun.

What had changed was me. I was different.

I thought of my grandmother, and wished she were here.

PART THREE

ISABELLA
1812–20

3

'**H**E'S A GOOD-LOOKING young man,' observed Mrs Ramsey. She peered out the window and observed with approval the carriage passing the window. The light shone on the waves across Loch Broom, and a wind splintered and diffused the bright colours of the day. High summer does not last long in Ullapool. Each day that the sun shines is a celebration.

Mrs Ramsey's hands rested on the cloth she was sewing.

'I said...'

'He's good-looking. I heard you,' said her daughter.

'But don't you agree, Isabella?'

'He's married. See, he has a wife.'

'What's that got to do with it?' Mrs Ramsey flounced.

'Everything and nothing.' Isabella straightened her back and, taking the scissors, snipped her thread with elaborate care.

'Really, Isabella. I don't know what's got into you. You act as if... as if...' Words failed her.

'Yes, mother?'

Muriel Ramsey was a plump woman who had the remnants of good looks under her fat. She tended to wheeze from being laced too tight. She wore life like a continual cross. The rot had probably set in long before, but of late her husband had concluded that the state of her disposition was due to the disappointment of a daughter whom so far no one had offered to marry, despite her being considered handsome enough.

Mrs Ramsey said that this was not so at all; that she was more than satisfied with the status of her sons' wives, who were delightful young women, and that she had beautiful grandchildren—what more could a woman desire? So although in private she complained, and needled Isabella incessantly, in public she was heard to state that how her daughter chose to spend her life was neither here nor there.

Isabella regarded her mother now with calm amusement. People said she had strange eyes. To look directly into them, they appeared to be blue, yet when she turned her head, in some lights they appeared astonishingly dark and the blue would be seen to be flecked with brown. She had a lean profile, and some said that her nose was a trifle too long, but Mrs Ramsey knew, all the same, that her daughter had been admired during her season in London.

'As if you are after every man that passes beneath your nose,' said Mrs Ramsey, lying broadly. Her daughter frequently appeared amused by her attempts to interest her in new partners, and the mother wished now to disguise her true intent.

'The good-looking ones need to be a little more accessible than Mr McLeod,' said Isabella, making light of the matter.

The carriage had stopped on the cobblestones, two doors along from them.

'They have a child,' observed Isabella.

'Don't stare,' said Mrs Ramsey, although no one from the outside could have seen them watching from behind the lace curtains. She thought secretly that Isabella's eyes were so bright and sharp that people would know they were being observed, however much they hid. 'What does the wife look like?' she asked. 'Has she a nice bonnet?'

'Oh my word no, it is, well, hardly a bonnet at all.'

'What d'you mean? A bonnet must be a bonnet. Is it fanciful?'

'Just the opposite. It is rather a pathetic little thing. A head covering, really. There is nothing elegant about Mrs McLeod.'

'Poor things. I've heard there's been a great deal of poverty in the north,' Mrs Ramsey remarked.

'Yes. I've heard that too.' Isabella continued to watch the McLeods.

'Well, they have a nice house to come to now, and the garden is looking a picture. All that book learning has been an asset to that young man. He must be quite a go-ahead fellow from all I've heard. With so many brains let's hope he's amusing.'

'I think you'll be disappointed, mother. I've heard that Mr McLeod is not the slightest bit amusing.'

'Oh dear. These Scots never are, are they?'

It may have been nearer to the truth than any other consideration that it was the matter of the Scots temperament which disappointed Mrs Ramsey, who was from the south. She had hoped that her husband might settle in London after their marriage but he had insisted on returning to his native Scotland, first to Edinburgh and then to Inverness, of which neither town had ever amused her particularly, and they seemed to be getting smaller and colder as they progressed northwards. Now, here in Ullapool, in the north-west of the Scottish Highlands, it felt as if they could moulder here forever and it would be neither here nor there to her husband.

Still, it was a comfortable enough living on the edge of Loch Broom, as a supervisor's wife. Mr Ramsey worked for the British Fishing Company, which had set up an establishment for the catching and processing of herring, said to be the best in the world. There were nearly a hundred houses in the village. The Ramsey's was one of the finest, with a panoramic view of the sea. It stood at the western end of Shore Street—

Sraid-a-Chladaich-An-Iar—in a row of solid whitewashed houses with blue slate roofs stretching out along a green point, hard to the edge of the loch, built so close to the water that on a clear day when a skin of light lay easily on the sea, the reflection of the houses could be seen. Beyond lay the Summer Isles.

The village was not short of amenities, for the company had built a pier, and there were two large stores, one to the right and one to the left of it. Up Point Street was the inn, named The Arch on account of the gateway to the courtyard, built high to accommodate coaches. Within the township there was a constant bustle, unlike the desolate and exhausted atmosphere of other villages in the north-west.

Altogether, though the routine of Ullapool was dull as far as Mrs Ramsey was concerned, she enjoyed the fruits of her husband's labours. She had some importance of her own. It was she who had been the moving light, amongst her friends, in obtaining the services of a schoolmaster. While living in Edinburgh her husband had become a member of the Edinburgh Society for Promoting Christian Knowledge. It was first and foremost an organisation for gentlemen but then her husband was a gentleman, at least in a minor way, one subject on which they could both agree, although Mrs Ramsey had never stopped to consider his position in relation to that of others. The belief that he was any kind of gentleman had been a great comfort to her in their northward migration. And he was sober, industrious and reliable, and took a little religion seriously. Mrs Ramsey was glad that he did not go to extremes over it, that would have been unmanageable. But his associations with the Edinburgh Society had certainly proved of great advantage when they settled in Ullapool.

The Highlands were in a joyless state of transition when they arrived and the settlers from the south were anxious to ensure a more comfortable situation for themselves than that of their neighbours. Poverty was all around them and seemed to rap at the doors of the town. It was better to ignore it if they could. Here, in this safe haven, where shining silver crossed the wharves in return for silver of a tougher kind, it was possible to think of other things. The Company's money built sturdy houses for the new inhabitants, they put up a church, built roads around the village, and applied for assistance from the Edinburgh Society in order to obtain their school. They had seventy pounds a year to offer the schoolmaster, a good sum, and only twenty pounds less than the minister earned.

Isabella had queried the use of the Society's funds. 'Don't you think it would be better to try and improve the lot of the labourers round here?' she said.

'Whatever are you talking about, Isabella?' Mrs Ramsey had asked the question with genuine astonishment.

'We could teach the children here ourselves.'

41

'But why should we?'

'Do you know that a man can work day in and day out hereabouts and earn a pound a year?' Isabella asked her.

Mrs Ramsey flinched. The cause of her daughter's problem, her single state, was all too clear to her. The girl thought that she had the head of a man. Mrs Ramsey sighed beneath her whalebones.

She noticed that her daughter still stared towards the road where the schoolmaster and his wife were unloading their possessions beside their new house.

'At least he is young,' Mrs Ramsey said, with fading hope.

'He is hardly a boy, mother,' said Isabella. 'He is thirty-four years old.'

Mrs Ramsey was threading a needle. She paused. 'It was old to qualify, I grant you.'

'Qualify at what? He is nothing more than a stickit minister.'

Because Mrs Ramsey already knew this and did not want to dwell upon the implications—after all, she and the Society had worked hard to bring Mr McLeod here—she did not reply. Nor did she ask Isabella how she knew so much about the teacher. She had not discussed these matters with her, and it disturbed her, the extent of Isabella's knowledge.

Her daughter turned back to the room and picked up her sewing. Presently she said, 'He has an interesting face.' Again, her mother did not think of asking how she could have observed this at such a distance. She did wonder afterwards, but by then it was the middle of the night when her indigestion was troubling her. She rolled over in bed and wished she had not eaten so much gooseberry fool at supper.

Isabella had a strange penchant for travelling unaccompanied. She rode well, and at first would set out into the countryside with escorts whom she soon left far behind. Later she went alone. She had moved much further afield than her mother suspected.

Once Mrs Ramsey's sister in London had been taken ill and she had hurried to her side, leaving Isabella in charge of the housekeeping for her father. At that time, he was totally engrossed in the supervision of the Company's best catch in years, and Isabella was free to spend her time as she chose.

Leaving their maid enough orders to ensure that the house ran smoothly, she had taken herself, day after day and sometimes by night, to the moors in the north. She had travelled by Lochinver to Stoer Point, to Gairloch, and even to Applecross in the south.

The women of Ullapool had looked askance at these disappearances, and among themselves sympathised with Mrs Ramsey at her daughter's strange behaviour. Yet they said nothing. In this respect Isabella was her own most influential ally, for she was adept at helping the women with their smaller children, and until the advent of the schoolmaster, teaching the older ones. She was spirited, they said, but being a young woman of certain breeding, she was unlikely to come to harm.

She met Duncan MacQuarrie on the Ullapool waterfront soon after she had gone to the town to live. He had been looking for work, but the Company was full up. She was twirling her parasol as if to shade her eyes from the glare, although it was not so great that she needed to bother. The point of the parasol had almost caught the eye of a man who stood, hands in his pockets, looking disconsolately towards the pier.

'Will y'be careful what you do with that thing?' he snapped at her.

Isabella put the parasol down and looked over the perpetrator of this insolence. It was beside the point that she herself considered the parasol a rather foolish toy which she had only brought to hide her face from the stares of the fishermen whom she had not yet learned to greet. She was not used to being addressed in such a fashion.

'I do not know you,' she said in her most haughty southern tones, acquired in London.

The man was heavily built although his skin hung too loosely on him for the size of his frame, and he wore more than a week's stubble. At first she thought he was an older man, a tramp from the hills, but as he looked at her, not cowed at all, she thought that he was much younger, maybe not past twenty-five or thereabouts, but lean and hungry and maybe very tired as well.

'I am Duncan MacQuarrie,' he replied. 'And your name, madam?'

She told him, attempting to give it with a flourish, though her voice faltered.

He spat on the ground then. 'Ramsey from the Company?'

'Yes.'

He turned as if to walk away.

'I'm sorry if you can't get work,' she said, the first thing that came into her head.

He turned back, his expression bitter. 'He's been talking about me?'

'My father? No. I guessed. From the look of you.'

'So you say.'

It was her turn to be angry. 'You do not know my father. He would tell you that he had better things to do than discuss the Company with me.'

The man regarded her with a hint of interest. 'What good would it do to discuss it with you?'

'It could be run better. They'd get a better return on their money if labour was structured differently.'

'What d'you mean?'

'They import too much labour. The cost is too high, bringing it up here from the south.'

'You mean we starving devils from the hills would take anything he offered us?'

'No, that's not what I said at all. He could pay more local labour the same wages without the outlay. For one thing, there's people already housed here that the Company's not drawing on.'

'If you could call it housing. Have you seen how the people live here? Eh? No. Well that's something you should see.'

'You're defeated before you begin.'

'Defeat. You make me sick, your kind. Ah, and to think you nearly fooled me. For a moment I thought you might have seen the face of the people out there. How could you? How could I have thought that?'

'I'm talking about business,' said Isabella.

'I dare say it's as entertaining a thought as getting a husband.'

'I beg your pardon?' The colour on her cheeks was high. 'That is hardly your affair.'

'Maybe not. But it lies heavily on your mind, I can tell by the look of you.'

'You don't...' She had almost been trapped into saying that he did not understand.

'For a moment there, I thought you might have a heart.'

His eyes rested on her, his lip lifted.

'How dare you...'

'Easily. I'm just an ignorant peasant with nothing to lose. You can report me to your father if you wish. It makes no difference. I owe him nothing and I'll be gone within the hour.'

He started to move away.

'Wait.' She saw that he limped.

He stopped, without turning back to her.

'It would be difficult to work on the boats if you were not sure-footed,' she said.

'There are harder things than that. If a man is to keep body and soul together.'

'Is it because of your foot that my father would not give you work?'

'He said the Company was full.'

She hesitated, choosing her words with care. 'I have seen something of what it is like near here.'

He turned to face her again, struggling to match her appearance with something he had heard. 'Are you the woman who rides alone?'

She started, embarrassed. 'I have been out once or twice.'

His hard gaze rested on her, trying to gauge her and not succeeding.

'When did you eat last?' she said abruptly, wishing to turn his attention away from herself.

'I didn't come to beg.'

'No. But there is no one else at home except a maid. I should like to share my lunch with you. Please. I have little enough company here.'

44

She thought he would refuse but he did not, as if he had suddenly come to a decision about her. Nor when he entered the house did he behave as if her benevolence was surprising.

'Where do you come from?' she asked over lunch.

'Stoer Point, to the north. It's rough land, a wild coastline pushing out into North Minch. You don't know it?'

'Not yet. Are things as bad as they say up there?'

He eyed her. 'You must know what they are doing to us here?'

'I have an idea. It's hard to sort out the truth of things, from where I am standing. I know about the troubles, of course, and I'm not impressed with what I see of the landlords.' She paused. 'But you must understand, people like my family take a different view of these matters. One hears such contradictory things.'

'The troubles were only a beginning.' He spoke with rage.

'Tell me.'

His hands hesitated over the soup which he was eating a little faster than he intended. He leaned towards her. 'How can I tell you?' he said. 'It is beyond words.'

She nodded, 'Aye. Then show it to me.'

It was high summer and a communion day when Isabella went north to meet Duncan MacQuarrie. She had not told her mother of her meeting with him. If she had been asked to explain the omission, she could not have offered a reason for it.

When next she heard from him, it was through a child, lurking in the Ramsey's garden. He was a ragged urchin of thirteen or so, with long unkempt hair and bare feet. Mrs Ramsey had sent him away with a stiff admonition which he had appeared not to understand. Afterwards she remarked to her daughter, 'He made me uneasy, I felt as if he was looking for something, the way he looked past me, into the house. D'you think these beggars from the hills will steal from us?'

'I've not heard anything of the kind,' said Isabella.

'They're said to steal food from the lairds.'

'Maybe they do, but haven't the lairds been taking from them?'

'That's dangerous talk. Who's been putting it into your head?'

Isabella sighed. 'Honestly, mother, I can't tell you. I know very little. But there's something wrong out there. I can feel it pushing against us. Can't you feel it?'

Outside, Isabella caught a glimpse of the boy her mother had seen, staring at the house, then drawing back.

'I think I'll walk along the sea front,' she said.

'Oh, I don't feel like it at all today,' said Mrs Ramsey. She massaged a plump ankle.

'I can go on my own.'

45

'Can you, dear? All right, but don't go far from the house, will you?'

'Are you afraid the wild men will snatch me up?'

But sometimes the effort of responding to her daughter demanded more of Mrs Ramsey than she could muster.

When Isabella went outside the boy leapt at her from where he had been sheltering behind a boulder.

'Miss Ramsey, ma'am.' He was almost unintelligible. She searched for her Gaelic.

'I won't hurt you. How d'you know my name?' she said softly.

'Duncan sent me.' He thrust a paper into her hand and disappeared, absorbed by shadows.

The letter asked that she ride forth to meet Duncan the following Thursday to attend a communion service near Lochinver. She was welcome to stay in the home of his sister Willina McRae, a married woman. The service would last until Monday.

Duncan was waiting for her as she rode by the mountain, on the road to the north, and when she came he did not exclaim or show surprise that she was alone. He was on foot, as she had expected, for few of the crofters owned horses. She dismounted and walked by his side. They travelled for mile after mile then, taking turns to ride the horse. Later, they sat on a rock and she offered him food from a basket she had prepared. She saw that he was uncomfortable.

'Does Mrs McRae expect me?' she asked.

'Oh, aye, of course. Not that one more will make much difference. Haven't you been to an open-air communion before?'

'It's different in the east, though I've heard of the services.'

'They expect maybe five thousand.'

She pushed the food towards him, surprised by his lack of enthusiasm.

'It is the fast day,' he said. 'We cannot eat.'

'I didn't know.'

'I thought you went to the kirk.'

'Well of course. But I haven't been to the Lord's supper in the open air like this. You will have to teach me.'

He looked at the food and smiled. 'You will know next year,' he said. 'As you are not prepared this time, perhaps we should eat after all.' He tore the bread with strong teeth.

'Won't you go in mortal sin?' she asked.

He looked at her. 'I'd hardly be going to the Lord's table with a pure heart, even now.'

'Mine is pure enough for both of us,' she remarked, lowering her eyes.

'Yours. Is it now?' He regarded her with amusement, then more seriously. 'Well. Yes. Maybe it is.'

'Why should you doubt me? It is true.'

'Aye. I know. My mockery was in return for yours. Never mind,

I won't approach the table this year.'

'Oh, but you must.'

He shook his head. 'I've already sinned in my head.' He touched her hand. 'You've got nothing to fear with me.'

'I know.'

'How did you know?'

'It matters not.'

'There are others to fear.'

'I shall be modest.'

'Yes. I knew that of you.'

They came round a corner and saw a valley near to the base of the hills, chosen as a site where the people could watch the proceedings and hear the speakers. In a quiet, expectant way they gathered on the grass, the young women bareheaded, the married women wearing mutch caps, and the old women with cloaks of muted colour pulled around their heads. Their faces were turned towards 'the Tent', a wooden shelter with a window for the clergymen, like a small stage where the ministers would perform their roles. Before the Tent was the communion table, which Isabella saw to be a plank on trestles, covered with white linen. The cloth glinted against the heath. Along each side of the stage there was a bench, and near that three posts. On the top of each post was a small box where the people would place their donations. Already the elders stood near the boxes, guarding them from theft. Their eyes were darting amongst the crowd as it gathered. One scowling man, with a crest of white hair and a bitter mouth, looked straight towards Isabella.

'Why does he look at me so?' she whispered to Duncan, although they were well out of earshot.

'He is watching for the wayward ones.'

'You mean there will be impropriety?'

'It is a holiday too, remember, and they come little enough for my people.'

'This is a strict parish, then?'

'It hasn't always been so, but times are changing.'

'Is there a reason?'

He turned fiercely towards her. 'Lax ways stand for the old church, which has done nothing for us here. Its ministers are the pawns of the landowners. They are in the employ of the men who have driven us off our lands. We are the dispossessed, the crofters who have nothing left. The sheep,' and he spat, 'the sheep have more than us. The black-faces. Did you not see them as we crossed the moor? Why do you think the land is so empty? Because the lairds have taken for themselves the place where we have always lived and sent us to the edge of the sea—there is scarce room enough there for a man and his wife and child to stand. There is nothing, nothing that is left to us.' His voice was rising, and around him people were listening and nodding their heads.

When he had finished, and the attention of those listening had been diverted to the latest arrivals, she said: 'But what of you? Are you strict?'

He shivered, as if a cold breath had touched him. 'I mean to be,' he replied in a low voice.

That night at Willina McRae's house the talk was the same. Duncan's sister was large and loose-limbed like him, without an ounce of spare flesh on her big bones, and her eyes burned from far back in her head. Rory, her husband, had lit the fire. It glowed with bog-fir, smoky and thick in the corners of the long room where more than twenty people were gathered. Behind a curtain the children slept. The conversation was punctuated with their stirrings and occasional coughs. Everyone present was staying for the communion. Some of them, whom the others called the Men, were neither ministers nor laymen. They came from wandering bands who acted as intermediaries between the ministers and the people. They knew each page of the Bible as well as their own names, although they had scant education. Catechists and mystics, their eyes held the gleam of fanatics. Each of them had long straggling hair and wore a black cloak over his shoulders and a spotted handkerchief around his head. Friday would be their day to speak. Already they were sharpening their oratory.

Some of the Men were to sleep in the McRaes' cattle barn. In the firelight, one of them stood in front of Isabella.

'You're a Sassenach?' he demanded.

She shook her head, trying not to show her fear or pull away from him.

Duncan spoke up. 'She was raised in the south. She is a Scotswoman.'

'You have English ways.' She saw as he spoke that his gums were bleeding.

'I was born in London but I lived a long time in Edinburgh, and then in Inverness. My family is of the Edinburgh Society.'

The man spat as Duncan had done earlier in the day, only this time the hatred was directed towards her.

'Moderates.'

'I do not know what you mean,' she said.

But the man had lost interest in her and moved on to others who knew what he was talking about.

'Tell me what he means,' she whispered to Duncan.

'It is to do with the division in the church,' Rory said, answering for him. 'There are ministers who do not attend to their business in a diligent way. They take advantage of the people. But now there are people outside of the ministry who are trying to lead the people back to the word. As God has told it. We don't have money to squander on a clergy who are idle, and drink. There is William MacKenzie at Stoer, one of the worst. He's nought but a drunken sot, and he gets rich for doing nothing. People perish every day collecting kelp. They fish when they can and starve the rest of the time. Sometimes they're allowed to till a strip of the poorest soil, and sometimes not. That's at the pleasure of the owners. We haven't even got time to grow our potatoes. The children are dying and the women are wasting away. And if we complain we get turned out, even from that. They've got us in the palms of their hands, with just enough money to exist, and if we leave them we're lost. They know how much they can get away with, for they still need us to gather kelp. Oh yes, they need us all right.'

'And the ministers do nothing?'

'Exactly. Bone idle, most of them.'

'They be bastards,' said one of the Men. He had not seen Isabella sitting alongside.

'Tomorrow the Men will speak,' Duncan told Isabella.

'And the ministers will allow that?'

'The ministers would not dare to stop them. The people will listen to them before the ministers. The ministers are afraid.'

One of the Men had risen to his feet. 'Will you sleep now, my friend?' called Rory.

'I go to the hills,' was the reply. 'Tomorrow I speak to the question. Tonight I will pray on the hilltop.'

Isabella stirred restlessly.

'D'you wish you hadn't come?' asked Duncan.

'One part of me is afraid. I didn't know it would be like this. But it's all right. I'm glad I came.'

'It's not as soft as you're used to.'

'It's something you'll have to become accustomed to,' said Willina, who had overheard this.

'What does she mean by that?' asked Isabella.

Duncan did not reply but got up to stoke the fire.

When she returned home, Isabella wrote to her sister-in-law in London, wife of her older brother, Marcus.

Ullapool, 9 July 1812

My dear Louise,

. . .it was the strangest experience of my life. The Men had their say on the Friday, and what they said was positively scandalous in terms of the company that was present. Any minister whom they did not think worthy of his calling, they got up and said so in no uncertain terms. As many as thirty of the Men 'spoke to the question' as they put it, on the Friday.

The day wore on and on. For a short time the sun blazed down and it was so hot I felt faint. Then, as suddenly, the wind changed, a cloud covered the sun, and within minutes there was a cold misty rain falling upon us. My teeth started to chatter, and we were all as good as soaked. Then again the sun came out, so that we all began to steam.

Oh, but the people are really poor here. I felt ashamed of my fine clothes, for they wear such pitiful threadbare garments, even the youngest and prettiest of the women. I wanted to apologise for my appearance—I was wearing that pink silk scarf which you and Marcus gave me the Christmas before last and I took it off and hid it in my pocket; I saw Duncan turn and smile a little at this: I had won his approval. Perhaps a little too much, but that is another matter.

On the Saturday, it was the turn of the ministers to speak. Not many of the 'Moderates' spoke. The breakaway movement from the Church of Scotland is flourishing in this parish. The object of hatred is one William MacKenzie, the terrible drunkard of whom Duncan and Rory had spoken.

It seems he took on an assistant called John Kennedy, or rather had him assigned, for the authorities could see that all was not well in the parish but were loath to remove MacKenzie. That's 'Moderates' for you, you see, this is why they are, and I think quite justly, seen to be useless and hypocritical—they make excuses for bad habits. Well, Kennedy was a fiery preacher—I say 'was' because all this happened some years ago—and he won a convert named Norman McLeod, who had been all kinds of spiritual adventurer in his youth: a Papist no less, for a short time, and then latterly a Haldanite before Kennedy came on the scene and led him back to Presbyterianism.

The story is most curious. McLeod, who was just a fisherman, was twenty-seven when he left to start training for the ministry. First he went to Aberdeen where he won a gold medal for philosophy at the university, and then to Edinburgh to train for his ordination. But they say he is not at all happy there, that he does not think well of his fellow churchmen, and indeed, when he had his say on Saturday, although not yet ordained he laid about him with some very harsh words. There is talk that he may never be ordained.

Meanwhile he has married a poor young woman who has waited for him for years. I've heard they were in school together and that she was cleverer than he is, which is saying something, for he is hailed as near to a genius. But she is never allowed to speak out for herself, so whatever brains she has, I'm afraid she must lack the equivalent in spirit. He's really quite a savage kind of fellow, all blazing eyes and stern jaw. A good figure of a man, the kind you could indulge yourself in dreaming over if only his expression was sweeter, but I do not think he would appreciate the idea...though you never can tell.

Duncan is truly in awe of him.

I meant to tell you more of all this but my writing arm is weary. The Sabbath was very holy and solemn, with the goblet passing up and down the tables from hand to hand and some people quite faint with the seriousness of it all. I did not take the cup, and true to his word neither did Duncan.

Duncan is a good man. He has a limp caused through an accident when the laird was out shooting and accidentally discharged a gun in his direction. He has fierce eyes too, but they are of a more tender light than McLeod's.

Much as I like him, though, I think it is time to quit this adventure. I find him disturbing and, because of a difficulty between us, I have decided to continue my explorations of the countryside on my own.

Yours affectionately, Isabella.

It had happened on the Saturday, when the ministers were speaking. The gaunt-faced men who guarded the donation boxes were watching the crowd with steely eyes. One of the breezes that constantly swept the crowd that day had risen with a sharp new intensity. Isabella shifted closer to Duncan. The guardian at the boxes, the same one who had looked at her so closely the day of their arrival, came over.

His voice was like flint. 'Woman, is this man your husband?'

'No.'

'You act like a wife with him, talking to him and casting him looks. When will the marriage take place?

'Come the end of autumn,' said Duncan swiftly. 'The lady stays at my sister's place.'

He did not look at her when the guardian had gone.

'Why?' she whispered, for what seemed like the twentieth time.

'Why not?' he had replied.

'We're not pledged to each other.'

'You came here with me.'

'Is that what you took from it?'

'We'll talk of it later.'

She began to get to her feet.

'No, not now,' he said, trying to restrain her by the force of his words. 'I am not one of the hypocrites of whom you speak.'

'You came here,' he repeated. 'D'you not understand what you have done, coming here with me?'

'You didn't say.'

'You did not ask. I thought you understood.'

She sank back on the grass, shaking her head.

Ullapool, 10 June 1813

Dearest Louise,

I feel so lost and confused within myself of late. I hope you won't show these letters to my brother, even though you're as life to each other. I don't understand what's going on in my head. I haven't felt easy since the time that I so foolishly—yes, yes, I admit it now—went into the highlands with Duncan MacQuarrie.

He haunts the town of Ullapool and his feelings around here are known, though he does not state them in public, he has too much respect. But people come to sense these things. His love is as great an affliction to him as it is to me who does not care for him in the same way, and of course father is even less inclined to employ him now than before. Although nothing is said to me, I know that there is encouragement in the town to scorn him. He is so poor, such an easy target, and with his game leg there is little he can do, though he labours on with the kelp. I keep referring to this accursed kelp; in case you don't know of it, it's a fine seaweed that grows around the shoreline here. When it's been gathered it gets dried out and burned on the beaches, so that there is a molten mass which is cooled into brittle blue layers, then *that* gets shipped off to the glass and soap-works in England. That's why the lairds are so eager for the people to be nice and handy to the icy sea—which is where they're living, thousands and thousands of them now, huddled near the beaches. A pretty sight? Does it shock you? I cannot bear it.

As for Duncan, I feel to blame for his worsening plight, through bringing ridicule upon him. I see now that it was natural for him to believe that I was pledging myself when I followed him. What else could he have thought? I did not understand enough their way of looking at things up here.

You may wonder that he asked me in the first place. Well, he is one of the terrible suffering lettered men, such as Highlanders often are, despite their poverty; placing learning above all things, and believing firmly in the equality of all men (I should like to say, of women too, but of course I refer to mankind, oh you will see what strain I am under at present).

Dear heaven forbid, I often think now, that poor people should be afflicted with knowledge and talent and intellect. Ah, that from me! No, don't listen, it is the deepest irony of which I am capable. But you see, he thought I was some kindred spirit, it seems, making a spontaneous gesture of my commitment. Perhaps I thought so too at the time, but now I do not know what induced me to go on that rash outing. It was an adventure, and adventuresses are not thought well of in this harsh and bitter land.

As if all that is not enough, and too much, I have had a most disturbing encounter with McLeod. It happened late one spring afternoon, although you would be hard put to think of it as spring for a small blizzard had blown up and died away, leaving in its wake a late fall of snow and the air was still damp and heavy with it. I had a great deal on my mind, on this evening of which I speak. I put on my fur-lined hood, and mittens, and set off. The snow obscured my view. Where there had been black rocks the day before, there was nothing, then the snow died away a little and the rocks began to move, or so it seemed. I cried out, afraid, and then I saw that it was the black-faces at large upon the moor.

I took a deep breath. When the snow cleared, I saw not only the foolish sheep blundering off at my approach, but also a man standing in my path. It was McLeod.

Sister, I feel that McLeod is part of my fate, that in him rests some overwhelming and mysterious power which will change my life.

My hands shake so much as I write, that I cannot go on . . .

He stood barring Isabella's way and this time she realised how tall he was; at least six feet or more. His black hair was worn smoothly and plainly, yet the plainness of its style could not disguise its thickness. His right eye had the beginning of a slight cast as if he were not looking quite directly at her, notwithstanding the intensity of his gaze. His complexion was of that darkness which distinguishes a man accustomed to be outdoors both summer and winter. But it was his mouth which she could not avoid looking at. It was set in a tight line with a downward inflection at the corners, as if trying to hide something, and as he spoke, Isabella could see that it was a fullness which might have been a tender curve had he allowed it full play.

'Why are you out alone in the snow, Miss Ramsey?'

Isabella stepped backwards, her knuckles grazing on a rock behind her, so that it was pointless trying to back further away from him.

'Who are you?' She was playing for time, making him explain himself, though she knew perfectly well who he was.

'Norman McLeod.'

'Oh, so you are. Yes, *the* Norman McLeod.'

'I beg your pardon, Madam?'

'I hear of you often. The preacher, no less.'

He smiled, or almost. She felt she had stroked a vanity.

'You haven't answered me.'

'How d'you know me?' she parried.

His look narrowed, and she realised that he was a person who did not enjoy prevarication, however much he might indulge in it himself if it were to his advantage. She straightened, and looked at him more boldly.

'I don't choose to fall into loose conversation with strangers, Mr McLeod,' she said. 'If you wish to speak with me, then I must know a little more of your interest in me.'

'I have no interest in you,' he said. 'Your name is known in these parts. You are talked of by men.'

He said this with so much accusation that she flinched as if he were attacking her, and in his way she could see that he was.

'I hope they speak well of me,' she said, but her voice faltered.

'Oh, the man who is so smitten with you, so foolishly running this way and that and deserting his parents and family who need him sorely, so that he can catch stray glimpses of your vain silly face and immodest ankle, speaks kindly of you. But that is to be expected of a man who has lost his mind. I speak of Duncan MacQuarrie, of course.'

He waited but she said nothing, and she felt his anger hardening against her.

'You know nothing of it,' she said, turning away.

'There are other men who speak less well of you.' His voice followed her relentlessly. 'They despair at the sight of a good man led astray by wilful and flirtatious unkindness.'

She turned back to him, placing her feet across the path like a man, as if she were the adversary.

'You have no business to speak in such a way to me, you, a student who is running foul of the authorities in Edinburgh from what I hear, for speaking out as if he knew more than the trained men of the church. Why don't you wait until you are one of them yourself before you start pestering young women who walk alone, minding their own business?'

'I am no longer at Edinburgh University.'

'Forgive me, I had not heard of your ordination.'

'It has not taken place. It will not.'

'You have failed the course? I had heard that Norman McLeod never failed in any of his undertakings.'

McLeod turned aside, and for a moment she glimpsed his weariness. When he spoke it was as if she was not there. 'I find I've done forever with Edinburgh, Madam,' and he turned back towards her and addressed her as if they had known each other all their lives and were very close. Afterwards she would recall that moment and wonder if she had misread him; at other times it occurred to her, as it did then, that in his own critical hour he had stumbled upon and recognised the kind of woman whom he most desired, one who would challenge him at every turn, and match his senses too. She would also come to understand, in the future, that he would never forgive her for having exposed him to his own vulnerable state. He spoke now, in a low and rapid voice. 'Miss Ramsey, I will never be ordained, so long as I live in this country, so long as the Church of Scotland and its clergy are so much in error in their interpretation of the Scripture and so lax in their moral behaviour. There are some people, ma'am, who consider me strangely singular, or even a touch fanatical, because I will not pronounce their shibboleth. I'm seen as a proud and insolent man, but that is as I am, and there is no other way. I will not seek favours or benefits, I will not flatter anyone in order to find an easy way. I chose not to go into the ministry after seven weary years of training for it, and I'm nothing more than a stickit minister, d'you know what that is? Aye, I'll tell you: a man without power or authority in the eyes of the law. But in God's name, I have no shame about this matter, and I know what is best for the people.'

'You're so very sure. I wish that I could be so certain of myself and what I believe.'

McLeod had by now recovered himself and his manner was again haughty. 'Then take advice from me. You are fallen, Miss Ramsey. You have only one recourse open to you if you wish to save your immortal soul. You must marry Duncan MacQuarrie.'

'I have done nothing. I've committed no sin.'

'Miss Ramsey, I saw you at the communion service with him, close to a year ago. You have led him to despair.'

'That's his peril. He's brought himself to that through a misunderstanding.'

'Then you should right it.'

'I have no duty to Mr MacQuarrie.'

'Man is head of the woman.'

'When she has chosen to be his wife.'

'Madam,' he said, and now it was as if they had barely passed more than a few words between them, 'you are past free will.'

The light on the alders was thickening into darkness. The young woman looked from side to side, seeking to escape McLeod. He stepped aside without bowing, wrapped his dark cloak more closely around him and began to walk away from her.

. . . Louise, it is hard to tell you this, and you may think I am abominable and strange, but I wanted to go after him. I wanted to tell him that I understood, and that when he spoke of free will I knew that he spoke for both of us. He and I are two of a kind, what's known as our own worst enemies. And we are due to make a closer acquaintance with each other, I suspect, for I hear today from Mother that he has been appointed schoolmaster at the parish school.

Sister, McLeod raises a fire in me.

Dispose of this letter. Burn it. Eat it. Well, at least, I implore you, don't show it to my brother.

Louise, would marriage really make me a better woman?

I hope all is well with you in London. We have heard echoes of the battle up here, and of course will all sleep sounder in our beds for knowing Bonaparte has been despatched at Waterloo. I gather that we may expect no further trouble on that front.

And I hear you are in a certain condition again, which of course gives Mother great delight. Bear up, my dear.

Yours, with love, Isabella.

P.S. Whatever strange passion McLeod invokes, I do not like him. That is quite different from what I have been describing of my feelings for him. But he is that strange kind of fellow who some would follow to the ends of the earth. I can imagine how it could happen.

In the year that followed, Isabella was consumed by a great industry, which she tried to explain to Louise:

Ullapool, 16 September 1815

...I can just imagine how busy you are with three little ones on your hands. I do intend to come south and see young Master Robert for myself, but it is surprisingly difficult to get away these days. Mary McLeod is with child again. I help her out with John Luther, quite a handful of a boy. Mary is such a slight person, and she looks worn already. Her ten-year wait for McLeod meant a late beginning to her childbearing. Do you know, she used to sit and spin wool for knitting into jerseys for him, and then when the winter was over she would collect up the jerseys and walk a hundred and forty miles to see him? No wonder she looks old already.

I do care for her very much, and since they have been here everyone has gone out of their way to make her life as comfortable as possible. All, that is, except McLeod himself, who seems quite oblivious to mortal needs. Still, she has a wooden rocking chair by the window and a small rug on the floor, and in the bedroom a big brass bed with a sparkling fresh coverlet, and she tells me that all of this is a great luxury.

I try not to think too much of my own affairs. I have not seen Duncan MacQuarrie for a long time. Sometimes I catch McLeod's eyes resting on me, but mostly his manner is very cold and I am most correct when I have occasion to speak to him. In the meantime, he and Mary spend a good deal of time on their knees in the bedroom.

She has told me that she often prays that they will so please God that they be allowed to preserve their present way of life, though it worries her that McLeod might get to know of this and think she is praying for material things. Must confess, I get a little tired of this, but she is very kind in her nature and it is true that she does have a good mind when she is not too weary to apply it to the detail of the moment. At her best, I find her a thoroughly good companion...

While Mary McLeod was on her knees praying for constancy in her way

56

of life, her husband was pursuing other ends. There was general enthusiasm in Ullapool for his teaching methods, and it was said that the children had acquired 'ever so much book learning in the shortest possible time'. The parents of some of the older children were heard to say with pride that at the rate they were learning, they wouldn't have to stay at school much longer; at which McLeod, in his turn, rebuked them sternly with the advice that while they might have learned like monkeys to read and write, he still had much work to do on their spiritual concerns and that would take a great deal longer. As for the parents themselves, there was much that needed doing for their spiritual welfare too; in all honesty, he could not see how they could expect their children's godliness to grow and mature if they did not look to their own.

These pronouncements were greeted with some astonishment by the local people at first, for as a rule most of them attended church on the Sabbath when the town minister, Dr Ross, was preaching.

'Come and join me and my friends next Sabbath day, and hear the true word of God,' McLeod exhorted them instead.

It had already been noticed since McLeod's arrival that the population did swell each Sunday. The visitors were people from the north, come to hear McLeod preach his own sermons.

'What do you think about Mr McLeod and his preaching?' a parishioner asked Dr Ross after his sermon one Sunday morning. The congregation had been very small that day, while across on the other side of town the overflow from McLeod's gathering could be seen spilling down the hill towards the sea, and cramming the street corners.

Ross was a small man with a plume of silver hair and a lean handsome face. He smiled. 'It is a phenomenon that will soon pass, you mark my words,' he responded with easy assurance.

'Dr Ross is nothing but a heathen libertarian,' thundered McLeod.

'Is it true,' whispered Mary McLeod, one evening later in the week, 'that you have offended Dr Ross and he is threatening to close down the school if you do not stop preaching on a Sunday?'

'It's nothing,' said McLeod. They were sitting at dinner. He took a piece of fried bread and used it to scoop the last of his fish into his mouth. Beside him, John Luther grizzled and pulled at his coat tail, hanging over the edge of the chair. He took the child on his knee and rocked him, reached over and took a morsel of bread his wife was toying with on her plate, and fed it to his son. The boy smiled and was still.

'You worry too much,' said McLeod, dismissing her question.

'But what of John's baptism? Who will do that?'

'Do not question me, Mary. It is unseemly of you.'

When his wife related this incident to Isabella, the younger woman was full of indignation.

'It's not good enough, Mary!' she cried. 'You should stand up to him. The way he's going on, Dr Ross is bound to close him down. I mean, can you blame him for being angry? There were only three people in church on Sunday.'

'And were you amongst them?'

Isabella shifted uncomfortably. 'You know I was listening to Mr McLeod.'

'And you are different from all the others who go?'

There was a silence between them. 'You're not married to him,' said Mary, finally. 'You do not know to what lengths he will go.'

Isabella looked away out the window. Her friend's eyes followed her. When she looked back, Mary had taken to rocking quietly in her chair. Under her hands the baby she was carrying fluttered, turned restlessly inside her. It is as well not to try and read her, Isabella thought.

After she had gone, Mary sat looking out to sea. It is all right for Isabella, she told herself. She is young, and she has always had enough to eat, so that her strength is not sapped. It's all right for her to have fallen under his spell, she has other chances and will get over it. I am too tired already to fight with him.

The following week McLeod announced to his wife that John Luther would have to be baptised at Loch Carron.

'But that's forty miles away!'

'We have walked further before.'

'But now?'

'I'll carry the child,' said McLeod. 'You will have no need to concern yourself about that.'

'Can't we wait for the summer?'

'We've waited too long already.'

'Then can you not appeal to Dr Ross? It is not the child who has offended him?'

'My dear Mary, do you not understand?' He spoke with a certain solicitude, as if she might be incapable of grasping what he was saying.

And indeed she did not understand him, but dared not tell him so.

McLeod explained seemingly with great patience, but there was an underlying agitation in his manner. 'Dr Ross is a man of the worst temper, to begin with, but that is not the point. We are talking of our son's baptism, the future of his immortal soul. The man who ministers such a sacrament must be worthy of that responsibility. Allow me to inform you, my dear wife, that last Sunday when Ross preached, he took the text "Ye are the salt of the earth" and all he had to say was about how salt is procured and processed. And the Sunday before that, the learned doctor preached on "Ye are the light of the world" and what did he talk about? Why, the planetary system! Hercules and Herschel and Neptune and Newton were the topics and personalities under discussion.

But of sinners and the Saviour, he spoke not a word. There now,' and his voice had assumed a note of positive triumph, 'surely you can understand that. Well don't you, Mary?'

'No,' she said, but not to him. It was Isabella whom she told of difficulty in coming to terms with her husband's philosophical scruples.

Privately, Isabella wondered how Mary would stand the journey to Loch Carron. The skin of her face was softly pleated around the mouth and her colour very pale. The small pulse in her throat throbbed constantly. She had seen it as Mary lay in bed, some days too tired to get up and attend to John.

'What would I do without you?' she said on days such as this, putting her thin hand on Isabella's arm.

'It will get better, you'll see,' Isabella had said, but sometimes she wondered if it would. It was not so much the state of Mary's physical condition that bothered her, although it was clear that she was not strong, but rather her total disinclination to oppose McLeod, whatever he said and even though his suggestions were often difficult to the point of impossibility. Or that was how it appeared to her.

Although when she had first come to Ullapool Mary had demonstrated a clear sharp brain if called upon to do so, lately it appeared that this required too much effort. More and more often if there were details about the housekeeping which involved McLeod, or extra bills to be paid, she would ask Isabella to tell him. McLeod would receive the information in silence, but he would invariably act upon it.

One morning as she made her way down Shore Street, Isabella realised with sudden shocked clarity that Mary would really like her to take over responsibility for McLeod. That she should be as a wife was beyond consideration, yet the day-to-day running of their lives, and perhaps even the matter of intellectual transaction, was something she appeared to be suggesting could best be attended to by Isabella.

'It will not be like that,' said Isabella with a grim force that made her almost speak aloud. 'She will not take me over and hand me to him on a plate.'

Besides, there were things Mary did not know of her and McLeod. The meeting on the moor would seem to have sealed their relationship into a cool and distant mould which McLeod, for his part, would be unlikely to alter. She wondered at times why he had accepted her presence so readily in the house at all, but considering its great convenience to himself, it would seem that he must be an opportunist as well as a dictator. It might even be that he had already mapped out her position as a retainer, growing older and more spinsterly before his eyes as the years passed; in that, he would achieve his ascendancy over her.

'I have to get away from here,' she said to her mother.

'Away? Where would you go?' Lately Mrs Ramsey had been enjoying a great deal of bad health. Isabella thought savagely as she plumped yet more pillows that her mother was almost in competition for her attention with Mary McLeod.

'I could go to London,' said Isabella, suddenly desperate to be away. 'I could stay with Louise.'

'Louise has plenty to do without looking after her unmarried sister-in-law,' said Mrs Ramsey.

'I could help Louise. You know I could. Besides, perhaps I could meet with a husband of my own this time.' Isabella hoped that her mother would not recognise her low cunning for what it was.

'Oh dear, I think it may be too late for that,' Mrs Ramsey tutted. 'And besides, who would look after me? No, it is out of the question. And,' as if reading Isabella's mind, 'I shall tell your father so, so please do not speak of it to him.'

Mrs Ramsey was playing a hand which Isabella found unbeatable. It was clear that her father would not entertain the thought of her leaving him on his own with his wife if she was not well disposed to the idea.

Sitting in the McLeod's small front room that faced the sea, Dr Ross sipped his tea, his finger crooked, and between each sip he smiled delicately at Mary, oozing kindly concern as if she were about to be struck by illness.

'Mr McLeod, I have a proposition for you.'

'Oh aye, Dr Ross?' McLeod tapped his fingers on the arm of his chair and waited.

'You might show a little interest.'

'It is you that is putting the proposition, Dr Ross.'

'You're a prickly fellow to be sure. What does one do with him Mrs McLeod?' Receiving no support from this quarter, he hurried on. 'Mr McLeod you have stirred up quite a following in the district. I know your heart's very much in it, you're a man of principle, sir, and I would not like to be seen to complain of such a man.'

'Yet you do.'

'I must confess it is not an easy position you place me in. But look, problems are there to be solved. It is part of your duty as a schoolmaster to attend my sermons. But I'm not strictly convinced that that is necessary on every occasion. Let us say, if you were to attend mine but once a month, put in an appearance if you like, then I think we could consider the matter settled. What do you say?'

'I say that if you were more strict in the discipline of those whose interests you claim to represent, then this situation might never have arisen in the first place. But that is the crux of the matter is it not, the scab that infests the whole Church of Scotland?'

'You refuse my request then?'

'Sir, if you have finished your tea you must excuse us, we have our devotions to attend to and the evening grows late.'

Vexed beyond endurance, Dr Ross cut the schoolmaster's salary.

When the McLeods finally set out for Loch Carron with their child in the spring they were already penniless. Before they left McLeod had stocked up with fish, smoked and dried, and flour, brought to him by his followers; outside was a huge pile of firewood, gathered off the moor. At least when they returned they would be comfortable, he told Mary, while he dealt with the problem of Dr Ross. Instead, they found a summons nailed to the door, issued in the name of Dr Ross, for the theft of the firewood from parish property.

'They will starve to death,' said Mrs Ramsey with what could only be construed as a note of satisfaction. She had been gravely embarrassed by the behaviour of her former protégé; entertaining Dr Ross to tea, she could not escape the thought that he might hold her responsible for introducing such an audacious and troublesome element into the parish.

'He did not steal the firewood, mother,' said Isabella hotly.

'Indeed, and whose side are you on? Although that should be obvious, the amount of time you spend with that rather sad little wife of his.'

'It is not a matter of sides, it's unjust, everyone knows it is. If you ask me, Dr Ross has done more to enhance Mr McLeod's reputation than to damage it.'

'But he has no job now, and he has to go to court in Dingwall. What will he do about that? And I hear he is very much in debt.'

'Let the magistrate decide what will happen to Mr McLeod. It is none of our business.'

'Well, I would have thought it was yours,' said her mother with a keener look than usual. She was sitting at the window, in her old place, as if the excitement of conflict had restored her spirits.

'At least that foolish fellow from the hills seems to have given up hanging around here. I suppose that is something to be thankful for.' She snapped her thread with pleasure. 'You know the one I mean?'

'I know,' said Isabella.

'Yes, I thought you'd remember. What was his name?' Her needle was poised over a cross-stitch.

'It is neither here nor there.'

'But you said you remembered him.'

'MacQuarrie, Mother, his name was MacQuarrie.'

'Ah yes, Duncan was it not? Yes, Duncan MacQuarrie.' She smiled, pleased with herself.

After the court case in Dingwall, when McLeod had been cleared of the charge against him, Isabella helped Mary to pack what was left of their belongings into two small trunks. Holding Donald, the new baby, as they waited for the carriage that was to take the McLeods away, Mary said, 'I cannot believe I will ever be so happy again, as I have been here on Shore Street.'

'So you have been happy?'

'But of course. Did you think I was not?'

'I'm sure you'll find things even better in Wick.'

'Oh you think so? With Norman away on the fishing boats again? It's not much of a life, you know.'

'He says he'll pay off the debts, Mary. I'm sure it will be better for you and the children than not knowing where the money is coming from.'

'It was my dream, this place.' She looked around the bare rooms.

'There will be other houses.'

'But where will they be? What's going to become of us? Perhaps I'll never see you again.'

'I'm sure you will.' Isabella felt a small knot of fascination inside her as she wondered whether it would prove to be so; and if it did not, what the rest of her life would be like: if she were never to see McLeod again.

'Isabella. He speaks of emigrating.' Mary gripped her friend's arm, and her eyes were frightened.

But there was no time to discuss this matter for the carriage had come. McLeod appeared, ready to lift the trunks aboard, then mounted the carriage steps without looking behind him.

'You have not said goodbye to Isabella,' cried Mary.

He turned, looking as if his neck was stiff, and bowed slightly towards her. Of late, he had taken to wearing spectacles, and now, behind them, his eyes appeared to be without reflection.

'Goodbye, Miss Ramsey.'

Mary craned her head back, straining to catch a last glimpse of the young woman who had befriended her. She saw her standing in the doorway of what had been her house and might have been forgiven for thinking that Isabella looked forlorn, though she supposed it must be an illusion. She had never seen Isabella looking really downcast; today, as ever, her hair was drawn back and nicely arranged, shining in the pale sunlight, and her large exceptional eyes were fixed towards the distant space that she and McLeod were now entering. Isabella did not raise her hand as they rounded the last corner, the carriage bearing them up the hill and away towards the east.

When they had gone, Isabella thought it is as well, I am pleased that they have departed. I have had enough of them. One way or another, they would have taken over my life, until there was nothing left of myself. Thank God, it is over.

But the truth was, that she felt very empty.

As she turned to pull the door shut, the shadow of Duncan MacQuarrie fell across the path in front of her.

4

THE DAYS AFTER Isabella's marriage to Duncan MacQuarrie had passed in a strange haze of decisions and quarrels and partings. It happened so quickly, and her parents swore on the still and sunny morning of its occurrence that they would never speak to her again, and upbraided her for her unnaturalness.

When she set off across the moors with her new husband striding along silently at her side, she half wondered if they were right, and if, in fact, there was something strange about her. It had seemed that her life was without purpose, and that no ordinary man would ever satisfy the hunger within her. At night the suffering face of Duncan haunted her, mixed up and confused with that of McLeod. In the mornings she would wake dazed and heavy, as if she hadn't slept at all, and wander around the town feeling aimless and lost.

The first time that Duncan had reappeared after the McLeod's departure she had been disposed to be briefly kind to him; too late, she had seen hope flare in his eyes. At once she became brisk and dismissive.

'I have work to do, Mr MacQuarrie.'

'What work is that?'

'It is just some things I have to do.'

'You'll have rather less to do, now that the McLeods are gone.'

'Well maybe that is so. But still, I'm busy.' When he continued to stand there, she cried out, 'Oh, it's none of your business, Mr MacQuarrie, now will you leave me alone?'

For a while he had, and when next she saw him he did not accost her, even looked past her as if indifferent. The days passed and she found herself wondering if she would ever see him again. Months went by without her daring to ask anyone if he was alive and well for fear they might misread her intentions.

When she had not seen him for six months, he came back to town. They almost collided outside The Arch, as she carried bannock cakes in a basket to Miss Ruby Quaid who was sick with the pleurisy. Grains of sugar gleamed on top of the cakes in a small bright rime. Duncan looked at them. His clothes were more threadbare than ever. She reached into the basket and handed him two cakes.

'Thank you, I will keep them until later,' he said, holding them awkwardly.

'I will marry you, if that is still what you wish,' said Isabella. It seemed like an astonishing thing to say, but she knew she had been rehearsing it for a long time.

He nodded, as if he were not greatly surprised. Taking her hand he drew it through the crook of his arm so that this way they walked to the water's edge, letting it be known for the sake of onlookers that they were united. When they reached the pier, she said, 'Well, you should eat now, shouldn't you?'

Gratefully, he ate her bannock cakes.

In spite of the bitter words that passed between Isabella and her parents when the marriage first took place, the couple did return to Ullapool after they had been north to announce the marriage to Duncan's family. Adam Ramsey had, at last, grudgingly offered his new son-in-law work with the Company, although he let it be known around the village that he had taken on a cripple out of charity, for the sake of his foolish daughter. Still, the wage he paid allowed the couple to live in what had been the schoolmaster's house.

In the months that followed, Isabella began to be glad that she had married Duncan and no one else. She had been a little afraid to move into the house vacated by McLeod and Mary, yet once in charge of it she had seemed to exorcise McLeod. She scrubbed and polished every board with relentless care the first week that she was there, and afterwards filled the house with flowers and the smell of her own baking. It was as if she had always lived there. At night when Duncan came home, it was him she saw and not McLeod. She felt alive, and beloved.

But as Mary had before, in this house, she dreamed that this was how her life might always be.

As winter drew near, the work on the boats became dangerous. Ice began to coat the decks and the men were required to work faster to complete their tally before the season was over.

She saw that Duncan was quieter, and that strain was developing in his expression. His hands were red and raw; at times he seemed to move with effort.

Mrs Ramsey, visiting her married daughter and enjoying a third snack before lunch, looked around the room. 'You do very well, all things considered, my dear.'

'Considering what things, mother?'

'Well. What has *he* done in the way of firewood for the winter, for instance?'

'It'll be done. He doesn't get much spare time at the moment, mother, as you know perfectly well.'

'Hmm. But he's not a great provider, is he, dear?'

'You know, too, how hard he works.'

'Oh. Oh really? Well, if you say so, Isabella.'

'Mother, is father saying that he doesn't?'

'My dear, I know nothing of these matters. Still. He did say that your husband let a whole netful of fish go over the side yesterday. Well, these things can't be helped, I suppose. A matter of looking where one puts one's feet, I imagine.'

That evening Isabella asked Duncan, 'Has father been treating you unkindly?'

He pushed his chair back and got to his feet. She saw that his gait was awkward. Something she had not observed before and supposed now that she must have overlooked, was that his limp was more pronounced. He was arranging his wet clothes across the fire.

'He has right on his side,' he said. 'I do what I can.' He turned back to her. 'It is not always enough.'

'D'you want to leave here?' she asked.

He knelt beside her, placing his face in her lap. She sat very still. In the years she had observed the marriages of other people—even her brother and his wife in London, who still behaved with decorum and great politeness towards each other while in the midst of their affection. She had never been given cause to imagine what it would be like to have a man kneel in front of her like this. She placed her hands around his face, so that he was forced to look up at her. 'I love you, Duncan MacQuarrie,' she said.

In the flickering shadows that lit the room she thought she saw a figure. She blinked and it was gone, but she knew that McLeod was back.

She wanted to call out and tell him to leave, that he could not touch her, but already he was gone. He will come again, she thought grimly.

In the morning when Duncan was preparing to leave for the boats, she said, 'Don't go today, Duncan. Let's pack our things and leave here.'

He looked at her. 'Are you sure that is what you want?'

'I am sure I do not want to stay. In the summer I'll help you with the kelp. If other women can do it, why not I?'

'What of the winter that is coming?'

'I have a little money, as you know.'

'Sooner or later, you'll be hungry. You've never been hungry before. And cold. D'you know what it is like to be really cold?'

'Well, we shall have each other.'

'Yes. Yes, that's so.' Already he was looking around the house, estimating how quickly he could gather up their belongings and be on their way.

In the company of Duncan's family that winter, Isabella found comfort and friendship with Willina McRae. The small amount of money the MacQuarries had brought helped all of them. The two women eked it out between them, so that although the winter had its difficulties, it was not all total despair. Armed with needle and thread, Isabella refashioned the children's scant clothes; as she fitted them against their thin bodies in front of the fire, she began to feel the stirrings of a need for children herself. I am a real wife, she thought, I will be a mother.

But then she wondered, what will we do with them if they come? Along with this new yearning there was mingled relief as the months passed and there was no sign of a child. And yet her body felt animated: she was sure that when it was ready, it would let her know. She was sometimes shy in the crowded conditions in which they lived, that Willina and Rory might detect the pleasure she took from lying beside their brother, behind the screen at the end of the room. But if they did, they said nothing.

In the spring they had to move. The food and money had run out and Willina was delivered of another child, crying and screaming a great deal, and nearly dying during the ordeal. Isabella thought privately that there must be some way to avoid such difficulty at that age of one's life. The only course, she supposed, would be to refuse certain acts, and she could not see how that was possible.

The McRaes said they must stay, that somehow they would all manage, but having made the decision before they had come north to become independent and work the kelp, and clear in the knowledge that they would all starve if they did stay, Duncan and Isabella pressed on with their plan to go to the beaches. Duncan built a shelter amongst the congregation of people who were coming together once more for the kelp season.

Isabella's feet were cut to ribbons the first day she entered the sea. Her wounds stung in the salt water, becoming worse as the days passed. She had nothing with which to bind them and soon they became infected, swollen and oozing.

Each day Duncan would suggest that she stay home, and each day she would return. This is what I chose, she said to herself, I knew, I knew.

But I did not know it would be like this. I did not know it would be so bad.

In the night she cried until towards morning, when she slept fitfully. The acrid smell of burning kelp filled the air and a continual pall of smoke hung over the camp. Eyes and noses ran constantly and the features of some of the kelp pickers became so swollen that they were virtually unrecognisable as the people who had arrived in the spring. Touching her own face, Isabella suspected that she was one of them.

'I am no sort of wife for you, Duncan,' she whispered one night when he had brought thin fish head gruel to her. 'Let me go back to my parents.'

'Do you want to go? I would understand if you did.'

'Of course I don't want to go. But what use am I here?'

66

'If you do not want to go, not for anything on earth will I let you go back.'

Before they left for the waves again, he helped her into her clothes each day. The clothes would still be damp, but he would have spent half the night, while she was tossing and turning, holding them to the fire so that they would dry as much as possible. Even so they were still rough with salt, abrasive, and rubbing her too-sensitive skin so that sores opened under her arms.

'This time, stay home. Please, you must,' he said one morning. He saw a hectic flush in her face, and knowing better than she did the signs of fever, he was afraid.

'I'm coming with you,' she said, struggling to rise.

'If you must go somewhere, go south. See if your parents will feed you.'

'You would have that? You said...?'

'I didn't realise the work would so nearly kill you.' He had been going to say, 'so soon', but did not. 'Oh what would I do without you?' he said instead. 'Isabella, you can't come with me today.'

'Will you stay here with me, then?'

'I cannot.'

A sharp early autumn shower beat a tattoo against the side of their shelter. She trembled, was overcome with shivering.

'I will rest today,' she said, capitulating, 'then tomorrow I'll go south.'

But by evening she was too ill to move anywhere at all, and Duncan, sitting beside her as the days passed, waited for her to die.

'It is pneumonia,' said Willina, come to take a turn sitting beside her.

'I know.... If only we could move her. That she should die like this, here, like a beached fish....'

'I will not die,' said Isabella in a loud distinct voice. Both the watchers jumped. Duncan leaned over to speak to her, but she was asleep.

'She will pull through,' said Willina thoughtfully. 'If the weather only holds.'

Isabella did recover and as winter approached again Duncan went, on their behalf, to ask her parents for food. Still weak and finding it hard to move around, she waited for him to return, full of guilty, greedy hunger at the thought of the food he might bring back.

She expected him to slink through the door on his return, for he had viewed his journey with considerable distaste. Instead, when she heard his footstep she did not at first recognise it, it was so jaunty. His face was alight.

'Duncan, tell me directly, what is it?'

'Eat first.' Which he did not have difficulty in persuading her to do. She tore at strips of meat and sucked some mutton chops dry, stripping them down to their marrows, and filling both her hands with oatmeal cake in order to stuff her mouth more quickly. She thought then how unlike her life before this was, that she was eating in this animalish gulping fashion, squatting on her haunches in a rude shack, with the sea pounding outside her door. Looking across at him, and the gangling set of his body, she thought, it could only be so with him. Not with anyone else.

'What have you to tell me, then?' she asked again, when her stomach had settled.

Even then he did not tell her at once, and when he did he chose his words with care. That day, in Ullapool, he had met McLeod.

'McLeod? But he is supposed to be in Wick.'

'He's paid his debts and he has money in his pocket. He is talking of emigrating.'

Immediately Isabella knew what was on his mind. Trust McLeod, she thought, to turn their lives around. Yet who else? It made perfect sense.

McLeod had told Duncan of a ship, the *Frances Ann,* which was to leave Loch Broom in the middle of the following summer, bound for Nova Scotia. It could take four hundred people. McLeod was planning to leave Mary and the children while he went ahead to find a place for them to settle.

'Would you consider going too?' he asked.

'Nova Scotia? Where is that?' she said, although inside her she thought she already knew the answer to his question.

'New Scotland? It is on the eastern seaboard of North America. A place also known as Acadia, for the French lived there a long while till the English chased them out.'

'America, eh? A big continent.'

'So what d'you say?'

An inner voice was asking her, can you bear it, close to McLeod? Can you be near him again? She saw him standing in the corner of the room, in the house in which they had both lived, and thought, will I get away from him by running? But she had known he would come back. Aloud, she said, 'I'll send for the money from my brother in London.'

'Maybe we can find it.... Well, yes, all right then. It will be the last time...we'll be free after this. Free, you hear me?'

'I hear you, Duncan.'

'D'you wish to stay in Scotland too? Until I have made things ready for you?'

'Ah, no, lad. You won't be leaving me behind. No, don't argue. I have no children to think of yet, as Mary does. And if I don't come with you now, we may never have them.'

68

5

WAVES OF MIGRATION had already begun, and word of the
departure of the *Frances Ann* swept through the Highlands.
Preparations to leave began as soon as the decision had been
made, and followed through the winter until the time to leave was on
those who were going. Weeks before the ship was due to sail, horse trains
began heading across the hills towards Ullapool. They carried the aged,
and children, in crubag packs, wooden frames with wicker baskets. The
trains were formed by tying each horse to the tail of the next by a hair
rope, in this manner taking both goods and people to the ship. They came
from all over, Strath Brora, Durness, Assynt, Lochalsh, Loch Carron,
Kilmuir, Kiltearn, Kinlochewe and parts beyond, as well as from the town
of Ullapool itself.

As the days passed, Isabella had grown stronger, seemingly by the
hour. I am changed by what has happened to me, she said to herself, and
by illness, but I am better, and better prepared for what is to come.

Still, at times she was overtaken by the magnitude of the adventure.
As she looked around the encampment of people waiting to embark, she
caught glimpses of what she was feeling in all their faces. She wrote then
to her sister-in-law:

Ullapool, 12 July 1817

My dear Louise,
. . . I get ready to take my leave of Scotland, and all the things I know.
Dear sister, think of me. Pray for me, if you will.

I am at once anxious to be away, yet at the same time afraid for our
well-being. I have been aboard the *Frances Ann*. They say she is being
made safe for us. Well, she could certainly do with some attention, for
you never saw a leakier looking tub.

Please tell Marcus that I have, to some extent, been reconciled with
our mother. We have had to stay somewhere while things were put to
right on the ship, and when it came to the point, she could not stand
to see us camping out in the open with the others—the shame of it, I suspect,
but as we do not expect ever to see each other again, she and father, all
of us, in fact, have made the best of it, and mother has given me some
household items to take with us, and those silver candlesticks that were

my aunt's. Mind you, mother has done a lot of weeping and asking God where she has gone wrong but her friends comfort her, telling her that it is not she who has made mistakes, and I will have my comeuppance. Her problem, of course, is that she will not be there to see it!

Well, it is a bright summer here, I have gathered plants and seedheads, sweet cicely from the manse garden, rose root and cloudberry, and I have been given some seed of the small wild celery that grows in the Summer Isles. I wonder, will they take root in Nova Scotia? I hear it is very cold, but doubt it could be worse than our winters here.

By the way, I have seen McLeod, but he remains a distant figure, totally preoccupied with preparations for the journey; indeed, we barely nod to each other. I think that is how it will remain, for which I am well pleased.

This really seems to be goodbye. . . .

With my love to you both, and the children, Isabella.

Two days later, Alec Roy and Dan Ban sounded the Coronach from the hillside above Loch Broom, as the travellers boarded the ship. The music unfurled like a dirge across the lake, nearly drowned out at times by the weeping of those who were left on the shore. Parents who were about to leave were wrestling with their own parents as they tried to drag children from their arms, believing that whole families were about to perish and some must be saved.

A woman standing next to Isabella as they were being jostled in the crowd while they waited for a rowboat to take them to the ship turned and cried, 'Why have we been driven out? Why is there no place for us here, in our own country?'

As the ship pulled away, McLeod, standing on the deck, broke into the old lament of McCrimmon, and in a moment the voices of everyone on board had joined with him and were soaring back across the water to the watchers on the shore—*cha tille cha tille cha tille me tuilleach,* return return return we never, in peace nor war return we never, with silver or gold return we never.

The Atlantic ocean was all around them now as the sight of land slipped behind them in the night. Packed side by side with the other passengers, Isabella found herself fortunate to have a bunk, although where she lay the side of the ship pressed against her, splintered and patched, one patch on top of another.

By morning there was already filth accumulating underfoot. The deck tilted this way and that, and sometimes it was to the advantage of the passengers as human excrement slid overboard. At other times, those caught on the wrong side of the boat found their ankles awash. Slowly, an order of sorts was established and passengers who were not so seasick that they were unable to help began a routine that was designed to keep their health and spirits intact.

For the first two weeks at sea the weather held and the ship appeared to make progress. Duncan and Isabella were among those who walked on the deck early each morning, glad to make their escape from the thick stench below, where they were forced to spend their nights. Glancing at Duncan, Isabella often surprised a look of happiness on his face. She saw too McLeod, bent in a curious fashion over charts. He appeared to be studying the position of the ship and the winds and ocean currents, as if he were the captain.

When they had been sixteen days at sea, they woke to find that the air outside had become strange and heavy. Emerging onto the deck they saw that the sea was dull and molten in its appearance, almost oily in its depths. The captain was up and down, checking charts, edgy and not speaking to anyone.

Duncan looked anxiously at the sky. 'I have told them I will help muck out in the hold this morning,' he said to Isabella. 'I think you should go below too.'

'Soon, if the wind rises,' she promised.

One by one, people were withdrawing into the ship, huddled in on themselves, as if they expected to be plucked off the deck by a wave at any moment. Alone on the deck, Isabella felt a growing exultation, as if she had the ship to herself. The first winds to touch it were little puffs, sharp, but not hard enough to worry about, she was sure, although the ship was developing an unpleasant short lurch. She was fairly certain that below the stench of sickness would be increasing by the moment, and she determined to stay on deck for as long as she could.

She heard a sharp voice beside her and saw the captain. He was a short, thickset man who had taken little notice of her on the voyage, as indeed he had not paid much attention to any of the women and children. He was an Englishman who so far had shown himself so uncouth that no one greatly minded his lack of interest.

'You, get down below,' he said now, indicating with his thumb towards Isabella. 'We're battenin' down hatches.'

'You think it will be a real blow, then?' she called across the rising wind.

His mouth was set in a hard line. He did not answer her but shouted orders to the sailors to shorten the sails.

The sun, what was left of it, suddenly vanished. It was almost as dark as night over the sea, only an eerie bluish light showing them the way. Then across the water there was a jagged flash of lightning tearing the sky from side to side like a skirt ripped in two. The west wind slammed down on them, and a solid rain exploded around the ship.

'Get below, woman, damn you, below,' the captain shrieked at Isabella.

Duncan's face appeared at the hatch. In a moment she was being thrown across the deck and was tumbling over, bruising her shins, as he forced her down. Her last glimpse of the terrible scene outside was a sail snapping, then flapping with thunderous roars; the captain taut in every muscle against the wheel and the men straining to control the rigging. And against the sky, the figure of McLeod, his body arched on the pull of a rope, his cloak thrown back, and the dark water cascading down his fisherman's arms.

Below, a commotion of sobbing had broken out. Isabella realised she was wet through and that Duncan was furious with her for not having heeded the warnings sooner. But there was no time now for reproaches or for changing clothes. Little children were being tossed around, bouncing from side to side of the boat. She began to gather up those who were unattended. Many of the fathers were as ill as their wives, and every man who could stand was being called to the pumps. With Kate MacKenzie of Durness who, like her, was still unaffected by the violent motion of the ship, she lashed the children into their bunks with bedclothes.

Outside the sea groaned, and the rain drummed, beating overhead. Through the portholes they could see it lashing as the ship heeled upwards, seeming to stand bolt upright with its bow towards the sky, then they would come crashing down again, until the next thing they saw was the water beneath the surface bubbling like a black cauldron, the fierce sea trying to force itself in upon them, then back up again, and the ghostly glow of another lightning bolt lit up the pallid faces of her companions. It was becoming impossible to tell whether the crashes above them were giant thunderclaps or the breaking up of the ship. They could only hear each other by shouting with all their strength.

Then, as suddenly as it had come, the wind dropped and it was over. Some of the passengers wondered if they were already dead, if this was the silence of heaven, although all around them the sordid evidence of their physical extremity suggested otherwise.

Soon there was a call for them to come out and they breathed sweet clean air under a sky like a pale bell-shaped dome. They looked from one to the other, smiling, touching each other, hardly daring to believe that they were all there, and alive, and that nobody had been lost.

McLeod stepped forward. 'Let us pray,' he began, and one by one they began to follow him, his voice a panacea for the terror they had experienced. Isabella wondered how long he would go on, for evening was coming on them now and a chill was in the air. We need hot food and dry clothes more than we need prayer, she thought.

But McLeod appeared to realise this as well, for he was soon finished.

Then the captain spoke, his complexion slightly more suffused than usual, and it occurred to Isabella that he had been giving himself some fortification while the rest of them had been praying.

'I must tell thee all somethin',' he said. 'I am about to turn ship around and return home.'

There was a stunned silence at first, and then the questions began, shouted from all directions. 'Why, why?' and, 'Captain, we cannot, we have nothing left to return to, you cannot take us back. We have paid our fares, all we have in the world.'

The MacQuarries added their voices to this clamour. Isabella was afraid that Duncan was about to use his fists on the captain; it would have only needed one of them to start and it would be a free-for-all.

He raised his hands. 'The ship be leakin'. We're closer to the coast of Ireland than we are to America.'

McLeod had been standing by, quietly listening to all of this. 'That is not so,' he said.

The captain looked surprised, but replied quite mildly. 'You suggestin' you be better sailor than I, Mister McLeod?'

'In this instance, yes, I must tell you that I am,' McLeod replied.

'Pray explain y'self, sir,' said the captain against a background of indrawn breaths from the onlookers.

'If you care to step below I'll show you on the charts that we are actually closer to North America than we are to home,' said McLeod. 'I can demonstrate to you most clearly that our chances of safety lie in continuing our voyage. And you will see, by morning there will be a wind from the east to help us on our way.'

'McLeod, that is enough, man. This is mutiny. I'll be placin' you in irons if there be any more of this talk.'

McLeod looked around them all, measuring his moment. Some of the passengers were close to falling at his feet in their anxiety that someone would continue to head the boat towards America. Others were wavering, confused and unsure whom they should listen to.

Isabella, sheltered from the evening breeze by Duncan, felt oddly removed from what was happening. She expected that they would do as McLeod said, and was grateful of his presence as an antidote to the captain. But it was clear to her, as she supposed it must be to McLeod, that reason alone would not compel the people to follow his instructions.

'I have seen a vision,' said McLeod, raising his voice. 'In my vision we stand on the edge of a new land, and God speaks to us through the act of merciful deliverance from the elements. Then in my vision, my head has turned itself around, and I see nothing, only darkness, and the everlasting canyon. Which is it to be, my friends, deliverance or darkness?'

Their voices went up in a roar. 'Deliverance.'

A woman at the back called out, high and clear above the rest, 'We are delivered by the father, our father, Norman McLeod.'

In the dusk, Isabella could have sworn that McLeod looked over their heads at her alone and fixing her straight in the eye, dared her to challenge him. It was as if he needed someone who would support him in his convictions, in the responsibility he was taking on himself for all their lives. She knew, too, that he needed her support amongst the women, for she had acquired a new stature herself in the last few hours.

Across the space which separated them, she closed her eye in a slow wink, certain that no one except McLeod could see her action.

His face filled with thunder, and then subsided. She wanted to laugh but touched her husband's arm, indicating that he should speak.

'I say we go with Norman,' said Duncan then.

'Aye. Aye. We go with him.'

The captain turned an ugly face on McLeod. 'If we ever do make land, Mister McLeod, the minute you set foot on it, you may expect they'll be arrestin' you and clappin' on the irons. I'll see to that.'

But by morning, as McLeod had predicted, a fair wind from the east sprang up while the sea remained gentle. The ship, set on a good course, flew across the waves towards America. All the men aboard helped to man the pumps, which could not be left for a moment if the sea was to be kept at bay.

On the last day of August but one, Kate MacKenzie who had become Isabella's friend, woke her early in the morning. Duncan was already at the pumps. Kate whispered to her, for all around them others still slept.

'I couldn't sleep,' she said quietly, 'so at dawn I went up onto the deck. Isabella, I swear I could smell land.'

'Land?' echoed Isabella, incredulous. She had almost forgotten that it existed. But Kate nodded her head with such conviction that she got up and followed her outside.

Kate stood on the deck and pointed, her red flag of hair gleaming in the light mist. And sure enough, it was not just the salt-laden air that they could smell, but a new scent of fresh pine forests. They peered at the horizon and there against it was a dark smudge.

In a few moments they were joined by Duncan, and Kate's husband Eoghann, and McLeod and the captain. They turned to each other, overcome with joy but also scared, both of losing the bonds which they had formed with each other on the voyage, and of the new life ahead. They reached out and held hands uncertainly, only McLeod and the captain standing apart.

'Well, McLeod,' the captain said, with as near a show of grace as they had seen on the voyage, 'I must say it is true. You're a better seaman than I gave you credit for.'

McLeod shook his head, haughty. 'Not at all. It was the Lord's doing. To Him be the praise.' Then he relented 'Come, we'll be friends.' He offered his hand, which after a moment's hesitation the captain accepted.

They all turned back to watch the coastline growing larger and clearer until in late morning the ship sailed smoothly into the harbour at Pictou.

6

I WISH THAT I could write to someone but there is only myself now. Nobody replies any more. To send my letters would be like sending them in a hollow log. Only the mice and the birds will find them...I'm alone. Duncan has gone to the woods to fell timber. We have a cabin that was left by lumber men last summer. I am thankful to God that we had somewhere to shelter.

McLeod rode past this morning. He was followed by a retinue of admirers. He has become almost like God Himself in this community. Everyone wishes to be his neighbour but they cannot all get land alongside of him. Personally, I am glad we do not live near him. I have been his neighbour once.

Duncan is not as happy as I expected. He wants to be close to the Man. Even the people who live here already, the ones who came before us, are flocking to hear him preach.

I would like to tell them, but I do not think that they would listen to me, that he is only a man.

Not that I have anything against men.

I am glad enough to be with Duncan. He is a good man and we've kept each other together body and soul all this long winter since our landing. We are kind to each other. I know the fierce side of his nature but it is not directed towards me. I am not sorry to have left Ullapool in his company. I think I am with child. I feel that I ought to know more about this subject. I always presented myself as a woman of the world. Yet out here, alone in the woods, it seems as if I know nothing.

I think the child is two, maybe three months along the way. I will have a talk with Kate. She will know what is what. I should have taken more notice but then it has been a long time since my marriage to Duncan, and nothing has come of anything. My breasts tingle, are painful. I do not always want him to touch me but he takes rejection so hard. At least he is not like McLeod who, I suspect, takes his way without kindness or respect for Mary. From what she used to say to me.

McLeod tells us that Mary is on her way to Nova Scotia...

How bright the sun is here, and yet it is very cold. In the shade there are still great lumps of snow. I hear them fizz as the sun strikes further in each day. By mid-morning the air is hissing and crackling. I am afraid to walk far around here, for there are abysses of water, small lakes quite unmarked and unknown to the stranger, which are still covered by ice, but it is thin and would not bear my weight if I were to stand unexpectedly upon it. I think the end would come very fast as the cold water closed over.

There is a strong smell in the air too, the sour sharp scent of vegetation which has been sealed over for the winter and is now uncovered. The old grass is a sickly yellow.

I hear a strange hooting. Yes, it must be, it is the spring peepers. Ross MacKay told me they would be out and about on the 21st day of April. I did not believe him, but he is exactly right. I have yet to see these little frogs, but I hear them, their voices grow louder by the moment, even as I write.

This is a different landscape to Scotland. Well, what did I expect? But the harbour of Pictou is not as jagged and broken as the shores of home.

Home?

No, I tell myself. This is home.

There are low banks sloping down to the sea and the narrow harbour entrance. The water is crowded still with drift ice, but it is receding. There is a bar at the harbour entrance which ships must navigate with care.

Already at the water's edge, on a small knoll rising above the shoreline, a cemetery has been laid. In the distance I can see it marked out by the clean-limbed birch and the shining spruce trees. It is the trees that tell me this is home. I can live with those trees.

There are three fresh graves in the cemetery. An old man died of a fever the week before last. It took six men more than a day to chip a hole for his coffin in the earth, but since then I hear it is getting easier. Last week, Samuel, a timber worker, was killed. . . .

At first, when they had found Samuel, the men thought he had been mauled by a bear; with supernatural strength he had pushed aside the tree and crawled some distance before he died. From his injuries it looked as if he had been torn apart, and bears were what they thought of first, out in the woods.

'Is there a gun handy? Has anyone brought one today?' said Grey Donald, kneeling by Samuel's body. He had taken his coat off and covered him, and in the brisk air he was shivering, and looking over his shoulder, as if the bear was waiting to pounce from behind a tree.

'You can save yourself the trouble,' said Duncan. He leaned against a trunk, and closed his eyes. At home, it would be different. There would be a scent of herbs in the air and trees in flower. Not many perhaps, not where he had lived, but from where he was standing now, under this dark shadowy tree, it looked like, oh it was so hard to remember already, but spring, and the scent of heather, and a breeze blowing across from the

Summer Isles. . . . The trees would be friendly.

'We have to find that bear now, while the scent of blood is on him. Otherwise, he'll get someone else tomorrow, you'll see.'

'It is not a bear,' said Duncan.

'Aye, then what is it?'

'Did you not hear the crash?'

'What crash was that?' Donald's voice held a touch of aggression.

It is only because he does not want to be told what he already suspects. Who can blame him? Who wants to know the truth, out here in the woods? It is easier to be able to shoot something than stop it falling out of the skies at a moment when it is least expected. Duncan ran his hand over the smooth grey bark of the tree he was standing beside.

'See the blood on the ground? See where it leads?'

Grey Donald nodded his head, which had been grey since he was a child. 'Aye.'

'It was the tree he was cutting.'

So they followed the trail back to where the tree lay and they could see that it was already rotten at its core, so that it would have been impossible to tell which way it was going to fall. The leaves were sagging as the life drained out of what was left of it.

'He was a good axeman,' said Donald angrily, a part of him still trying to refute the fact of the fallen tree.

'He was too.'

'Better than all of us.'

A knot of men had gathered around them now. Donald turned to them for confirmation of what he had said. They nodded, shifting uneasily.

'Best get him back then,' said Duncan. 'You might as well take your coat, Donald, more use to you than him. Who wants pneumonia?'

Not home, just back, that is where we are taking him, he thought, as they loaded Samuel's body onto a sling made of branches and a canvas bag meant for carrying tools. It felt as if he and Samuel were alone in the woods together.

'His missus'll take on,' remarked Harry. Harry was an Englishman who had joined up with the Highlanders. They did not know where he came from, and did not ask; he was simply one of the men from the waterfront who came along with them one morning and stayed. That was how it was in Pictou, you never knew who you would be working alongside from one day to the next.

Duncan felt a profound sense of irritation with the small nuggety man walking alongside of him, jabbering. What did he think Samuel's wife would feel? They all knew that she would 'take on'; as they drew nearer to the settlement, each and every one of them was trying to undo the knot of fear in their gut, praying that the man in front would take

77

it on himself to knock at the door and summon her outside.

And who would hold the children back from her skirts while she looked down on his dead face?

The men broke open a puncheon of rum after that, and some of them went home the worse for wear, Duncan amongst them. Isabella had never seen him drunk before. It was not the way of Highland men, unless they were drunkards and layabouts who were outside the pale of ordinary men. Besides, there had not been money for strong drink.

In Pictou it was different. Rum was being run from the West Indies and it flowed like water. Every family had it on the table, and Isabella had tried it more than once. In the winter, it seemed as if there was nothing like it to warm one. It was cheap too, and for a day's work and a return of five shillings, a family could buy enough to last a month. In spite of hardships, already many families were of the opinion that the living was easier than in Scotland, though it was said that it had been even better ten years ago, and that the last few seasons had been hard.

But spring was bringing close to them the danger that lurked in the woods. It was not just Samuel's accident. The snows were melting and the rivers rising. The lumber was floated on the fast-moving waters, down the rivers, to catch the ships at the port. When the logs jammed the men raced across them to free them, and if they were not sure-footed, they fell between them to their deaths.

'. . . How preoccupied I am with dark waters. But how can I be otherwise? Duncan is not sure-footed, that is the trouble.

'He says, "Give me a couple of seasons and there will be enough money for good land, this is the only way to do it, to raise money fast. There has to be a reason for us coming all this way." When he says this, there is an edge of bitterness in his voice which I do not like. I think he is sadder about our move than I am. But he was closer to his family than I was to mine. I say to him, write them and tell them to come too. He says that he will, but I know that he will not until he has something to show for it, and so he pushes on in all kinds of conditions in order to make our fortunes.

'For those who work in danger, it is little wonder that they turn to rum for comfort, and to blot out fear of what they do.

'Truth is, they would rather it had been a bear that ate poor Samuel.'

Isabella was shaking mats outside the cabin one morning early in May when McLeod stopped on the path outside.

He was riding an excellent horse, at least sixteen hands, and still his feet appeared low in the stirrup. The animal flared its nostrils and pawed the ground. She let the mat she was holding fall, and for an instant a thread of excitement passed through her. It was a long time since she and McLeod had been face to face with each other, and alone at that.

'They say there'll be snow again before it's really summer,' she remarked as he sat there looking down at her.

'Aye, I've heard that, Mistress MacQuarrie.'

'D'you wish to come in?' she asked, noting the edge of danger in his voice and beginning to wish him away from her.

'No. Thank you, Ma'am,' he added, as an afterthought.

How strange it is, here in the woods, far from our beginnings, as if it were only yesterday that I was wiping up beneath his son, and my home was next door to his, and the fishing boats were tied up at the back door. How odd that he was beholden to me, that I was in charge of my life, and in a small way the lives of those around me. Certainly I was beholden to no one, and free to make choices. It is not like that any more.

For now it appeared he was the one in charge.

'Would you tell your husband that I should like him to call upon me, at his convenience.'

'Why would you ask him to do that?'

'There is a private matter which I would like to discuss with him.'

'But I am his wife. Surely you could give me a message for him, that he may know why you wish to see him?' She saw that the cast of his right eye was more pronounced than before, as if he had been reading a great deal and it was strained.

'I hope you'll get settled on a piece of land as soon as possible, Mrs MacQuarrie. I am sure it would be the best for both of you.'

'Thank you for your concern. But I'm sure we can work something out.'

He put his head up a trifle then. It irked her, the way he was adopting a superior attitude; it was as if he were treating her and Duncan like children who needed guidance. She suspected that he had come to give Duncan a piece of his mind over something and it was on the tip of her tongue to tell him that he had no right to do this, that he was only a lay preacher, but there was something about him that made her keep silence.

After he had gone she put the mats back in the cabin and stoked the fire, trying to put him out of her mind. In the town of Pictou she knew that he was attracting such vast hordes of people each Sunday that the local minister had thrown up his hands in despair and gone to preach somewhere else. Things were much the same as they had always been, only now it was not enough to do as one chose for oneself, you had to be totally for him or you were no one.

'But it is not fair,' she said, speaking aloud. 'If Duncan drinks too much that is a problem that is between him and me. McLeod cannot understand that Duncan is afraid of the depths below.' Fleetingly, she wondered if in truth it was simply that McLeod had no imagination at all, while Duncan had a great deal too much.

And McLeod's eye had been cold as he looked at her. As if she were in some way responsible for Duncan rolling down the path. She had wanted to say, 'Look you, McLeod,' (for she would not bow and scrape and call him Mister, he owed her a small favour or two which in itself was something he probably found intolerable), 'my husband is working hard and prayer is not enough to keep the Devil at bay in the woods.'

It passed through her mind that she and McLeod could become enemies. She was shaken by this thought. If anyone had asked her until then she would simply have said, 'McLeod? Why, he and I are old friends.' It would have been God's truth, in spite of many hesitations about the depth and meaning of that friendship, but now she was not so sure.

When Duncan lay down beside her that night they had buried Samuel, he dropped off into a deep sleep, snoring and snorting like a pig at trough and clutching her with an abandon which shocked and excited her at the same time, not that it had come to anything before unconsciousness overtook him. She had lain beside him wide-eyed, not wanting to disturb him. The lamp was still burning, but she thought she would leave it on a while, and then she must have dropped off to sleep herself, for when next she opened her eyes it was to feel Duncan beside her heaving in a different and terrible way, and she heard him racked with sobs.

'Why?' she said at last, touching his face. His tears seeped through her fingers. She wanted to weep herself, though she did not really know why.

He shuddered and then lay still. 'We are all lost,' he said, and in the flickering lamplight his face looked gaunt and sad and truly desolate.

'I'm with you,' she said.

'Don't ever leave me, don't ever die without me.'

'I'm not going to die,' she answered him. 'Not for a long time yet.'

'There would be nothing,' he said. 'Nothing without you.' The shadows were shot with dusty orange-red light. His tears looked like blood.

7 May 1818

Is McLeod so busy with God that he is unaware of the daily terror and dangers that lurk in the woods?

He has such a way of turning everything to his advantage.

He is putting on weight since he arrived here, a fact that had not escaped me, although it is not much commented on. But Kate, who is much more diligent about attending the services than I am, tells me that last Sunday his coat would not button around him. He tried to pull it together, suddenly feeling the cold, and it would not meet at the front. Some were hiding their faces a little, not daring to laugh though much tempted. He puffed and spluttered a little and then remarked, 'I am so full of the Holy Ghost that my coat will not button on me.'

Nor are the advantages which he is accumulating ones which simply serve his pride. Although he has done a fair bit of work building a cabin, McLeod is taking a lot of time from the men round about, especially those who came with him on the *Frances Ann,* getting them to do labouring work on his account in return for his preaching, and a little teaching of the children. Well, he is right to watch out for me, for I'll have none of that as far as Duncan is concerned.

I mentioned before a third grave in the cemetery but I try to pretend that it is not there for if anything makes me afraid it is this. But the fact is, a woman in the village has died in childbirth. How often one hears that phrase! It is none the less terrifying for its familiarity. Especially for women who are a long way from home, in rough cabins cut of the woods.

Especially to me. I do not want to die. I have promised that I will not.

10 May 1818

The snow is gone. The sun has a little warmth. Duncan has turned some ground and I have planted grain.

The rivers run clear. There are fish to be caught. It makes a change to our diet. I am learning to set nets. Trout, salmon, gaspereaux. When we sit down to food like this I feel as if we are lairds.

'Don't you feel as if we are in a castle of our own?' I said to Duncan the other night. We were eating a fine plump salmon. He had a line of juice on his chin from eating too fast. He is like a wolf when he comes in from a day of cutting timber.

He looked at me intently. 'I would not live in one.'

'Oh come,' I said. 'We don't need to have airs and graces just for enjoying ourselves a little better.'

'It would be immodest,' he said.

'That sounds like McLeod to me.'

He sighed then. 'You don't like him do you?'

'He's all right,' I said, 'but you mark my words, *he'll* have a grand house before long.'

'I wish you'd come to his services, at least. The people who came on the ship with us will think we don't care about them any more.' He was folding his napkin and wiping his mouth in a very deliberate way, so that I knew he had steeled himself to say these things to me.

'They might be head over heels in love with him, but I'm not. He's not ordained, you know.'

'You make too much of that.' I could see it going through his head that this was the difference between us, that my family were of the Edinburgh Society, and perhaps he thinks that sooner or later I will show some high and mighty ways of my own.

'I want Holy Baptism for our child,' I said. 'Who'll do that for us, if we have been running after him who is not entitled to do it?'

There was a silence. Then, a silly sleek smile on his salmon-flecked mouth. 'You're not having one of your jokes? It's the truth now?'

'Aye, it is.'

Pushing the plate away, holding me, letting go of me, not knowing quite what to do, as if I were a piece of bone china he had grasped too eagerly.

'Come along then, I'll leave the table till morning,' I said, inviting him to the bed.

'No, don't tempt me, you're in no condition.'

'It won't hurt. I'm better now than I was when you didn't know about it.'

'You're wanton, you're a bad woman.' His face full of nameless joy. And desire. I am full of power. I am sure that everything is going to be all right.

20 May 1818

I am watching the nets for we have lost salmon the last three days in a row. There are only remains left when I go to gather them. I have been told it will be the eels, evil-faced creatures with jagged yellow mouths, they flick to the surface, vanish, a whiplash of black slime. Some people eat them but I would have to be desperate.

I sit on a large smooth boulder. I have been told that I must not take my eyes from the water if I am to see the eels at their work but I feel I must put all of this down. There is so little time to write a journal, so much to do in this new country, and some day I want to be able to tell the children what it was like. At the rate we are going we will soon live in a large house and they will be raised in comfort. It is easy to forget what one's life was like a six month ago when it is in steady transition. So I write of the black slab table, the shining cloth, the rough floor, the pale mayflower at the door. Each is a symbol, one against the other, darkness and light, like our lives emerging out of one and moving on to another state. It cannot be an accident, not entirely coincidence, that at last I am to have a child, that I have conceived in this wilderness which is yet so full of hope.

An hour has passed since I wrote that.

The water mesmerises me. I had not meant to sit here so long . . . .

Well. A large salmon in the net, thrashing about. I should have gone straight to it, that was the whole point of this, but all of a sudden a large eel, it looked about the thickness of a man's arm, and perhaps three feet long, although it was difficult to tell from the way it writhed and contorted in the river, it appeared as a dark streak and straight away it was at the salmon's shining body. I could do nothing but sit and watch, not just because I was afraid to put my hands in the water to try and pull the net in, but also because I felt compelled to watch this spectacle. I have never seen humans eat so neat and at the same time so fast. First the eel nipped smartly at the head of the fish so that within seconds it was still and unresisting; then it began to devour the flesh. To my amazement, I saw that it disdained the skin, and so when it had eaten but a little way in, all of a sudden it turned the fish inside out, tearing its skin straight off as quick as a man in a hurry to take his clothes off, then nip nip and swallow and before long the backbone was exposed, without a single joint being broken and in minutes it was as clean as the bark of a spruce tree, and the eel had vanished back into the depths—I would like to say he waddled after consuming our dinner so rapidly, but not a bit of it, he looked very spry and on the lookout for another meal, and all that was left was the sad little bundle of skin and bone.

It made me shiver. The sun went behind a cloud, there were suddenly long sable shadows on the ground beside me. I remembered that there had been a year—the one before we arrived I think it was, when the sun had not shone all year, they called it the year without a summer and the crops had failed. I am not superstitious, like Duncan's people, or so I tell myself, but I did not like it. I felt afraid again, in a nameless way that I cannot describe. I got to my feet and my bones were very stiff.

Behind me, in the woods, I heard a crash. And then something moving. At first I thought it was the branch of a tree fallen part way and shaken by a sudden wind, but the noise seemed to continue and move away.

I wondered if I had been watched by a bear. I have not told Duncan about this, but I am determined to be more careful, and keep a good listening ear. I don't know what I would do if I met a bear.

22 May 1818

It is raining. I would like to go out but the downpour is too steady, a permanent glaze of rain on the cabin window. I feel trapped inside.

This is ridiculous I know, but I feel as if there is something out there. Something watching me.

24 May 1818

It has stopped raining outside but, in a contrary fashion, I have not wanted to go out. I asked Duncan last night about the Indians. There are not many in the area he tells me, but they are all called Micmacs. He assures me that they are not in the habit of hurting other people.

Kate and Eoghann came to visit us last night. Duncan offered them some rum which he still enjoys, though he is so much more content, now that he knows of the child, that he is not so set upon drinking the stuff. But it keeps the cold out, he says, though I'd have to say that such an excuse does not hold quite so good now that winter's past. Anyway, his offer of hospitality was turned down with an embarrassing firmness, and I saw our friends glance at each other as if he had done something rather dreadful, especially Eoghann who seemed very firm indeed.

On an impulse, I asked after McLeod, and was not really surprised when they began to extol his virtues and loudly sing his praises. As if by accident, almost, they went on to say that he was gathering a group of people around him who were prepared to renounce the Devil and all his ways in the face of all the immorality in Pictou.

I certainly felt then that I had been reproached.

In the next breath they asked would we come to service next Sabbath for the baptism of their new baby boy. I was on the point of saying something about McLeod's lack of ordination, but I could feel a look from Duncan burning the side of my face. Of course there was nothing we could do but say yes.

It is all a bit difficult, for Duncan has not been to see McLeod as he had asked. I think he would have gone, were it not for sharing with me, for the moment at least, the feeling that we can stand on our own feet. Now there is a feeling of confrontation in the air.

They walked into Pictou on Sunday morning, a distance of nearly three miles.

'I must see about getting you a horse,' said Duncan.

'There're more important things. Walking is a good exercise for me. See how strong I am? I'll get weak and fat if I start riding around everywhere.'

'You do get tired sometimes,' he said anxiously.

They approached the waterfront and already a large group of people were gathered on the foreshore. The size of it surprised Isabella. It was almost like the communion days of old, back in the Highlands.

Searching around the crowd for the sight of familiar faces she spotted Mary McLeod, the first time she had seen her for more than a year. In her arms she held another child, born as she had been about to leave Scotland. She looked more pale than ever.

Isabella made her way over to speak to her and she raised haggard eyes, scarcely seeming to know her old friend at first.

'How goes it with you, Mary?' said Isabella, reaching out to take her by the hand.

'Oh, well enough. I'm not impressed with sea travel.'

'Was it a bad crossing?'

'What is a good one? There were storms day after day, and I was ill near most of the time. So were the children. Look at this one, his name is Bunyan. Did you ever see anything sicklier?' There was a hint of bitterness which Isabella had never detected in Mary before. 'I tell you, I watched this child night and day, expecting him to die every minute of the way.'

Privately, Isabella did not think that he looked a great deal better now. She thought of the hours she had spent with Mary on the edge of Loch Broom, and was sorry for her. She tried so hard to be the kind of wife McLeod desired, but there seemed little thanks for it, or, for that matter, little hope that she might ever achieve her ambition.

Shortly after this, McLeod began to preach. Thinking on it afterwards, Isabella found it difficult to recapture his exact words. But they were very harsh, and critical of almost everyone in and around Pictou. He spoke against the Church of Scotland, harangued other ministers who were working in Nova Scotia already, and catalogued such a list of sins amongst the inhabitants of the town as she had never heard described before. Then he turned his attention to the congregation. He started with drunkenness and Isabella saw that Duncan was hot and uncomfortable, sweating in his best clothes. For a time it looked as if McLeod was going to pursue this line, but then he switched quite suddenly to the sin of adultery.

A deep blush passed around the assembled people. They were not used to such matters being aired in public.

'The two matters, drunkenness and adultery, inevitably will go hand in hand,' thundered McLeod from a makeshift pulpit, constructed from a cabin trunk and two kitchen chairs up-ended on each other, 'one thing leading to another. You have only to look at the example of Mr James McOnie down there lurking at the back of the congregation, trying not to show his face, although he is wont to show his more lewd and unseemly parts in circumstances beyond the ken of decent men and women. The name of the circumstance has to be identified however as that of the woman called Maude, who is fat and frowsy and a whore to boot, Mr McOnie, and what have you to say for yourself about that?'

There was a loud cry from the back of the congregation and at first Isabella took it to be McOnie himself, but it was not. It was his wife, learning for the first time of these accusations against her husband. McOnie had fainted clean away.

Isabella thought of her fish, turned inside out and with its bones stripped bare.

It was a wonderful and terrible drama, and she could feel the excitement in the air, as if the Men had just spoken. Again she told herself that it was only one man, that it was McLeod. But she could see now why they were calling him the Man, on his own account, and why they flocked to hear him. It was a grand performance.

Beside them, Kate and Eoghann's baby stirred in its woollen shawl, reminding Isabella and Duncan that it was on account of him that they were here. An expectant hush passed through the congregation as McLeod announced that the MacKenzies had brought their child today for baptism. On being called to bring their child forth, Kate and Eoghann stood and made their way to the front with Isabella and Duncan following them, to stand beside them while the child was given the sacrament.

Isabella looked up at McLeod perched on the cabin trunk, meeting his gaze. The right eye hovered to the side of her face as he cast his misdirected glance towards her. She wondered if it was as bad as she believed or if it was just her imagination which exaggerated his squint.

When they were all standing ranged in front of him, he looked from one to the other.

'Oh yes, the MacKenzies,' he said, his voice tart. 'Well, what is holy in the eye of one man may not be in another.' He sniffed, as if savouring the scent of the salt-laden air.

The four of them waited, their anticipation turning and growing into uneasiness.

'I do not think you are worthy enough parents at the moment to have your child accepted for the sacrament,' said McLeod softly, yet at the same time, loud enough for everyone in the congregation to hear.

A shiver of shock passed through the MacKenzies. Isabella, standing a little to one side, saw but did not share it. A surge of anger and humiliation on her friends' behalf flooded through her, but with it came little sense of surprise. It was what she might have expected from the now all-powerful figure of McLeod.

'It is the child, man,' cried out Eoghann in anguish. 'I do not know what it is that we have done, but whatever it is the child has not. He is full of the innocence of the newborn.'

'You must examine your hearts and see if they are truly pure, and when you have completed that exercise, remind yourself that the child depends upon its parents for spiritual guidance. The child can but fail in the circumstance it now finds itself in.'

Kate opened her mouth to argue, but the magic of this unfolding drama was gripping the onlookers again and she felt herself caught in their stillness, aware of them listening, waiting for her to beg and plead, and so was silent.

As they walked back between the rows Isabella remembered the child that had been refused baptism at Ullapool. There will always be someone who has to pay for what was done to McLeod, she thought. If that is God, full of vengeance, I am not sure that I want too much to do with Him.

Beside Mary McLeod, John Luther, a sturdy toddler now, trudged up to his father who was dismounting from his pulpit. McLeod picked the child up and holding him in his arms, popped a piece of molasses candy that he had taken from his pocket into his son's mouth. The child sucked and smirked with glee at the onlookers, who were now reluctantly beginning to disperse.

Without speaking to the MacQuarries, Eoghann and Kate walked away, bewildered and bowed. Eoghann carried his new son in his arms while Kate led Martha, their older child, by the hand. They did not look back. Isabella could tell by the tilt of Kate's head and the hunch of her shoulders that she was crying.

2 June 1818

Duncan is unhappy. He thinks Kate and Eoghann's child was refused baptism because it is we, who are their friends, who are unworthy. I have heard, however, that McLeod is refusing on a grand scale. I will not listen to Duncan. I have told him that the true reason that McLeod will not baptise children is because of not being ordained, and that he knows within his own sinful heart that it would be an abuse of the sacraments if he were to undertake baptisms. Look, I have pointed out, he cannot marry people—of which fact everyone is aware—because it is a legal matter, rather than one of religious conscience and principle. McLeod mystifies the issues in order to confuse people.

But Duncan sits, dour and quiet, and does not touch a drop of drink in the evenings. I wished he would stop, but now I almost wish he would start again. McLeod's meddling has not brought about a desirable result. Duncan's temper is stretched to breaking point.

I am little better. Our hard-won peace seems to have melted like butter in the sun.

I tell myself, when the child is born, it will be better. But that is still a five month away.

And the woods, which I had grown to like, still feel unfriendly.

5 June 1818

If this goes on I think I will go mad. I have to get out of the cabin, yet I cannot escape a feeling of menace out there. I tell myself it is my condition and Duncan's frame of mind but still there is this unease. I gathered wild strawberries today. In the wood nearby there was a crackling in the undergrowth. I wonder if I could learn to handle a musket? A bear's muzzle fetches ten shillings.

6 June 1818

Truth is, something is going to happen, and I do not know what.

7

Pictou, 20 June 1818

To the Justice of the Peace in this County

Sir,

It is, as you enquire, properly reported to you that my wife Mrs Isabella MacQuarrie suffered grievous injuries at the hands of an unknown male assailant on June 10. I returned home from my work that evening to find her lying on the floor of our cabin in a most distressed state. She had sustained injuries, both cuts and bruising, to her throat and body. She was barely conscious when I arrived and throughout that night there were times when I believed she would die. Friendly neighbouring women have nursed my wife since then. There have been periods of delirium and high fevers. I cannot allow her to be interviewed about this incident at the present time, although I realise that it would be in the interests of catching the offender. As you said in your communication to me, the longer it is left the less hope there is of apprehending this foul creature.

But she begs me not to have anyone ask her about the matter and I am afraid, sir, that she will go off her head if anyone should come near her.

My wife has since lost a child she was carrying at the time of this incident. It was our first, and we were much looking forward to the event. Her distress is heightened by this loss.

Please do not ask me again about seeing her. Take my word for what has happened.

No sir, of course my wife was not violated in the terrible manner you suggest.

Yours etc.

Duncan MacQuarrie, resident of this County.

(Copy of a letter found by Maria McClure enclosed in her grandmother's journal.)

8

HIGH SUMMER, yes it is high summer indeed.
He knows. He pretends it has not happened. Some days I do too.
What else can I do? Other days it will not be put to one side.
Let us re-examine the matter.

Let us go back to that day in June. I say us, as if I am addressing a crowd. A crowded courtroom, perhaps. No, that will never be. I am actually addressing the record.

So. It is a June day. I see the beautiful harbour as flat and blue as a man's shirt when it is ironed, lying between the gentle hills. I am happy. Although the sun is bright, the night before has been cool. There are ashes in the grate, I kneel to sweep them up. My belly has started to swell, soon I can feel that it will be awkward to stoop so far.

Then I hear that noise again, a scuffling in the leaves outside. I try to ignore it. Every day for a week now I have heard movement. I do not think it is the bear any more. There is too much stealth about it. A bear would not have guile. It would crash about more. A porcupine, I wonder. I am told there are plenty of those in the woods, and they would move more quietly through the undergrowth perhaps. So why does it stop, start, appear to move closer and then move away?

That morning had been different. The movement was close to her, and out there, she heard a sneeze. An ordinary human sneeze.

So it was true. All along she had known that it was a man.

Isabella went to the door and called out. 'Hullo, who is it? I know you're there, you might as well come out.'

There was a hesitation in the air, then all noise ceased. It had become so quiet that it seemed as if the birds might have stopped their singing too.

'Are you lost? Do you need food?' She tried to speak in a brave voice, but the silence was frightening.

'Is it you Duncan?' she heard herself say, and then suddenly she was aware of herself whimpering in the back of her throat.

For she had seen him. A man in a heavy jacket and buckskin pants. He was swarthy, with sharp ferrety features, and not much taller than she was. He looked strong though, with long arms. She thought of apes, which she had never seen, but heard discussed in London. The man moved towards her and pulled his lips back in what she took to be a smile. His teeth were bad and stained with tobacco.

'You're hungry, are you?' she ventured. What women think of, when all else fails, she explained to herself. Feed them, that is what men like. It is softening and kind to offer food. She reached for the bench. There was a pot of cold potato and some scones left over from supper.

The man nodded. 'Yes, I'll eat,' he said, and sat at the table without waiting a further invitation. He had an accent which at first she could not place.

She began preparing the food, keeping one eye on the door. He was between her and it.

I cannot be in danger. If it is only food he wants. Surely? He has no reason to harm me...But why has he watched me?

'Are you from around these parts?' she asked him.

An indifferent smile hovered at the corner of his mouth. 'You have rum.'

It was a statement not a question. He reached out for the tankard and helped himself. There was plenty there. Duncan's lately more abstemious ways were in this man's favour. He threw down half a tankard, gargling it a little as he did. It was a disgusting sound. And she was aware of his smell. It was sour, rather like rotting vegetation.

'Bon. Ver' good,' he said, and this time she recognised his guttural accent.

'Were you born in France, or here?'

'You ask too many questions. Get the food.'

'Here, I should think. You're a descendant. Was your father stationed here? At Louisberg, perhaps?'

'The food.' His tone was angry, as if she had trifled with him enough.

'I haven't got much. I'll have to light the fire.'

'No.' He stood, seizing the food out of her hands and stuffing it into his mouth, then snatching more rum to wash it down.

She moved to the door. His hand shot out, grabbed her arm; she pulled away, resisting him.

'Why have you been watching me?' she cried. At the door, two more men had appeared. They were both rough, looked like lumbermen. One was tall and red haired, the other an older man with rumpled greying hair. She tried to think whether she had seen the redhead in the village. She was sure, as she looked at him, that he was a Gael, though no one whom she knew, or could remember seeing before.

'There's food,' said the first man, waving at the bench with his free hand, while with the other his thin tobacco-stained fingers still gripped her arm.

'Not much,' said the redhead, a note of contempt in his voice.

'Please,' said Isabella, turning to him, and appealing, 'you're one of my countrymen. I'm happy to give you food, but ask your friend to let go of me first.'

'Let her go,' he said. He was laughing, his mouth already crammed with scone.

The Frenchman dropped her arm and she drew back into the corner. But the redhead's hand was falling upon her. She could not take her eyes off his hands. They were stumpy and thick, white with feathers of red hair along the backs of them. His hand ripped her skirt in one sharp motion, splitting it from the bodice. She heard herself begin to wail, a thin high sound that she would go on making for an hour or more, even though her mouth was hit repeatedly to stop the noise.

'I told you you'd like her,' the redhead said to the others.

She knew then that it was he who had watched her, not the Frenchman. 'But she's mine first.'

'I am with child,' she said quietly, as he closed in on her, forcing her legs apart. She tried to grip her ankles around each other, but one of the men flicked them apart as easily as slicing a twig, and then she was on the floor, the planks digging into her back as he entered her.

That was the pain she was aware of at first, being bruised as she was pushed backwards and forwards on the boards, but then there was the tearing between her legs, the dry pain which increased as her terror and humiliation mounted.

'Don't fight me,' he snarled, interrupting their rasping connection to spit in her. He came at her again but by now she was raw, and a blaze of pain scorched her. She tried to muster spit in her own mouth to shoot in his face, but found herself as dry there as the rest of her. Her hatred and her cowering were beginning to tell on him, and he was losing heart for the act he had started upon with such deliberation. It took him a long time to be done with her.

His companions had become impatient. They had drunk more rum as he panted and snorted on with what had become a chore. It occurred to her that if it were not for them he would abandon this mortal act.

At last he was finished and his seed swelled out of her; it made it easier for the others. The Frenchman took her three times, lapping in this puddle, the swollen aching entrance that was all she could feel of her body. The rest was numb as if her sex was surrounded by a void.

In the respite before the grey-haired man descended on her she felt a surge of strength returning and tried to push him away. His punishment was swift. First he stood and kicked her on the floor while he undid his belt. Then he knelt down and seized her by the throat, his thumbs pressing the breath out of her. He took her then while she was choking, the spittle running out of her mouth and blackness filling her brain. She had become so limp that he had to hold her to him like a rag doll.

'Tell that thee like it,' he commanded. She had thought before that he was a north country Englishman, but he had spoken little. It was not that she cared what this motley bunch were, or where they came from, only that she could make sense enough of what they were saying to obey their commands and escape with her life. If there were point even to that.

'G'arn wi' thee, tell that you like it.'

'I like it,' she whispered, with all that there was left of her voice.

'Ah, you would bein' whore,' he muttered and set to work on her again. He was quick, too quick for his own pleasure, and not pleased with his performance in the sight of the other men either. He rewarded her with blows to her head. She could not cover it, nor see him either as her eyes closed up, and then she felt the snap of bones, ribs and an arm as unconsciousness blotted out the rest of what was done.

Later, when the sky was darkening outside, she was roused by greater pain than any the men had inflicted on her. Struggling to remember what had happened, and feeling the board and the smell of new timber against her cheek, she touched the sticky mess on her body. There was dried blood all over her, but where she touched herself now, there was fresh blood. The pain was worse than she had thought possible. It was beyond endurance. Or so it seemed to her then.

But she was still alive. She must have endured it after all. How unfortunate, how very unkind. Death would have been the better, the surer answer.

There had been four sovereigns in the jar on the mantelpiece. They had been taken. Those, and a puncheon of rum would be enough to tempt robbers, it was agreed by the neighbours. But not enough, surely, to provoke such a beating?

Isabella did not tell them all that had been taken. Neither did her husband.

'How many?'

Duncan stood at the door. He was on his way to the woods. More than a month had passed. Isabella sat by the fire, her left arm still in a sling, but otherwise outwardly as she had always been.

She said nothing in response to his question. They had had this conversation before.

'Tell me,' he repeated, 'how many?' His face was working and she thought he might hit her. He had not done so yet, but so much boiled and seethed within him that she did not know what would happen from one day to the next.

'Have you gone dumb? Did they take your tongue too?'

She got up and crossed to the bench, so as to be seen to be doing something. She picked up a bowl with her good hand and awkwardly dropped a cup of flour into it, starting bread with an exaggerated care. He walked back to her.

'You know what I mean. I want to know how many men there were that day.'

'What difference does it make?' she said, breaking her silence.

He touched her shoulder, more gently than she expected. 'Nothing can mend what happened, whether it was one or twenty. I need to know.'

'And I need to forget.'

'How many, Isabella?'

'Two,' she lied. She didn't know where the lie came from; it was something that had sprung up when he had first found her bleeding on the floor. Dazed and half conscious she had nonetheless known that she must save him from knowing that which she knew. Or all that she knew. She had wondered many times since why this should be so. He was a man, and this thing had been done to her by men. Then she would think how much she loved her husband. She was confused, no longer knew what she ought to think. And every time she did think about it, it seemed sillier than the time before, that they should be bothering whether it was one man or ten who had done this damage. It was like some crazy ritual, something he could not force out of his head and in a kind of madness needed to keep adding to the horror and disgrace of it all, letting it hang there between the two of them, filling his mind with more and more pictures to pass his days.

His shoulders bowed. 'For the last time. I will never ask again.'

She was tempted to tell him then, to lean against his strength. Afterwards she would wonder whether it was because she did not believe in it, thought that he would buckle before the truth. For the truth stuck in her throat and she said, 'Two. There were two men.' She turned back to the dough that she was mixing, trying to anchor the bowl with her injured arm.

He straightened, walked back to the door, stopped again.

'There were three tankards on the table that night,' he said. His voice was flat. He walked out the door.

He had known all the time.

She stood at the bench for a long moment. Too long. For when she went to call him back, to ask him to help her or let them help each other, however it could be done, he was gone, and the woods were silent again.

So that she was left alone with what felt like guilt, except that she could not decipher its cause, nor think of anything she had done which might cause her to feel this way.

20 September 1818

I often think of dying now. It will be winter soon. We see no one. Duncan sits drinking rum by the fire in the evenings.

Last night Duncan sat by the fire (we have begun to burn coal, this is a new marvel here; once I would have delighted in it, so very modern) and he drank until he no longer recognised me. After that he came to our bed and for the first time in a three month or more, lay with me as my husband. Only it was like a stranger in my bed. It was like that morning in June. He staggered out at first light, without a word.

She remembered as if it were a long time ago, though she thought it was only three weeks or so, the day they brought him home from the woods. She had been hanging out the washing. She could still see each garment, like a patch against the sky: the bright linen of their bed; the dark blue shirt that Duncan wore on Sundays; her camisole, delicate and cream though much mended, bought in London and the remnant of some other life she could no longer believe she had inhabited; and a bright plaid blanket, full of reds and yellows, that she was airing before the winter. The wind plucked them up and flipped them towards the sky. The wind was in the trees. She heard them sigh and creak. Yet their movement somehow gave her hope. She had been desperate for so long, so still within herself, that she was relieved when she felt some stirring within her, as if in some distant place in the heart there was an intimation that she might live again.

So she listened to the trees, trying to read their message. Then she walked down to the river where Duncan had set a net that morning. They had had no fish for a long time; almost, she thought, as if the fish were shunning them too. But there was a fish that morning and she hauled the net up and dealt with it, a fine speckle-bellied trout. She took it to the cottage and placed it in the baking dish, banked up the fire to get the oven hot. There was a pan of milk set and she skimmed cream from the top. She thought she would bake apples in the oven alongside the trout. It was time they had a feast again.

As she finished spooning the last of the cream into the bowl she felt dread descend on her like a hard hand. She stood upright and the first thing she feared was that the men were coming to get her again. She looked wildly around the room without seeing anything, as a blind person seeks when danger is near, sniffing the air like an animal, for she knew that she would smell them if they came near her again. She had thought that they would not come back, that they would be far away; perhaps to the south, in America or the West Indies, for she had decided that they were men off ships. She had even wondered if they were convicts, such a various group of vagabonds travelling together. Now, in panic, she thought they were returning and ran from one wall to another, clawing to find an escape while all the time the door stood open.

She stood still again, certain that this time she would die. The air was fresh with the scent of spruce and she could smell nothing alien on the breeze. It was very cold, though. The fall that year had seemed like endless summer, but it was drawing to a close. The nights held a touch of frost. Isabella reached for her shawl and wrapped it round herself. She sat down to wait for Duncan, but she didn't think he would come.

Soon she heard men's voices. They were familiar voices, and she heard Eoghann call her name, then Grey Donald's, and six or more of them emerged out of the trees, carrying between them the body of her husband.

She ran forward to meet them, big awkward men with nothing to say, Duncan's clothes on his still body were soaking wet, his face already like marble and twice as cold when she reached out to touch it.

Eoghann made tentatively to take her hand.

'There was nothing we could do, Isabella. He was under the water too long before we could reach him.'

'It was a log jam,' said Grey Donald. 'He went out to free it. His foot slipped and was caught between the logs. They rolled on, taking him with them, and he went down between them.'

She could see then his lame foot which he had always tried to ignore. He had worked it so hard that it was almost as strong as his good one. He should have known though, she thought, it was never meant for jumping logs on fast-flowing rivers.

Oh but he would have known. She knew that he did.

So that the next day she walked through the green leaves of the woods with the men and a filigree of shadows fell around them as they carried the coffin to the cemetery.

'We will look after him,' said Eoghann, meaning that she did not need to walk so close beside them as they carried him. But she kept on walking in their midst with her hand on the wooden lid, and, looking at her face, they decided that it was best to leave her be, to let her do it in her own way.

3 November 1818

The nights grow longer and colder, the dark comes early, the first snow has fallen, the fire dies out. Although I am not asleep I know I am not awake either. I know I must move and cover myself or I will die on my own hearth frozen by the cold maybe there is nothing wrong with that . . .

8 November 1818

McLeod came to the house the other morning. He had brought me money collected by the people who had come out on the *Frances Ann*. I took it from him, then he suggested we kneel in the fresh snow by my door to pray. I looked at him then and told him to go to hell. When he had gone I took the money inside and counted it, two pounds and three shillings. It is not a fortune, but it will buy some meal for the winter. I think I will be able to shelter here until the spring but after that I do not know what will become of me.

December, date unknown

I saw a fox streaking across the snow today, its brown-gold fur was gleaming and its eyes were like coals in the reflected light of the dying day. I would like to slope off over the snow, over fallen branches, through the trees, leaving no trace of where I have been or where I am going. I have had enough of this adventure. I want to get away from it all.

Towards Christmas

Eoghann has brought me a hen. It lays well. It can winter in with me.

My body has a curious familiar sensation about it. As when I was having a baby. The candle streams over my page; pale light and a room full of fallen shadows. While I am feeling like this, I think I will survive. That, at least.

New Year's Day, 1819

It is true then. A quickening in the night. So that is what is to become of me. I am not alone after all.

9

ISABELLA'S FACE WAS chalk white and she scarcely seemed to recognise Kate MacKenzie and Dolina Finlayson, the midwife, when they arrived at her house. The baby's crown was already showing and she had stopped shouting, intent on finishing her task. A few minutes after their arrival the baby came without their help, a tiny boy with wizened features and a club foot.

'Like Duncan,' said Isabella, gazing at her child.

'His foot was from an accident,' said Kate sharply.

'It is fitting though, don't you think,' said Isabella, gazing at her with her odd-coloured eyes. They seemed at that moment to be without expression.

She did not speak to anyone else for many months.

At nights Kate would stand and look out the window of the cabin into the summer darkness. There was nothing to see, but sometimes Eoghann caught her with her head tilted on one side as if she were listening, waiting for some sound above the night wind.

'What is it? What are you listening for?' he said one evening.

Behind the curtain which divided the cabin across, one of the children cried out as if in a dream then subsided into sleep again, but she did not seem to hear him.

'I don't know. I think of her.'

'Isabella?'

'Yes. It must be hard to bear. To be so far away from God.'

'Is that what you think?'

'She's so far from humans, I cannot imagine that she is any closer to God.'

'God is everywhere.'

'Well maybe, but she'd walk right past Him without seeing Him at the moment, if you ask me.'

'Is her child all right?'

'He's perfectly healthy... except for his foot. I saw him smile the other day.'

'Do you know what she's called him?'

'She doesn't say anything. There's no point in asking her. Still... I opened her Bible when she was putting out the wash. There is a new

97

entry there. Duncan. Well, what else would she call him?'

The pale stars suddenly darkened as if touched by green and scarlet lightning; then the sky flickered and glowed. Together they watched the northern lights, wild tongues of brilliant colour licking the heavens.

They tended to blame Isabella for a pervasive unease they could not shake off, although they both knew that this was unfair. It was nothing they could identify, but they both felt there was something amiss in Pictou. On the other hand they scoffed at wild reports that were being circulated by McLeod's more ardent followers.

They had not attended one of his gatherings since their child had been refused baptism, and in this they were joined by a number of families who had suffered the same fate. The pain of his refusal had eased a little once they began to realise that McLeod was indiscriminate in the manner in which he chose to dismiss parents from the prospective baptism of their children. Not only that, but there were some who had enquired about Holy Communion only to be told that there were none amongst them who were worthy to receive tokens for admission to the Communion rail. Yet in spite of this, and his increasingly harsh denunciations of individuals, the crowds which attended his sermons were swelling in numbers each week. And word was growing that soon those who wished to follow McLeod would be moving on.

Eoghann told Kate of this rumour one evening as she was serving up potato cakes. She looked tired, her coppery red hair scraped back into a straggly bun, and she limped, for she had worked that day shelling dried oats with her feet in a barrel; her swollen toes were pinched and cramped in her boots.

'McLeod is said to be done with Pictou,' he said. 'Says it's not a fit place for his children to live.'

'So where's he carting Mary and the children off to this time?'

Eoghann held his finger a moment longer than necessary over the pipe he was tamping. 'It is not just his own children he is speaking of.'

'Oh?'

He thought she wasn't listening, reflected, then spoke more to himself than to her. 'All his followers now, he calls them his children in the sight of God. They're calling themselves Normanites.'

'Well, if you must call yourself something, that is as good as the next name, I suppose.' She began to poke morsels of potato in the baby's mouth. Eoghann could tell what she thought of what he had been saying.

'It's not just what they call themselves,' he said at last. 'They're planning to build a ship to carry them south to Ohio. It's meant to be a more moral atmosphere down there, more sympathetic to McLeod's way of thinking. They mean to call it *The Ark*.'

'The ship?'

'Aye.'

He sensed a gleam of humour in her eye. He was surprised then, when she said, 'Maybe he's got something.'

'You mean that?'

'Ah well, it sounds mad to me, but what's a bit of madness? Maybe that's what it takes to change things.'

'Some think McLeod's really crazy.'

'Is he?' She sat down heavily at the table and took the baby, Ewan, on her lap. 'I remember he saved us on the ship. I can't dismiss him that easily.' She observed how closely he watched her and lightened her tone. 'Ah, come Eoghann, we can do without him. We're strong. We can stand up for ourselves, eh?'

'But you would think about it?' he asked, showing his hand.

'Is that what you're wanting? Oh Eoghann, he's naught but a narrow-minded bigot when it comes to it. It's one thing to be grateful for good turns done in the past. But this is Nova Scotia... All things are new, are they not?'

He nodded, but she could see that he was not convinced.

'Look what he did to us.'

'Aye, but perhaps we took it too personal. He has things on his mind, you know, Kate.'

She sighed. 'Well, I shall think about it then.'

When next he spoke of it to her again, he could see that she had indeed been thinking and perhaps talking with the women. He approached the subject with care, uncertain of their common conclusions or whether they might reach any.

'They say that quite a few are thinking of following him,' he said.

'That's true. I'm surprised at the number. More than I thought.'

'Would you, Kate?'

'I don't know. I can't sort out right from wrong any more.' Inside her head, a small voice warned that she was being led on to say something that was expected of her, but she could not stop herself for what she was saying had some measure of truth in it, was getting close to what she felt.

'I like this place well enough. But what's it going to be like when the children are older? Well...I don't know...some strange things go on here.'

'What sort of things?...Isabella?' His voice was tinged with anxiety.

'Oh...her. Oh, I don't think so. Well, not just her. She disturbs me. But she chooses to be alone. She is...herself. I wish I knew...oh well, what is there to know?' She pushed a strand of hair back into her bun. 'I've heard John Munro is going with McLeod.'

'That bothers you?'

She shrugged. 'He makes a kind of sense of this place. And if he thinks there is cause to leave...well.'

His hands lay on the table. She saw that they had become stringy and tough with horned nails. 'Aye, there is something in that,' he said, after a time.

'And Norman McDonald. And Squire Donald McLeod.' They nodded, counting up in their heads all the people who had followed them to Nova Scotia since they left Scotland, people they had grown up with and respected. The same people were McLeod's friends. 'And then,' she said, 'there is this hanging that's to be done.'

'Who told you about that?'

'Oh Eoghann.' She looked at him a trifle scornfully, as if he were being foolish like one of the children. 'You think I wouldn't hear a thing like that? It's the talk of the whole town.'

He banged his fist on the edge of the table then. 'I did not want you to hear.'

'They will hang Donald Campbell on Saturday,' was all she said.

On Thursday afternoon a gallows was erected on the site of the house where Donald Campbell's father and stepmother had lived, and where, it was said, he had killed them.

The High Sheriff of Halifax arrived in town on Friday night and put up at the waterfront hotel. Outside, a rough and ready band consisting of three pipers and some fiddlers made a commotion they described as 'a tune or two' along by the seafront, and were followed by youths clapping a beat and shouting their heads off.

'You must stay inside tomorrow, Kate,' Eoghann said that evening. He stood by the window, drumming his fingers on the sill.

'I've got no intention of going out. Will you stay here too?' She was asking if he would witness the hanging.

'Yes,' he replied at first. Then he said, 'But there may be law and order to be kept on the streets.'

'Let someone else do it,' she said sharply.

'I thought you were worried about the way things are going in Pictou?'

'Perhaps it is true,' she said wearily and with traces of anger in her tone, both for him and for the way things were. 'Maybe we have no place here.'

'Aye, maybe,' he said.

In the night he lay awake, sweating one moment and cold the next. He lay closer to Kate, pressing against her flannel-clad back, but in a moment she would turn over in his direction; they seemed to swivel and turn from side to side all night. Towards morning he slept, but there was the sound of people passing in the woods as the dawn broke. He felt his wife lying tensely beside him, awake but trying to keep perfectly still so as not to disturb him.

In the grey light he saw that her eyes were wide open and that the skin beneath them was blue and taut.

He put his hand out and took hers. 'I think you should get right away from here today,' he said.

'And you?' she asked, still trying to arrive at some position, some positive indication of what he planned to do that day.

'I'll help you get the children away,' he avoided her. They had three children, a girl and a boy who had come on the ship with them, and the baby. The eldest, Martha, was six, and had an enquiring nature that bordered on the inquisitive. They spoke fondly of her cleverness but there were times when she seemed a handful, and she had the physical presence of quicksilver as well. Aboard the ship, when she was still toddling, Kate often thought she would never have survived the journey were it not for the watchful eye of Isabella MacQuarrie.

She thought of Isabella now. 'We could perhaps go to Isabella's house,' she said.

'I wondered about that,' said Eoghann. 'Is she the best you can think of?'

'The houses of everyone else whom I know well enough, or who are likely themselves to be home, are towards the waterfront. Or there are the McLeods.'

'We cannot go there now, not when we've stayed away so long.'

'I suppose not.'

'Besides, I expect McLeod'll be marching up and down proclaiming his own saintliness to the crowds.'

Even the younger children were quiet over breakfast. Only Martha, who was in a talkative mood and not noticing her parents' silence, demanded her mother's attention.

They had barely finished spooning the last of their porridge down when Kate began bundling them into warm clothes. She was longing to hit Martha and did not trust herself to hold her tongue, at least, any longer.

As they made their way through the woods, people streamed towards them. Kate was shocked to see that many of them were folk they were acquainted with, taking their children in the direction of the waterfront.

'You'll always get those who feed on others' problems,' Eoghann growled, but by now she could see that he too was looking back over his shoulder.

'Is it a misfortune to pay for a dreadful crime?' she asked.

'If you want vengeance why don't you go down there and see it for yourself?'

Suddenly they were quarrelling. What did she want, he was asking, she must make up her mind one way or another, as if it was she who was hankering to go there.

101

'It is you who wants to go so much, so why don't you leave us,' she responded, two high points of colour burning in her cheeks. The children were tripping in the undergrowth. She dragged Martha by the arm across a log and the child screamed at her in a fury, sporting blood on her shin.

Another group passed them and called out in high spirits that they were going the wrong way. Kate was beginning to think that they had, in fact, misjudged the direction of Isabella's cabin when they came upon it in the trees.

'You can leave me here,' said Kate.

'You'd better make sure she's there.' Eoghann was trying to contain his anger, for Kate was on the verge of tears or attacking Martha. Neither of these responses were in her nature and he was alarmed by the depth of her rage. We are all unhinged, he thought. This hanging that is to take place is not just an occasion for punishing wickedness. Rather, we are celebrating the death of a simpleton. For that was all he knew of Donald Campbell who was to swing that day.

Glancing around Isabella's house confirmed what he had first thought, that it was empty. No smoke issued from the chimney, and there was a tight and shuttered look about the place. He tried the door. It had been bolted.

'She'll be hiding inside,' said Kate, shaking, and more afraid now that she realised their journey had been in vain and that they would have to retrace their steps. 'I know her tricks, that's what she does.'

Eoghann was rattling the door and banging on the window now. 'No, I don't think she's there.'

Kate stood still and listened, though it was not exactly a sound that she was seeking. On other occasions when she had been there and guessed Isabella was hiding from her, it had been a certain awareness of her presence which she could neither describe nor define. This morning it was not there. A hen scraped in the dust outside. Apart from that the place might have been abandoned for years. There was no sign of the baby's clothing hanging in the sunlight to dry.

'I should never have come here, we should have stayed inside and locked the doors at home.'

'We'll turn around and go back,' said Eoghann. 'Come on, we should hurry.'

He was urgent now for he had no wish to join the crowd surging through the woods. A weary repugnance overwhelmed him. It was as if some calamity was about to befall them all, his wife and his children, if he did not take them to shelter as quickly as he could.

But their return was not going to be easy. People kept coming towards them. All the backwoods dwellers from far beyond Pictou appeared to be converging on the waterfront. The way they had taken was becoming choked with carts, some of them rough handcarts in which old men and women were being pushed along. There was an air of festivity and Martha was becoming infected with their gaiety.

'Come along mother, father,' she urged them, believing that they were heading for the same destination as everyone else.

'Quick, come quickly, this way,' said Eoghann, drawing them towards the stream bed over to one side of the track. They stumbled as he pulled them along in the new direction, but it was no use. There were more people coming this way too, and now he and Kate could see that their way home was cut off by the crowd. Suddenly Martha disappeared. They panicked, looking towards the stream, but in a moment they saw her again being borne away with the crowd in the company of a child she knew.

Now they were forced to join the horde and so themselves became a part of the drive towards Roger's Hill, where somebody alongside of them said the condemned man was about to appear at the church.

'Martha. Martha, come back,' Kate called out, her desperation mounting. The child looked back and saw her mother's face. In terror she tried to return, understanding now that this was no ordinary game, but she could not move back through the crowd and they all continued to be pushed forward.

A wheeled carriage appeared and a body of militia headed by the High Sheriff marched along at its side. The fiddlers who had cavorted the night before began to play a jig, and a brass band started up a ragged march in opposition: *oompah oompah pah pah*. Behind the bands followed a group of clergymen.

'Where's McLeod?' Kate asked Eoghann.

'Would you believe it, they say he's working down at the waterfront on *The Ark*, a half dozen of them, as if nothing were happening.' Eoghann was listening all around him, even as they struggled with the children.

They looked at each other and recognised in their complicity that they had agreed to go along with the crowd now and not continue with their efforts to turn back, even if that were possible. Martha ducked through the legs of a group of people in front of them and rejoined them; they began to float along, not fighting the crush any more.

The carriage had stopped at the church, for this was as far as it could go before the track ran out. Then Donald Campbell was lifted out and a great sigh, half moan, half exaltation, went around the crowd. The bands and the fiddlers stopped their racket and in silence broken only by the lapping of the sea and by indrawn breaths from the crowd, the fetters were taken from Donald Campbell's legs. He was a sallow, thickset man with eyes placed back under the shelf of his forehead. His face was implacable as he began the walk towards the hill of execution. When he reached the gallows, one of the clergymen, Dr McGregor, stepped up to him.

'Do you admit to your crime, Donald?' Dr McGregor beseeched him. Donald Campbell spat at the ground, taking excellent aim so that the spittle appeared to skim Dr McGregor's face.

The clergyman stepped back. 'For the last time, will you tell us before God that you are guilty, and ask Him for your forgiveness?'

'Oh aye, I'm guilty all right,' Donald Campbell replied.

'And your repentance?'

He turned his face away from them towards the gallows. 'Oh that. You can do that for me.'

'Donald, I believe nothing will ever melt your heart,' said the reverend gentleman, and exhorted the crowd to pray. Kate wondered whether he was praying for Donald who, it seemed, needed none of it, or whether it was for all of them who were shamefully committed to each other in the spectacle of his death. She tried to pray for Donald Campbell but she found she was praying for herself and her children who were about to witness this event.

The Sheriff ordered then that he be placed on the gallows but Donald Campbell was already preparing to mount them himself. As he stood waiting for the executioner to draw the bolt the excitement began to turn to terror amongst some of those who had gathered. It was one thing to see the dead, and there were few amongst them who had not seen death at first hand, who had not been at a parent's bedside or watched a child taken by a fever, or a friend or a neighbour struck down by the elements in the harsh and violent lands they had inhabited; but none, except perhaps for seamen and visitors to the port, had ever witnessed the deliberate taking of a man's life. Whimpering erupted from sections of the crowd and some began to push backwards, not wishing to see after all. Kate, holding her younger son in her arms, felt as if she was having the breath crushed out of her. Eoghann was struggling with the older boy, Roderick, who was playing hide-and-seek with another child among the people in front of them, and at the same time trying to pull Martha back from where she now stood at the front of the crowd.

The executioner was hooded but it seemed that his identity was known, for some were calling out, 'Come on, Mac,' as if they knew him from other Macs who were there in their hundreds, 'get on with it, what's keeping you?'

He was wrestling with the bolt but it was yielding only slowly to his efforts. The trapdoor fell at last with a heavy clang, but appeared to tip sideways so that instead of plummeting straight through it, Donald Campbell's feet slipped to one side and the knot skewed round to the back of his neck. It was clear that his neck had not broken and that he was choking for breath.

'Let him down, let him down,' some of the mob were screaming while others shouted, 'Do it again, do it again, make a proper job of it.'

The rope uncurled, so that the man swung round to the spectators, his face blue and contorted. His heavy breathing could be heard over the crowd, while his body twisted on the end of the rope, as if the rope were being skipped.

Kate felt vomit rushing to her mouth and tried to stifle it, but where she succeeded others did not, and moaning and stench began to fill the air, adding to the horror of the spectacle. She looked round for Martha and saw the child coming towards her. Her eyes were staring.

'Why did you bring me here, mother?' she said.

And why did I, Kate asked herself, why do we start with so many good intentions to save our children from the world and from themselves, and then we let them down so easily? What have I done, that I followed here with so little resistance when it came to the point? She looked for Eoghann, and caught him staring at her as if he hardly knew her; a gaze so dreadful, she knew whenever she looked at him again some memory of what was happening now would pass between them.

For Donald Campbell was still alive, and the executioner was blundering around the gallows making helpless little motions as if asking for someone to tell him what to do next. The Sheriff was strutting up and down, puffing out his chest and trying to look as if everything was going to plan, though it was clear that he had no more idea than anyone else what to do. For a moment it seemed as if he might try to have the man taken down, but by now Donald Campbell was more dead than alive. If he went ahead, a decision would have to be made whether to put him up again and finish the job more tidily, or whether to try and revive the dying man, thus thwarting the path of justice.

This is what they thought, those who were watching, or thought afterwards that they had thought, for no rational conclusion could be reached at that moment.

At last Donald Campbell's thrashing ceased and his blue face began to relax into the contours of death. The crowd held still, calmer now, as the last death throe subsided.

Then a woman's cry, long, bitter and anguished, rang out across them all, a thin single note, and looking to where it came from, Kate saw that the woman who had made that terrible sound was Isabella. She thought that Isabella was about to fall, holding her baby in her arms, but instead she stared wildly from side to side, and the next moment, dishevelled and thinner than Kate could have thought possible, she slipped between the crowd, which parted to let her through, and then she was gone.

When they looked back to Donald Campbell, he was at last, undoubtedly and mercifully, dead.

The following morning Kate and Eoghann joined those who went to hear Norman McLeod preach his Sunday sermon.

10

From a sermon by Norman McLeod, lay preacher at Pictou, in the year of our Lord eighteen hundred and nineteen.

'THOUGH IN GENERAL you have been kind friends of mine for a long time now, I see, plainly, different traits in your characters and habits that are both very deep and dark, as well as very dangerous. Some of you are so self-conceited in your own wisdom, and so headstrong in your temper and disposition that I fear very much how far you can conduct even a Christian plain dealing. The Lord looks down upon the strong and selfish minds of people who are without real conviction or brokenness of spirit from their cradle. How will God's precepts avail in our eternal concerns without the powerful light and life of the Spirit of Jesus Christ!

I see all around me not only self-importance, but the fast and open signs of degeneracy in this place, and amongst our neighbours. Pictou is a fearful place. It is ripening and fast improving in wickedness. In truth, I am loth and fearful to remain within its boundaries. I experience an awful and uncommon dread in my heart and spirit concerning the increasing audacity of the inhabitants, as well as the approaching appearance of the tokens of God's displeasure.

I tell you now, this is a branch of Sodom. I have heard from eyewitnesses of the prevalence of great filthiness, particularly at the shipping place, where it is customary to see women accompanying sailors during the night. And with my own ears I have heard the sound of empty religion and the filthy song of the rioting drunken swearer, going hand in hand. With the same mouth to bless God and curse men, excited one of Heaven's ancient complaints against similar sinners. And then there is the matter to consider, of dishonest and deceitful modes of transaction, particularly in lands and horses, carried on without a blush of shame.

And still another thing alarms me sorely, which is a maddened itch for immoderate dressing, an example of the extravagance of the times, more notoriously in reference to females. There are two or three amongst you here today who will surrender your head-dresses to the elders at the door as you leave, and your foolish bonnets will be shorn of their ribbons, the better to remember that such vanity is not acceptable before God.

Oh Pictou, Pictou, thy sins are fearful. I humbly desire to bless the name of the Lord, for having given me, and those of my friends who choose to join me, a gate to escape from this place while there is still time. Our ship sails for Ohio soon, north up the coast of Cape Breton, and veering south then to America. Some of my oldest and best friends will be accompanying me on my journey, and on this first mission we will stake our claims on the lands which our friends in the south have assured me are awaiting us; there we will flourish amongst godly people, like-minded to ourselves. Once again with thanks and humility we will regain the means of salvation.

I urge those of you who have not already made up your minds to leave Pictou, to examine your hearts and minds in our absence and consider with such wisdom as you are able to muster, your course of action.

My God has already spoken to me.'

11

IN THE MOUNTAIN there are caves. The mountain is made of limestone. I have come to live in a limestone cave at the foot of the mountain. Does that sound mad? I am sure it does. Let me tell you something. It *is* madness. I have come here to hide it. No one can see my madness now except for my child, and he suckles me with a blind forgiving mouth, and his eyes are only for me and whether or not I can provide for him. Because I can, he smiles at me.

The cave is very long and cool but it is not draughty. I think it is nearly a hundred feet long, but it is quite narrow, in places not much more than six feet. I know these things because while the child sleeps I pace backwards and forwards, and I count my paces and add up the distance. The cave is not as dark as you might think, for I am not the first person to have lived here. Someone has made a rough floor, and a door and a window. It is almost comfortable. And beautiful, it is so beautiful. There are columns of limestone hanging from the ceiling of the cavern—is this what is called a stalactite?—they look like ice, they shine where the light strikes through, glowing at night by the gleam of candle light. I half expect them to start dripping down the back of my neck.

Through the floor of the cave runs a stream of the purest cleanest water I have ever tasted. By day I go out into the woods to gather berries. I have a net which I brought from the cottage and my skill at fishing stands me in good stead. I think that I, and Duncan son of Duncan, little Caveman, may stay here forever.

What drove me mad? Do you know, *I* don't know any more.

Was it the wild men in the woods? Men? What men? I don't think there were any men. They were figments of my crazy imagination. No, no. I never saw strange men in the woods. Ghosts perhaps. I remember my mother, long ago, telling me at night that there were no ghosts, or only ghosts for people who had been bad. Now what did I ever do that was bad? McLeod would say I was proud. Perhaps that is what it is. Perhaps I did not pray heartily enough to God. I have tried it here in the cave, but I do not know what to pray for. Even God does not bring husbands back to life.

Poor Duncan. To think that I killed him. Now that is a sin. Driving *him* mad and driving him away with wild and fanciful tales of men in the woods. I still remember him saying to me the strangest thing. He said, 'There were three tankards on the table.' Who could have put them there? I must have. I must have been expecting company. Yes, that was it. No one had visited me for a long time, and I kept hearing bears in the woods, and thinking it was friends passing by, so I put out the tankards.

Poor Duncan, yes. That was what a crazy woman would do. I have to look after his little baby for him, little Duncan Cave with the funny foot. He will have to be watched over in the woods, for he won't be sure-footed like the other children. Other children? Now, how silly of me, there will be no other children, we will live in the cave and the woods forever. No one will ever find us.

I wash his little clothes in the pure water of the stream and hang them in the branches at night. What would they make of me, the good people of Pictou, a wild cave woman, with tangled hair, my skin burned brown by the sun? How my complexion has changed. I can tell this by the colour of my hands, though I cannot see my face. It is as well not to see it, I might be afraid of the burning eye which greeted me in the glass. But I feel the sun's rays on my face, and it is a warmth I lap up like a cat.

I am strong too, for I climb trees and set snares for birds. Last night I roasted a pigeon. Ah, but that was delicious, the fat dribbled down my chin as I tossed the little bones away and they got washed along by the stream, taken gently away out of the cave mouth.

Why am I mad? Oh haven't I answered that yet? No, no, I am still working that out. It must be my badness, my driving Duncan away to his death. I miss him, poor lovely pale-skinned Duncan, poor lost Highland man who was never happy in this strange land.

I am. I think. Why should I not be happy? I am simply mad, but that is not a problem for me. It is only other people who find it difficult. That is why I have gone away, so that they will not be unhappy when they see me.

Little Duncan Cave will not be unhappy. He won't yearn for another home. This is his home, yes. He is brown too, he will be like a little Micmac boy. I took him to town one day. I thought I would go and collect one of my hens. In my flight from the cottage, I left them on their own. Poor things, they will be lonely, so sad for hens to be on their own, and I like their eggs. One morning I woke, and I was yearning for eggs. So I said to my little man, my baby boy, let's go to Pictou and find a laying hen, so mother can eat eggs.

But when I got to the town, the way was barred. There were people everywhere. We were pushed and shoved, and finally pulled along with the crowd who were all excited and full of some momentous event.

I could not turn away, I was drawn along with them too. I was taken willy nilly to the hill where they were hanging Donald Campbell. I saw a man step forward, with a black sack over his head and slits for eyes, just as if it were the Tower of London itself. I was close to the front of the crowd, and I saw the hangman raise his hands to undo the bolt. They were short thick hands, and red hairs sprung in clusters along the backs of each finger. Now where have I seen hands like that before? I do remember, I cried out when I saw the hands of the hooded hangman...

There are no men in the woods. There are no ghosts. There are only hands. Here in a long narrow cave I can keep my back to the wall all the time, I can keep watch. No hands can reach me here.

Ah baby baby mother will keep you safe!

Rain outside, a cold soaking rain. I must gather wood for the winter fires. I must hurry around as soon as this rain is over and make sure I have plenty, and get it as dry as I can...

It is still raining, and I think the rain is turning to sleet. Oh the autumn cannot be over yet. I should have kept better count of the days. There must still be time to gather wood and food for the winter.

What if the snow blocked off the entrance to the cave? Could it happen? Surely not.

There, I am saved. It is sunny, the day's like a polished sovereign. I am full of hope, I have been given more time to make ready. I have washed at the stream like any good housewife of Ullapool or Pictou. World to world, it is all the same. I make my cave ready.

11 October 1819—written at McLeod's house in Pictou

This morning McLeod came to the entrance of the cave. A cool misty rain was falling outside. I had been to collect Duncan Cave's clothing from the branches outside. They were very damp and I had put stakes by the fire, hoping to dry them. I saw a long shadow and heard a voice I knew. It was as if I were a girl, back in Ullapool, when I was full of spirit and fire, and knew all about everything, and the whole world parted in front of me as I strode through it. I was back in that night on the moor when McLeod stood in front of me. He announced who it was, reassuring me as he stood at the entrance to the cave, but I knew already it was him.

He had taken a sweeping look around him. Isabella snatched Duncan Cave to her, thinking perhaps that he had come to take him away from her. He squatted beside her then, and it occurred to her that she had never seen McLeod kneeling so low before although they had been close neighbours for all that time, and she had travelled so far with him. He put out his hand and touched the baby's face.

'He is like his father, then?'

'Can you see it?' she said, wondering, for her strange little baby of the woods did not seem like anyone she had ever known.

'Aye, he's like Duncan.'

'He is named for his father,' she said. Then, on impulse, she opened the blanket that was covering him and showed his foot.

'He has his mark on him,' she said.

He looked hard at the foot then. 'I had heard,' he said, and touched the misshapen limb. 'But it is coincidence. Duncan's lameness was from an accident.'

'Or is it the will of God?' she said, and she could hear the hard edge in her own voice.

'Oh aye,' he said. 'But that has nothing to do with you.'

She sat very still. She had not realised that anyone could read her thoughts so clearly, but it occurred to her that if it was to be anyone, it would be McLeod.

'How did you find me?'

She thought he smiled then, but it was such a rare sight that she could have been mistaken.

'Who said I was looking for you, Isabella MacQuarrie?'

'It was no accident. Things are never an accident with you, Tormod,' she said, making bold with his name. What did it matter, she asked herself, especially for her, who had nursed his babies and washed the sweat from his wife's brow in times of her illness; she, who had followed him across the Atlantic. Besides, what difference did it make? They were just a man and a woman who knew each other, kneeling together on the floor of a cave with a baby between them.

'I have seen the clothes on the branch a number of times.'

'You've passed here before?'

'Oh yes.'

'You didn't know it was me, though?'

'I guessed that it would be you. There have been people out looking for you, you know.'

'Do they know I am here? Have you told them?' Isabella glanced quickly around her, seeking a way of escape; now her cave seemed like a prison. She began immediately to imagine that he had reinforcements lined up outside, waiting to capture her if she should try to get away.

'Of course not,' he replied easily and got to his feet. He knelt again by the stream and scooped a handful of water to his mouth, then took his handkerchief from under his cloak and wiped his hands carefully, as if he was giving himself time to think. It gave her fleeting pleasure that he should take such care with her. He was not in the habit of choosing his words.

'I've told Mary that you're here,' he said. 'That is all. You trust her, don't you?'

'Of course I do.'

'She needs help with the children. We're moving on, you know.'

'To America?'

'No.' He smiled at her, a warm smile at last. She had been waiting for him to start praying over her, but she guessed now that he would not. 'Even my plans go astray sometimes, Isabella.'

'What's happened then?'

'*The Ark* took us, of its own volition, it seemed, to a spot on Cape Breton Island. It's called St Ann's Bay. It's very beautiful, very unspoilt, only a handful of settlers living there and a few remains of French settlement. It's not so far, as the crow flies, from Louisburg. There is much good land there, and although I suspect the winters will be very hard, when we saw it in summer weather nothing could have been more tranquil. John Monro and Norman McDonald were with me, amongst others. We've agreed there could be no more splendid place for us to settle.'

'And what of the religious brotherhood you were seeking?'

'We'll make our own, Isabella.'

'Our own, or yours...?'

'Oh, they call it Normanism, but no one is forced to follow my ways.'

'Not true. You're very hard on anyone who doesn't do as you wish.'

'Ah yes, if they choose to follow me, then they will do as I say, or as I tell them according to God's law. And how I wish that more of them would listen to the word! But I forsake only those who persist in being Godforsaken and leave them to their own devices. Those that come with me, well, they follow absolutely. Do I make myself plain?'

'It's naught to do with me,' she said, and felt a shiver pass down her spine, for she knew now why he was here.

'You can stay with Mary. She'd be glad of your company and your help. You always knew how to manage our children, and she's in ...delicate health again. Our fifth child. She says she only wants you, Isabella. It would be no charity. And you need not see anyone until you're ready. Kenneth Dingwall lives with us, employed as my manservant. Oh...and there is another man, Fraser McIssac, who stays with us for the moment doing labouring on the farm. He's a quiet man, keeps himself to himself, and is most godly and prayerful, you wouldn't need to converse with him at all. When the summer comes we'll all sail for St Ann's.'

'I can't come with you,' she said, trying to sound reasonable. 'This is my home.'

Outside she could hear that the soft rain had turned to a steady downpour. Duncan Cave began to wail. She turned away from McLeod and put the baby to her breast to quieten him. She did not want to hear what was coming, for she knew he would only repeat the same insistent thoughts that she had been trying to push aside now for days.

'You'll freeze to death in here,' he said. 'Come, you know that's the truth. I'm not just trying to frighten you.'

'That might be my choice.'

For the first time he looked stern. 'Do you have the right of free will?' He looked at Duncan Cave.

She thought of the summer, and the wild berries, of birds she had snared in trees, and of fish she had netted from the river. She looked around her castle of minarets and spires, her floor of flowing water, she felt its echoing in her skull.

Then she looked at Duncan Cave in her arms and back to McLeod. She knew it was all lost to her.

'Thank you,' she said, and in spite of herself she was grateful. He stood watching her as she gathered her few scraps of belongings into a bundle, saw his piercing grey eyes flick over them and rest on her journal.

She tried then to see herself in his eyes; fleetingly, and for the last time, she thought of running away from him.

'You can go back into the world in your own time,' he said, reading her mind again.

'Do they know I'm crazy?'

'Are you?'

'You can see that I am.'

'I can see only my old and valued acquaintance.'

'You don't know what's happened to me.'

There was an impenetrable silence. 'As you are coming with me,' he said, after a time, 'it would be best to put it out of your mind, whatever it was.'

So she followed him into the sodden afternoon. He helped her mount the horse, holding the baby then passing him up to her. She wondered, as she had done once before long ago, if they would be friends like this again. But whereas in Ullapool she might still have entertained that possibility, here in this country, where he had become so powerful in such a short time and her own life had fallen into chaos with equal speed, it seemed unlikely.

As the horse plodded on they did not speak and she had time to reflect. He had told her to put things out of her mind. She glanced from side to side and told herself she could see no ghosts.

'Well there seems to be plenty to be done around here in return for my keep,' Isabella wrote in her journal that night, 'but what did I ever expect? At least for tonight I have come in for a little cosseting and nobody has reproached me. A little while ago Mary came into my room here and clucked over Duncan Cave.

' "What will you do, Isabella?" she asked me, and I saw that she was asking, what was I going to do about my whole future, which was at least more than McLeod had done, who simply assumes that I will follow wherever they go. And having left the caves, what else can I do? I did say to Mary that I had thought of writing to my parents for my fare home, although, in truth, it was a thought which had just struck me out of the blue, that instant. I suppose it is a possibility, but there is no guarantee that they would want me back and therefore no compulsion for them to send the money. I am not even sure that I want to go back, or that if I did it would ever be my home again.

'On the other hand, I do not wish to stay with the McLeods for the rest of my life, that is a decision I came to a long time ago, in another country. This evening, McLeod roared through evening prayer, back on form, as if today had never been. My eyes were supposed to be closed, but I looked around me from beneath lowered lids, catching sight of Kenneth Dingwall, a young man who already looks old, and very suspicious of anyone who comes within a ten foot of McLeod. He has a cool, sour eye and watches everyone.

'As for the other man, McIssac, he is a heavy sweating fellow, a bit overweight, and pompous. McLeod suggested, all sweetness and light, that I should teach this fellow to read, which brought him down a peg; indeed, I could have sworn he glanced at me with positive dislike between a prayer or two.

'I think McLeod must have observed more of this than he let on, for when he had completed his delivery, he glanced from Fraser McIssac to myself and said, "How good it is that you two have met."

'His manner could not have been more pleasant, and yet I shuddered.

'After dinner, I saw him speak quietly to the man, obviously telling him to do some task for which he was not prepared, for he scowled deeply. Later I saw him sitting on the step polishing his boots, with a great deal of spit to help them along.

'I feel strangely calm and sensible, as if the events of the past year or more are over, and as a sober and industrious widow faced with the plain facts of my situation I can see that I must do whatever is best for this child sleeping beside me.

'Cape Breton Island, eh?

'Well, I expect we will make something of it.

'Could it be that McLeod now sees all his debts repaid to me?'

Wild flowers and twigs and bits of ribbon and recipes for succotash and forach fell from Isabella's journal. But the place where it opened with ease each time Maria McClure picked it up in her house in Waipu was marked not by Isabella but by Maria herself. It was sticky with tea and grains of sugar and pieces of biscuit from all the times that she had opened it and read it, sitting at her kitchen table or lying in bed reading last thing at night when she had her evening snack, sometimes leaving the yellowed pages open and face down on the coverlet while she slept.

The next entry, written at St Ann's, Cape Breton Island, was in a hand that pressed hard into the pages with angry flourishes, the hand of Isabella McIssac: 'So that is the price of my keep. In the end, it was I who was in McLeod's debt. When we sat at table today, after this wretched marriage had taken place, I could have sworn there was complacence in his eyes. As if he had buttoned himself up for once and all. I have been betrayed by my own people, or those, who in the absence of all others, I had come to think of as mine.'

PART FOUR

ANNIE
1838–55

12

FOR AS LONG AS Annie McIssac could remember, the house and the church on the knoll overlooking the inlet of Black Cove had been the centre of her life. The house was that of McLeod, where the Man lived and ruled.

He ruled the church too. It seemed vast to Annie, a huge edifice sixty feet long and forty feet wide, with walls twenty feet high. From the ground level there were four entrances, and inside the church two stairways led to galleries built round three sides of the building. There was seating for twelve hundred people, and it was never enough for the congregation. Or the audience, as Annie's mother once called it, but then her mother, Isabella McIssac, was known for outrageous utterances. It was a source of great shame to Annie, who knew that to be liked and well thought of, and to get on at school in the master's schoolroom, one must behave well in and towards the church at all times.

Yet what her mother said could not be denied altogether, for the church did slope towards the front as in an auditorium. The light from the six arched windows was designed to fall so as to make a pool of brilliance around the central character. And plain though the furnishings were, the finish of the church showed the care of the master craftsmen who had worked in St Ann's learning their skills over the years, in particular building ships. Now they had brought them to bear on this building. There was magnificence in its arches.

The church towered even above the three-storeyed mansion which stood beside it. It looked like the house of a wealthy man, although passers-by might have found it paradoxical that high on the front of the building, set in a circle of glass, a cross proclaimed that this was the house of a clergyman. In Nova Scotia, and particularly on Cape Breton Island, clergymen were not prosperous as a rule. Indeed, the clergy who had been sent there by the Edinburgh Bible Society were known to lead lives that were harsh and difficult in the extreme.

'It is their own faults,' McLeod's voice clanged from the pulpit, for the principal actor was in full flight this very minute, caught in a vortex of light, a wry sunbeam turning his mane of thick white hair to an illuminated gold crest. He swaggered, he strutted, he leaned over the edge of the pulpit like an eagle arching over its prey, dazzling them with the sound of his voice. Only it never seemed to stop.

Tormod Macleoid. As in the Gaelic which he now spoke. He styled himself with one word, one name, like Paul, the Apostle of old. McLeod. Annie's mother Isabella referred to him with a reckless flourishing carelessness which shocked her daughter.

'It is certainly the fault of these foolish young men,' cried the Man, which was what his congregation called him, as he fulminated on about the pathetic young clergy from Scotland. 'I have said it more than once...'

Indeed, he had said it more than a hundred times. And not blushed a single time that he should repeat himself in such a fashion.

'They are pawns in the Church of Scotland's *grr-aand de-signs*. De-*signs*, and the stup-*id* women who put their noses into the business of men. For, *yes Lord*, it is known indeed that it is women, and especially Mrs McKay from the Edinburgh Bible Society, who are behind all of this, despatching witless young men to do their *duty* in the colonies, yes, and unsettling and dismaying the whole community of men who live on this island, with the exception of ourselves, my good friends, and now let us pray, saying, Our Father...'

But it was not over yet.

Sitting inside the church beside her father, Annie was wrapped in a cocoon, as the voice of McLeod rolled over her. If McLeod said that people were stupid then there could be no question but that it was so. She was eight years old and the world was full of absolutes.

Just sometimes, the light that streamed through the windows would change and the pattern and shapes of things would seem to shift, and Annie would be overcome by some pale intimation that goodness and purity might not always hold. On the other side of her sat her brother, little Black Hector, so named because he had been born with a shock of jet-black curls, although they had long since turned to a thatch of rather mousy brown hair. He was a heavy, thickset boy, with long arms that would be powerful like his father's. When he spoke his voice was ragged around the edges, breaking already, although he was just thirteen. The two of them formed a strong and solid phalanx; she was a wisp, like a dragonfly caught between them, whom they must hold together.

She had sat still for more than two hours that morning and her bones were invaded with a cramp that she dared not admit. Whenever her attention wandered she fixed her eyes on the elders at the front, in their black suits with their silk hats beside them on the pew, and recited their names inside her head: John Munro, Squire Donald McLeod, Norman McDonald and a dozen others whose faces were as familiar as the church itself. These were the men who governed the church. Their presence restored her sense of security, her belief that nothing ever changed. That, and the bodies of these two males between whom she sat, her father and her brother.

Really, her world was complete. There could be no doubt that she was safe.

She felt herself drifting, yet at the same time her heart soared with glowing certainty that when she was older she would be a faithful worker for the church, who would come and clean it twice a week and sew altar linen. She promised herself to read an extra chapter of the Bible over and above the two to which she had already committed herself each day. The air seemed green. It was as if she was swimming under the water of St Ann's Bay. A wave broke over her head. Oh it is lovely, she exclaimed inside herself. It is what heaven must be like. I am so happy.

She pressed her knees together, pushing herself up a little straighter on the seat, and without thinking, lifted her hands out of her lap and put the palms against each other, the fingers pointed upwards to form a steeple like that of the church itself.

On either side, two hands descended on hers, prising them apart with a vice-like grip upon her wrists, and the faces of her father and brother glowered down at her.

Annie knew that she must not cry for if she did she would incur even greater wrath the next day. Perhaps not today, not when they had finished in here, for it was Sunday, and chastisement was a duty to be performed with other tasks on other days; but sooner or later it would happen and either it would be painful or so arduous that she would wish herself dead before it was done.

The edge of safety shimmered and dissolved around her.

It is unfair, her heart cried out, and she was almost swallowed up by the injustice of it all. If only mother were here. But it was cruel precisely because mother was *not* there.

And it was no good complaining about it, not to anyone. Not to her father, who would pretend he had not heard, or to her friend Peggy McLeod whom she loved like a sister and was the daughter of the Man, because she might tell her father; or even to God, who did not seem to bother Himself about the doings of her mother. That was the hardest part of all, that her mother got away with it, with not coming to church, while Annie went and had to endure for the sake of them all, and for everything.

The McIssacs lived further down the inlet from the McLeods in a small plain house which Fraser had built soon after the arrival of the Highlanders from Pictou. It was white and square and without adornment, like the other houses in the neighbourhood. The central room was the kitchen, where in a large stone fireplace flames consumed log after log throughout the winter. A spinning-wheel stood in the corner of the room, and down the middle ran a long table, so that in its appearance the kitchen too was much like those of other people who lived at St Ann's.

Yet there was a certain difference about it. Annie could never work out exactly what it was. Rather than anything specific, it was an accumulation of small things. The curtains at the window dyed brighter colours than those of their neighbours; a picture on the wall of men and women congregating together in elegant dresses with frills around the hem, twirling parasols and smiling up at gentlemen, which had once been given to her mother by Aunt Louise from London, who was now thought to be dead; a shawl thrown over a chair with a casual flourish, as if to make it appear more sumptuous than it really was; a fur rug on the floor.

All of this was to do with why she felt she must work harder than almost anyone else at school. And although nobody ever said so directly, she must not grow up like her mother and so worked harder still.

Each evening the family gathered around the long table. They folded their hands and Fraser said grace before they began their meal. When they had finished, he read the Bible aloud.

'Quite fluent,' her mother sometimes said, and Annie could swear she raised her eyebrows at Duncan Cave, her half-brother who lolled at the end of the table and appeared not to take the slightest notice of what her father was saying.

Annie hated it when they flicked comments like this from one to the other. She would see her father's face burn dull crimson then as he was overtaken by bouts of speechlessness. Although Isabella had not said so in front of her, Annie could not avoid the knowledge, because somehow her mother managed skilfully to impart it, that it was she who had taught Fraser to read.

Now it was time. The remains of their meal lay on the plates in front of them, threads of cold meat. Being Sunday, the meal had been prepared the day before so that Isabella would not be seen to have laboured on the Sabbath. It was a custom which she had come to find a great convenience.

Duncan Cave had left more on his plate than anyone. He pushed it aside and stretched his long frame back in his chair, looking up towards the smoky ceiling. His young man's face was thin and his eyes bright. A smile appeared to hover at the corner of his mouth.

'Was the food not good enough for you?' Fraser demanded.

'There is gristle.' Duncan Cave looked down the length of his finely turned nose. 'It's more tolerable when the meat is hot.'

'It is more tolerable when the meat is hot,' mimicked Hector from where he sat, close to his father. His admiration for Fraser was boundless, and he was quick to seize whatever opportunity presented itself to gain favour with him. Yet already Annie sensed that Hector was doomed to be less a man, in the sense that a man is implacable and unbending in the matter of his duty. Hector would falter and flounder and end up even less understanding of why he must do these duties, and even more determined, therefore, to perform them.

122

Yet she loved him. It is as well he has me to understand him, she thought. For mother does not. But then who would understand her?

For her mother, sitting at the opposite end of the table from her father, somehow both glittering and brooding at the same time, did not seem to understand anyone in the world except her club-footed son, Duncan Cave.

'I will make you fannikineekins tomorrow,' she said to him as he disdainfully turned the piece of offending grey gristle over on the plate.

'It is just that I am tired of what meat looks like,' said Duncan Cave, sighing.

It was his stepfather's turn to smile, at once amazed and supercilious.

'May I have some fannikineekins too?' said Annie timidly. For she really would have liked some but beyond this was afraid that someone might shout at someone else, and that by saying something she could stop them.

'You. You played up in church today,' said Hector.

There was a stillness around the table. 'Did you now? Was it not much fun in the kirk today?' said Isabella languidly.

'Did the Man rabbit on a bit, eh?' Duncan Cave asked. He looked around them. 'Well tell us. Mother and I are dying to hear what hellfire and damnation he has in store for us this week.'

'That is enough,' shouted Fraser, banging his fist down on the table so that the milk jug hopped. 'You,' he said, turning to Annie, 'you will rise at five each morning this week and chop wood for an hour before you begin your devotions.'

'It will be dark,' said Annie faintly.

And oh, she was so afraid of the dark.

'Quite so, you may have a lamp,' said Fraser, as if to soften the punishment, although clearly it had not occurred to him until that moment that it would prove ineffective otherwise.

And so much for Hector. So much for love. He scowled at the table-cloth now, pleased with himself on the one hand, but on the other afraid that he might also have stirred up a bigger storm than he intended and that its fury might at any time round on him.

On his side of the table, Duncan Cave seemed to lift his shoulder, certainly an eyebrow, as he looked at his mother. Annie studied the table-cloth, not daring to peek, supposing Isabella as aloof as always.

In fact, Isabella had been studying her daughter's face.

'We shall read from the Book of Isaiah,' intoned Fraser.

'So we are on about the landlords in Scotland again?' said Duncan Cave.

'They robbed us. They were drunken and committed all manner of sins,' shouted Fraser. 'Can you not understand that, you...you worthless doodler?'

'Yes, yes, I understand very well. I am interested,' said his stepson.

'Isaiah is so very political, that is all,' said Isabella.

Fraser's hands were trembling as he opened the book and began to read. There was a mist in front of his eyes, curiously like tears, as if the heat in the room were affecting him. Sweat collected on his brow and ran in runnels down his forehead. It was hard to see when he was taunted like this. He swallowed, cleared his throat, and began to read: 'For all the tables are full of vomit and filthiness, so that there is . . . *no place clean.*'

Ah, this was better, he could cope with them now. He even paused, looked over the top of the book and around the table to make sure that his words were having the right effect. He saw with satisfaction that his wife was flinching, and that the child Annie was white and shaken. He avoided looking at Duncan Cave, as Annie had avoided her mother's eye.

To Annie's surprise, Isabella stopped in her room that night when she came to check that she was in bed. Usually she glanced around and said a firm goodnight before she closed the door. But occasionally she would come in and sit by Annie and talk quietly with her; when she did this Annie would wonder why she was so afraid of her, for in truth, Isabella never raised her voice towards her, or punished her for things. If there had been things for which to punish her. Only Fraser had the capacity to discover evil doings in Annie. Annie desired only to be good, to be loved, to be like the McLeods. Or even to be better than the McLeods' own children.

But it was hard with a mother like hers. It was whispered amongst her friends at school that Isabella did not believe in God.

Now, as Isabella sat beside her, staring intently into her child's round face with its prominent eyes and somewhat failed chin, Annie dared to ask her, 'Is it true, mother?'

'Is what true?' Isabella stroked the top of Annie's hand with an idle finger.

'That you are a heathen? Well, that is what I have been told.'

The magnetic finger paused. 'By whom?'

'Oh I can't remember,' said Annie hurriedly. The finger waited. 'Margaret McCabe.'

'Oh. Them.' Isabella's expression embraced an entire family. The finger resumed its gentle, hypnotic action. 'Now do you think that I look like a heathen, eh?'

'No. Because heathens are dark and don't wear clothes. Heathens are savages.'

'Then you've nothing to fear, have you?'

'Not a witch either?'

'And who told you that?'

'No one, nobody told me that.'

'Ah yes they did. Come on, dumpling.' When it suited Isabella she was known to be an excellent cook, for which it was suspected that Fraser forgave her much. Although she remained lean and lithe herself, he and the children, with the exception of Duncan Cave, had a tendency to plumpness. In what passed for her better moods Isabella was wont to refer to them by whatever culinary inspiration came to mind, sometimes with a touch of malice that mostly went unnoticed. As she had intended, she provoked her daughter now.

'I'm not fat.'

'Maybe not fat, just a little round and fluffy, eh? That's what mother's dumplings are like. Now the truth, I want the truth, huh?'

'Peggy McLeod.'

'Hmm, I thought so. You believe everything Peggy McLeod tells you?'

'She's Reverend McLeod's daughter. She's my best friend.'

'Oh yes, the minister's daughter and his darling. D'you know, she can do no wrong, that one. I'll guarantee she gets no punishment from his high-and-mightiness.'

'Are you, though?' Annie, embarked now on this course, could not withdraw from it.

'A witch? Has she seen me riding my broomstick? Casting spells? Tell her, yes I am a witch and I turn girls into curds on the top of the milk, thick and yellow like fat blobs, and they melt and run away into the grass and fall down into the pits of hell where they sizzle, and never come back.'

'Mother!'

'You're too scared to tell her, aren't you?'

'You wouldn't want me to, would you?'

'I don't care,' said her mother, and laughed.

'I might tell father, though,' said Annie.

Her mother stood up and blew out the candle.

'Mother, don't go away. I won't tell him.'

'You must tell him whatever you choose,' said Isabella, and her voice was cool and even as it moved away and then her footsteps faded on the stairs.

They stopped outside Duncan Cave's room.

'Is it you?' his voice called softly in answer to her knock.

He was bent over his desk, a pen in his hand. Papers were spread around, and each of them was covered with delicate line drawings, pictures of plants in leaf and in flower. They lined the walls above his bed, and Isabella felt as if she was entering a garden, as if petals were showering down upon her and bushes were brushing her ankles, so accurate and exact were these drawings. She could have sworn that she felt the tremble of the air shifting the foliage.

Duncan Cave held up the drawing that he was working on. It was of a rock covered with lichen.

'What a thing,' she exclaimed. For though she liked it, because he had done it, it was not like the more living vibrant plants that scattered the room.

'It is the rock where Bunyan and I used to sit when we were lads,' he said, his voice stretched and edgy. 'He would like to see it again.'

Her heart turned over heavily then. It hurt her to hear him speaking of himself and his friend as if their boyhood were long past, and yet she could see that this was how it must seem. Bunyan McLeod was dying and no one could save him now from what was to come.

She remembered the delicate baby whom Mary McLeod had nearly lost on the ship, and whom she had helped to nurse when he was small, only a little older than her own first child. They had been friends all their lives, and neither had had other friends. Now, at any hour, they would be parted.

'Will you come and see him tomorrow?' asked Duncan Cave.

'Aye, if that's what you want,' she said, inwardly recoiling, for she did not like to visit the house of McLeod.

'I should,' said her son, who had the shape of a man but was still a boy. He is too young to bear so much, the mother thought. She put her arms around his shoulders where he sat, and he turned towards her, burying his face against her hip.

When she had left him, she glided on down the passageway and paused at the next door. She hesitated and passed on. There was nothing to be said between her and Black Hector, who chose not to please her at all and would prefer to think that as Duncan Cave had another father, so he might have been borne by another mother, before she came along.

Would that it had been so, was her own grim rejoinder when she thought of him in the darkest hour of the night. So she walked on, away from the one amongst her children who must work harder than all the others to please his father, because by odd chance he was also the one who did not have the protection of the McLeods. Whereas Annie, unprepossessing though she might be, was dutiful and kind, and a willing handmaiden to the ebullient Peggy McLeod, while Duncan Cave could do whatever he pleased simply because of his love, unrehearsed and without guile, for Bunyan who was dying. Hector had no such friends in the house of the Man.

She would have sought a room of her own if there had been any left spare, but they were all taken up with these children of hers. In the room where she must lie down for the night, her husband lay waiting.

As she sat on the edge of the bed he opened his mouth, issuing forth a belch stained with grease. Instinctively she moved down the bed an inch or so. His hand fell on her shoulder.

126

'Where are you going?'

'Nowhere. I am going nowhere.' Have nowhere to go, she might have added, but did not.

She thought, as she had before, I have endured worse. And survived.

Annie lay and felt the breath of the house and held her own for as long as she could, as if the act of breathing might cause some explosion of all the elements that mingled under the roof of her home. Then, where the moonlight struck the boards, she watched the floor with fascination, certain in her heart that the Devil would rise through it one night and seize her by the ankle. Would he break open the floor with a mighty crash (she hoped so, for even then it might not be too late for someone to hear and save her, though who had ever been saved from the Devil when he was so poised to pounce?). Perhaps he would slide through the floor with stealth and presence like that of the Holy Ghost who, she was sure, could appear in a room like a breath of fog on a moor, like steam rising in the kitchen from a pot of potatoes.

But though she watched and waited, in the end she slept.

In the afternoon Peggy and Annie sliced and creamed their way across the ice, their skates whistling as they practised turns. It was an early snow and the lakes were solid already, and soon the bay would be as well. When she was flying over the ice like this Annie felt free and cleared of all responsibility. It was a heady, giddy feeling, like madness, as if there was a space behind her eyes. It was a harmless thing to do that no one complained about, skating across the ice, yet the very pleasure it gave made her doubt its rightness.

Today, Peggy was hugging the importance of impending death to her like a treasure.

'We are fortunate,' said Peggy as they carried their skates home, 'that we have several children in our family. It's always useful to have more if any should die.'

'I suppose it is,' said Annie doubtfully.

'You haven't really enough in yours,' said Peggy.

'No,' said Annie humbly. 'I can see that.' Immediately her burdens became greater. 'I shall make up for it when I'm grown,' she said.

'Oh yes. I shall make sure that I have plenty too. What will you call them?'

'Oh, I hadn't thought. Well, Fraser of course. And maybe Hector. And I will name one for its father.'

'So what shall that be?'

'Oh Peggy McLeod, how can I know that?'

'You could marry one of my brothers.'

Annie had already considered that and wondered about naming Edward, but the idea of an actual living person as a husband was

127

embarrassing; besides she was afraid that it might seem like impertinence to suggest a McLeod for herself. But Edward was clever, and so good to look at she could have eaten him with jam whenever she sat across the table from him at the McLeods. His eyes seemed to rest kindly on her, unlike those of his six older brothers, whose glances were bold and sharp as they looked at each other, sly as they moved across their father's face. They were said to run brandy from the island of St Pierre.

As if reading her thoughts, Peggy said, 'Edward is our second Edward you know. We had another one, but he died too.'

Annie remembered the grave at Black Cove which bore the brief inscription, 'Short spring, endless summer.' It was a terse comment for someone as vocal as McLeod, and it occurred to her with surprise that it must be the work of Mrs McLeod. She hardly knew Mary McLeod, although she spent so much time in her home. Often the minister's wife did not rise from her bed for days at a time, and when she did sit at table with them her face was like flour and her eyes fatigued. They roamed across the tops of her children's heads, and Annie could have sworn that she saw none of them. Her hands lay between her knees, the fingers threading themselves round and round each other, a ceaseless rhythmic motion contained in the circle of her lap.

'Well I suppose you must have enough Edwards now,' said Annie, hoping that the subject of naming children was over.

But Peggy was inexorable. 'What would you call the girls?'

'Eh?' Annie was surprised. 'Oh, I don't suppose I shall have girls.'

'You might. Somebody has to have them.'

'Aye. But I think I will be having boys, you know.'

'But if? What if?'

Annie divined that Peggy was waiting for her to say, like any best friend, her own name Peggy, or Margaret.

'Maria,' she said, suddenly perverse. As soon as it was out she regretted it. But it was too late to take it back. 'I would call a girl Maria.'

She comforted herself with the thought that if she persisted with her goodness it was a problem she might not have to confront. Sons must certainly be her reward.

So they made their way to the house on the knoll above Black Cove, where Bunyan McLeod lay dying.

Bunyan was propped by a mountain of pillows. His high forehead shone like marble, and although he was barely twenty his hairline had receded. Within the recesses of his skull his eyes blazed, a dark unnatural colour, and yet Isabella who, as she had promised, was visiting him too, could not escape the thought that Bunyan, of all McLeod's children, was the most like his father.

'How are you today then, Bunyan?' she asked quietly.

'I am as well as can be expected, thank you, Mrs McIssac.'

'How have you been passing the time?'

'Oh, I've plenty to think about, and Duncan tells me all that's happening out there in the world, and what he thinks I cannot see in my head he draws for me. I am very fortunate.'

'I am glad that you are...' But for the moment Isabella could think of nothing to say. Had she meant to say happy? Or to agree that he was fortunate? Neither would do, and yet it seemed that Bunyan would find either acceptable.

It occurred to her then that although Bunyan knew he would die, he was experiencing the stars and the clouds, the woods, the lakes and the sea as they were told of to him by Duncan, and that her son already knew more than she had learned in a lifetime. Somewhere in the last bitter years she had thrown away hard-won knowledge and a spirit of adventure, vamping up her manner with toughness and a quick and cynical tongue.

The woman wanted to possess this young man, as if what he knew could change her; owning him, she might extract what he knew.

'I am excited by what I will find,' said Bunyan.

'What if there is nothing?' she blurted out before she could stop herself.

He smiled. 'Well, at least I shall know.'

'What does your father say?'

But he was tired again and turned his head away, his eyelids drooping.

Behind her stood Mary, whom she had not seen in a long time. She was surprised to register that she was looking better and calmer than she had for some years, though noted the slight oddness of her appearance, with a headscarf knotted under her chin like the women of old when they appeared in a church.

'You're managing, then?' she said, when they had withdrawn to the room next door.

Mary nodded. 'But I must. Who else will, if I don't?'

'You've changed, Mary.'

'Have I? Oh, I don't know about that. Perhaps I am just more myself.'

She is still strange, thought Isabella, and remembered the times when Mary had been alone over the years. For it was in those times, when McLeod had ridden into the wilderness to preach his word, or the happy year when he had gone to New York State to be ordained so that he could marry people and legally represent himself to the Governor in Halifax as a minister, that Mary had had small brief summers of her own, seeming to keep well and strong and manage her children as she never did when her husband was home.

It was only when he was there that she withdrew into herself, going out little and not appearing in church where, on occasion, McLeod had

129

berated even her for immodest ways.

Looking at her now, Isabella guessed that at present she felt as if she was alone and was the stronger for it. Still, she was unable to resist asking her a further question.

'Does Norman comfort Bunyan?' she said. For although it felt improper, she experienced a vague, uneasy excitement, as if a new dimension on McLeod might be revealed.

Mary blinked, seeming not quite to have heard. 'Thank you for the conserves, Isabella. You are always so kind to us.'

Behind them, Peggy and Annie ran down the passageway, chanting a spelling rhyme.

'Should I keep Annie home?' said Isabella.

'Oh she is no trouble, no trouble at all,' said Mary. She clutched Isabella's hand as if possessed of a quick thought and as if they had had no discussion at all about McLeod. 'I have to tell you, Isabella, I cannot help but wonder if Bunyan's view of the eternal differs from that of his father.'

Bunyan did not die until the spring and it seemed to those who watched like the longest winter since the world began.

On the day that he was buried all the men of St Ann's gathered at Black Cove. Of late, some who dared had stayed away from the services, tired of the absolute power that was McLeod and querulous with anxiety about the corruption which they saw but dared not name amongst his sons.

Now, out of a tender regard that they believed they had forgotten, they came back to him.

Isabella watched Duncan Cave, pale as milk and dressed in black, set off limping on his game foot across the fields to where the burial would take place. The death of Bunyan felt like a blow beneath her heart.

'What of Bunyan?' she had asked Duncan Cave the night before. 'How was he at the last? Was he at peace with himself? Did his father give him comfort when he needed it?'

But Duncan Cave had been either too removed from her in his grief to be reached, or he did not know. It was all the same; he did not answer her.

Behind Duncan Cave, Fraser and Black Hector had followed. 'Who does he think he is, setting off without us,' Fraser said to her as he did up his collar stud.

'It was his friend, understand he wants to be alone,' said Isabella, for once placatory.

'Hmph. McLeod's an older friend of mine. Those two boys did not know each other as long as I have known McLeod.'

'But it is the boy who is dead,' said Isabella patiently.

At last she was alone, for Annie would spend the day with Kate MacKenzie where grief was not so thick on the ground as here. Isabella knew that Annie secretly would have preferred to stay with her, and that she had been unkind to send her away. She is a child, she said to herself, children do not understand the meaning of grief in the same way that we adults do.

She knew that she was cruel.

She leaned and stroked her cat, of which she was more than a little fond. She called him Noah, though quietly, for fear that some, overhearing her, might be offended. She did not know where he had come from. One day he had simply appeared at her door, sleek and rather overfed. Yet nobody had laid claim to him, and so he had come to live with her. He had wide eyes like a slice of the moon, and his coat was long and black and fluffy. Under his chin there was a bib of white which gave him a slightly petulant air, as if his lip was drooping. He loved Isabella with a passion which she might have found embarrassing had he been human.

But today, there being nobody around, she stretched herself in the sun, revitalised as if in forgiveness for the winter and the death of Bunyan, even though neither were anything to do with her or anything that she had done. She felt her body steal back to life. As warmth soaked through her, she felt that she could do anything, walk on water if she must, and at first such a strange and hectic notion, so apparently frivolous in regard to the Scriptures, frightened her. But then she thought, why should I not have confidence in myself, why do I have to believe that I am subservient to the will of others. And even if I am not brazen enough to confront them with such confidence, I can nurture it in private, and what harm does it do anyone, especially if it will make me feel so much better?

So she stretched there, letting her skin soak up the heat of the spring sun, and the cat leapt up beside her, nuzzling under her armpits, driven wild by the accumulated sweat in the matted cloth of her winter garments. He nibbled fiercely as if he were having a meal, then folded his body down the length of hers, purring a loud noisy dribbling purr until he slept so deeply that they both entered a long period of stillness. She was anchored to this spot, fearing to disturb him, and an hour or more passed this way with his body curled along hers.

It grew cooler as the sun dropped away from midday, and Noah stirred, stretching out to his full length before he gathered himself tidily together and minced down the path, looking for a bird.

Then, confused by the sun and guilty for such indolence on a day committed to sorrow, Isabella sank back, her lethargy overtaking her again, until Noah redirected his attention towards her.

In the garden she heard his high piping miaow, a kind of *nya, nya,*

nya in the back of his throat as he flung himself at her. He landed on her back, digging in all his claws, seemingly determined to injure her yet loving her as well as he kneaded his paws backwards and forwards in her flesh, only a stray claw reminding her that he was not to be trusted.

So this is what I have come to then, she thought, communing with a half-wild animal that has sprung from nowhere and taken over my life.

No wonder her daughter was in the habit of eyeing him with positive dislike.

It was shortly after the death of Bunyan that Isabella began attending the revival meetings that were taking place in various parts of Cape Breton, giving rise to the notion that she was truly out of her mind or else truly wilful and without concern for the consequences of her actions. But it had begun more accidentally than the people of St Ann's believed.

On a summer day she was sitting at the front door with Noah in her lap, with the house behind her so quiet that she believed it to be empty. As she was about to stretch in the sun there was a footstep behind her. She knew without looking that it was Duncan Cave, for it was a different footstep from that of anyone she knew and there was no way he had ever been able to disguise it from her, landing with a thump on his left foot even when he danced.

Only today he was not dancing, and his face was gaunt.

'I thought you had gone out,' she said.

'There's nowhere to go.'

'You can't stay in that room forever.'

'Why not?'

'You have to do something.'

'Why? What do you do?'

She regarded him and he looked back at her, an unblinking mirror of her own face. They never quarrelled, and yet there was a trace of accusation in his tone.

After a while, she offered, 'There were things that Bunyan said.'

'Mother, I know what Bunyan said.'

'Did he tell you to stay moping indoors for him all through the summer?'

He was silent.

'I know you heard what Bunyan said, but I heard only some of it. Now I see ghosts.'

'You do, mother?'

'And creatures in the woods. They come at me in dreams, I don't know who they are, Duncan. Sometimes I think they are real, and then I'm frightened, but other times I'm not sure if it is just a craziness that I have. We came out of the woods, you and me, Duncan Cave.'

He shivered.

She sat, reflecting. She recalled how once, in a cave, McLeod had come to her. It must have been McLeod, she was sure, for who else could it have been — a tall man on a misty afternoon, a man wearing a cloak, taking her away from a place where she was calm and happy. He had led her away on a horse, saying that she must put all that had befallen her behind her. She could not remember what he meant though, for the past was like a dream. In that cave there was lightness, and whiteness, and whatever it was that frightened her had disappeared. But now, at the edge of her consciousness, there was fear again.

And she wondered, but could not explain to Duncan Cave, whether it would all have been different if McLeod had been Bunyan, if Bunyan was not McLeod reborn as he might have been. Only now Bunyan was dead, and she would never find out.

'I think I should go back into the woods,' she said. She took his hand absently in hers. Beside her he lifted his face to the wind, as if the answers might be on the breeze, as if something was stirring far back in his mind.

Next time she saw him come out of his room it was Sunday, when the house was empty of the rest of the family again. This time he held a sketching pad in his hand. Waiting until he was out of sight she walked slowly across the field to where Fraser's second horse was standing and saddled him up.

It was a long time since she had ridden, but the horse seemed pleased of the outing and the forest felt friendly. There was a clean scent of pine needles and the tang of spruce in the air. Deeper in amongst the trees snow was banked up comfortably against the trunks like fluffy white pillows, even though it was almost midsummer, and there were creatures wilder than Noah wherever she looked. They stood stock still when she appeared, before scampering into the trees—squirrels, muskrats, and an occasional fox.

She was glad to be on horseback though, for although she was no longer afraid of bears as she once had been, she preferred not to meet them on foot.

Soon she was aware of other stirrings amongst the trees and realised that she was far beyond the perimeters of St Ann's. She had lost all track of time and distance and found that she was caught up amongst a large group of people converging on the one spot. At first she was afraid, for it reminded her of the way people had congregated around the hanging at Pictou, even though to remember that was in itself a relief. That is why I am here, she thought, confronting what has lain buried for so long.

Encouraged, she turned to a stranger by her side, a stocky woman with her bonnet pushed back from her head, laughing amongst a group of people.

'Where are we going, then?' asked Isabella.

The woman looked at her as if she was simple, but seeing that she really did not know, she said, 'To Peter McLean's communion service.'

'A real communion service?'

For McLeod did not administer communion, considering that none were worthy of receiving the sacraments, in the same way that even now the only children he baptised were his own.

By the time Isabella arrrived at the meeting by the sea there were perhaps two hundred boats anchored in a bay and at least five hundred horses tethered in the woods. The service had already begun. At the front stood a weatherbeaten man wrapped in a buffalo cloak preaching in a way that was passionate and full of emotion. Isabella took this to be the Reverend McLean and settled herself on the grass to listen.

'My friends,' the man cried, and there was a ripple of pleasure around the congregation, 'we do not all have to suffer eternal damnation, whatever we have done on earth. There is a *possibility* of pardon. And of divine grace.'

When the people stood up to sing Isabella found that she was crying. She stayed a long time amongst the crowd, mesmerised by its ardour and by the intensity of it all. And when it was time, she took the cup.

She couldn't be sure of anything, of course. One never could. But as McLean had said, there were possibilities.

She went again on other days, travelling further overnight by Little Narrows to Whycocomagh, and from there to Lake Ainslie and Mira, arranging in her absences for Annie to stay with Kate MacKenzie. The second time she was away she collected stone root and indigo, and other plants and herbs that she remembered from long ago, and made potions that relieved the illnesses of her women friends. When she had been for the third time she saw Annie look strangely at her and guessed straight away that she understood her defection. Her daughter's friends, who had never made a great practice of coming near, now stayed away altogether. Annie seemed to be almost entirely enfolded into the McLeod family, so that it became unnecessary for Isabella to make other arrangements on her behalf.

'Do you really go to the meetings, mother?' she asked her one morning as she prepared to leave for school, as if hoping that there was a final chance that she might not have to believe in it.

'Yes, it is true.'

Isabella saw the bleakness in Annie's face.

'Does father know?'

'I don't know.'

'You don't care, do you?'

'He wouldn't stop me.'

'You mean he couldn't. You do what you like.'

'Should I not? Do you think?'

'He is afraid of you.'

'Oh come. Who has been putting such ideas into your head?' But she laughed, and could not hide a glimmer of satisfaction in her voice.

Still, she looked at Annie, and wondered what would happen next between them.

She wrote in her journal: 'I am saddened that in order to find some peace of my own, we may be more or less finished with each other, especially as I doubt that I will attend many more of these meetings, the thoughts being in my head now, rather than any benefit to be derived from hearing their constant reiteration which, in the end, is the way of all churchmongering. But then, Annie has never felt as if she was truly mine. She finds more favour with her father these days. Yet she is my child, and my daughter at that, and I would that there were some part of her that I could hold onto, some way not to lose all of her.'

In the church at St Ann's, Annie sat between her father and Black Hector and listened to McLeod. Although when she visited his house no reproaches were ever laid on her, now she felt that he spoke directly to her about her mother.

His voice rolled over the church and up into the high arches.

'There are people who go to the revivalist meetings and are wildly extravagant in their be-*hav*-iour, *and* immoral, with illicit procreation and sexual intercourse going on on all fronts. The women screech and scream, they screak and shriek, falling down prostrate, springing monkey-like from place to place, roll around and rave. Oh, I have seen rabid females in the United States in such transports. It is a terrible thing, some of them even believing that they possess the word of God in their own mouths, and are followed in their hysterical ways by others. *That* is what the Church of Scotland and its emissaries are *doing* to the state of religion he-ere! Still, what comes with the wind goes with the rain. These matters are but a specious flutter of the wing, and will all pass. Our modest ways at St Ann's will prevail...'

There were rumours about that Isabella McIssac had taken a black-and-white cat for a lover, and wore the milk teeth of her children banded round her neck, beneath the collar of her dress.

13

ONE SEASON PASSED into another, chasing each other, as golden rod faded, snow fell, banked and melted away and sweet spring skies unfolded, followed by another high summer and the ripening blueberries, an unfaltering procession of the years.

Hector McIssac was fifteen. His face wore a dark fuzz of beard in the mornings which made him proud and embarrassed at the same time. McLeod decreed that beards not be worn in St Ann's and so by the time he left for school he was clean-shaven. But he knew he had dark hair on other secret parts of him, growing in fine strands still, straight along his body. His private dream was of when it would curl along his back and shoulders as it did on his father.

At school, which young men often attended until they were eighteen or even more if they chose—for the Man set great store by a good education—he often glanced sideways at Miss Martha MacKenzie, the sister of his best friend Lewis. He wondered if she could see how old he looked.

Of course she was a grown woman, an old maid in fact, and was only at the school helping with the small children and observing how a classroom was run in preparation for becoming a schoolma'am over at Sydney Mines.

Her being unmarried, and so old, he couldn't even admit to anyone that he thought her pretty, but the truth was that her hair reminded him of nasturtiums, and he could not help but notice that the skin of her arched throat was the colour of cream, and he would have liked to bite it.

'Why is she to be a teacher instead of getting married?' he asked Lewis.

'Oh she was good at Greek and algebra,' Lewis explained seriously. 'But she had more trouble with the New Testament.' He added this as if it excused her cleverness a little.

'Is it because she is a woman?'

'Aye, she cannot be expected to understand such profound matters, Mr McLeod has told my mother. But as she is set on teaching awhile, he has said she can learn about the infants in the schoolroom.'

'It is philosophy that confounds females rather than language,' said Hector. 'That is what the Master says.' He flipped an apple core into the lake and watched it float.

'Oh aye, he says Martha would be better off married, but who would have her now? She is twenty-six.'

'It is all her own fault,' said Hector, not wishing to pursue the subject of Martha with his friend, who sometimes saw through him when others did not.

'He is unbiddable in his ways,' sighed Isabella to Kate MacKenzie, speaking of Hector.

'Oh he is just a boy,' said Kate, who had brought up two sons before Lewis, the one she had not expected to have and had grumbled about when he was born, but had grown soft over as he grew older.

Eoghann muttered at times that she treated Lewis like a girl, but she took scant notice. Her husband was so much a man of the church these days that he had little time to attend to family matters and it was mostly left to her to bring up their last-born.

'Well, Hector is like his father,' said Isabella. 'You would not think I was in charge of him at all, he is so malicious.'

'Isn't that how you like it best? You have said before he is his father's son?' Kate reminded her gently. For although she had tried to understand, she had not always approved of the way Isabella conducted her family's business.

'Have you heard the news of Donald McLeod then?' said Isabella abruptly, sensing the reproof.

'That he is to build a ship and make everyone's fortunes selling timber and produce in Scotland?'

'Aye. Would you trust Donald McLeod with your fortune?'

Kate shrugged. 'The ship is not built yet.'

'It may not be, but my husband is talking of putting money into it.'

'So is mine. There is nothing you can do that will stop it. Unless you have some secret power that I do not.'

'Oh, I've none of that where Fraser McIssac is concerned. But I don't know that there will be fortunes here for the taking for much longer.'

'What d'you mean?'

'Haven't you seen the colour of the potatoes this year?'

'They're not at their best, but what has that to do with it? They'll be better next year. Perhaps there is too much fat.'

For some of the women were becoming complacent. You could see it in their eyes.

Kate was uneasy all the same. Sometimes Isabella knew too much about things which she did not. 'Norman McDonald would have had something to say about Donald's scheme.'

'But Norman McDonald is gone.'

'Well he had had enough. And now McLeod has fallen out with the Squire too.'

The women glanced at each other, and looked away again.

Presently, Kate asked, 'Is Annie doing all right at school then?'

'Annie? Oh, as far as I know. You know how it is, she spends most

137

of her time with the McLeods.'

'She seems a good girl,' was all that Kate said, unsure whether more was required.

In the night, at McLeod's house, Annie heard a man scream. He screamed from some deep and terrible inner torment, and his scream rang on for a minute or more.

She sat bolt upright, and knew that the Devil had visited someone. Peggy stirred beside her in the bed.

'He is coming out of a dream,' she murmured and fell back to her own dreaming.

Annie lay awake, trembling until morning.

'Who was it?' she asked Peggy as they brushed their hair before the mirror.

Peggy's eyes flickered and the light in them cooled.

'Who was what?' she said, looking away.

At breakfast, everyone seemed as they always did, gathered around the board. Annie tried to examine the faces of the brothers, of McLeod, but she could read nothing in the expression of any one of them. Only Mary, Peggy's older sister and not favoured by her father as Peggy was, looked drawn and smudged.

But it was a man she had heard in the night.

It was Kenneth Dingwall who followed Annie's eyes with his own. He smiled a quiet, sly smile. The tailor who served McLeod and answered his every need saw also every gesture and glance that passed in the presence of his master. He raised his plate of porridge to his mouth and a small slick of it escaped and dripped down his chin, shiny and coated with milk. He put the plate down and rubbed his chin with the back of his hand.

Lately, Martha had seen that McLeod watched Annie in the schoolroom. It troubled her, for the child was one of the quietest and best behaved there. She noticed how often he called on her, and how she flinched when she could not answer, for work as she might, she was an average student who found it difficult to do better than pass the halfway mark.

She sat near to Isaac, youngest son of McLeod's oldest friend, the mystic-natured Squire Donald McLeod who had followed him from Scotland and whom McLeod no longer considered to be his friend. Isaac could answer anything he was asked, but however often he put up his hand to answer now, McLeod ignored him. Seeing Annie's discomfiture Isaac had more than once leaned over to whisper an answer to her, feeling it wasted if it was not of use to someone.

'Why are your parents not friends any more?' she asked him during a lunch break, made bold by his kindness, although he was much older.

'It is because my brother and Mary McLeod are in love, and he thinks my father is helping them to meet.'

'But what is the matter with being in love?' cried Annie, indignant for the cause of romance and suddenly angry that her friend had not confided this family secret to her.

'There is nothing wrong with love, I am sure,' said Isaac, 'but it matters much with whom you are in love. And our master does not permit love within his family. Haven't you noticed that none of his sons has married anyone?'

He leaned over and whispered in her ear, 'They love brandy and money more than they love women.'

Stung, Annie had pulled away. For a week she had pretended that Isaac did not sit near to her, and turned her eyes away when he whispered.

But one afternoon McLeod had called on her, and would ask no one else for the answer she could not provide.

'It is a simple matter, surely, for you to tell me, in the words of St Matthew, Annie McIssac, what has the Son of man come to save?'

In the silence that followed, McLeod cast his eyes around the room.

Seeing Annie's stricken face, Isaac leaned over and muttered the answer, that which is lost.

Annie herself looked lost. 'Who? What?' she whispered piteously.

'Did I hear you ask someone for the answer to that question?' said McLeod. His tone was ominous.

She did not reply.

'Will you not answer me?'

Annie's head hung lower.

'Answer me, young woman.'

Isaac, grown frightened, looked from McLeod to Annie and back again. He had never heard McLeod refer to a pupil as a woman before. The girls were simply girls or children. Now he saw that Annie could well become a woman and that McLeod, who had whipped many boys before but never a girl, was about to strike her.

'Come...out...here.' His face was taut and strained to the point where the threads of veins in his temples looked about to burst. The room was very still.

Annie stood up and advanced towards McLeod with her hand outstretched.

'I am ready,' she said when she reached the desk.

Isaac could not decide in the seconds which flashed past him whether she believed McLeod would pull back at the last, or whether she expected to be hit. He glanced down the long benches which lined the schoolroom, to Hector McIssac who was now staring out the window as if nothing were happening at the front of the room. Looking back to Annie and McLeod, Isaac could see that the schoolmaster was committed to his course of action, and perhaps too, that he wished to hit Annie harder than he had ever hit anyone before.

In the far corner of the room, standing at her post, Martha MacKenzie had become frozen like a tree in winter. A small cry escaped from her and her hand flew up to her beautiful creamy throat.

Unable to stop himself, Isaac leapt from his seat, throwing himself across the short distance that separated him from McLeod and Annie as the cane was raised. Reaching up, he tore at the rod in McLeod's hand, but McLeod anticipated this even as he flew at him, and hung onto the cane; his arms had not lost their strength even though the boy was young and so full of rage that he held on like a grim terrier. A furious see-sawing began, backwards and forwards across the room.

'You will pay for this, pay for it, d'you hear me, boy?' shouted McLeod.

Above his voice, Isaac was making a sound like a screaming seagull, a boy's voice of high terror yet exulting in his own magical and new-found strength. Behind them, Annie stood with her hands in front of her mouth.

Suddenly the rod whipped out of McLeod's hand and Isaac was holding it aloft before he brought it down on his knee, snapping it in two. He threw the pieces at McLeod's feet.

'You will pay for that,' McLeod repeated, but now his voice was like cracking ice.

'Not in this room,' said Isaac. 'I've done with you forever.'

When he had gone and Annie had taken her place again, McLeod resumed his lesson.

'What has the Son of man come to save, Miss McIssac?'

'That which is lost,' whispered Annie.

Martha MacKenzie looked as if she were about to faint. When school was out she approached McLeod.

'Minister, may I have a word?'

He turned stony eyes on her. 'What is it?'

'When I was a pupil here it was not your policy to whip the girls. Has that changed, pray tell me?'

'I will tell you nothing. You are not here to question me.'

'But I wish to know. If I am to be a schoolma'am, I need to know what is done in classrooms nowadays.'

'You will not find out here.'

'I do not understand.'

'I would trouble you not to return, Miss MacKenzie.'

She lifted her chin. 'It would seem that your classroom is emptying fast, Minister. No doubt the more liberal schoolhouses of Mr Munroe, and people like him, are filling. But that is your problem, sir.'

She lifted her skirt as she stepped out the door.

'You should have let him give it to you,' said Hector as they made their way home. 'He'll blame somebody. Probably me,' he added, gloomily kicking a stone.

'I would have let him,' said Annie. 'I wanted him to hit me.'

Annie learned to milk cows. It was women's work which she knew Isabella disliked almost more than any other chore. It made her hands red and sore and the skin round her fingernails often split, causing large, ugly sores. If she became the family milker, Annie figured, she might be seen as more diligent and worthy, and her mother might become more amenable. Or take more notice of her, a treacherous inner voice suggested. She pushed the thought aside. She did not need Isabella's approval. It would be enough if the community of St Ann's saw her as a young woman beyond reproach.

Or if, indeed, the family of McLeod would again see her thus, it would be sufficient.

She sat at the stool then, with her face pressed against the flanks of the cows. She hobbled each animal the way Isabella did, with one leg lashed up against a tree so that it could not kick the pail, and squeezed and pulled until milk appeared. At first it seemed impossible that the animals would ever yield to her. They shifted restlessly as she squeezed harder, their bloated udders giving up an occasional drop because it was impossible for them to hold back entirely.

'Stroke it down, stroke it,' said Isabella behind her. 'Look,' and she made a circle of her thumb and forefinger, and drawing the other fingers in towards the base of the palm, flexed gently, making a fist. 'Remember she's female, it hurts her to begin with, letting down the milk, go gentle, that's right, and she won't be able to hold back. Ah, that's better. Your fingers are a little short for the old girl with her big fat teats, but she's one of the easiest, once you know how to start her.'

Annie felt her face burn at the mention of women's functions but it was like her mother, what she must expect from her. Soon the milk did begin to flow, and though her hands became as raw as her mother's had been it got easier each day. She clenched and released in steady rhythms. The milk pulsed like a vein down the length of the teat and the cows stood more at ease.

And so the milk drummed frothing into the pail, the girl and the animals bonded together, the cat Noah at her side, its greedy mouth open to catch the drops. There was the quiet splatter of shit beside her, the warm earthy smell of the cow's dung: she felt close to them as she laid her face against their flanks.

Her mother was gentler with her and made sure that she did not milk all the time. She also complained less about the task when it was her turn at the stool. Sometimes at night, in the house, mother and daughter would startle each other by candle-light on the landings, or even by moonlight, for Annie, like her mother, was already a restless sleeper. There, in the different and stranger illuminations of night, they might look into each other's eyes.

Isabella wondered then if she ought to try explaining to her child that neither of them need be called to account for what lay between them; that it was just that love itself seemed to have stopped some time before Annie was born. It was as if she was outside of love and all its possibility.

Back in bed, by her husband's inert body, she would say to herself, it is for the best. It is good training, a little loneliness. Nobody should let her think it was going to be easy.

14

I T WAS A NIGHT of fine mists and autumn rain when McLeod sent a runner from the house to summon Eoghann MacKenzie before him. The MacKenzies had been picking rosy Cape Breton apples in the mellow afternoon. Towards evening the weather had changed, a winter bite in the air, and the fire leapt in the stone fireplace as Kate announced dinner.

Eoghann said grace; Kate lifted fresh flannel cakes off the stove and placed them on the table. Lewis's hand shot forth first as always, and as always Kate reproved him. At the same time she admired the way he was filling out. She thought that he would not stay long at school now, for he spent more time on the farm with Ewan than he did at his study. Ewan was the next in the family above him, an easy-natured and pleasant young man, sitting across the table from her. Lately, Lewis preferred his brother's company even to that of Hector McIssac. Quietly, this pleased her.

The knock at the door shook her thoughts. There was nothing in it to startle her, for it was neither insistent nor loud, and yet as soon as she heard it she knew that there was something wrong.

Eoghann was already at the door. 'The minister wants to see me,' he said, collecting his coat a moment or two later.

'Can't it wait till we've eaten?' Kate asked.

'The boy says not.' Eoghann looked troubled. 'He wants Lewis to come too.'

'What have you been doing, lad?' she asked, lightly touching his hair as she passed by his chair to collect Eoghann's dinner. She would put it to warm in the oven.

'Nothing,' he said. 'Do I have to come?'

'It sounds urgent,' said his father. 'You've been doing all your homework, have you?'

'Of course he has,' said Kate, too quickly.

'He'll have to do his own answering if he's been up to anything,' said Eoghann.

But Lewis looked so mystified that, although Kate and Eoghann exchanged puzzled glances over his head, neither of them could seriously believe he had done anything amiss.

When they had gone, Martha said in a quiet, tight voice, 'I'll kill him if he does anything to Lewis.'

'Martha! What are you saying?'

'I have come to know what McLeod is like,' she said.

Kate glanced at Ewan, but he shrugged. 'It will be nothing of importance I imagine,' he said, and rose to attend to cattle that he had put in the barn earlier in the evening.

'I have crossed McLeod,' said Martha evenly. 'Someone must pay for that.'

Kate shook her head, but her voice lacked conviction. Something was being admitted which she knew but did not want to think about. Something she had known for a long time, and knew very well.

'Then why Lewis?' she asked.

'Because he would prefer not to be seen punishing me.'

'But that's wickedness.'

The air was heavy. 'Yes,' said Martha, 'it is, isn't it?'

'You're imagining things,' said Kate, as she picked up her sewing and moved closer to the fire. There was a ringing in her ears; she was faint from it.

Much later that night, Eoghann and Lewis returned. Martha had gone to bed. 'There is nothing to wait up for,' Kate had said, and seeing that her mother wished to sit on her own, Martha had left her.

Lewis' face was tear-stained. He went past Kate and straight to the room he shared with Ewan, so that she barely glimpsed him.

Eoghann sat down beside her. Age and despondency were all about him as he settled his bulk on the chair.

'The boy's been stealing,' he said.

Kate's sewing fell out of her hands, her astonishment genuine. People did not steal at St Ann's. The greatest insult one neighbour could inflict on another would be to lock a door, whether absent for an hour or a month. Each home was open to the next, so that if anyone was short of an item, be it food or a blanket if there was a passing traveller, or an iron pot for extra preserving, nobody need ever ask. Theft was not to be considered.

'Lewis? Our boy? There is a mistake.'

'No mistake. Murdoch Morrison had money taken this morning. Fraser McIssac saw Lewis pause there on his way to school.'

'Fraser . . .? I don't believe what I'm hearing. Where was Hector . . .? Does Lewis admit this?'

'Of course he doesn't.'

'Why of course? Lewis doesn't lie.'

'That we knew of.'

'Well, what has he done with this money?'

'I don't know. Look don't you start asking me questions, I've had McLeod at me for hours, over and over and over.'

'It's a lie.' Martha was standing at the door in her nightdress.

'Martha, please, it is a mistake.' The ringing in her ears threatened to overwhelm her.

'I tell you, it's a lie.' Martha's voice was rising.

'Tell her to get out. Has she no modesty?' Eoghann's voice was hard and rough.

'Father, you don't know.'

'I will send you myself.' He was on his feet, his hand raised towards her face. She cowered and disappeared into the shadows.

'May God forgive you for that,' said Kate.

'You too? Have you all turned into madmen and thieves? The evidence is against him. Don't you see that? You can't protect your children forever. You have to let them stand on their own feet. Take the consequences, answer for themselves. Face reality.'

'This is reality?' Kate asked him.

The silence between them now was one of shock. Eoghann had never questioned their lives at St Ann's, and Kate, looking at his expression, suspected that he never would. Thinking back to the day of the hanging, she remembered him as he had been before. He had seemed to think for her and the children, made decisions; stood in judgment of those who did not, or who failed in their undertakings. After that day, he had stopped thinking and let McLeod do it for him. Though now she saw that McLeod had simply made decisions which Eoghann followed, while it was she, Kate, who had done the thinking. As Martha was doing too. Well perhaps she should leave it to her. Or someone. She was too tired to keep on doing it for them all.

In the silent house their old clock chimed midnight.

'What do you think we should do?' she said at last.

Eoghann sighed with what she could see was relief and she understood what she never had before, that he could not see that she was thinking, or that she would think of doing things other than his way. Even when he had asked her to consider coming to St Ann's, it had been a kindness extended to a young wife. Really, there had never been any choice.

He was speaking. She had to concentrate to make sense of what he was saying.

'There's to be a meeting of the school trustees tomorrow night. Norman will preside as magistrate, to decide what's to be done. He suggests Lewis should go along.'

That was another thing she thought of, and it increased her anger. McLeod was everything, minister, teacher, magistrate, there was nothing except trading—which he left to John Munro—that he was not in charge of, and every facet of their lives was controlled by him. They could do nothing without first turning to him.

'You'll go with the boy?' she said, containing herself.

'That's not necessary.'

145

'But Eoghann...'

'Don't you understand? What it has been like tonight? The shame? They'll decide on a punishment that fits, and that will be that. Mine is to live with what he's done.'

'Mine too, it seems,' said Kate.

He turned to go upstairs, waiting for her to follow, but she went back to the fire. 'I'll come up later, I've some sewing to finish.'

When finally she did go and lie beside him, he put out his hand to take hers as he used to do when they were young, but she turned on her side and pretended to fall straight into sleep. So it was they passed the night until towards dawn, when they slept fitfully.

In the evening, Kate spoke to Eoghann. 'Has Lewis said that he will go?'

'I am seeing to it that he does. I have told Ewan to accompany him.'

'And it will be no shame for him?'

'He will find it educational,' said Eoghann grimly.

'What do you think will happen?'

'Oh a good dressing down I expect. He may have to do some extra work for the Man. You worry too much,' he relented towards her.

In the schoolroom they were gathered, school trustees and elders of St Ann's. They had come to discuss theological matters and a working party to provide more slates and books in the school. They sat in long rows down the side of the room as the children did. McLeod sat at the desk in front. Well, there was nothing unusual about that, only why was he convening a court at this hour of the night? There was a shuffling amongst them. It was already late. Some of those gathered had not heard that there was trouble in the district, but they had seen Lewis MacKenzie brought in by a side door at the beginning of the meeting.

Now he was ushered forth from the side room where he had been waiting with his brother.

McLeod leaned forward. 'So tell me, boy. Do you practise self-abuse? Come, speak up?'

'No, sir.'

'Have unnatural thoughts?'

'No, sir?'

'You are sure now?'

'Yes, sir.'

'You are not going to cry, are you? Come, you are a man. Aye, that is better. But it is true, is it not, that you stole Mr Morrison's money? Climbed through the window? Eh, now that is how it happened. Speak up, Lewis.'

At the back of the room Ewan MacKenzie half-rose to his feet and was pulled down by hands on every side. McLeod nodded his approval to those who had restrained him.

'Speak to me, Lewis. You have not lost your voice have you? You have told me that you are not girlish in your ways. Haven't you?'

'Yes, sir.'

'And you took the money?'

'Yes, sir.'

'Sire, I demand to speak.' Ewan's voice rose from the back of the room.

'Young man, you will be removed from this court if you speak again.'

McLeod tipped himself back in his chair now, closing his eyes in contemplation of the matter before him while the hush in the room held an air of mystery and excitement. The men leaned towards one another and away again. They had not expected this tonight; blood sang in their ears as they looked at the youth before them.

They watched him and they watched McLeod, perched hawkishly in front of them as he tipped his chair back then forward again to hunch over the desk. His hands were held prayerfully before him.

'There are kinder punishments than whipping or the stocks,' he began, 'both of which would be meted out in Sydney town if he is sent there for further trial. Or they may send him to jail. He is young, and the way things are in the jails there he may perish with the cold at this time of year. I think we can deal mercifully with this matter here amongst ourselves. What do you say, my friends?'

They had drunk warm sweet tea all evening. They had nothing to say to each other as they waited for their sons, this man and his wife. Towards eleven, the door opened and Ewan came in. He went straight to Kate without looking at his father and touched her shoulder.

'Where is he, Ewan?'

'Outside.'

'Why doesn't he come in?'

'He wants me to tell you, before you see him...that he is hurt.'

Lewis stood at the door. One side of his head was covered with blood and his eyes stared somewhere beyond her. He held his scarf awkwardly near his face.

Eoghann's face was terrible as he took his son's hand and drew it away. Where once there had been an ear, now there was only part of it.

'How?' he said.

'With the sword,' said Ewan, speaking for Lewis.

Eoghann touched his son's face, then reached out for Kate's hand but she snatched it away. 'I am sorry,' he said.

'Sorrow will never be good enough for this night's work,' she said.

'I will ride to Sydney tomorrow to see the best lawyer I can find.'

'Will that restore his ear?'

She placed the shocked youth before the fire, fetching water and a bandage, heating a poker to cauterise the wound. The voice she used to Eoghann was hard, but to Lewis she uttered hushing noises as if he was a bird.

'I'll have his innocence defended.'

'Oh his innocence now, is it? Eoghann, go outside and tell that to the night air. Tell it to the moon and stars. You're easily bewitched. Or is it that the wizard got your tongue when you had the chance to defend your son before?'

In the morning, when she was sure he had gone, she climbed out of bed and went downstairs to make up the fire. Martha was already there poking around in the cold embers.

'I hate him,' said Martha. She was on her knees with her back to Kate.

'We thought he was like God when we were young,' said Kate as she poured water into the kettle and scooped out flour to begin the bread. Her back ached, a long score of pain along her spine. So many parts of her hurt, she could think of little except the pleasure of rest.

'Your father still thinks like that.'

'It was my father I was speaking of,' Martha replied. She straightened. 'How is Lewis?'

'Still sleeping. I gave him a powder last night, some roots that Isabella McIssac ground up for me in the summer. He should sleep awhile yet.'

'Isabella McIssac! That woman.'

'It won't be her fault. She may be strange, but it is the men in that family who are warped. Or most of them.'

'It is fair enough to say that.'

They spun round at the sound of Isabella's voice at the door. She stood waiting to be invited into the room. Martha and Kate wordlessly stood aside.

'I have some news for you,' said Isabella as she shed her cloak.

'What has the boy done now? What is the latest felony?'

'Wait.'

'Oh don't tell me. McLeod is cutting off arms and legs now. We should line our children up outside the door to make it easier for him.'

'I have come to tell you that it was not Lewis.'

'I know it was not.'

'But not everyone had your faith. They weren't his mother. . . . Well. It was a peddler, Kate. That fool Murdoch Morrison showed him where the money was. Or as good as. The peddler came to Murdoch's door and he bought something from him. He took his money out from where he keeps it, in full view. In all his excitement, running around telling everybody he had been robbed, he forgot about that.'

'How has it been found out?'

148

'Grey Donald saw the peddler climbing through the window as he was on his way to Boularderie. He stopped there the last three nights and not knowing of Lewis's trouble did not mention it to anyone until he got back here this morning.'

'Aren't you sorry?' Annie asked Hector.

'It was only a little bit of ear,' said her brother. He was staring moodily out of the window, unable to think of anything to do with himself for the day. Nobody spoke much to each other in this house these days, and now even his father was unusually silent.

'But he didn't do it.'

'Well he might have. Just because he *did* not do it does not mean that he *could* not do it. It is like a warning. We should all take heed of the warning, Annie.'

'But I try to be good.'

'Yes, but you still get into trouble, don't you,' he said, in triumphant confirmation.

'Lewis was your best friend,' said Annie timidly.

'Oh that was just a childish thing. I am grown now. He is a sissy.' He breathed on the pane of glass and watched it mist up, drew his finger across it, then wiped it clear again with his sleeve. Something had caught his eye in the distance outside. 'Like him,' he said pointing to Duncan Cave walking across the early snow towards them.

She stood by the window with him and together they watched their half-brother who had not yet seen them, carrying a sheaf of papers under his arm. Hector slouched over on his side and executed a couple of clumsy steps across the room.

'He will never be a man,' said Hector. 'He is his mother's darling too. Well, isn't he, Annie? Isn't that the truth?'

She nodded, dumb. She wanted to cover her ears but he was irresistible. Still watching out the window, she saw not Duncan Cave, for he was part of the landscape, but rather the landscape itself, full of shadows and fallen light, the flounces of snow on the garden, and the immense sky pressing in on them full of heavy banners of cloud rolling towards the house, promising further falls, and the shapes of trees blurred by winter. It occurred to her that she was not a part of it but merely an onlooker who was yet to discover some mysterious place in the scheme of things, and wondered if she might spend the rest of her life standing behind glass.

'If we're careful, you and me, we will be all right. It doesn't have to be like it is. People will forget that there was our mother and him.'

She nodded. She did not like to admit to this strange grown-up brother of hers that this thought, or intimations of it, had already visited her many times.

149

Detecting agreement in her manner, he pressed his advantage. 'We don't have to be different,' he said.

Now that Lewis did not require a defence, the lawyer Eoghann had consulted turned his attention towards the prosecution of McLeod and the school trustees. There were differences of opinion when a sheriff appeared from Sydney to arrest the trustees said to have held Lewis and cut him. They were bound over to appear at the next term of the General Sessions at Sydney.

'That will fix McLeod,' said Kate with a mixture of hope and bitterness in her tone. For the moment she had put aside her quarrel with Eoghann.

'Oh, I'm afraid he will fix them first,' Isabella said. For already she could see it all unfolding, McLeod earnest and unrepentant, defending his actions as having been in the common good.

'What do you mean?' Kate snapped. 'Even McLeod must pay for his folly some time.'

'It's not McLeod who's been arrested, though. Oh Kate.' Isabella was distressed; Kate looked so drawn and dreadful, her face ash-coloured and deeply lined, as if she had grown old in a matter of weeks. Her mouth trembled and her hands flicked over her knees, picking at invisible threads in her skirt.

'McLeod's got out of trouble before,' said Isabella as gently as she could. 'I saw him get off a charge brought against him in the courts at Dingwall long ago, when he was a young man.'

'I have heard of that. But it was different.'

'And now, it is not even he who has been charged.'

'Do you want him to get away with it?' Kate cried. For she could not forget that it had been Fraser McIssac who had begun this appalling chain of events, even though Isabella was her friend. Until now, by tacit agreement, it was understood that Isabella and Fraser's actions had no common basis.

Now Isabella turned her strange eyes on Kate. 'I should like...' She paused. 'I should like to see a victory,' she said. 'But I do not expect it.'

On an evening soon afterwards and muffled up to his neck, his heavy cloak over his shoulders, McLeod came by dark to Kate and Eoghann's house. At the door, seeing Kate, he asked, 'Will you allow me to enter, mistress?' Without his usual presumption that he might come in at once.

'May we speak alone?' he asked Eoghann, once he was inside.

Eoghann glanced at his wife.

'He is my son too,' she said.

'Nevertheless, my heart's as heavy as a dead codfish, and I cannot bring myself to speak to you more than one at a time.'

'Oh do what you wish,' she said, without stopping to wonder at herself speaking so carelessly to him.

When McLeod and Eoghann were settled in the parlour, Martha came down to the kitchen from her room to join Kate.

'He'll talk father round, won't he?'

Kate took a stick from the fire and burnt through the thread she was using to darn. 'It will be to your father's regret,' she said.

The room the MacKenzies claimed as their parlour was used more to do accounts than to sit in; or sometimes to discipline children. It was a small, poky room with a fireplace that backed onto the kitchen's chimney. The fire was rarely lit, for it was prone to smoke, and the room stood dank and cold for months on end. A high-backed wooden chair stood on either side of the hearth. Eoghann and Norman McLeod had taken one each and sat facing each other across an impasse as physical as the stone from which the fireplace was built.

McLeod's face was sunk low in the tall, white collar he habitually wore, his cloak thrown back at the shoulders, as if presenting a penitential profile to his companion.

Eoghann waited for him to speak.

The minutes wore on. Eoghann looked at McLeod but he was sitting perfectly still, as if he was waiting for Eoghann.

'What have you to say...Minister?' said Eoghann at last, unable to bear the silence any longer.

'Oh...aye. Nothing at all,' replied McLeod.

Another ten minutes passed.

'You cannot have come here to say nothing,' said Eoghann. His hands were sweating and he could feel perspiration accumulating all over his body, yet he was very cold.

'Hmph. Mmm.' McLeod made little sucking and drawing noises under his breath.

'Are you all right, Minister?' said Eoghann, very frightened now. He wondered if he should call his wife, but McLeod looked perfectly well, and had not altered his position.

'Do *you* feel better?' said McLeod, as if from a long way off.

'I want.' Eoghann began to say something, but he could not remember what it was he wanted. When McLeod had walked through the door he had wanted some kind of revenge, but sitting here beside his silent form he could hardly remember why. Now, he wanted to be forgiven. He was sure that was not right, that he did not, for once, need forgiveness, but he felt that it would be easier to ask for it than to sit in silence like this beside McLeod. Reason seemed to be slipping away; there would be others who would not forgive him, but he did not know how to rescue himself.

As if reading his thoughts, McLeod said, 'Shall we pray, friend?'

In a moment or so the two men were kneeling on their stockinged knees beside each other. 'For what we are about to receive,' McLeod began, and Eoghann knew that he was lost.

After what seemed like an eternity of praying, for the health of stock, for clement weather, for the sins of others, for the salvation of the wicked who had abused the Church of Scotland, for the denunciation of other clergy in Nova Scotia who were leading the people astray, for education and for good fishing, and a list of other bounty both actual and spiritual, the two men rose from their knees. Eoghann thought his had disintegrated on the hard floor and hobbled a step or two to ease himself, but McLeod stood straight up and drew his cloak around him without flinching.

'Well, Eoghann,' he said in an everyday manner. 'It is all for the best, don't you think? Your boy, I'm talking about.' There was a touch of impatience in his manner, as if Eoghann was a little slow. 'Even if he did not steal on this occasion, he will never be tempted to do so in the future. Wouldn't you agree?'

'Yes, Minister,' replied Eoghann, so low he was barely audible. He opened the door for McLeod who swept past his host, barely glancing at him.

But seeing Kate and Martha by the fire, he turned to them. 'Good night, Mrs MacKenzie,' he said. His voice was fulsome. Kate looked at Eoghann but he did not meet her eye.

'Good night, Minister,' said Kate, and closed the door behind him.

McLeod preached a curious sermon on the Sunday following his visit to Eoghann. It was an exaltation, almost mystical in its allusions, to a good man amongst them, who for his meekness and gentle ways could expect an easy passage to heaven. Heads began to turn as slowly the congregation recognised that it was Eoghann to whom the sermon was directed.

'But what if they had put Lewis in jail, or he had been whipped?' Annie asked Hector as they walked home from church. They were a discreet distance behind their father and there were some last things that she wished to understand, for once and for all.

'Oh I don't know,' said Hector, kicking out at an icy boulder. He was bored, and restless, and Martha MacKenzie wasn't in church, although the last time he had seen her she had looked like a real old spinster and wasn't fun to spy on any more. He had watched the elders in church and thought how long it was going to take him ever to climb the ladder. He looked ahead at their father's stolid back and bent head, and reflected on how little piety seemed to have done for him.

'But seeing he didn't do it,' persisted Annie.

'Well they didn't.'

Brother and sister stopped in the snow, looking at each other.

'They didn't put him in jail. Or whip him.' he said. 'So it is all right. There is nothing to worry about.'

So the two of them trudged on, and Annie thought that there must be someone in whom you could place your trust, and for the moment it might as well be Hector.

John and Murdoch McLeod had finished building a ship out of black birch. They named the ninety-ton barque the *Maria*.

Now that it was done, their brother Donald, Norman's second son, loaded it with timber cleared from the land of the settlers and set sail for Scotland.

McLeod seemed careless of all that had gone before in the months just past, and as near to a state of happiness as he cared to admit when the ship departed.

It did not return. Donald did not send back silver or gold or pounds. In St Ann's they heard that he had sold the ship, but after that nobody knew where he had gone. For the time being he had vanished from the face of the earth.

15

THERE WAS FAMINE over the island for the crops had failed. A blight had ruined the potatoes for the third year in a row, while wheat fly attacked the grain. There was no seed to replant; the stored potatoes were soggy black piles of foul-smelling muck that killed the cattle if it was fed to them. Most of the beasts had been slaughtered anyway, to tide the islanders over for food. There was almost nothing left. It was a creeping malaise that had caught up with them, spreading from west to east across the island. At St Ann's they said it could not happen, but it had. McLeod decreed it the fault of indolent and idle people in the rest of Cape Breton, who were more interested in baccy and toddy than they were in tending the fields, but before long he could not say that, for it had overtaken them all. When the famine did catch up with St Ann's, some said that it must be God's punishment for pride. McLeod still had his followers but only the most faithful were above cynicism when they spoke of him.

It was now several years since Isabella's first premonition of the hunger that was to befall them. She remembered the strange dark green spots on the leaves of the potatoes that year, and how quickly they had turned purplish-black, how disgusting the potatoes tasted. She had known there was something amiss, but apart from her comment to Kate she had dared not speak; if it had spread then, she knew that the trouble would be attributed to her. There must always be someone to blame. It stopped people from being so afraid. She had already seen how they looked at her when things went wrong.

At the ports there was panic as the people scrambled for food. Thirty thousand Scots now crammed Cape Breton Island and few had brought any resources of their own. Farmers began signing away their lands in 1848, hundreds of acres at a time, for a bag of meal that would last only a month or so. Some were becoming sceptical about the blight ever lifting as their bellies crawled, as if with maggots, and their children walked around miserable with distended stomachs. Often they had running diarrhoea although there was nothing inside them.

A few had noticed that the blight appeared worse during tides of unseasonable weather, months of dampness and higher heat than was normal, but if there was an association between the two nobody knew what to do about it. Or were too tired. Or hungry.

As the famine moved relentlessly towards St Ann's, Isabella laid in stores of food to last them for as long as possible. She picked wild rosehips after the frosts and dried them across the veranda of the house, hoping to stop the scurvy in winter, and went searching for wild yellow cloudberries on the edge of the bogs to make bakeapple jam. Though what use is this, she wondered, as she brought the fruit to boil with the last of her sugar, for who will eat jam if there is no bread to spread it on? She began to feel helpless for the first time.

When the pigs were slaughtered that fall she guarded their heads in a way that she had not done before, to make head cheese. One hog's head, one hog's tongue, salt, pepper and sage; at least if you had the pig to begin with, it was cheap. She cleaned and scraped the head, covering it and the tongue with salted water, simmering them until the meat fell from the bone. Then she drained and seasoned the meat before packing it into bowls.

She was helped from time to time as she worked by her daughter Annie, serious and grown up. Such a responsible young woman, people said. But when Annie was not in the kitchen with Isabella she was ensconced in the sitting-room knitting, and talking to Francis McClure. She had acquired a range of knitting patterns from Peggy McLeod with whom, after a break of some years, she had resumed a friendship. She had also been introduced to Francis McClure by Peggy.

He was a heavy young man, not unlike Fraser McIssac in his appearance, only he wore a thick, full, dark moustache over his heavy upper lip. And, his eyes, blue and narrow, sparkled a great deal. The young woman spoke in a quiet restrained way and showed him her patterns, of which he appeared to approve inordinately.

It rankled with Isabella that there was another mouth to feed.

'Your drawings are quite remarkable,' Isabella said to her first son.

'You're biased in my favour, mother.'

'But they are. Oh what a big success you would have made in London, Duncan.'

'How do you know?'

'Well, I have been there. They recognise quality in that city. What if I were to write to your uncle Marcus and send him some of your drawings to be looked at by . . . by the Academy, or one of the famous painters there? What if he were to send for you?'

'Mother, you don't know that he is alive even.'

'If he saw your drawings . . .'

'He would reply to your letters? How many have you sent that have gone unanswered in twenty years or more?'

'Something must have happened to him. Some accident befallen him.'

He touched her arm gently where it lay on the edge of the table, turned her hand over, dirty under the nails where she had been digging for roots.

'What would I draw in London?'

She sighed.

'I know you're trying to tell me something,' he said. 'You don't have to explain. There is not enough food to go round here.'

'We'll find enough.'

But it was not true. Fraser thought she had not heard him speak to Duncan Cave the night before, when her back was turned, but she had. 'It is all I can do to feed my own children,' he had said, 'without catering for layabouts who are not mine.'

'Don't go,' she said now. 'I want you here. What would my life be if it were not for you?'

He gripped her hand hard. 'Come away with me, then. There's nothing here for you.'

The thought of going somewhere, anywhere, was tempting.

'How can I?' she said dully.

'Why can't you?' He turned her hand over in his. 'Think of the things you've done when you wanted to.'

'There's Annie. How can I leave her?'

'Ah, Annie.' His voice could not disguise his ambivalence.

'People think I'm unfeeling. I do not always know what I feel these days, but I feel something. Besides, I'm getting old. I'd be a millstone for you.'

'No, not you. Away from here, you'd do all manner of things. We could go to Boston.'

'Let me know where you end up, and maybe I'll come.'

He looked at her in the lamplight, and speaking levelly said, 'Yes, mother, I will tell you where I am.'

In the morning he was gone. She sat for a long time wondering whether she could be bothered to look for food again. Noah brought a mouse in. He, at least, still had a full belly. He looked at her, not understanding that she would not share it with him. 'It may not be long before I do,' she said to him, and scooped him into her arms. 'Fat old cat, there is still you.'

Kate had caught sight of her face unawares in a glass and been aghast. She had not looked at herself for years. It was bad enough to feel the seams of flesh on her face. She could see her hands mottled and disfigured and had no reason to think her face would be better, but still it came as a surprise. Some days she thought she would die before evening.

'Are you ill, mother?' Martha would say with solicitude.

'I don't know,' Kate answered each time, and it was the truth. Pain moved through her like a hot poker but never seemed to settle in one place for long, so that she wondered if she was imagining it. She wanted to hide her discomfort from Martha who, it seemed to her, worried about her out of all proportion to other interests in her life. Whereas once she had feared that Martha would marry too soon, or unwisely, now it caused her regret that she had not married at all. Although there were times when secretly she wondered if marriage was a good idea for anyone, if there might not be too much potential for disappointment.

At nights she woke from dreams she could not recall, remembering only that they had imposed some great dread upon her, and reached out her hand to find Eoghann's friendly one. In the darkness there was only the emptiness they had imposed on each other years before.

Sometimes when they were at the table she would look at her husband covertly, to see if there might be any way to shift from their mutual exile. Now he was an elder of the church, always engrossed in the attacks that were brought against it and against McLeod by the clergy beyond St Ann's who called on him frequently, and in public now, to prove his ministry. Eoghann's face had become harder, more weathered, the mouth thinner and the lines about it were more deeply etched. His eyes were bright and cool. He rarely looked directly at her, and if he did it was in an appraising, distasteful way, as if she was someone he had to put up with.

On a spring day, perhaps when she had been thinking of Lewis, who had worked now for a long time in a lumber camp to the south without returning to St Ann's, Kate disappeared into the woods.

'She's a grown woman,' said Eoghann, when Martha told him that she was gone. 'What am I supposed to do about it?'

'Look for her,' said Martha.

'I am due at the church.'

'Please, at least allow Ewan to look for her. She's not well.'

'It's in her mind,' he said. 'Oh do what you wish. But remember, your mother once appeared to have some wisdom. You could be losing yours even before you have properly come to it. Don't look for sympathy when you go off your head.'

They found her sitting on a log in the woods. She was less than a mile away though she believed she had travelled much further.

'What were you looking for?' Martha asked her when she had brought her back home.

'A way out,' said Kate.

'A way out of what?'

'A way out of here. To find the church.'

'You know where the church is.'

'Not that one, not McLeod's. I have heard. Hear, you know. Once Isabella. Isabella told me once. There is another one.' Her hands shook, and her lower jaw had become convulsive as she sat and stared at the fire. She stayed like that from that moment on, moving only when eating and sleeping made it necessary.

157

She ate greedily when food was placed in front of her and grew fat; when the food was not put there fast enough, she cried like a baby.

A traveller stopped at their house one evening and asked for shelter. He was tall, his face smooth and closely shaven, and there was an air of languor in his brown eyes. His hands were well manicured and he placed the tips of his fingers neatly together when he spoke. He had read books and even met the abominable but entertaining Mr Charles Dickens on his visit to Halifax the previous year. Martha was fascinated. Eoghann was doubtful at first, and shocked by the presence in his house of a man who had read novels, but as it was Saturday night said he would have to stay until Monday; they could not provide food to take with him on Sunday. That was no trouble, their guest responded. He was a widower, lately a clerk of Sydney Mines until the death of his wife, and he was looking for a change. He had not found one yet and there was no hurry. In fact he would welcome the opportunity to accompany such a pleasant host to the church next morning.

Later, when Alexander McWhirtle had been there for a month, he declared himself willing to relieve Eoghann of the responsibility of his unmarried daughter. He would even, he said, for a consideration be prepared to live with Martha in the cottage vacated by a cowman on Eoghann's land, so that Martha could attend to her mother.

Often Martha felt as if she had twice as many children as anyone else she knew, for she bore one each year for the following three; her mother cried louder than any of them as the food on the farm began to dwindle, and Eoghann regretted the proliferation of mouths which the widower had inflicted on him.

'The situation is grave,' said Fraser over their meal. Isabella looked at their plates. Considering what was before them, she felt it to be an understatement. Each person had a helping of suet to take the edge off their appetites.

'If we can last until the spring I can catch fish. I was good at that,' she said, turning to Annie.

'Annie would drop them,' laughed Francis McClure.

'Oh I would not.' They gazed at each other as if oblivious to food. It was as well for Annie that they were half starving, Isabella thought with some malice. It had done her appearance the world of good. At the same time she determined to give less if she could to Francis. She found him disagreeable. Even Hector, sitting on the other side of him to Annie, appealed more, morose and even uglier in his temper than usual, no doubt because his attentions had been refused by yet another young woman.

'I was not speaking of the food situation,' said Fraser, rubbing his stomach. It had occurred to Isabella frequently of late that he did not seem to be losing weight at all. 'The Minister is getting a very hard time of it from those fanatics and fugitives that roam this island.'

'Oh you mean those poor clerics! What have they done this time?'

'It is not a laughing matter. It is in the papers now, the things they are accusing McLeod of.'

'Well what does he say of them? What names does he call people who oppose him? Suckers and swindlers, was the last I heard. Tipplers and tavern-hunters. Bankrupts and bigamists. Which of those are you, Mr McClure?' she said, turning to Francis.

'He does not oppose Mr McLeod,' said Annie swiftly.

Francis beamed proudly back.

Ah, the conversation is so deadly dull here, Isabella reflected. If only Duncan Cave were here.

'Have some more suet pudding,' she said to Fraser. He looked purple. 'I have saved you some.'

He gave one of his customary hiccupping burps. 'I have had sufficient. Thank you.'

'You're fortunate. Did someone feed you at Baddeck today?'

'I had a good lunch there, yes, that is so. At the house of Mr and Mrs Finchwilly.'

'Willyfinch, eh? What did the old skinflint have in his larder to spare?'

'You are mistaken. They are a most generous couple.'

'Really. I could have sworn they took meanness as a challenge. But forgive me, I am always misunderstanding people.'

'I had suckling pig, roast very tender,' said Fraser, indignant, and before he could stop himself.

'Suckling pig, you do not say so, Fraser McIssac. Suckling pig. They killed that for you?'

'You do not understand,' he shouted, the veins in his throat knotting. 'That is what I said to him, that is a great sacrifice, but he said no, not at all, it be drooned in the brook.'

Isabella looked around the table. If one of them would laugh. If only just one of them would laugh. But they all stared at their plates, and now she could see that Francis McClure had remembered that he was hungry. She was afforded a momentary pleasure that there was nothing left to offer him.

'I think the Master has had enough,' ruminated Fraser, subsiding from his rage and unaware that he had said anything amusing. It was clear that he was unusually intent upon imparting some piece of information.

'So what will he do about it this time? Who is he planning to take to court now?'

'He is planning to emigrate.'

He paused and looked around him, enjoying the greatest effect he had had on the conversation of his family in years.

'Where would he emigrate to?' said Isabella, trying to conceal the tautness in her voice.

'Australia, I do believe. He has had a letter from Donald.'

'Donald has turned up? Now there is a swindler for you. How long is it? Eight years?'

'He says the climate is very good there in Australia. He's spoken favourably of the prospects for farming.'

'McLeod would go on his own? At his age?'

'Oh no, he is talking of everyone in St Ann's going. He is planning that a ship be built to take us.'

As if to appease her for his indulgences, he slaughtered a thin cow the following week. When Isabella had fed herself, with stealth she fed Noah.

His lower jaw chattered uncontrollably at the sight of meat. His yellow eyes gleamed, as if it were all her doing, that she had invented meat especially for him. His affection overwhelmed her. I am buying him off, she thought, but it didn't matter. She knew he would eat her if he could, so long as there was enough of her left over to continue serving his needs and comfort.

He stretched, reached out his paw to her. His tongue was hanging out of his sweet whiskery little mouth. She could not resist him. She leaned down and touched the tip of his tongue with her own.

The spring came and she ruptured the ice, brought out eels from the river. Such delicacies, such riches, she thought as she stewed them in her largest pot. And remembered, not for the first time, how they could strip a creature to the bone.

Standing alone at the bench, she pressed her hands over her ears as if to shut out an old voice, or voices. The trembling fractured ice she had broken that day, and the dark water above which she had perched herself, had opened something up again, something that would never go away. The smell of the fish nauseated her. She had sworn once that she would never eat eels. Now it seemed that she must, or die.

'I do not want to be alone,' she said, looking wildly round the kitchen and gripping the table for support. Annie appeared in the doorway. 'Are you all right, mother?' she asked.

'I am perfectly all right,' said Isabella. 'Why don't you go and entertain your young man?'

When it was time for Annie to marry Francis McClure, Fraser McIssac traded some last thin beasts and seemed not displeased, perhaps enjoying the prospect of long relief from feeding his daughter. From the sale of the beasts he gave her money so that she could purchase a quarter bolt of white cotton, sprigged with tiny blue flowers, for sheets and nightdresses; some white calico, for aprons; a pot; a tripod; and a hanging lamp.

Isabella gave her her aunt's silver candle-sticks and a white linen table-cloth.

'It is all I have,' she said.

'It is enough,' said Annie, turning the objects over in her hands. 'Thank you.'

And might have said more, but did not.

16

A T THE BITTER HOUR of their leaving, those who were to stay behind
stood on the hillsides and wept.

The *Margaret* lay trim and ready in the bay, the *Highland Lass*
anchored close by. This would be the first ship to sail. Her prow was
carved in a fair and smiling likeness of Peggy McLeod, for whom McLeod
had named the vessel.

There was little time to waste. October was upon them, and if they
were to leave this year, it could be put off no longer. Delays had arisen
and the ice was due to close in over the bay. The ships had already been
on the stocks for more than twelve months, complete and ready to sail,
but unable to be launched for lack of funds to purchase gear and fittings.
During that time McLeod had often called together the three hundred
people who had declared themselves willing to emigrate with him.
Although most of them had land to sell, no one wanted to buy it, or was
able to, after the famine.

McLeod had appeared supremely unconcerned. 'The Lord will
provide,' he purred whenever he was tackled.

Which, in the middle of 1851, He did. Or a fair likeness of Him,
according to McLeod, in the shape of a businessman from the south who
offered to buy the McLeod house and property for three thousand dollars.
This started a wave of buying throughout the district.

So the passengers carried as many of their possessions on board the
ship as there was room for. Those, and food—potatoes shredded and
evaporated in birch-bark wrappers, dried codfish, pickled meats, and bread
made without yeast.

Then Mary McLeod fell ill; they waited for her to recover, and reloaded
the ship. Now the time had really come. For until this moment there
had been an understandable element of procrastination, of fear in the face
of the unknown.

Isabella was among those who watched from the hillside. Annie and
Francis were boarding the ship that late autumn day, the brilliant red
and gold leaves of the Nova Scotian woods already dusted with the first
hint of frost. Close by her stood Fraser and Hector.

'Don't you wish to go?' Fraser had asked her.

The kitchen had been steamy and fogged over with an atmosphere
of homeliness the night he enquired. He sat in the chair opposite her in

an uncommon display of companionship. She had held her hands around her mug of tea as if it was a crystal ball in which she saw her freedom. *At last, when he goes and I am left, I will be free of the shadow of McLeod.* Then she looked across the fireplace at her husband, and wondered whether freedom existed anywhere.

'Our daughter is going,' he said, breaking into her silence. 'And no doubt our son is thinking of it too.'

She could have said, *but my son will be here, on this continent,* but stayed silent.

She stroked the cat instead. Although he was old his coat was still full of crackling and fiery sparks.

'You're more interested in that creature than you are in our future,' said Fraser, so angrily that in order to avoid his outburst, she began to compose a reply in her head.

'There are others, besides those who are going on the first ships, who are talking of going if it is all a success,' she said. 'They say they will build more ships. Can't we try a little caution and see how things proceed?'

He appeared ready to remonstrate; she would have to be more convincing than this.

'After all, what if our children don't find it to their liking, and want to come back? There will be nothing left for them to return to. Or if we got to the other side of the world, and there was nothing there for any of us, we would simply be a burden to them at our age. But if we are here, minding what we have, we are insuring a safe passage for all of us sooner or later. If it is meant to be.'

She must have sounded full of sweet reason, because for once he nodded attentively and seemed pleased with what she had said.

And yet she knew that he had not banished the idea from his mind.

Closer towards the waterfront, John Munro, who ran the trading post, stood watching the passengers taking their place, his face inscrutable. Of all McLeod's friends who had ceased to call him that, Munro was the one who had seemed indestructible in his loyalty.

And might still have been, had not McLeod rounded on him too, describing him as a brandy smuggler, and bringing a boycott down on his warehouse in the midst of the famine so that Munro's fortunes were in a state of collapse. In vain he had written letters to the paper explaining that McLeod's sons did exactly that of which he now stood accused, but McLeod had mocked him. *The money-lenders will trump up any excuse for their greed,* he claimed.

And that, Isabella reflected, has as much to do with why these ships are leaving here and tearing families apart as any number of things which McLeod may claim to be the reason. While people had fared worse on account of the boycott than they might otherwise have done, McLeod made intercessions to the government on their behalf for rations. But it was clear to many, when they looked back on that time, that if they had stood by Munro their plight might not have been so bad.

So there were those who were for Munro, and those who were for McLeod, and all things became much clearer. It was a question of who should have absolute power. It had always been so. Only now, Munro wore the face of the clergy. One person must stand, eventually, for all that McLeod opposed. Because Munro was the strongest, had stayed the longest, it had to be him.

Now she saw Annie taking her place behind the ship's rail, for her daughter had been one of the first aboard earlier in the morning. Annie, her married Annie who obviously felt so much more respectable now that she was not so clearly aligned with her mother. She had had a child which did not survive its early birth in that first year of marriage, and Isabella had held her daughter as she wept. The next one will be better, it was for the best, this one was not meant, I am not the first to whom this has happened, Annie had said to her mother. Isabella, with her arms around her and liking the feel of her for the first time that she could remember, wondered if there might be depths to Annie that she had not plumbed.

And would not, she supposed. For Annie's face had closed again, and now she was standing beside Francis McClure, ready to go to Australia.

On the other side of her stood Peggy. And beside Peggy was Hugh Anderson, whom everyone, except McLeod, knew was her lover.

Mary Fraser's parents stood agonising whether to board the ship or not, for Mary had vanished that morning and travelled by fast horse to Boularderie to be married to the man she loved, in order to escape the migration. Now they put their feet tentatively on the gangplank. 'Will you forgive me?' their daughter said, standing by the ship with her new husband. 'Oh aye,' her mother had said, 'it is all right, yes, this is your home, now I must go to mine.' But it made no sense at this minute, they had no idea why they were leaving.

Donald and Catherine McGregor.

Roderick 'Og' McKay and Jessie and their babies.

John 'Ruadh' McKay and his wife Ann and their twelve children.

And Kenneth Dingwall, who had stayed constant to McLeod since the days of Pictou, and grown thin and held together by his skin.

Mary, McLeod's daughter who had finally been allowed to take a husband, Roderick Ross, and their children.

And five of McLeod's sons, all of them except Donald, who was already in Australia.

Kate and Eoghann's daughter Martha, and Alexander McWhirtle her husband, Martha walking away from her mother as one in a dream, or a nightmare.

And more of them by the score, until in all there were close to one hundred and forty aboard.

And the sky and hills streamed round them in the blue swimming light, and beneath them the sea.

Then Mary, McLeod's wife, who had knitted jerseys to take to her husband when he was young, and walked in the snow to meet him.

And at last, there was McLeod.

Who that morning had ceded his church to the new Free Presbyterian Church of Nova Scotia. It had not been in the church itself that he had preached his last sermon, but on the hillside overlooking Black Cove. Boats carrying well-wishers were dotted around the bay. He had stood with his back to the hill, his face radiant, like an apostle of old as he traced their wanderings up until this point.

McLeod with his hair streaming in the wind.

McLeod with his voice lifted.

McLeod.

Tormod.

His name on every lip.

McLeod, like Moses.

He put up his arms. 'I have chosen that we gather here on the hillside where I can see all your faces and the harbour for the last time. For thirty-one years we have lived together as one community, one people, one beating heart. One hundred and forty of us are now taking to the high seas to answer God's call, to go on a pilgrimage twelve thousand miles away. My son Donald, known to you all, will meet us in Australia and guide us to new and profitable holdings of land. There we will found a new community. How can we continue to live as one if we are scattered across the world? I trust that that which we find will be a fitting home, so that we may all be together once more. God has been with us in all our wanderings. Through the troubles and trials of the old country. And he has saved us twice from shipwreck. He has rescued us already from seeming despair in our present venture. I know with a conviction beyond all earthly doubts that we are following His will, crossing the sea.

'Those of you who remain must resist the devilish temptations that provoke the soul of man, you must remain pure in heart and in all your actions, and if you do not, you must expect the terrible judgment which befalls man when he crosses the great divide.

'Remember the godly ancestors, the men and women who held converse with God. Follow their examples and rest assured that neither principalities nor powers will overcome you.'

Kate MacKenzie, who had not spoken for nearly a year, suddenly cried out, *'Oh Dhia nan gras mailler rin,* merciful God be with us!' and fell to the grass.

McLeod's own tears, which they had believed impossible, whipped away from his face on the wind. 'Goodbye friend and foe. Goodbye to the house of God. May we be protected until we build Him a new house. Blessings with all those here and His people everywhere.'

Shaken by his rhetoric, a wailing rose from those who were assembled, an ancient litany of sorrow, soaring above the hillside. It seemed that everyone wanted to go, that there was no one left behind who did not think, now, that the migration was a splendid idea. Isabella found herself snuffling into her handkerchief, and turned her head away so that John Munro would not see. But she caught his eye, and saw that it was watering too. She was astonished at them both, and almost smiled.

'*Beannachd*, farewell!' they called, but already, even as the anchor lifted and the bell tolled, the plans to build more ships were crystallising.

The gangway lifted, the mainsail unfurled, and the *Margaret* moved from her moorings. Those on board and on land sought each other's face.

'Return return return we never *cha tille cha tille cha tille me tuilleadh*, in peace nor war return we never.'

Through the sea of faces, Annie saw her mother, clutching her scrawny cat. Isabella, dry-eyed now, sought her daughter and wondered if she could have loved her better.

'I'll be on the next ship,' said Hector, turning to his father.

Fraser nodded, his hands gnarled round the top of the stick he had taken to leaning on in the past year, his eyes towards the ship skimming away into the distance.

Too late for Martha to see, Eoghann at last took his wife by the hand and led her shuffling and staring away from the water's edge.

Isabella and Fraser walked beside them, but apart from each other. Isabella felt still and alone. It is all too late, for all of us who are left, she said inside herself. McLeod has gone, and his damage is left behind him.

The weather remained good, and by tropical waters, by St Jago in the Cape Verde Islands, and by Cape Town, the *Margaret* made her way to Adelaide in Australia. The old rules still held, yet as the warmth soaked through them an air of gaiety began to steal through the prayers. When McLeod retired to bed at nights a fiddle would appear, or the *piob mohr* would be played in wild abandon as the ship glided on across the equator.

Annie and Francis walked on the deck, arm in arm, although with an air of careful reticence. Married couples were expected to set examples of restraint to the single, she reminded him.

'Annie. Annie, you're sure you still care for me?'

'But Francis, how silly you are, why should you think I would not?'

'You're strange, you turn away from me. No, don't say otherwise, it's true, I have seen you.'

'Nonsense, it is just the motion of the ship and the closeness of the people; it is nothing, you fret too much...'

Donald McLeod was not waiting to meet them. Nor was there land to be had in Adelaide.

A letter, yes, there was that.

It was from Donald, who wrote that he had gone on to Melbourne.

17

MCLEOD LED A GROUP inland to explore the territory beyond Adelaide. His five sons were included in the party. The sun beat down relentlessly, a sun of such heat as they had never experienced. On the dry branches of dead trees birds sat and gasped for water; the blue-grey spikes of strange plants were dotted against the red earth.

'I think we have gone far enough,' John McKay said when they had travelled for two days. 'This heat is not for the likes of us.'

'You don't care for this landscape, then?' McLeod asked them.

'These parched and barren lands won't grow much grass. There's no water. How many rivers and streams have we seen? Hardly a one. It won't suit me, friend,' said John McKay, appearing to speak for all of them except John Fraser who poked away at a patch of soil a distance from them.

Because there was nothing else that he could think of for them to do, John McKay asked McLeod, 'Why don't we join your son in Melbourne? I heard at the port that it is an easy and safe journey around the coastline.'

'He said that he had followed prosperity,' Kenneth Dingwall slipped in, as if this was what he had been waiting for someone else to say.

'It's exactly what we should do, I'm sure, father.' Samuel McLeod's eyes were alight at the prospect of new adventure.

'Besides,' said his brother, Alexander, 'I have heard there is gold there.'

'That is not what we have come looking for,' snapped McLeod.

They all looked at him then. They were in a gully where the white bones of trees stood against the red landscape and McLeod, seventy-one now and older than they understood him when they saw him in their mind's eye, shocked them with a flicker of uncertainty across his face.

'Sometimes I wonder if you're my sons at all,' he said, looking around at the young men. They laughed, white teeth flashing against the newly acquired tan on their faces. 'Gold and adventure, what kind of talk is that?'

It was talk too naked, too unlike McLeod, some of them thought privately. It unsettled them to hear him speak like this, even if it was a family matter. It reminded them, as if they needed it, how strange their surroundings were, and how frightening.

'Melbourne could only be better than this, whichever way you look at it,' said Edward, the youngest, soothing him.

'Aye, that's true, lad. Are you all in agreement then?'

'I think I'll stay here,' said John Fraser, who had rejoined them. 'It may be possible to farm here; there are patches that don't look so bad.'

'And be parted from the rest of us?' McLeod asked incredulously.

The terror of the unknown was taking hold, but affecting each of them in different ways.

'It may be our last chance,' said John Fraser. 'Perhaps all the good land in Australia is already taken.'

'That's nonsense,' said McLeod. 'It's a vast continent. We are only on the edge of it.'

'Still, I came for land, and I'm not sure that wandering on and on is going to make much difference.'

Francis McClure, who had said nothing and stood at the back of the group, felt them waver.

'I am going on, father,' said Samuel. The brothers ranged themselves across the head of their convoy and all except John Fraser fell in naturally behind them.

'It is God's will,' said McLeod. 'We go to Melbourne.'

It is not God's will, thought Francis. It is the will of McLeod's sons. They talked so much of God that he felt like a simpleton and a stranger amongst them. He was a sensual man who had been surprised and pleased by his wife's enthusiasm for him, and was now disappointed that abortive childbearing and the passage to Australia seemed to have conspired against her interest in him. He had no idea why he was standing in a desert far from home.

He found himself thinking of summer on Prince Edward Island, where the air was as crisp as an apple in the mornings and bees tumbled stupidly above flowers in the afternoons. He had been innocent then.

In the tent cities of Melbourne where the gold rush had begun they paid high prices for food and shelter, and most of all for water. Donald, reunited with them, was apologetic that there was no land to be had, but he was sure that if they were patient something would eventuate soon.

The heat sat inside Annie like a fever and when Francis rolled over towards her in the tent she cringed, cowering in the corner, wedged against the canvas as if he might reach and violate her.

'We're married, aren't we?' Francis said sharply as he pulled his boots off in the shelter of their tent awning, tired from a day's labouring.

'For the procreation of children,' she muttered.

'Aye, surely. But as we have no children, shouldn't we be trying harder?'

She turned her bleak face away.

Outside, the tall blue-gum trees rustled and shivered and her skin crawled.

Across the earth crept blue carpets of flowers. Patterson's Curse. She was certain she, too, was afflicted with a curse. She glanced at herself to see if her skin was turning blue. It is the madness taking me, she thought. It comes to us sooner or later, it is in my family, this was bound to happen.

She wrote to her mother:

'. . . it is very pretty here. I am sure you would find it all most interesting. So much colour, so much light, such intensity.

'There are days, though, when the light on the stones is so bright, that you would think for a moment, when you opened your eyes, that it was snow. A strange kind of illusion.

'The air is full of birds, red and grey galahs everywhere, which soon remind us where we are. At night the sun fans out across the sky and is scarlet, then it drops away out of sight, and suddenly it is dark. All you can see is the outline of saltbushes. Often the dingoes howl, a weird noise if you are not accustomed to them.

'Oh well, mother, one does become accustomed to many things in this life I suppose, and I hope that all is well with you and father and my brother, to whom I trust you will give my love. It might be better for Hector to wait awhile before he comes out here, for I am not sure what Reverend McLeod intends for all of us to do, just yet.'

From where McLeod stood, it looked like Pictou again. Melbourne was bawdy and dirty; bushrangers roamed the landscape and highwaymen lay in wait for miners returning to town with the receipts for their gold to be cashed at the Treasury. Already he had spent one night against his choice in the company of such men, and been permitted to pass in the morning when he said prayers to them. But whereas once he could have imagined people applauding his courage in the face of such danger, now they simply laughed and said how pleased the bushrangers must have been to be rid of him.

The people were scattering, the dream sliding from his grasp. Those he had known since they were born frequently were unable to recognise him because they had had so much to drink. And now that the *Highland Lass* had arrived there were more people for him to give of his attention, spread out almost beyond his reach unless he moved night and day. He scurried round Melbourne with hectic fervour.

Out in Canvastown food rotted, shit lay in piles on the ground and the water stank.

The typhoid came then. It came to the tents like a romp in the night, not scrupulous in choosing its victims, dancing its way from one tent to another, then doubling back the way it had come in the dark.

Week by week, in the inhospitable shelter of Canvastown, the symptoms spread. The McLeods were not excused. First Alexander became ill, then Samuel, and then Edward, bright and eager and the cleverest of the McLeod's children. The flush on their cheeks turned to a rose-coloured rash. Their tongues became dry and brown, stiff like old leather. They wasted, picking at black spots which passed before their eyes, as if at flies on the wing, their hearing fading away.

Annie prepared lemon juice made from fruit begged from a ship at the docks, made wine-whey from a good port added to boiling milk and cooled, and prepared animal broths thickened with rice and a little bread. These were the things said to be for the best and she was surprised that she learned so easily what to do, as if these remedies were in her bones. Some were helped by them, but the McLeods' sons were beyond anyone's help. One by one, the three youngest of them died: Alexander, then Samuel, then Edward.

Mary McLeod had appeared in some miraculous way to have been restored by the voyage. It was as if, being old and of little consequence in her husband's sight, she had less reason to watch her ways. Bundled amongst friends young and old, the children who were sometimes frightened at nights turning to her for comfort, she appeared to her companions to have found a new independence. Those who had expected that she would not survive the journey had, instead, watched her grow in strength.

On the goldfields when her sons lay dying she asked them to live, and when it was clear that they could not oblige her, it was she who organised their burials. One by one.

'*Is a Dia fein a's buachaill dhomh,* the Lord's my shepherd, I'll not want,' she said.

McLeod, alone and terrible in his grief after a life of total certainty, faced the possibility that he might have offended God.

With the strength of a much younger man, he strode night after night through the dirty streets of Melbourne, asking himself in relentless pain if his sons had been the price of his pride.

It was in a dream, he told the people of St Ann's at last, that he saw a way through what had befallen them.

They must now, he said, proceed to New Zealand. Donald, inclined to letters and journalism, had had correspondence with people there and confirmed that New Zealand was a suitable solution to their problems. The dream was in order. McLeod had written to Sir George Grey, the Governor of New Zealand, and been informed that there was much good land to be had.

'We all pay for our sins,' Annie said as she and Francis prepared to leave Australia.

'You're not so keen on him now?'

'Eh? Of course I am keen, as you call it. He's our leader, struck down, that is all. We learn that even the greatest fall. And that we learn from their deliverance. But we must all suffer for our sins, sooner or later.'

'Aye Annie. But come closer, eh? The nights are a bit cooler; you can't go on complaining of the heat forever.' His voice was pleading, though not hopeful.

At his touch she became rigid.

'Francis,' she whispered, 'it's too soon.' For she had lost another child which she had buried herself in the hard earth.

'Aye.' He turned himself heavily on the sacking bed strung between poles which they shared.

'I repent my sins, Francis,' she whispered.

'Hey, what does that mean?' he said, turning back to her, and fearing even before he looked at her to see some end between them, even though they were tied to each other forever.

It was as he had expected.

'There was lust between us,' she said earnestly

'But his sins are not to do with us,' he floundered, trying to relate her line of thought, and McLeod, to their estranged bed.

In the dark her voice was confident. 'But of course they are, Francis. His downfall is an education to us all, we who are so much less than he will certainly be punished if we do not heed the warnings we are given. Obedience, chastity, Francis. Passion is a curse. We must mortify the body. Oh Francis, I despise myself.'

'But I don't despise you. You're so clever, so capable. Don't you know, Annie, you're becoming admired? The way you had hoped. You're respected.' And he said these things to her not only because they were what she wanted to hear, but because they were true.

At the same time he was overcome with desolation.

'We will do better if we go about things in a modest way,' she said. 'You do see? Yes, of course you must...Now let us go to sleep, and in the morning we shall go to New Zealand.'

Looking up through the awning of the tent, she could have sworn she saw a black-and-white cat, smiling and licking its paws, riding the antipodean sky.

She lay there, her eyes closed as if she was asleep, and thought of her mother. She would have liked to be able to tell her things, but Isabella never seemed to have heard what she had tried to tell her. Would she listen now? On the ship to New Zealand perhaps she would write to her. She remembered how her mother had sat with a secret look on her face and composed entries in a journal which she did not show to anyone.

Had she shown Duncan Cave? Who knew the secrets of her mother's life?

She wondered if anyone would ever want to know about her life as much as she longed to know about Isabella's, or if it would ever mean as much to anyone else. She thought of the children she had had, and who had already died before they drew breath, and now that her husband was snoring beside her she began to weep a little.

After a while she decided that this was an indulgence; that it was no good preaching to him if she in herself was not strong.

Later, from New Zealand, she wrote to her mother:

Waipu, June 1854

...We have at last settled down from our wanderings. The Reverend McLeod petitioned Governor Grey for holdings while we were in Auckland, where we have been this past year or more, waiting for the allocation of this land.

We knew this was the place for us, for we had seen it from the sea as we approached New Zealand, and it looked like the shores of Nova Scotia. Yet, now that we are here, it is not really like that at all. It is lush, almost as I think you would imagine the tropics (perhaps that is only the opinion of someone who has seen the tropics, I do not know whether I would have been able to visualise them at all before I left St Ann's). But the growth is so thick, there is no snow all year round, although a considerable amount of rain, and things just grow and grow. We have several cows and we fell a two acre of land about every week. Come the summer there will be a great burn-off of the bush.

We have built a house from cabbage tree planks, but soon we are to have better, Francis has said.

I have had another child but it has gone the way of the rest. Don't worry, I will be all right.

Your affectionate daughter, Annie McClure.

To which Isabella wrote back:

...I hope that your brother has now settled in New Zealand as well as you have.

You will be sad to hear that my black cat Noah has died.

Did you get my letter advising of your father's death? It has not been so easy here since that event, though the neighbours are kind. There is a small brigantine, to be named the *Spray*, which is being built here for the purpose of travelling to New Zealand (and I believe that there are still more planned). People are clamouring to leave. They say the fire has moved out of this place, from north to south, now that McLeod has gone, and in spite of myself, I think they are right. Now that John Munro has left on the *Gertrude* things are very quiet indeed. Certainly, I was surprised that he went. There is an opinion here that if even he were prepared to pocket his pride and go, then it is virtually pointless to stay here. I made early application for a berth on the *Spray* and have been successful. If you do not have room for me, no matter. I have a little money from the sale of the farm, and I can set up on my own. The balance of the money will be forwarded to you and Hector through your father's solicitors.

By the way, Duncan Cave has come back from Boston, and I am sure you will be pleased to hear that he is coming with me. The ship sails next month, and by the time you receive this, we will be on the high seas.

Yours, kindly, Mother.

P.S. Be sure to sleep on a good hard bed the next time you are with child. Some prescribe opium for miscarriage. I am against it. On no account have relations with your husband while you are carrying.

PART FIVE

MARIA
1898–1953

18

IN THE MORNING *Maria thinks that the bird has flown away. She opens her eyes, hoping that it will still be there, peering at her from some corner of the room with its dark sharp eyes. She plans to give it crumbs from her toast for its breakfast. But at dawn the birds outside begin their morning oratory and she hears a stirring in the room, as if the bird, guided by them, is preparing to take its leave, finding its way back by the way it has come. She looks around and the room seems empty except for the curling newspapers on the walls and the old dresser that has stood in its place for a hundred years, the cracked pitcher in the bowl, the disintegrating crochet work, and a tiny yellowish picture of a man and a woman, tacked above her bed. Even now, this morning, she reaches up and touches the face of the young woman. In all the wide world she does not know where the young woman is. She is her talisman still. Some day she thinks the young woman will come.*

There is a humming in the air. She cannot place the sound though it grows and swells around her. It is a pretty sound but it holds a touch of menace too. She turns uneasily in the bed. 'I am not afraid,' she says to herself. 'Nothing can frighten me any more.' Later, she says, 'I am too old to be frightened, it doesn't matter what happens to me now.' Only she wants to know what it is. 'It will be all right if I know,' she murmurs aloud. Her fingers curl over the edge of the blanket, holding it tightly against her chin. After a while she falls asleep again, although it is not like her to sleep late into the morning.

When she wakes the bird is sitting perched on the pillow beside her. She reaches out to touch it, but it hops out of reach, flies up to the rafters again, sits and stretches its wings and delivers a white turd on the floor beneath.

The morning began with milky streaks in the sky, turning to marbled cirrus clouds, then the light changed to rose pink and glowed. It was perfect weather, almost as warm as a summer's day.

Watching from her window, Maria wondered if later she would be allowed to sit in the sun and soak up its warmth or if she would be watched. This was how it was each day. Alone in the house, she was aware that there were always people close by. It was as though they were afraid she might break loose and inflict some terrible damage if she walked past certain perimeters that had been laid down for her.

The young woman thought that they were probably out there

watching her now. Well, they wouldn't have much to watch today; she could not run very far.

She began to wash herself at the bowl, massaging the soap over her tightening stomach. The skin felt as if it would split, and at its base there were purple marks like lashes developing. She did not know what these marks were and wondered if the child was preparing to break its way out through these angry-looking welts, or if the welts were in fact the mark of God. Or Satan.

They said that Satan had taken her soul. Her uncle Hector had said she was a witch.

So be it. She had danced at night with the Devil, and she was made of fairy air which was rising inside of her now. Last night a cat had stalked by and she had called out to it. For a moment the cat had paused, sniffed the wind, and made as if to go inside with her. Beyond, in the dark places where she could not see, where bush still pressed against the edge of the farm, something, or someone, called it back.

The watchers.

How afraid they must be, that they must deny her the comfort and company of a little animal!

Dreaming, she recalled her grandmother talking of her black-and-white cat in far-away Nova Scotia. She had laughed when she told Maria of it, her near-toothless gums revealed shrunken and naked, as she shook with mirth, remembering how the old people had been afraid of Noah. Then, with a gleam in her eye, she had raised a saucer of cream to her lips and sucked it with greedy smacking, satisfying the insatiable longing of the old for rich food as she lapped like a cat.

'D'you think I'm a witch, then?' she had demanded of the child.

Maria had shaken her head, not knowing what to say.

'Come on, little pumpkin, tell me, don't be afraid.'

'Yes, grandmother,' Maria had whispered, and Isabella had touched her head with love.

'Yes, yes. Come and I'll tell you the secrets.'

But Isabella was old. She would start on one thing and then her story would trail away. When Maria was very small she had told her of the migrations, the great movements from country to country, and of storms at sea, but now she would begin to tell of fairy people who dwelled in caves and in the woods. Only nothing much seemed to happen, and if Annie caught her speaking to the child in such a way she would put her mother to bed and leave her there for a day or so.

'It's only a joke, Annie,' Isabella would complain, but her daughter would bang the butter pats together with extra vigour, or take the mats outside and have a real session beating them. If she was particularly displeased she would give her mother plates of thin gruel while she and Maria ate rich-smelling baked meats, wild pork, or a sweet fillet of beef from a steer freshly killed by Hector on his farm. Annie watched her daughter then with a special cold, clear eye when she was administering what she described as a 'drop of sense' to her mother, to make sure that she did not conceal any tidbits.

So, in time, Isabella spoke no more of witches and fairies. She sat for days in silence, turning her catechism over in her hands as if to please her daughter. When there was nothing else to do she even rehearsed Maria in hers, so she might get meats and sweet dishes too. Then Annie would make custard for her, and Isabella would sit for hours afterwards, silent and preoccupied. Maria thought she was reliving the secrets, but really she was counting the hours until she might ask for more custard with some reasonable hope that Annie would give it to her.

Hector's land was adjacent to Annie's homestead. Long before, after the death of Francis McClure, he had absorbed her land into his. In return for the land he had guaranteed them a good living. He had kept his word, though he told Annie that their mother should not be indulged nor be a law unto herself. 'We have,' he pronounced, 'come a long way to begin a new life, we must bring only that which is good into it. Our mother is a cross, no life is perfect, some suffering must be endured, but not too much.'

Hector festered with boils in middle age. Rose anointed them with ointments but nothing worked. Isabella was disdainful of his wife, the New Zealand-born daughter of a Liverpudlian butcher, and Rose in turn was afraid of her mother-in-law and avoided her whenever she could.

'Who does she think she is?' Hector would rage at what he believed was his mother's superior attitude, although in truth he had been surprised at himself for his hasty marriage in Auckland after he had arrived on the *Gertrude*. With hindsight, it was not quite the union he imagined himself entering into in Nova Scotia, but a change of latitudes did strange things to a man. Rose was, he comforted himself, of good British stock, and one of the hardest workers he had ever met. When first he knew her, he could put his hands, fingertip to fingertip, right around her waist, and she had curly dark hair which covered very small ears.

'It is atrocious, the way our mother speaks to Rose,' he fumed, both to his wife and to Annie. 'I don't know why you don't stand up to her,' he would say, addressing Rose. Then proudly, he would add to Annie, 'It is not as if she is not a woman of spirit, my wife, you know.'

Rose always looked away, and said even less, terrified that she might be forced to meet with Isabella. 'It is not suitable for our sons to visit that woman,' she told Hector.

On a rare occasion when Rose was forced to visit the house when Annie was ill and Isabella bedridden, Isabella enquired with a certain amount of relish after the state of Hector's health. Learning that he was indisposed as usual, she whispered that sow-thistle—or puha as she now

179

called it, since she had come to New Zealand—might usefully be included in the poultices which Rose made for him.

On the way home Rose hesitated and wondered. She could not bear her own curiosity. She gathered the plants and that night pressed them through a sieve before applying them to Hector's fierce pustules. By the week's end, they were gone.

'I have a miracle come on me,' Hector said that Sunday, and gave thanks. Fearing that he might too thoroughly proclaim the poultices to be the work of God alone, and afraid that Isabella, laughing at both of them, might get to him with the truth first, Rose confessed the source of her remedy.

Hector railed bitterly against the works of the Devil then, and wore no more poultices. His boils came thicker than before; he swore, again before God, that this was his mother's work performed out of malice, and did not speak to her again. Isabella smiled if the subject of his cures was raised in her presence, and was heard to say that she wished that she truly possessed such powers. Then she left the matter alone. Three of Hector's boils broke as he carried her coffin down Cemetery Road and the skin rubbed raw on his shoulders and neck, so that even stronger men might have been expected to cry or put their burden down, or hand it to someone else. But Hector walked on, his face red and suffused, until his mother was safely in the ground.

His boils cleared then, and he told Annie that the poison in his system had been put to rest with their mother and that was a good place for it, too.

Sitting looking out over the land which linked the family even in their fiercest divisions, Maria thought of Isabella and wondered who Hector was really concerned about now. Was he watching her, or in his heart did he still watch Isabella? What would Isabella have made of me now, Maria wondered. She touched her dress where it was tight across her stomach. Taking up scissors, she began to make some alterations.

She was about to turn from the window when she saw what looked like a cloud dissolving in the sky above, but as she watched it erupted and fanned out, growing darker by the second, and she saw that it was smoke; it looked as if there was about to be a burn-off.

So they were going to have them again this year; this year of our Lord 1898, going on into April, or so she calculated. It seemed important that she measure the passing of time, though she was uncertain where it was all going, or what it meant; soon, she was sure, her mother would come back and tell her. Like Isabella waiting for custard, she would be forgiven if she sat quietly and waited.

In the meantime, for today at least, there were the fires to watch. She thought they might not have had them this year, for the farmers had become uncertain of their value and some said that they did more harm than good. It was a quick way to clear land when the settlers first arrived. After months of felling trees, the men set fire amongst the stumps and those trees that were left standing. The fires raged like storms across the land and whole stands of bush fell before them. Clouds of smoke hung in the air for weeks and billowed across the ocean, so that ships far out at sea claimed to have had their way lit back to land by the glow in the sky.

After the fires died and the earth cooled, the farmers laid seed amongst the cinders and a long time afterwards the grey land would turn to green, pale scarfs of colour first, turning deep and lush in time so that cattle could graze and fatten on it. Those who were against the burn-offs said they robbed the soil of fertility and that it would be short-lived riches, and that the shipbuilders were growing restive as they found it harder and harder to get timber for their trade. Logs were having to be brought from far inland, pushing up their costs. Some years there would be fires and others there would not. Spring was usually the time of the fires, but this was to be a year of fires and the fires were to be late. Who but a fool would burn now?

The sky erupted, flames shooting up and exploding like scarlet dahlia petals against the bright sunlight. Maria saw that the seat of the fire would be close by Hector McIssac's homestead.

It had now gone eight by the black clock in the front room, but already the house was hot and she knew it was not the heat of the sun. The fires were sweeping down the fenceline within sight of the house, where green nikau and a stand of kauri grew.

She cried out in horror; this was the retreat she had known all her life, the trees where she had hidden her secrets from adult gaze when she was a child, talked to God when she was growing up and addressed him like a lover when she knew no better. Where, in secret consultation, she and Isabella before the latter grew infirm had noted growing things and the complex and intricate nature of ferns and leaves in their adopted land, had listened to birds that sang with different voices. They had tracked butterflies, and once discovered a swarm of wild bees near the edge of the cleared land, residing in a hollow log. It was Isabella who had gathered wild honey, and all the long summer they had feasted on it like kings. Even Annie had been pleased.

And now the fire was eating into the heart of the trees. Before her eyes Maria saw the largest kauri become a pillar of flame, a vast torch poking upwards into the sky. Exploding branches hurtled to the ground, the sound whistling through the air and punctuated by bangs like gunshots. Above the fire birds were shooting upwards trying to escape the holocaust; caught in the down-draught, they were sucked back into the fire. The sun was getting brighter, and against the light the fires paled to apricot with a touch of blue, then coloured up again as the smoke

181

rose so high that the sun was nearly blotted out and the day became dark. A wind sprang up, lashing Maria's face at the open window where she stood crying, hot cinders raining about her. One landed on the curtain and smouldered there before she tweaked it with her fingers. So this was the hell that had been made for her! Soon the Devil would claim her; she should submit to the flames and be consumed by them, and that was how it ought to be.

Coming towards her now across the paddocks, through the dry grasses, the brown top and rye from Nova Scotia that had come with the people in their mattresses and spread throughout Waipu, the tongues of fire snaked their way towards the house.

She opened the windows wide, holding them apart at arm's length so that the flames could reach her more easily. Below her she saw men wielding sacks, beating their way across the paddocks. The men were dark and sooty and wore handkerchiefs round their heads. They were calling, panicking, as the fire raced out of control towards her, threatening them all. Beyond, more men had formed human chains to the river and buckets were being passed from hand to hand. Just when there seemed to be no hope of containing the flames, there came a sudden wind change and the fire whipped away in the direction it had been intended to take; turning inwards on itself it began to die almost as fast as it had sprung up.

Maria pulled the windows shut as the men stood easy in the blackened paddock, but there were some who looked upwards, even as they fought the fire. That, they said, was how they would always remember the witch, with her arms stretched out like some unholy cross and her shameless belly pointed towards the flames.

Maria lay down on the couch in the front room. It was cooler there and the windows faced away from the destruction of the bush. It was very quiet. No birds sang. The crickets were silent. The wind had dropped, and she felt totally alone.

What had brought her to this solitary state in a house of hewn timber with a sharp pitched roof, full of devils and ghosts and with her mother's possessions around her? Ringed and almost consumed by fire, why was she shunned by all who had ever known her?

She touched her stomach. Like one of the wild birds trying to fight its way free, she felt the movement of the child under her hand.

I will tell my mother when she comes, Maria thought. She will understand this, she will put her hand there and stroke my hair and call me her bonnie lass and forgive me.

That night, by candle-light, Maria pulled open a trunk in her mother's room. A forbidden place, it housed her grandmother's things. 'One day we will have to get rid of grandmother's things,' Annie had said, but noting the look of reproach in Maria's eyes, she had done nothing.

What *were* grandmother's things? Dusty books that looked like ledgers, and bundles of letters tied up with pieces of black ribbon and twine. The shadows were raking the walls as she opened one of the books. It was not a ledger but a notebook full of close handwriting. A journal; the journal of Isabella Ramsey turned Isabella MacQuarrie turned Isabella McIssac. The letters were in her writing too; they had been sent back to her from England by the daughter of one Louise Ramsey to whom they were written, after her death in a fall at the hunt more than forty years before.

Opening the first book Maria stared at the words. The handwriting was a beautiful copperplate. The candle wavered, dangerously close to the curtain.

I have been betrayed by my own people.

She watched the candle, thinking how easy it would be to let it burn at the end of this day of fire.

'Mother, where are you?' Her voice was reedy and thin in the quiet house.

She moved the candle and picked up the book again. It was on top of the pile, though there appeared not to be any special order. *I have been betrayed by my own people.* Here, then, were the secrets, the mysterious answers.

19

MCLEOD HAD DIED one yellow afternoon and the world carried on. True, some would become emotional recalling his last days when he lay by his window and blessed them as they visited. In the final hour he called aloud, 'Children, children, look to yourselves, the world is mad.'

He was buried beside Mary in the cemetery by the sea. The settlers had cleared land there soon after their arrival, so that those who died could lie close to the ocean, a reminder of all the oceans they had crossed in life. The day that he was carried down the long white road to the cemetery, Angus Finn stepped forward to relieve the McLean men who were taking their turn at carrying the coffin.

'Let me give a hand,' Angus had said.

The McLeans stopped, their feet puffing up dust around them in the tracks they had made, and Murdoch, a tall bony young man, sweating with the effort and strain of it on a hot March day, looked at Angus whose father had turned his back on McLeod in Nova Scotia twenty years before. His eyes blazed. 'Do you think I would let you touch his coffin?'

Angus shrugged, an elaborate gesture of contempt. 'All right then, you can take him to hell yourself,' he said and turned away.

Those of the onlookers who expected him to be struck down were disappointed.

But there were changes. The divisions at St Ann's began to repeat themselves. Angus Finn had spoken for those newly liberated from the shadow of McLeod. An iron railing like a palisade was placed around the graves of McLeod and Mary to keep them safe inside. Others said that it was to stop McLeod from getting out.

Looking around them now, many found it difficult to perceive a world quite as mad as it had been described by McLeod. They worked and prospered; on Sundays they did go to church, but there were cows to be milked afterwards and cream to be set, there was dinner to be cooked— for dinner would not keep in summer heat—and if there was a boat to be loaded with stock before a tide, all was done. In Auckland not everyone subscribed to the same beliefs and shipping companies were impatient of delays. The Nova Scotians may have experienced a thrill of fear as they challenged the past, but there were some things best kept to themselves. It quickly became clear to them that to set themselves apart from the world in matters of trade was self-defeating.

Annie, for her part, belonged among those who would never forsake McLeod. Neither could many of the other women. They sat carding wool together, calling their gatherings 'the frolicking', and there, in a comfortable way, they cogitated on the sin of the world. There wasn't much they could do about it, they supposed, and the men of course had a finer appreciation of sin than they did. But in talk new rules imperceptibly emerged, relating to prosperity and its temptations.

Godliness brought its own rewards and married well with wealth. There were plenty of opportunities for their daughters' virtues to extend to new horizons. They could see that the young women would become comfortable matrons without the hardships they had suffered, and given that they avoided cards and Catholics, kept chaste, and made sure their children learned the catechism, they could make a most equitable peace with the Lord. It was even conceivable that the old people might all enjoy more comfortable old ages as well. Money and land, and dutiful wives, offered themselves as simple solutions to the restlessness of their sons.

In moments of perversity Annie sighed and asked why God had been so unkind to her. 'It's a hard land,' she would sigh, wiping her face and knotting her strong eyebrows in a gesture of resignation. Her concerns varied in those days. 'Are you afraid of the Maoris, Annie?' her friends asked her one afternoon when the wool was flying through their hands and they were replete and buttery after she had fed them. Hers was a popular house, spacious, quiet and free of children. Not that they said this.

'Oh I never see any to be afraid of,' said Annie carelessly. She slipped more fleece amongst the bent wire teeth of her carding tool and watched the action of her hands with satisfaction, for she was faster than any of them. Yet she felt their eyes on her and was uncomfortable. She reached up with an instinctive touch to her white ruched cap, as if reclaiming her respectability. She wore the cap like a badge, the mark of a married woman. 'Maybe Martha does.'

Her eyes flicked across the room to where Martha McWhirtle sat in a corner. The afternoon sun had been making her guest even drowsier than she usually was. It was rare for Martha to join them, for there was little respite between the annual bouts of childbirth which had continued since her arrival in New Zealand, and when she did come she was quiet and abandoned, for the most part, to private thoughts. Her once magnificent hair straggled from under her cap, rusty-coloured and streaked with grey.

'Yes Martha, tell us what you have heard,' they said, turning to her now. 'Is it true that people are building tunnels at Omaha down to the river banks in order to escape the natives when they attack? Should we be afraid?'

'I've heard that people are doing that. They can't have much to do with their time,' said Martha, forced to rouse herself from a reverie. The tearing of the cards and the whirring of the spinning wheels dropped away. 'The Maoris seem perfectly friendly to me.'

'Well you would know better than we do,' said Annie briskly, and wondered why she had addressed Martha, for she guessed what she might say before she had spoken.

But it was too late to retrieve the situation, for Martha looked around them thoughtfully and said, 'Duncan Cave has told me that the Maoris were given small change in return for their land. They were swindled by Busby. I think they have cause to be annoyed.'

'What do you mean? We have paid for our land.' Annie's voice was sharp. Her afternoon, her lovely day which she had planned with such care, was not going well. She always regretted inviting Martha McWhirtle and had not expected her to come.

'I was not suggesting you did not. It was Busby I was referring to.' Martha picked up a fleece and began winding it around a card with unusual determination. 'Forty pounds in gold, sixty blankets, ten coats, ten black trousers, twenty-five white pairs, four cloaks, five pieces for gowns, fifteen handkerchiefs, three hakimana...'

'What is that?'

'Guns,' said Martha without altering her inflection. 'Twenty hoes, fifteen iron pots, some axes, some bags of shot, and a bit of tobacco. That is as much as I can remember. But that is about all there was.'

'It is a fortune,' said an outraged voice from the back of the room.

'It depends on what it is required to purchase.'

'I have never heard such nonsense,' said Annie. Her tone was bitter. 'That is what I would expect of that fellow.'

Everyone in the room knew that she meant her half-brother, and that she would not refer to him again by name if she could avoid it.

'It is not Duncan who has told me of it. It is Riria, who is his friend and has come to assist me with the children. She is a great help. I don't know how I ever managed without her,' said Martha, looking around them with a mild gaze. 'Now at least I can go visiting from time to time. It is nice for me, don't you agree?'

But the thought of the stranger who at this very moment was caring for Martha's children was too much for the other women to contemplate. They frowned, and fumbled amongst the wool, turning back to their work.

'Of course,' said Martha, continuing in her contemplative fashion, 'it is neither here nor there to us, we have no land.'

'I am sorry for you, Martha,' said Annie, and knew she had gone too far. The older woman was not without friends, especially those who remembered her in the schoolroom when they were children.

'Alexander is not inclined to own land, that is how it is,' responded

Martha, as if the conversation was quite natural. 'But there, he is talking of going to the Coromandel soon. He has always had a mind to gather gold, and often wishes we had stayed in Australia. So it is just as well that we have accumulated so little. Except children.' She smiled in a rueful way and was silent again.

'How sorry my mother will be,' exclaimed Annie, flickering delicately with pleasure and wishing to end the conversation there.

But soon her friends began to leave and in her raging heart she could hear them talking about what they had heard, imagining themselves safely out of earshot. She vowed to tell Hector about it at the next opportunity, and ask him what he would do about Duncan Cave, whom they also called Duncan Clubby, raised like Lazarus by their disreputable mother when she had thought him gone forever.

When she had recovered herself, she realised that at least the diversion had saved the women from asking after Francis, and maybe that it had all been for the best. For Francis had compromised Annie with the reality of change long before the death of McLeod. She had often felt compelled to stay silent when sinful ways were discussed. Francis, stout and comfortable, had filled their house with tobacco smoke and a beery breath. And there were other matters which gave rise to sideways looks and extra cups of tea; these she preferred not to contemplate.

In the end, the problem of Duncan Cave had not been with them for long. His reappearance was short-lived and when he died he was easier to cope with in the grave than he had been out of it. The same was true for Francis, though his departure took much longer. Time and death would enhance both men's images and Annie would take her place with those who reviewed the effects of sin.

When Isabella had been accounted for as well, there was only Maria to contend with in the battle for moral superiority.

Until the dark man from the diggings swept away all the edifices which she had so carefully built around her daughter.

Maria dreamed of her mother. The air outside was acrid with the smell of ash and burnt vegetation. Here and there a lick of fire erupted amongst the stumps of the broken trees. A watcher slipped towards it and wielding his wet sack disappeared into the shadows.

In Maria's dreams she saw her mother as she thought she might have been as a young woman, dark with a touch of stateliness in spite of her rounded shape. She could smell milk on her as she sat on a stool in a barn in Nova Scotia, her face against the flanks of a warm and restless cow, her hands stripping and pulsing, her dreams as yet unrealised. What did her mother dream of in those days? And had the dreams come true?

She opened her eyes for a moment, wondering where she was. It was the same bedroom that she had slept in all her life. What was the sound outside? Snow banking against the roof? But it was the wind and the sound of the trees shaking, and the earth in pain from the blight of fire. She called to her mother but no one came. She did not believe that Annie would not come to her, that they would stop her from coming now, after a day of mortal danger.

She thought she heard a voice but it did not answer hers, was some other person who watched in the night.

Sleeping, dozing, waking for periods, gradually becoming conscious as another milky dawn crept under her curtain, she relived her last meeting with her mother.

'You're very fancy to be going to church, young lady.' Annie's voice was sharp.

'It's only a bit of ribbon on my hat,' Maria studied her reflection in the mirror. The ribbon was pale blue. She had considered something brighter, but it seemed unwise to draw too much attention to herself. Besides, the blue was cunningly bright against her straw-gold hair and her blue eyes that held a hint of green. 'Just like her grandmother,' Annie had remarked more than once, noting those shifting, elusive colours that were neither one thing nor another. She said it as though it tainted her admiration for Maria.

'Only a bit of ribbon. D'you know what the Man would have said to that?'

'McLeod? Ah mother, McLeod's long gone, you don't want to be dwelling on that forever.'

Annie's face grew dark and Maria thought that she really believed he was listening, that he could hear her.

'Let the Devil take McLeod.'

Her mother's hand flicked out and Maria turned quickly away, narrowly avoiding the blow. But the warning was there. Annie had never struck Maria. Remembering this, Maria was afraid. It was not just what she had said, but all that had gone between them in recent weeks. Her mother was stretched to a state of almost unendurable tension.

Maria wanted to soften the moment. 'I'm sorry, Mother. I didn't mean it. Truly.'

'He turned many a woman out of the kirk for her vanity.'

'I know.'

'What makes you think you're better than the old people?'

Stung then, she retorted, 'Perhaps you'd like me to shave my head?'

The two women exchanged despairing looks.

'Don't be cruel, Maria.' It was Annie who broke first. 'I'm old. You hurt me too much with talk like that. Oh your hair, that anyone should touch one strand of it.' She could not resist touching it, running her fingers through it, and Maria, knowing she had won, stood allowing the

188

privilege. 'Don't ever say that to me, not in jest, or anger. Heh, it's so beautiful, such fine lovely hair, why d'you need ribbons and bows when you've got a crown like that to wear on your head? Eh? Eh, tell me, bonnie girl?'

Maria smiled at her mother then, through a tangle of starry brown lashes. 'There, mother, it's a wee bit of ribbon really.'

'Oh. Oh you. Well go along. I can't say anything.'

'Come on then, we'll be late.'

'Aye, and keen for kirk too, ah that's better, yes.'

The congregation had settled and the minister ascended into his pulpit. Light filtered through the tall tree outside, through the ungarnished windows, as the chamber echoed with the responses of the congregation. In the pew across the aisle sat her Uncle Hector, and behind him his sons and their new wives. The Minister, Kenneth Falconer, was a young man with an ascetic face, filling in for a year while Aeneas Morrison, a disciple in McLeod's footsteps, was visiting his mother in Nova Scotia. Some said that it was this young man, however, who had a visage like McLeod's and that his sermons were full of a fire that reminded them of the past. His frequent sharp remarks appeared to be aimed at members of the congregation, striking to the very heart and causing blushes of shame such as had not been seen or felt for thirty years. The old people nodded their heads and glanced sideways at each other. There was a certain half-forgotten malice in the air. The church had been fuller each Sunday than it had for years.

The minister was very tall and leaned towards them from the pulpit, his light hair already thinning, steel-rimmed glasses perched precariously on his high-humped nose. He had a piercing voice which made Maria uncomfortable. She was sitting at the end of the pew against the wall and she leaned her face against the cool planed wood, as if it might block out at least a half of what was being said. She longed to look around but dared not. The unconfirmed presence behind her made her restless, so that she had to restrain herself from squirming in her seat. Perhaps it would help if she were to concentrate on the sermon?

She raised her eyes towards those of Kenneth Falconer, and it seemed as if he were leaning forward to address her directly. Clearly others in the congregation thought so too, for although they were trying not to look in her direction, imperceptibly their eyes were being drawn.

'*Timothy* Chapter Two,' intoned the Reverend Falconer.

There was a rustle amongst the people. 'In like manner also, that women adorn themselves in modest apparel, with shamefacedness and sobriety; not with braided hair, or gold...or pearls...or *cost*-ly ar-*ray*...'

Up and down the pews, flashing looks across the aisles now, the old people remembering the word of the Man. Or God. Wearily, Maria supposed that you could take your pick. They were one and the same, were they not?

The faces around her had taken on an alien look. They were no longer the faces of the people she had known all her life, but set countenances, with eyes looking across snow and ice and storm-driven seas, eyes set in networks of fine wrinkles, the women with mouths drawn and sucked in to small tight lines, the men stern and ramrod straight, grown like strangers. She wanted to duck their eyes, to look away from them, but she was afraid that if she did she might be seen to be looking at the man she knew now was sitting behind. The man who had come to look at her.

Instead, she held their gaze.

Afterwards they would say she looked back at them as bold as brass, as a brazen woman would.

'Let the woman learn in silence with all subjection,' said Kenneth Falconer. 'I suffer a woman not to teach, not to usurp authority over the man, but to be in silence.'

Beside her, her mother's face was pale as glass and her eyes like those of a frightened animal. Maria reached out with a small gesture, which she hoped was inconspicuous, to take her mother's hand, but what she touched was cold and unresponsive, shaking like the hand of someone who has lain asleep on a limb and woken to find it beating round wildly and without feeling.

Kenneth Falconer's voice was very soft now, drawing them all in so that they listened to every word. 'For Adam was first formed, then Eve...'

Not a word spoken now in the church; there was only a silence that seemed as if it would never end. Then Maria heard someone scrape past a pew behind her, breaking the silence and scrambling to leave. Footsteps rang on the wooden floor and every eye except hers and Annie's followed his departure.

Kenneth Falconer raised his chin slightly, his eyes which were a washed-out grey seeming to glint and shine a little more brightly behind the polished spectacles. 'And if a woman has no man in her immediate family, an unfortunate situation which some people sadly, through death or circumstances, should find themselves in, until the time when she is taken in holy wedlock to be spiritually guided by the rightful head of her household...and her *Bo*-dy, then she must take counsel from those who are close and dear to her, and from the influence of the community which has nurtured her. Let me recommend the reading of *Timothy* 1 to all of you who might fall into this un*us*-ual category of people. Of course,' and here he flashed a sudden smile of wintry light around him, 'I have known this flock for only a short time. It may be that there is no one to whom the wisdom of Timothy particularly applies at this moment, but still it is worthwhile for all of us to reflect upon such matters,

190

and all those women amongst us who are of fruitful years may take comfort from the concluding words of that chapter, in which we are reminded that the woman in transgression shall be saved by childbearing, if she should con*tin*-ue in faith and charity and holiness and sobriety, Glory be to God Amen.' With this flourish he concluded his sermon and Murdoch MacKenzie who was layreading stood up to give the notices. It was over, or so Maria thought, for the rest of the proceedings passed her in a blur of sound of which she was no part, just a fly against a wall, and the figure of Kenneth Falconer was the giant spider with his eyes magnified and multiplied behind his glasses.

As they rose to file out, Annie appeared to have recovered herself. She held her head high and her step was firm. She strode from the church, looking slightly to the left and right and nodding good morning to her neighbours, as if what had occurred was of no account to her at all.

At the door she stopped and shook Kenneth Falconer by the hand as was her wont. 'A fine sermon, Mr Falconer.'

'Thank you, Mrs McClure.' He nodded his head gently up and down.

Trapped now, Annie could not leave without saying more. 'It reminded me of the old days and the Man himself. Well, you've heard speak of the Man here, of course.'

'Indeed, oh yes I have,' he agreed.

'I was reared at his table,' she said stiffly, as if he had not understood her connection.

'Really? Well, no one ever told me that.'

'Why then, you must come to lunch, and I'll tell you more of it,' said Annie. 'I've fresh bread baked last night, and cold meats prepared yesterday.' She wished him to be aware of her consideration for the Sabbath, and that she knew how the old people did things.

He was dismissing her with such smoothness that for a moment she might have thought there was a hint of warmth in his voice, but in the unusual quietness of her friends, who were pretending now that they were not listening to the conversation instead of engaging in their usual lively Sunday discourse, she knew she had imagined it and that she was alone.

But still there was Maria who must pass Kenneth Falconer. Now the forced conversation around them fell completely away. Maria could nod her head and pass with downcast eyes and they might yet forgive her. Especially those who had always known her and remembering her as a small and shining child without a father might recognise in her the troubled woman whom they could yet protect. They were close enough to put out their hands and hold her.

Instead, she stood in front of the minister and looking into his multi-faceted eyes, said, 'My mother is a widow, and a good woman. Did you deliberately set out to cause her pain?'

191

'Miss McClure, I do not understand you.'

'Was it the way of Christ to inflict public humiliation on a defenceless woman? Really, Mr Falconer, it seems to me that whatever business you may think you have to do with my mother and me, and in my opinion you have none, that it should be conducted in a courteous and private manner.'

'I was discussing the scriptures in my sermon. And I do not think that women, young women such as yourself in particular, are fitted to discuss the scriptures, Miss McClure.'

'Minister, I do not agree with your view,' she said, lifting her chin.

'I have nothing more to say to you. Good day, Miss McClure.'

'Oh Mr Falconer, but it is not for you to decide when our conversation is to end. Who pays your stipend? Is it not we, the people?' Maria opened the bag hooked to her wrist, and drew out three pence from it. 'Mr Falconer, I despise you,' she said, and threw the money at his feet.

Under the tree outside, Annie stood clutching its trunk. Those near her resumed their talking to cover what they had seen but nobody came to join her. Across the distance that separated them, Maria looked at her mother and turned to walk away. She will follow me, she said to herself, it is the only way, I have broken with them all, but she will not break with me. We are tied to each other and beyond that to the grave; to Isabella my grandmother, and to all women who have suffered and borne children and succoured each other. She will follow me down the road and I will tell her goodbye, that I must go with Branco, who has returned for me.

Under the tree Hector McIssac had at last joined his sister. His sons William and Neil and their wives stood uneasily for a time watching their cousin before moving away from the crowd. William, the elder, looked apologetically at his wife, as if to ask forgiveness for having embroiled her in such a family mess. Neil, however, smaller and always quieter and quite unlike his brother in appearance, with eyes and a nose akin to Isabella's, looked over his shoulder after Maria with an anxious frown. Beside him his new wife Stella, tiny and bubbling with the excitement of the drama that had been unfolding before them, clung to his arm. He appeared not to notice her and continued to watch after Maria. At last he raised a puzzled shoulder and shook his head as if dismissing what he had seen.

Coldly Hector was offering Annie his arm.

'The roadmender was in church,' he said.

She nodded, and a way between the people parted to let them through. The horses stamped their feet and their carriage drew away in the opposite direction to that which Maria had taken, detouring by a back road as he bore his sister towards his home.

The sun was high and burning as Maria walked. She was surrounded by the bright clear light that fills the north in summer; a time when the surf beats on the long line of the beach known as the Cove; when out at sea a purple haze lies over the Hen and Chicken Islands, and all along Bream Bay from the Head to the Tail the fishermen cast their lines or gather shellfish. The blazing pohutukawas had spilled their spiked petals over the banks above the sand, the grasses moved in a soft and constant rustle and only the stands of bush, increasingly isolated by the advance of the axeman and the fire, offered cool refuge.

She faltered. In the bright light and the quivering gold air she seemed to be walking into black spots. Red lines raced before her eyes and she thought she would fall. She knew, without looking, that her mother would not follow her now.

A carriage passed her, and another. In the carriages were girls, young women she had studied with at school, riding beside their parents. Their eyes were studiously averted; they were putting more effort into avoiding the sight of her than she ever remembered them applying to literature or needlework.

She reached a stand of totara and stepped into the trees. The air was filtered and green where the beginning of a clearing had been made. She sat on the ground and put her head between her knees. She did not know why she had behaved as she had. Indeed, reviewing the past few months of her life, she did not understand any of it. She thought about Branco, who had come back to look for her as she expected he would, and there was an odd dead weight inside her, as if he was untidy luggage that she would like to find somewhere to put down. Since the beginning of winter she had carried the thought of him around, brooding on him every moment of the day, and now she did not want to do so any more.

The revelation was frightening in its implications.

It appeared that she had just divorced herself from her own community on account of a man she no longer wanted to know. She turned the idea of him carefully over in her mind, trying to work out why she felt so disinclined towards him and whether in fact she had ever cared for him at all.

Is it the difference of him, she wondered. Perhaps it had got to her at last, the way the people looked down on the gumdiggers. For a moment she felt ashamed.

Then it occurred to her that it was difference that she had sought. It was neither race, nor the faith of either of them, nor occupation, nor language which separated them; it was all of these things, but it was also these considerations which had drawn her to him. If this was what using someone was, then she had used Branco to drive herself to make a

193

declaration of her independence from the community.

Now, it seemed, she had finished with him.

Sitting under the tree, away from the gaze of passers-by, she was less than impressed with what she saw in herself.

The black spaces accumulated.

'He was there to look on you with your airs and graces, wasn't he? Well, answer me. Wasn't he?'

Her uncle's pink face, rimmed with frosty whiskers, was thrust towards hers. She could smell his breath, heavy with a sourness she could not identify. Behind him, in her old chair but like a guest in her own house, sat her mother. She really is old, Maria thought. Not just getting old, the way she's always talking about it, but an old fat tired woman.

'I couldn't have stopped him from coming. It's a public place of worship.' Wanting to placate her now, ready to give in to anything in order to win back her love.

'And you're not ashamed that he defiled it on your account? You would know he's a papist?' Hector's jowls quivered with indignation.

Looking from one to another, Maria felt herself slipping into the darkness again. Part of her wanted her mother's forgiveness, but another part of her was suggesting that it was time to shake the dust of Waipu off her shoes. She had dreamed of the wider world; now might be the time to find it. Even if it was no further than Auckland, that would be far enough. She could learn to dance, and be presented at Government House; she would like to walk in wide streets and look in shop windows; perhaps she might even study at the Institute some higher form of learning, as she had heard young women were doing these days.

It began to crystallise in front of her, a gleaming prospect.

'Maybe he wants to change his faith,' she said wearily.

'You have been seeing him then? You know what's in his mind?'

'I didn't say that.'

'Then what are you saying, pray?'

'There's no need to set on him, on me. It's nothing. Give me a chance and I'll show you.'

'A chance. We'll give you a chance.' Her mother and her uncle exchanged heavy looks across her head. Maria started towards the door in involuntary escape but her uncle stood to bar the way.

She hesitated, knowing that she was about to lose something, to capitulate to something from which she might never recover.

'Go into your room, Maria.'

'Mother, I am not a child.'

'You are still my child.'

'I will not.'

'She is like our mother,' said Hector, turning to Annie. His voice

194

was regretful.

'If I do not?' asked Maria.

'You will be put there.'

'For what?'

'To think about your wicked ways. And to put you out of reach of the beast that stalks you.'

'Mother.' She was entreating her now.

'After a time, and when you have said your catechism for a month or so, we will think about what's to be done with you.'

Looking at Annie, Maria could see with terrible clarity what she had never truly divined in her mother before: a sense of outrage at the ways of the world, and how personally she took them.

Her mother and Hector could not contain her if she resisted them. But if she were to run, there was only the bush and the river to which she might flee. Who, of the riverboat men, would take her aboard? And she was without clothing or money or supplies. A departure must be on her own terms. The vision of her uncle and his sons advancing upon her in a paddock, or as she cowered like an animal behind a tree, rose up before her.

Her voice sounded like a child's in her ears. 'I'll go to my room now, mother,' she said. 'We can talk about this when my uncle has gone.'

It was a long walk, from where she stood to the doorway, but she hoped to achieve it with dignity.

Then blackness overwhelmed her, and when she woke she was lying in her bed with the door closed. Through the window, stars held steady in the darkness beyond. Soon it would be light, she thought, soon this blackness will go away. But even as she raised herself on her elbow her head swam. It was next day before she woke.

From the kitchen she smelt sour skimmed milk which her mother placed near the fire to warm until curds were formed. There would be a cheese at lunchtime. The bread had been baked too. All was well. She strained her ears for the sound of her mother's movements. When she heard nothing, she got out of bed and put on her robe, keeping her own movements stealthy although unsure exactly why she should. Still there was no sound from beyond the door. She took the handle but when she tried to turn it she found it locked.

On the other side of the timber dividing them, her mother's voice raged.

'That's where you'll stay,' Annie shouted, 'and your uncle's coming with bars to seal the window, and you'll read your Bible and think it through. There now, kicking'll do you no good, nor screaming. Oh Maria, Maria,' and her voice turned to keening, full of grief. 'It'll do you no good, I can't relent now, and it's all for your own good, my darling girl, now there, no more, I know what is good for you, I do, I do. I know.'

20

THE BIRD BEATS *itself against the window, again and again with terrible force. Something has frightened it. Maria does not know what it is, or what she has done. She thinks that the source of terror is outside the house. She understands this and feels helpless, unable to reassure the bird. Now it flies up to the rafters and dashes itself there, falling stunned to the ground. Maria moves to pick it up, but it opens a bleary eye, shakes itself, hops up on one foot, and takes off again, its beak extended in a silent shriek.*

There is a ledge between the end of the rafter and the top of the wall. The sparrow takes refuge here, and sits with is wings half extended, quivering all over. He holds his leg in such a way that Maria wonders if it is damaged.

'You'll do yourself a mischief, little bird,' she whispers. 'It's no good going on like this, there's no way you'll escape. We have to work at it together. Why don't you just sit quietly there while I find you a seed or two, something to keep your strength up.'

The bird sits still on its perch, utters a cheep. She thinks she is getting through to it.

'I'm a witch, you know, witches don't hurt wild creatures, they're wild creatures themselves, yes that's what we are. Don't you know that, little bird? Eh? There, there, you're settling. There, you're not so frightened. I'll just sit here quietly and see what you do, wild one. No, I know you're not ready to come down yet, I won't move, you're safe here.'

For a moment she thinks she can walk over to the bird and kneel beside it, before she remembers that she is on the floor and he is in the ceiling. This is an old dream, where she walks around the room at the level of the mantelpiece, or higher. Many times when half awake she has believed that she is walking across the world, above rooftops, her feet slicing cleanly along, the air holding her up. In dreams like this it has always taken her a long time to wake up.

Maria woke to hear her mother's voice behind the door, as she had each morning since her incarceration. She had almost lost count of the days. It was a splendid year; the sun shone continuously and corn and tomatoes were ripening faster than they could be gathered. The people shook their heads and spoke of an Indian summer, and how it looked like there would be no winter at all, the rate they were going.

From her room, Maria watched the blue sky through the bars that

Hector McIssac had placed over her window.

She did not scan the ground below, as those beyond the room might have expected, waiting for her lover to appear. She supposed, now, that she would never know what had become of him. This mattered to her, because he was someone who had been prepared to take risks for her. Too late she had realised that she didn't care.

In the end it was she who had taken the greater risk. Though they had turned over his hut, they would not touch him. Now he was gone and she did not expect to see him again. What mattered was the passage of this month. Then, maybe, she would be allowed to live her life unhindered again. And sooner or later she would go away, however painful and difficult that might prove.

Her term in the room must almost be over. She had counted four Sundays, days when a door banged, a carriage called, and the house had gone quiet as her mother went to church. Even now, she would keep up appearances. She could see Annie walking up the aisle with her head held high beside her brother and his wife, taking her seat in the usual pew, following the prayers for the faithful, and walking out again with a 'good morning' here and there.

In that way, Maria guessed, she would leave a path which her daughter might follow after a suitable time had passed.

And now the fourth Monday morning. She had woken earlier than usual, for lately she had had great trouble waking up. At first she thought her mother was speaking to her, but Annie was talking to someone downstairs. A man's voice, just after dawn. Maria listened. It was Hector. Now his voice grew indistinct. She was not certain whether he was still in the house or had gone outside.

'Maria,' called Annie.

An exchange took place between them each morning; Annie would pass food to her and in exchange Maria had passed her out the chamber pot. She had considered the idea of escape, but by now she knew that Hector or one of the boys lurked nearby for most of the time. It was between her and her mother, she had concluded, and nothing was to be gained, no dignity or power for her cause, from ill-considered breakouts. She would see it through, pursuing her own plan. As the days passed she stitched her clothes and put her wardrobe in order. When the time came to leave, she would be prepared. At least this was what she told herself, although some days she was so sleepy that she would nod off over her needlework.

Although she had been expecting a change in her routine, now that it had come she was unprepared for it. Something more than she had expected was afoot.

'What it is, mother?'

The door swung open and Annie stood there, dressed in the black mourning clothes she had worn when Isabella died. She made no effort to stop Maria walking past her.

'So where is my bodyguard, my precious uncle? Aren't you afraid I'll escape?'

'I wish you would. I wish I had never set eyes on you.' Her mother's voice sounded like mud sliding along a riverbank, full of disaster.

'Mother, when will this ever end?' asked Maria. 'What's happened is over. I've sat here, and sewed, and made no complaint to you. I've accepted your will. What is it now?'

'A month. A whole month you've sat in there. Yes.'

'It was a month you suggested. I can't stay in there forever. Can I?'

'Come out here to the kitchen, I have something to say to you. Your uncle is waiting.'

'Can I not speak to my own mother without that man listening to us? Mother, this is crazy.'

Yet she followed her. She saw the room as it always was, except that this morning there was no fire burning and it was cold. An unusual and early frost lay outside on the grass. Through the window she could see again the garden she and Annie had planted. She felt as if she had crossed from one world into another, rather than from one room into the next.

Her uncle stood by the window, looking out with his hands folded over each other behind his back. He did not turn when she entered the room.

'Good morning, uncle,' she said, although she would have preferred not to speak to him.

'Good morning,' he replied, but he did not turn to face her.

'A month, Maria,' said Annie again, in that same dead heavy voice.

'I do not understand this at all. What are you trying to say to me?' Maria searched first her mother's putty-coloured face, and next her uncle's unrelenting back.

'I did not know when I sent you there...' Annie faltered. 'It did not occur to me at first. A thought so dreadful that even as the weeks passed it seemed impossible...Do you know what that month means, Maria?'

'A week, a month, it could be a year, mother. Time's lost its meaning. Perhaps you've destroyed time.'

'There was no bleeding in that room, Maria.'

Silence then, and the unlikely frost outside. Her bare feet, cold on the floor.

'Did you hear what I said? No blood.'

'I heard.'

'No bleeding at all.'

'Would you have me cut my veins then?' whispered Maria. 'I've felt like it.'

198

She was playing for time, avoiding the moment when she would have to tell herself that it was true, that some half-known secret about the life of women would become hers.

'You are with child, Maria McClure,' said Black Hector, from where he stood at the window.

Their faces, both of them, then the whole procession swimming before her, of people who lived good lives and did not toy with fortune, with straight mouths and eyes like the frost. Outside.

21

'I'M WATCHING YOU, *little bird. Wild ones are good to each other, hush come quietly, little sparrow.*'

Kenneth Falconer had said, '*For all flesh is as grass, and all the glory of man as the flowers of the grass.*'

The bird looks stiff and sore, as if it had been beaten, which indeed it has.

Maria observes it, hardly breathing lest she startle it, imagines the tiny web of veins like threads in its wings, visualises the miniature structure of its body as complex as that of a human heart, muscles like fine shells pumping minute quantities of blood, the brain no larger than grains, its response to the world as finely tuned as her own.

'*In the morning we will find a way out of here for you.*' *Her voice becomes uncertain.* '*Perhaps, perhaps.*'

And after a while, '*Or perhaps you would like to stay here with me. Well, now there's a thought. Hah. How foolish that would be. No, let's get you better, stay here another night, yes? And in the morning you'll be restored, it's nothing more than bruising, I can tell that, nothing broken, and when you've had a rest you can hop along to the open window and set off again. That's what I would do if I were you. I think. Yes, I think so, though it's hard to remember, wouldn't you say. Ah, bird.*'

She closes her eyes.

'*The grass withereth and the flowers thereof fall away,*' *says Kenneth Falconer's voice from across the years.*

The hole in the window is jagged. To enter or leave by that hole is tempting the worst kind of tearing and disablement, a terrible aftermath of scarring in its wake. She will encourage the bird, with great gentleness, to take the proper path.

Sparks still spat and hissed where once the bush had stood.

This, the book of secrets. Maria's hand on the yellowed page of Isabella's journal.

I have been betrayed by my own people.

The front room, where Maria had passed her days since her mother's departure, smelled of smoke.

'Aren't I the one who should leave the house?' she had said to Annie and Hector before they went.

'And where would you go?' Hector had asked her.

'There must be somewhere,' she had said, casting around. 'Somewhere in the bush, perhaps there's a cottage, some place I could stay.'

She could see the idea had some appeal, may even have occurred to her uncle. 'It's understandable that you should wish to hide your condition,' he said stiffly.

'So you'll consider it? You'd look for somewhere?'

'There is afterwards to be considered, when the child is taken away. You would have to come back.'

'It's my child.' She was overwhelmed by this new knowledge and oddly excited as well. A child, and her own. 'You can't take it away,' she said.

'Of course it will be taken,' said Hector as if she was simple. 'It will be illegitimate.' His tongue trembled around the word. Maria saw his Adam's apple convulsively at work in his throat.

She thought, I must be careful. All of this is so new, so unexpected. I knew so little of what I was doing, but now that it is done I must work through it, one step at a time. She cast her eyes towards the floor.

'I wouldn't have to come back,' she said, adopting a meek tone. 'I could go away for good.'

Annie sagged, almost falling.

'Not too far away, mother, somewhere that you could reach me...if you wished.' She had been going to say 'me and the child', but she restrained herself.

'I would never want to see you again.'

'You don't mean that? Mother?'

Annie looked down the garden, to where the last tomatoes were splitting their skins and the vine turning black as the frost melted in the morning sun.

'Your mother needs rest and care,' Hector said smoothly. 'She will find it at my house. She can hardly be expected to receive it under this roof with you. She can stay with us until a place is found for you.'

'Are you ill, mother?'

'Of course she is,' said Hector, as if Annie had lost the power of speech. 'She is heartsick. It wouldn't surprise me if you were the death of her.'

It was true that Annie did look poorly, her face puffy and swollen and her body trembling from head to foot.

'It is as well, then,' said Maria. 'I would rather be on my own.'

After they had gone, she took kindling from the box beside the fireplace and set the fire in the stove. Although the sun had come up outside the room was still very cold. As it took on a glow she realised that she was very hungry too. She opened the flour barrel, taking out flour to begin the dough for scones. Her next move was unclear but she was not going to do anything on an empty stomach. She realised how important food had become to her of late. It crossed her mind that she might die.

Perhaps that was what was expected of her, that she die by her own hand? A proper penance, no half-measures; severed limbs and a broken body. That was the price of sin. She looked at the rafters, and then at the narrow ladder-like stairwell that led to the upstairs rooms, and she thought that it would be easy enough. There was cord in the kitchen cupboards, or sheets which could be torn into strips. She shivered, not so much from fear of killing herself, but rather that she might fail. Her mother had once told her in hushed tones of a man in Pictou, before her time it was, but her grandmother had been there so she'd been told—not that Isabella ever told her herself—who had only been half hung in a public execution, a bungled job, he choked in front of everybody and his face was as blue as cornflowers before they got it over. It was no way to go, not even for a common criminal.

But something joyous was welling inside her, pushing aside these uglier visions. She was not going to die. She would not give up her child. The thought was stunning.

Not that it solved anything. An image of Branco swam before her. His child too, even if her feelings towards him had changed. And the thought surfaced: he could help me. It wouldn't be perfect, it is not what I want now for myself, but together we could make this baby safe, which is all that matters.

The grass was brown and yellow in the autumn light, there were hawthorn berries colouring up on hedges planted round the cleared paddocks and the air smelled sweet and clean after her long month indoors. Wasps blundered around and near her, groggy in the cooler atmosphere, tumbling towards their deaths. At first her legs felt shaky from misuse, but she was so overjoyed to be abroad again that soon she began to run. Across the paddocks she sped. The river surged past her and her feet felt as if she was flying. There was not a soul in sight. The startled birds rose in a flock beside her and she believed she was as free. For a moment she forgot why she was running across the paddocks, or if she did remember it seemed like a lie, it had nothing to do with her and she was not afraid of it. She was a young girl without a care in the world. Down the rough track which had been worn by their feet, and now she could see that it was overgrown and hardly existed at all. Round the corner to where his shack had stood.

It had gone, and in its place was a pile of ashes. She stood stock-still, not believing for a moment that she was in the right place. A slight breeze flattened the tops of the grass and caught a small eddy of the black ash sending it skywards then dropping it again onto the smoky bed. Standing in Maria's path were Hector and his sons. A little behind them stood two more men. Five men, fanning out and barring her path. Across the distance which separated them William McIssac caught her eye and looked away.

She was of course grateful to them. The thought of asking Branco for help had been a fleeting one. He seemed like a dream, a phantom who had played some part in the events which had overtaken her but was without form or substance.

She reconsidered this now with a certain grim amusement. As the last two months had passed, it had become increasingly clear that she could not have dreamed him up. The evidence against this was too real, too increasingly tangible. But that she preferred to be without him, to be on her own, was still the truth and she had been relieved by her relatives of the need to consider his return.

Except that she never was alone. The shadows of the watchers haunted her from the trees.

And now the trees were burnt. Everywhere she turned, it seemed there was fire, so much had been destroyed. They would destroy her if she let them. Alone in a house ringed by fire. A funeral pyre, perhaps. Her rations had been small the past week. Maybe they thought that one way or another they could make the child go away. But the child moved, it was alive.

Still, when all else failed, they would take the child. Fine words, to say that she would keep it, but she knew how hard she would have to fight. They would do what they believed was best for her. And then what? The punishment would not end there. She would be shunned forever. At nights she dreamed of her resistance, but when she was awake she could imagine little action that would be effective against them.

Now, her hand lying on the book.

What drove me mad? Do you know, I don't know any more. Was it the wild men in the woods? Men? What men? I don't think there were any men. They were figments...

Isabella, grandmother. What did you know all those years?

(undated)
A letter from the caves (near Pictou)

Love and all its ways have deserted me, or I have deserted them. I do not expect ever to leave this cave in which I now live with my child. In the absence of response from my beloved sister, or of any opportunity perhaps ever to communicate with her again, I write letters to myself. I dwell on the nature of love, and the feeling I have for men. I ask myself, if I am the rib of man, why does he inflict so much pain upon me? Doesn't he, therefore, suffer it too? It is not merely that I have been left alone, but that in the presence of man I had insufficient dialogue that satisfied me. I was never sufficiently held in thrall. And as for man's most base desires, I can feel only outrage. I think I have been dealt a sorry hand. Body and soul, I am a poor vessel for the aspirations of man. A return to the world would demand too great a compromise. Could it be that

I ask too much of myself?

My child weeps in the corner of the cave. Some would say, he's bawling his head off, but it is that, and something else, as if in infant sleep he has woken crying from a dream. What can one so young dream about? His tiny ribs surely cannot encompass woman. I wonder, could it be that he is both man and woman in one body? For that matter, am I? What kind of woman lives in caves, eating birds and berries? I am happy in this cave. If I were taken away from it, I would leave part of myself in it.

Grandmother, a message from the grave. There are caves in the hills behind Waipu. I have heard tell of them. They are full of stalagmites and stalactites and glow-worms which shine like a million candles. They are little explored, being both a place of enchantment and one of fear. All these things that befell you, and I never knew. I really am like you, grandmother. I have been exploring too, and ended up in a cave.

No wonder, Maria thought, that the people, Annie and the women, had sought to keep her apart from Isabella. No wonder they would have had her take her grandmother for a fool.

In her mind's eye she tried to envisage the rugged terrain that led to the caves beyond Waipu. The difficulties to be encountered were another potent reason that the caves were so little visited.

Deep in these thoughts she did not hear the footsteps outside. When she was roused by banging on the door, her first thought was to refuse to open it. Her uncle's voice called out to her.

'Open up, Maria McClure.'

'Why should I? Did my mother send you?'

'She did not.'

'I am waiting for her to come back. I will not see you unless you bring her.'

'Your mother will never return.'

In the night, fraught with smoke and the aftermath of fire, she detected an elegaic quality which filled her with foreboding. She unbolted the door and pulled it open, half expecting to see several men come to get her.

But Hector stood by himself on the doorstep, a heavy coat, more like a cloak, wrapped around him as if he were one of the Men of old.

'I do not wish to see you,' she said.

'Yes. Better to hide your face in shame, I agree.'

He stepped inside, closing the door behind him.

'Where is my mother?'

'She is dead.'

'No...Another trick...?'

But straight away, she knew it was true. His eyes bored into her, red-rimmed with smoke and exertion and the day's fires.

'When?'

'Last evening.'

'But why? How, Uncle Hector?'

'Her heart. Broken. She said it was broken before she died.'

I must keep calm, she warned herself. I must not let him see into me. Aloud, she said, 'That is nonsense. People die of disease. Or of age. Not of broken hearts.'

'Believe what you wish.' He lifted his shoulders, dismissing her comment.

'Had she been ill for long?' Maria whispered, faltering in spite of herself.

'Since the day she left here.'

'I would have tended her.'

'You.' His manner was full of contempt. 'Much good you could have done. You killed her.'

'You've been burning fires all day. As if nothing had happened.'

'Your mother was beyond earthly help, there was work to be done.'

'When will she be buried?'

'It is already done.'

Maria sat down suddenly, her body determined to betray her.

'You couldn't do that.'

'But we have. She was buried at sundown. It was agreed that the sooner she was taken to her rest the better for all.' He paused with heavy significance. 'In the circumstances. Your condition is known of round here.' He looked at her. Her clothing gaped across her bulging stomach, and her ankles were swollen. No wonder she was unable to stand up properly. 'Your condition was further advanced than we suspected. You could have informed us of that, at least.'

'I didn't . . .' Her voice trailed away. They would never believe that she had not known, that she had undertaken a season of delight in innocence. As if the pleasure conferred knowledge. So, she was a liar too. Not that it mattered. She was now totally alone. She tried to shut out his insistent words.

'God will wipe away our tears and there will be no more death, nor sorrow nor pain,' Hector was intoning, turned biblical in his phrases now that he had accomplished his task.

'Did my mother . . . did she have a word for me, uncle?'

'None.'

'Nothing at all?'

'What word would a dying woman have for the likes of you?'

'She was my mother. She loved me.'

'She did not. She despised you.'

Maria wanted to argue with him, to try to prise an admission from him that her mother had not spoken harshly of her at the hour of her death, but his face was so set, so certain, that she began to believe him. I will never know, she thought with despair.

'I will go away from here,' she said dully.

'You will stay.'

'Surely that's for me to decide now?'

'Count yourself fortunate that you are left with a roof over your head.'

Her heart hammered in her chest as she tried to assimilate each new piece of information that her uncle was offering. She endeavoured to look him in the eye, to meet his pale hard gaze. For a moment she detected in it something akin to excitement, as if all this activity and the crowding in of events had taken him out of himself, made the blood race a little. His gaze flickered away. Perhaps he guessed at what she could see?

'So I am a property owner,' she said.

'To an extent,' he admitted.

'What do you mean? Either one is a property owner or not.'

'Before your mother's death we discussed your future. She agreed with me that you were not fit to take possession of the land around you and try to administer it. Your age is against you of course, and you have shown no signs of a mature outlook, such as your mother enjoyed at the time that your father, God rest his soul, departed this world. At the same time, having brought you into this miserable life, there was a responsibility for your welfare which she recognised. Accordingly, she made the land that the house stands on into my name, and the house into yours.'

'But that's monstrous. Did you have a lawyer witness that?'

'A lawyer? Young woman, it is neither here nor there to a lawyer. Any lawyer would recognise that we have acted in your best interests.'

'My best...oh uncle. You do not know what you're saying. I will see a lawyer myself in Auckland. I am leaving for there in the morning.'

'I have told you, you will not.'

'And I have told you, it is not your decision now.'

'You will be prevented from leaving.'

'How can you prevent me?'

'You will not cross my land.'

He smiled at last and her thoughts turned to the kindly uncle on whose knee she had once sat when she was a child. 'Poor little bairn,' he had murmured then, 'nothing but a poor fatherless little bairn, hush don't fear, you have uncle to care for you, pretty child.' Hector and his wife had no daughters.

'You understand,' he was saying, his voice as soft as velour, 'in order to leave the house, you must cross the land which is mine. That is not allowed.'

'I see,' she said, as if she really did. 'Uncle, I am trying very hard to understand your attitude towards me. I'm finding it very difficult. I'm offering to leave here. I can hardly expect you to be pleased with what's happened to me, nor am I pleased with the situation myself. There, you see I'm not without regret or penitence. But I'm prepared to be responsible for what's happened, now that I'm on my own. Don't think I'm without sorrow for my mother. I have hardly had time to comprehend what you've told me. But now she's gone, I don't wish to stay here. You speak of my best interests...I tell you, that for all of us it is better if I go.'

'And even if you crossed the land, then you must consider who would take you away from here. By the boats? I hardly think so,' he said, almost as if she had not spoken at all. 'Food will be placed regularly. You will not go without. The compensation for the land which was your mother's is the price it will cost to keep you, Maria McClure...When your confinement is due, place a white cloth at the window and a midwife will attend you.' He smiled in a melancholy way. 'I am as your father now, Maria, heaven preserve and keep me.'

'Tell me, tell me why you're doing it,' she cried out. 'Oh please tell me why you won't let me go.'

'Rebellion is as the sin of witchcraft. And stubbornness is as iniquity and idolatry. *Samuel* I, chapter fifteen, verse twenty-three. I recommend it to you, Maria.'

'Witchcraft? You think I'm a witch? Oh I don't believe this, you call yourself a Christian. You cannot believe that?'

He opened the door to take his leave. Against the night his coat was like the burnt trees as he turned away from her; an obdurate back, no quarter given. Above him the new moon hung like a crystal. I must not look at it through the glass, thought Maria, but already it was too late, for she knew no luck in the world was going to save her.

'Uncle,' she called piteously down the path after him.

He paused but did not turn back to her. 'What is it?'

'Did she say nothing at all? Not even my name?'

'She did not,' he replied, speaking into the night. 'She would not speak your name in my house. We brought better things with us, better morals to this country than you have found here. Our journeys were not made in vain to be sacrificed to such mischief. Your name will be as a curse under my roof and within my hearing. Goodnight, Maria McClure.'

At the gate he paused. 'You may till the garden if you wish,' he called.

Later, she woke again from one of her dreaming sleeps, the names ringing in her head...from Assynt in Sutherlandshire from Applecross and Skye, Lochalsh and Harris, the Man said I must be patient Maria. And were you patient mother? Oh aye, I was. And I was the child mother?

Aye, yes you were the child, the grass Branco it smells so sweet, the sweet scent beneath us, oh but why d'you need ribbons and embroidery when you've got a crown of hair like that Maria oh mother it is a little bit of ribbon...

all flesh is as grass...

...my own fair lass, my bonnie girl...

the grass withereth...

...from Loch Broom and Loch Tollachan, Dunrunie and Badinscallie from the Summer Isles and Corry Halloch, return return return we never, streaming on across the seas, to Nova Scotia across the Atlantic, to Pictou and St Ann's to Australia by the green Indian Ocean on the good barque *Margaret* and on the *Highland Lass*, by the Tasman Sea, and the *Gertrude* and the little ship *Spray* and on the *Breadalbane* and the *Ellen Lewis*, the sails of the ships billowing before fair winds and bad, great white canvas sheets on the rigging, mother I dream dreams as you must have dreamed and my grandmother before me...

I am betrayed by my own people.

Grandmother, why did you leave the cave? How can I live my life out in this place? How did you? Grandmother, they will not keep me forever, will they? Isabella, oh Isabella, I wish you were alive, or that I were dead.

Later again, it came to her that this could be her cave, safe and secure, where they could never reach her. Towards dawn she took the candle and opened the book once more, reading what Isabella had written of McLeod's arrival at the cave to prevent her and her child from perishing in the woods one winter long ago.

Watching the sky lighten she thought, so this is what it has all come to. And wondered if McLeod had seen his followers perverting the course of morality. Or had he long ago lost sight of what it was all about himself? What natural savagery had overtaken a community which had begun with such kindness in its intentions?

But Isabella had been a married woman who had been taken against her will. While she was a single woman who had lain, from choice, with an enemy. For that was how they must see him, though she did not. No enemy you, Branco, nor yet a lover; a friend between seasons.

Perhaps McLeod would have left her in the cave?

I am the last sacrifice.

Taking her cloak from behind the door, she stepped outside amongst the dew. Across the paddock, a watcher waited. She turned the other way and another dark shape loomed against the scarlet tongues of morning. To her left, another. The house was surrounded. She made to run, but the child kicked inside her with such force that she staggered. Again the world loomed black. While she could still stand she made her way back inside.

It will only be for a little while, she told herself. I will stay here for a short time, until the child is born. They cannot watch me forever.

Just a little time.

Did she imagine it, or did one of them call to her?

You are a murderer, Maria.

No. No. I didn't kill her. Mother, where are you, tell them I did not kill you.

As if with an axe, Maria, as if with an axe.

The voices, maybe they are in my head. Perhaps there is no one out there.

Was it the wild men in the woods? Men? What men? I don't think there were any men...No, I never saw strange men in the woods. Ghosts perhaps...mother, long ago, telling me at night there were no ghosts, or only ghosts for people who had been bad. Now what did I ever do that was bad?

Just a little time, alone in the cave.

Maria's hand brushed an object, like beads only rougher. It was lying beneath a packet of the letters. She uncovered it and saw that it was beads of a kind, though not like any she had ever seen before. It was a string of human teeth, the teeth of young children.

She took them out, fearful, fascinated, and half-disgusted at first, but the shiny teeth were smooth like small white shells on the outside, and only the crowns rough, with a few brown pits here and there, old toothaches preserved forever, and the roots curved down to sharp scratchy little points.

What would they say, if I told them that I wore my children's teeth strung around my neck?

She counted the teeth and in all there were fifty-six, three complete sets of milk teeth less four.

Her eyes widened. In her hands, as if they were flesh, so alive had they become, were the teeth of Duncan Cave who had died before she was born, of Annie her mother who was now dead, and of Uncle Hector.

She held the beads in her hand a moment longer, then carefully placed them around her neck and covered them over with the collar of her dress.

22

THROUGHOUT THE WINTER Maria made fires, collecting wood from the paddock around the house. The boundaries were clear and she no longer sought to cross them. At first she had thought of staying inside so that she would not have to touch the soil that her uncle now claimed was his, but that seemed self-defeating. She needed warmth and food if she and her child were to survive. The real battles must wait until after the baby was born.

She put her arms around her belly then. I am holding you now, she told the baby. Whatever her uncle might have accomplished over the land, she thought he might have more difficulty convincing the law that they should take her child from her, even if it was considered the proper thing to do.

Often Maria returned to the journals of Isabella. It worried her that Isabella had survived for so long in the cave only to succumb to McLeod in the end. She kept likening her own situation to that of her grandmother's, in spite of the clear differences between them. Isabella had chosen to leave her community but McLeod had coaxed her to return to it. His reward for her compliance had been to ordain the course of her life. And it seemed to Maria that it was McLeod who breathed on her, too, ordering her days and the progression of her life.

In the mornings she baked bread, as her mother had done, although she could never eat a half of what she made and took to feeding the birds with the crumbs on the rough lawn outside. Seven wax-eyes and four fantails came early each morning before the arrival of the blackbirds and thrushes, busy and outrageous in their behaviour.

At lunchtime she cooked meat that was left for her twice a week by darkness at the gate. As winter had come and the flies had vanished during the cooler weather, it usually stayed fresh, though sometimes when it was delivered it smelt as if it had been hung overlong. One night a brace of pigeons was waiting for her; she had a curious conviction that they had been left by a different person from the one responsible for the other provisions. She plucked the birds with care and stuck the brightest feathers around the edge of the mirror. There, baby, she said aloud, those are for you, feathers and finery you'll have, my pretty girl.

Girl. Yes, it will be a girl, she decided as she prepared a sweet pigeon pie. I wouldn't know what to do with a boy. All my life I have lived in the presence of women, and my dealings with men have come to difficult ends. I have little faith in men. She shook her head. That is unfair. You haven't really given them a chance, Maria. Oh but have they given you a chance? Well, I can't altogether blame Branco, I gave him plenty of chances. Pshaw, Maria, it wasn't a man you were after, it was an escape. Well, he didn't help much, did he, look at you now.

Ah, but you did, Branco, for look what we made. Now there is you. And again she would touch her stomach and under her hand a fist or a foot would bulge against its walls.

Whoever prepared her provisions appeared to think carefully of her requirements. On another day there was a parcel of soft white wool. She sat down straight away and began to knit, her hands busy again, plying the soft yarn as she made garments like cobwebs for the baby. The next time there was a towelling cloth to sew into napkin squares and a note which read, 'The baby will be going south, it will need to be dressed warmly when it leaves.'

By the fire that night she put down her knitting. 'I do not want this baby to be born,' she said aloud. 'There is no way I can keep it to myself except that it stays inside of me.'

Later she lay in the dark and placed her hand on the fluttering bird-like creature within her, counting its heartbeat. Wind blew through the cracks in the bedroom wall. The bright summers of the past, and the billowing fires, had dried the timbers in the house and all winter it creaked and crackled, talking to her. We are a good trio, she thought, the house, the child, and me.

She was glad now, that for the time being she was there.

Winter ran on that year, frostier than usual in a climate where children were in the habit of running barefoot summer and winter. She could see them passing along the track that led past her gate, and from where she stood they looked pinched and buttoned up more tightly this year.

None of the children looked in her direction. Often she saw ones she knew, the younger brothers and sisters of her friends, and once or twice she called out to them, but after the first time or two she knew better. They looked straight ahead and pretended they had not heard her.

One night seed potato was left by the gate. 'It is early to sow,' read the note left with them, 'but when the frosts are over you should turn the ground and plant these.'

So they expect me to be here for the summer, eh? To lay in provisions for the next year? She turned the note over inside the house, for she never showed any sign of interest where they could see her in what they left.

'When is your time?' said the next note.

She smiled to herself with pleasure. There was something they did not know about her, after all. She, too, would like to know. Though she had an idea now. She had cleaned the house for a fortnight. It should be spotless when the midwife comes, she told herself as she turned out cupboards.

She sat back on her heels then, almost toppling with the effort, and wondered why the midwife might look in the bottom drawer of her mother's chest where her old clothes were stored.

She sat on the floor then and wept. In the drawer were the clothes she remembered, a navy dress in fine wool, worn at the elbows, white collars which had become yellowed with age, a mob calico hat which her mother wore on wash days, and a shawl which came as near to being ornamental as anything her mother had ever worn, made of dark green handwoven cloth which she pinned in front with a large cairngorm. The brooch still lay in the top drawer of her mother's chest. So much that was familiar, so little that was memorable. She had been her mother's work of art, her ornament, and she had failed her and destroyed her. Or so they were saying, and she supposed that in a sense it must be true. She could remember the last days when she and her mother lived together, how Annie was often short of breath and her colour bad. Why hadn't she noticed? Her mother must have been ill for a long time, all that summer when she was unable to find Maria on dusky evenings.

The drawer stuck as she tried to push it shut, jamming against a hard object at the far corner. She slid her hand inside and running it along the edge came to a book. Another of Isabella's journals.

For a long time Maria sat looking at it.

'I am not ready for it yet,' she said aloud. The past already felt as if it was cramming her head from all sides. 'Enough is enough. When I can bear more, I will read it.'

It was difficult to sleep at nights. There was no way she could arrange herself comfortably in bed. Three nights in a row she walked up and down. In the morning she would forget to light the fire, and the sight of food repelled her. Half-frozen, she would scrape out the ashes and set some kindling. When the fire was alight she put on a log big enough to burn all day and sat there until it was ashes, then shivering, made her way to bed. Within an hour the walking and pacing would begin again. Pain spiked the small of her back. Her legs felt like jelly. Weals stood out across her stomach. She half expected to see the skin begin to break as the child emerged but it only stretched more tight and hard. On the third morning after the marks appeared she took a handful of butter and smeared it on her stomach, rubbing it in to soften the skin which looked as if it would surely split that day. This gave her relief straight away, but when she sat by the fire the butter soaked through her clothes and she could smell herself then, rancid and sour. Her hair felt clammy as if she had been sweating and hung in lank matted knots around her face.

'Please come out, please,' she said to the child.

Immediately she regretted her comment, fearing that the child had heard her and might obey and they would be parted. 'But at least I'll see you,' she commented, relenting. 'And I will take care of you. I will. And you can love whom you will, lass. Eh, will you be a girl? Will you have fair yellow down on your head like a young chick...oh that's my own mother's voice for you...or will you have a black crown, like— him? Like my mother herself? Or my father perhaps? Now there's a thought for you. That, the greatest absence in this house. Perhaps it's as well. Or would it have made a difference? Strange how little I think of him, your father. That is my injustice. And Annie's. He had a right to be heard.

'Yet I can hardly recall his name or where he came from. Francis McClure of Prince Edward Island. Well, it's neither here nor there. It is nothing...Except a half of me, and who I am. Fancy, I had not thought of that. Was he a wildcat, a joker in the pack? I've heard he was a quiet enough man. Were there things they did not tell me? Ha, was it easier to blame it all on poor old Isabella?

'That's who this baby girl will be like. Isabella. Yes. And I'll call her Belle. For her. Belle, yes, come out little one. We'll work something out, you and me. We'll keep the midwife at bay, and when it's all over there won't be much they can do about us, you and me together. Who's to know, eh little Belle? They stick their noses in the air and come by dark...well you and I can do a little of that.'

The birds waited outside on the grass but she did not go out to them. They would have to get used to not seeing her around; they and the watchers. If indeed there were still watchers. Perhaps they knew she would not stir for now. Maybe they had gone away. But she could not take a chance.

The japonica bush was flowering, its blooms like blood spots on the shining tangled branches which needed cutting back. The flowers shimmered as she stood looking at them, but the more she stared the more harsh and urgent their colour became. She felt as if she had taken opiates, and she needed to go to the lavatory but it was too late, the water gushed around her feet and now there was blood as well and at the same moment the first pain began.

It was night. The pain had passed. The baby had stopped moving inside her.

'I think you ought to fight a bit,' she murmured to it. She lit the candle beside her but her eyes blurred. It was curiously difficult to see.

Then, like a tidal wave, the pain came surging again and she felt like a ship far out at sea hit by a monstrous wall of water and having nowhere to go except run with the elements. Maria thought she would drown.

But she knew now from where the baby would come. In the mirror above her bed she could see herself thrashing in the raging shadows of her room and she remembered the white cloth at the window.

In the mirror's reflection she saw herself, her knees drawn up and parted, and her body open. In its entrance, a sleek wet crown of hair amongst her own matted and bloody bush.

She needed them then, the watchers outside.

They can come if they will save us, she thought. The pain washed back, receded again. I can bear it, she told herself. I will not call them. They think I'm beaten but I am not. There. There, see how it goes. We will be all right.

But in the next wave she was lost, and abandoned the hope she had held so briefly. Mother, where are you? They cannot have taken you away without seeing me. Mother, I know you are listening to me, why don't you come?

Panting then. Not this bad, please not this bad. She pulled herself upright on the bed, squatting on her haunches. Pushing down, it was easier now, rocking backwards and forwards on her heels, triumphant as the crown began descending into her hand.

No, I will not take the white cloth. I will not put it in the window.

She shouted then to whoever might hear. 'I need none of you, you hear me, none of you.'

Then it stopped, the baby wedged inside her. Too weak to bear down now, she collapsed forward on her hands and knees. She could hear her voice, whimpering far away. Asking them to come.

They cannot have heard me. Or surely they would be here. Do I have to beg them? Is it that? Yes, it has come to that, I want them. The white cloth. The white cloth. Too late, I cannot get to the window, oh dear Lord. Mother. Oh please God.

A small wailing voice replied. By the candle-light, she looked down on the blanket and saw the baby lying between her legs. There, it was done. Joy, like a fresh wave, engulfed her. It will be all right, she said to the baby. I have you now. She slept again, and heard in her sleep the songs of the Gaels, and the echoes of a lament.

When she woke she was stiff and cold, and between her legs there was a cold solid mass. She could not remember for a moment what it was that had so tormented her in the night. The candle had burned down and gone out.

She put her hand on the baby, knowing without looking that it was dead.

A quiet still voice inside her said, 'There isn't any God.'

And then she repeated this blasphemy aloud.

With the spade she turned the hard earth. The paddocks were misty and cool but they held the fragrance of approaching spring. The curious wax-eyes stood a careful distance away from her.

Maria scraped the last loose earth over the grave, turned the spade over, and tamped the soil firm with the flat side.

'Maria McClure.'

At Hector's call, she leaned on the shovel. It startled her, but at the same time she had been expecting him. The watchers may have failed at their task, but she knew they would not miss a sight like this. She looked at him without speaking.

'What are you doing?' As if he did not know, could not guess.

'Burying my child. What does it look like?'

'So you killed it too?'

That was what they would think. She had known that. For two days she had lain, feverish and too weak to move, expecting her own death. She had risen once from the bed and its mess to wrap her daughter in a blanket, clearing mucous from her face. Such a pretty face it could have been, skin like pale morning, slanted eyes and a well-defined mouth, clenched though it was in death's grimace. A touch of Gael and the gumdigger's mark upon her too, a new race, my little princess, a different breed we might have brought about, if I had not failed you. Around her neck the tell-tale cord, if only she had known, could have held onto consciousness a minute, or five. A killing of sorts. A failure of will at the critical hour.

This morning as Hector stood accusing her was the first time since the birth that she was not feverish and that her legs would hold her up. She was not in a mood to argue.

'She died soon after the birth.'

'You didn't call us.'

'She came too quickly.'

'I think you're lying.' His closely shaven face gleamed as brightly as the surface of a pond. The blue eyes were chipped stone.

Maria did not answer.

'Oh not with your bare hands,' he said, 'no, I wouldn't say you killed her like that. But through your pride, which is worse.'

'If you knew what was happening in that room, uncle, pray why did you not come to my aid?'

He studied her with dislike. 'Perhaps it's better, what has happened.'

'Is there nothing you wouldn't say to me?'

'There's such a thing as natural law. How could you allow the child to die? Unless it was meant. Was it deformed?'

As he studied her, it occurred to her that this was what he expected, that the child would have some monstrous malformation through the crossing of races. She thought of the slanting eyes.

'She was perfect in every way,' said Maria evenly.

'Then it's true. You have killed twice.'

'I can't change what you think.'

'You're guilty, all right. Two deaths.'

'I wish she was alive. Not that I expect it means much to you.'

'I can't say that it does. Except, if it's true, it might take down that overweening pride of yours. Your soul is in danger.'

'My soul is my own business.'

'There is your Maker, Maria. Think on that. He can never cure you of the sickness and evil that has afflicted you. That is there for all time. But I've no doubt the Lord will do His best with you, if you say humble enough prayers to Him.'

'Your Lord may do as He chooses with you, uncle, but He need not worry about me or my business.'

'I should beat you, Maria. Only your feebleness of mind and body prevents me.' His expression registered disgust at her filthy appearance and unbuttoned clothing. Her hand flew to her throat, clutching her collar higher. She could not be sure whether he had seen the row of teeth lying against her skin.

'Do as you wish,' she said. 'You can always ask your Lord to forgive you.'

'You're sick. I can't even begin to understand you.'

'There's no great effort involved, uncle. You may consort with the Devil and all his works for all I care, it doesn't make a scrap of difference to me. There is no God, and there is no heaven and there is no hell, except that which men and women make for themselves and each other. And having known both already in my life, and knowing that my grandmother, and maybe even my mother, have known things which I know now, I have nothing more to say on this subject to you. Or to anyone else. Now, I have things to attend to, not least my appearance and general condition which so clearly troubles you. Will you excuse me?'

'It is a terrible sickness,' Hector said, but his voice was uncertain.

When she reached the door of the house, he called after her, 'When do you plan to go away?'

'I do not plan to go anywhere, uncle.'

'You will not be stopped from leaving.'

'I need time to recover my strength.'

'I see.' His agitation was growing. 'Very well. Provisions will be sent for as long as you need them.'

'That may be for a long time. I recall there is a rather large credit owing to me, uncle Hector McIssac.'

She closed the door behind her. After standing indecisively for a few minutes, Hector started to walk back to the path where his horse stood tethered, but when he had gone a few steps he came back to the gate and cupping his hands, shouted up to her. 'We wouldn't fail you at this

216

moment. You must be in torment, woman.'

By way of an answer, the curtain at the upper bedroom window was drawn across.

'We'll get you a doctor, Maria.'

The curtain was flicked back again and a pan of dirty water pitched down the steep slope of the roof below the window.

'Witch,' he screamed then. 'Witch. Witch.' He ran backwards into the paddock, stopped and seized a dry cowpat, spinning it discus-like as the schoolboys did to each other towards the door of her house.

Across the paddock by the burned-over ground, figures moved.

Watching from behind the curtain, Maria thought, he is not the only one. There are watchers who watch the watcher.

There were things for her to do. Now she would clean the house and put things in order. The grate would be emptied, the brass polished, the table shone. The cracks in the wall must somehow be papered over so that the night winds could not reach her.

Food continued to be delivered regularly to her, and whatever other provisions she needed. She left a note of what she required each week on a piece of paper under a rock by the gate. Often on sunny days a lizard crouched on the rock, as if guarding her messages.

Sometimes in the weekly provisions there would be a newspaper or two. She did not know who had placed them there, and was certain it was not her uncle. Well, whoever you are, this is a last reading, she decided as she scanned the headlines: King Dick had made a speech; it looked as if the Maoris were dying out; a new art society had been formed in Auckland. The price of butterfat was holding steady. There had been a ball at Government House. She hesitated at this last item. Gavottes or waltzes?

She would never know.

In a pail she mixed flour-and-water paste. Now she took the newspapers and pasted them over the cracks in the walls. When the first layer was dry she pasted another over the top. Soon the upstairs rooms of the house were solidly coated with newspapers.

A wind came up that night and whistled round the eaves. It did not enter by the cracks in the timber. Maria lay in bed and looked around her.

That was it, the year of 1898. It was far enough.

After that, she took the newspapers out of the box the next time they were put at the gate and left them there. When she had done this a time or two, they were not sent again.

23

Y OU'RE SITTING QUITE *still now, little bird. We just watch each other. And the wind's rising, can you hear it? See the tree moving out there? How that tree's grown. Maybe you should try the elements in the morning. Brave it, you know? What d'you think? It's good that you rest, but not for too long. We might hypnotise each other. That's what I think McLeod did to people. Aye, he hypnotised them. It must have been that. And me? I didn't think I was under his spell but perhaps I was all along. . . never moving. . . fixed by the Man's dead eye. . . . Hmmm, sooner or later one of us will die if we just keep sitting here looking at each other, little bird. One, or both of us. Do you mind dying?*

Some do, some don't.

Fear's a strange thing. You can be afraid of all sorts of things. The wrath of God, other people's way of looking at things, of Maoris and Dalmatians, of distance and separation, and yes, certainly, of death itself. But these are as nothing, these are conquerable fears, if one is not afraid of oneself. If one observes a certain truth in dealing with one's own conscience.

She had time now to read the journals, all the time in the world. At first she went over them often, but after a while they were printed in her head and she returned to them without opening the books.

The accounts of her mother's life, as seen through Isabella's eyes, appalled her. She thought over and again of the tall big-busted woman with the plain face, all jutting eyelids and high colour, understanding too late how alone she had been. How she had pursued the notion that somebody might eventually love her. No wonder she felt betrayed by her daughter.

Sometimes she almost hated the grandmother who had cast such a long shadow. And whom she was like.

Then she would go back to the journals again, read the words as they were written on the page.

Journal of Isabella McIssac, 4 January 1858

New Year has been and gone. What a pleasant occasion it was! In this house by the sunlit sea I feel as if I have lived in New Zealand forever. Such things that I can grow here, vegetables, and a profusion of flowers. Plenty of fruit to be had too. The beach beyond is known as the Cove, a shining strip of sand where the boats pass by. It is a place of wild open space, and a good deal of skulduggery goes on, which I find most entertaining. What quantities of rum are smuggled ashore! I wonder if anyone has told McLeod.

As well, there is cattle loading on a regular basis; I dish out a mug of tea to the men now and then, and in return we have a bit of a chat.

In the village the women meet, but nowadays I would just as soon leave the frolicking to Annie. It relieves me of having to see her, anyway.

Though of course I do visit her from time to time. She and her husband are very busy making money these days and to some extent prosperity takes her mind off herself. I try to avoid going when my son-in-law is there. He is a boring man, given to drink and womanising. It is hard to tell whether my poor religious ninny of a daughter is aware of these failings. Francis is so puffed up with his own prowess in the sport of catching girls in barns that he acts with that terrible complacency which fools the innocent and ignorant.

Poor Annie. I did not do well enough by her. But there, she was her father's child, a solemn creature in love with images of McLeod and his scriptural fantasies. I thought coming here we might make up for some of the failures of the past. I expected too much from both of us. She enjoys misery and I persist in enjoying myself.

Still, she is more agreeable than Hector. He's one to look out for, to fear. As punishing as McLeod, without his brains. I think he would like to make trouble for Duncan Cave, denies brotherhood with him, and is out to spread a foul rumour or two. He is no different from when he was a boy. I wish he had stayed in Nova Scotia. He is the only thing that really bothers me here.

Duncan Cave is strong now, more than a match for Hector. He works the scows that ply the coastline. I can see the boats passing from my kitchen window, and sometimes he runs his shirt up from the ropes so that I know he is aboard. For the most part he lives in Auckland and has found compatible friends. He has been introduced to botanists and other naturalists who have put his drawing talent to good use, both in his spare time and while at work on the scows, where he has an opportunity to observe coastal plant life and crustaceans in their habitat. He draws them for these researchers and is getting quite a name for himself. He is so happy.

Oh yes, Hector will have to work hard to harm him. And I have heard that Hector has a little trouble of his own on its way. He has a new wife called Rose, and they do not treat each other kindly.

Well, I should not enjoy his problems so.

No, I must deny that I do, I am simply a harmless old woman. I am batty, I live by the sea, I make plants grow. It is indeed a wonderful life.

On a night of sudden spring storm when the wind funnelled into the sky and the macrocarpa lashed at the window, Maria was disturbed by a knock at her door. She had been dozing by the fire, her knitting fallen from her lap. That year she had shorn two sheep which had appeared at her kitchen door and stayed a season. All the wool had been spun, and a large pile of it was looped around two kitchen chairs.

At first she thought the knocking was a branch come loose, banging against the side of the house. But in a lull in the storm there was another clear rapping and a man's voice calling, though it was whipped away by the wind rising again.

She put her knitting down, afraid now, her hand on her chest.

'Go away.' She listened to the sound of her own voice. She often spoke aloud to herself, but she had been outside the society of other human beings for so long that she did not know how it would sound in their ears or even if she would be understood.

'It is better for you to go away, whoever you are.'

'Please, I want to come in. I won't harm you,' called the person outside. It was the voice of a young man.

'You don't frighten me,' she lied. 'It is you who should be concerned. I'm the witch of Waipu, don't you know? Are you a stranger, or mad, that you come here this dark wet night?'

'I am your cousin, Jamie McIssac, and I must see you.'

She opened the door a fraction then. It was never locked, in the way of the people.

On her doorstep stood a young man dripping water in rivulets from heavy oilskins. She judged him not more than twenty, his hair plastered to his skull making him almost babyish in his appearance. His eyes were luminous in the light, and startled wide, terrified of something beyond or behind him.

'Please.'

'Well. All right, then, drowned rat. The winds are sweeping high and rough over Bream Tail tonight by the sound of it. But be quick about your business.'

She shut the door behind him and motioned him to the fire. With the door closed he seemed more at ease and she saw his glance flick around the room, inquisitive and darting, in spite of whatever it was that had driven him there.

'Cousin, then. Whose child are you?' Her voice was coming out quite normally. It didn't sound strange, or if it did, he appeared not to notice.

'Second cousin,' he said, as he began to untie the strings of his oilskins. 'I'm sorry about the mess.' He stood awkwardly away from the rug.

'It will dry. I do not know my second cousins.'

'The son of William McIssac and grandson of Hector.'

'Hector. Hmph. That devil. What's he been up to?'

The boy looked shocked. 'He's long dead.'

220

'Eh? Well, fancy that. I suppose he would be. It makes no difference. I can do without the McIssacs. I've nothing to say to any of them.'

'Neither have I, cousin.' Again the young man's eyes widened, as if he expected to be followed into the house.

They took stock of each other. The woman stood her distance in the shadow of the lamp by the long kauri table. She was taller than average, with fair hair turning grey bundled up behind her ears. It was very thick as if it had not been cut for a long time, or ever, and might fall at a whim. Her skin was very fine and slightly olive, as if she spent time outdoors. She was solid and well built; a slight thickening around her waist suggested that she was no longer young, and under her chin there was a tell-tale crêpiness. Otherwise she was ageless. Only her hands, large-boned and raw-knuckled, suggested any hardship.

The young man's teeth began to chatter as he considered his surroundings and the woman opposite to him.

'I'll put a log on. There, you'd better get stripped down and a blanket about you.' He blushed and she smiled. 'It's all right,' she said. 'I'm old.'

But with a sense of shock she guessed that was not how he viewed her. It was so long since she had seen herself reflected in anyone else's eyes.

'Go on,' she said firmly, hoping not to give herself away. 'It's all right, I'll get the blanket and start a mug of tea while you're at it. But you've nothing to worry about. I've seen a man's body before. A grown man's, and you're no more than a slip of a boy.'

'I'm twenty-three.'

'Are you, now? A great age, yes. The way you're shivering I'd have put you at half that. Not so brave now that you're actually here alone with Maria the witch.'

She filled the iron kettle and placed it on the hob, passing close to him as she did. 'I've got my back turned.'

'I don't know much about you, cousin. I was a child when you started living here by yourself.'

'So how is it then, that you come running to me when you're in trouble?'

Her bluntness unsettled him. 'I did not say I was in trouble.'

'You did not, but it's written all over you. Jamie McIssac, I am going now to get a blanket from my room, and while I am doing that you had better decide what you want with me, for I'm not standing round making small talk. You have a minute or so to think about it. Or else you can go.'

'If I do not?'

She turned at the foot of the stairs and looked at him, observing his thin chest which he had stripped. Again she smiled. 'You would threaten me?'

The wind howled, and beyond she thought she could hear the sea beating. The night was turning to a gale. He dropped his eyes, bright and clear in an otherwise quite ordinary face. Yet the way he held his head and moved were uncomfortably familiar, though she could not identify his appearance exactly with that of anyone she had known. Except, perhaps, her own reflection. She shivered in her turn and hoped he would not notice.

'No, of course I would not,' he was saying. 'I meant what I said. You have nothing to fear from me.'

She went upstairs then, but her heart was beating rapidly.

In the upper room she leaned her face against the glass. A corner of iron on the roof had worked loose in the storm; it rattled and shook above her. What will I do about that, she wondered. I have no ladder to get up there. It is easier to think of that than what is down below.

She could not tear herself away from the window. Night after night she had looked through the same pane of glass. She knew the stars, every one it seemed, although occasionally they surprised her. Sometimes they fell from the sky, shooting down so fast she half expected them to whistle past her, but there was no sound and they never seemed to touch the earth at all in the end. Another time, one had trailed across the sky for many weeks and she had wondered if the earth was on a collision course with the moon or sun, but that too had gone away, a shining fan of starlight that she missed when it vanished from the heavens. Tonight there were no stars, just the raging wind and the sound of the river below the house, and in the light of the sullen moon shining from behind the irresolute clouds, the gleaming filaments of toi-tois that stood along the river bank. I must get rid of him, she decided. Viewing the immensity of the night sky and the dark storm, she decided also to make scones.

She turned to face her mirror, and in spite of herself and her determination, was drawn to look at herself. She touched her hair and a strand of it fell, snaking down nearly to her waist. She drew her fingers across her skin and it felt polished and firm. What could the young man see that made him start and blush the way he did? Sometimes she had pretended to herself that she could not remember her age, that she had lost track of the years, but it was a lie. She was thirty-seven years old.

Her thoughts embarrassed her. Besides, there was too much that she knew.

She took the blanket which was folded over the foot of the bed, shook it out and returned down the narrow stairs.

Her footstep was silent. She startled him with his back to her, only the towel around his waist. But this time his discomfiture was momentary.

'You never really left, did you?' he said, pulling the blanket around himself.

'What do you mean?' she said, as she lifted the kettle. She would have liked to give him a good rub down, his skin was so goose-pimply.

222

He scratched the inner calf of one leg with the toe of his other foot. 'You were banished, weren't you?'

'If that's what they told you.'

'Why did they?'

'I can't remember. Oh, it doesn't make much difference, does it? Whatever they say, the choice is mine now. I could walk out of here if I wanted to. At least I think so. They can't watch me forever. It sounds as if poor old Hector doesn't get much of a chance these days. Unless they pickled his eyeballs and put them in a glass jar on a fence post.' She saw his expression then. 'Ha, don't speak ill of the dead, eh? . . . You're easily shocked.'

'No. No, I'm not. You surprise me, that's all.'

'Do I now? Well, I surprise myself too. I've spoken more words to you in the last half hour than I've spoken to any human being in—oh, I don't know—how long has it been? What year is it?'

'1914.'

'Ah, yes, so it is.'

'Don't you really know?'

She was sure he would recognise her craftiness for what it was. 'I was just making sure. Sixteen years or thereabouts.'

'It's a long time.'

'Aye. But I could have worse company than my own, and the birds, and the rustle of the grasses in summer, and the falling of leaves and the rising of the wind in winter. And the odd wild creature that saunters in on me. Like yourself. Not that it's ever been human before.'

Maria lifted down mugs and filled them with tea.

'You're not like I thought.' He looked larger, more rakish now, his light brown hair drying out in a wavy tangle and the blanket around him like a cloak.

She resisted the temptation to ask him just what it was he had expected. I am being too easily drawn, she sensed. He was avoiding an explanation of himself as he began to adopt a comfortable attitude, sitting beside her fire, drinking tea. She turned uncertainly to the bench.

Taking her largest basin from the cupboard she opened the flour bin and measured out three cups. 'Why are you here?' Her hands kneaded butter into the flour, dough collecting under her fingernails. She had never cooked for a man, nor watched her mother do so either, for that matter. Something women did for men in spite of themselves, she suspected.

Jamie hesitated. She was aware of the old house and the rainy night pressing in on them. The winds might have blown from off the Highlands, through the brown machair grass that bent beside the Atlantic, or through the elegant grey branches of the birch trees stripped in winter on the coast of Nova Scotia. Across the world, the winds and the voices tramped.

We are alone, trapped at the end of our destiny at the bottom of the world.

'Why, cousin Jamie, why are you here?'

He had to answer her now. But he lifted his head, turning it this way and that, as if fearing attack on open ground.

'They would have me go to war.'

'War? What war is that?'

'You do not know?'

'Tell me of it.'

He shook his head, disbelieving. 'You have heard of the Boer War?'

This time she was ashamed to admit her ignorance, but she straightened her shoulders and said with a touch of defiance, 'I have not heard of it.'

'It was in Africa.'

'Africa. That is the way we came.' He stared at her without comprehending. 'The way our people came, by Cape Town, which is at the end of Africa. Nice country, I've heard, though very dry.'

'I don't know much about that journey,' he said.

'Oh but you must, the old people always tell of it, of how they came here.'

He turned a shoulder up, a puzzled gesture. 'We don't listen to the old people so much now. There are other things happening in the world.'

'So it seems. So...what is this war in Africa?'

'No, that's the one my father went to, and his brother. This is another war in another place. What I'm trying to tell you...since the Boer War, they're patriotic here. Everyone goes to war for the sake of the country.' He saw her pause for a moment at the bench, as if sensing his uncertainty. He hurried on. 'Oh it's right enough, I suppose, we must defend our beliefs. The values of the old country.'

'Like Culloden?'

'Culloden? Now that is an old war.'

'But is it like that? Are those the things you're fighting for?'

He told her then of the war sweeping Europe, of the press across France, seemingly to England's borders. All the time he talked to her, he was watching her strong hands at work in the dough, moulding it, dividing it into squares, and her back, very straight, held against him. The war, he said, had already been in progress for many months, for they were now into September, and the German troops had come close to Paris. All able-bodied young men were being called upon to serve, although the ones who worked on the land were exempt so far, unless they chose to go.

'And are you not on the land?' she asked, closing the oven.

He shook his head. 'My two older brothers are on the farm. I'd begun studying medicine.'

'You had chosen that? Why?'

'I'd rather heal than kill.'

'Ah. So you don't want to go to this...this war?'

He looked miserable, as if she had seen through him and might disapprove.

'I see. I do see.' She sat down on the chair opposite him.

And to his relief he felt that she did see, although he did not understand why he should think this of an odd reclusive and uninformed woman, such as Maria was.

'So you stood up to them,' she said.

'Yes.'

'And what do they say about that?'

Although he smiled, he appeared to mock her when he replied. 'They said I was like you.'

'They did?' It seemed very hot in the room. She felt threatened by the fire and the noise of the storm. And yet she was amused, enlivened by a memory of the past. 'Wild? Rebellious?' she asked.

'Aye, and headstrong.'

Suddenly they were both laughing.

'Did no one teach you better ways?'

'That's exactly what they said. You see, I've never done what they wanted. Studying medicine costs money. I was to have gone into the timber trade. But that's not what I wanted, so I've worked my way through university, loading cargo on the wharves down south at Port Chalmers, and in Auckland in the holidays. Then this war came. I stayed away from home, but word was sent that my mother was ill. I can tell you, she recovered fast enough when I got back, or at first she did. Then my father started on at me about joining up. They'll let me finish my degree father, I said to him. I'm so nearly finished, and then, think if I did go, how much more use I'd be in the war.'

'Did you believe that?'

'Yes, in the beginning, because it was the truth. But all he could see was the shame of me staying at home, and I began to question why it mattered so much. I came to the conclusion that it was just his pride.'

'I know about pride.'

'You know what I mean about him, then?'

'Oh aye, but pride has its merits too. It's knowing when to stop that's important. What happened then, did you give in?'

'Aye. My mother fell to vapours again and in a weak moment...well, I enlisted.'

'So now you have to go?'

His voice was grim. 'It means I am a deserter. I can be arrested and taken away.'

'What makes you think I would harbour you?'

The rain outside had stopped and the air held an unnatural stillness, marking the passage of the storm down the island.

'If we are alike, as they say, I thought maybe you'd help me.'

There was a pause in the conversation. 'So you are William's son,' she said idly, as if picking up the conversation somewhere else, and although he had already told her this. 'What of Neil?'

'Neil and his wife are childless. I am William's youngest son. The dispossessed.' As she raised her eyebrows in puzzlement, he added: 'The landless one. Not that it matters, I wouldn't make a farmer's shovel. Do you know my father?'

She shook her head and knelt to gather scones from the oven. It seemed that all her life was concentrated in small actions. She needed time to think. It was clear that he must stay the night, but in the morning she would make him go. She must for her own sake. What became of him was neither here nor there, if he went in the morning. If he stayed longer, she might desire his company. She could see that this might be possible, though she had thought that it was not. She had stayed a long time, guarding the grave of her child under the japonica bush; there was no other constancy, no known way that she could change her life now. She did not want anyone to come in and change it for her.

She spread the humped brown scones with red jelly. No mountain ash or cloudberries here, but there were japonica apples to collect from the bush, which did as well. Everything in her life had an order, a way of doing things, each act marked the progression of her life; she knew, more than this young man could ever know, what day it was and where the moon would be each quarter and what the state of the grass would be outside from one season to the next. She could call up birds and milk a cow and pull its calf (for there was a cow that ranged free from the herd that cropped at her boundary). Quietness was the only peace she sought and already Jamie's voice filled her house. Her ears were having difficulty in coping with the sound of him in the room. Beside the fire, he seemed to fill all the spaces which she protected. Air and clean space around her, that was what she wanted. And no, she did not want to touch or be touched by another human being, not ever again in her life.

Some nights, towards daybreak, she thought her daughter spoke to her; when she did, she answered back and told her the old tales, stories of men and women who set sail across the seas, who built log cabins and toiled in snow and embarked again towards heat and open plains. She heard her voice in the river and on the wind that stole over the hummocky hill across the way and rustled in the toi-toi answering her, and this was all the conversation she needed. She did not want those voices stilled by the presence of another.

She watched him eat, found herself savouring the pleasure it gave her and wished that it did not. 'Are you afraid to die, then?' she asked Jamie.

He stopped, put the food carefully back on the plate. 'I am afraid to die a pointless death,' he said at last. 'Does that make me a coward?'

She considered this. As she reflected, he noted the poise of her head, and it was as if he had always known her, for everything about her was familiar too.

'I can't see that it does,' she said at last. 'There's a difference between you and me, isn't there? You see,' she said, hurrying on, 'I have expected to die more than once. And then, I have been twice accused of causing death. In that I am sure that I have more experience than you.'

'They can't really believe that of you,' he exclaimed. 'It's like witches, and burning at the stake.'

'Oh I call up storms, and make milk curdle, and cause the crops to fail, you don't know.' She was on the verge of laughter again.

'But that's what they do say.' Immediately he wanted to bite the words back and he lowered his eyes.

'Of me? Of course they would. It was what the old people said of witches.'

'Did you? Kill those people?' He attempted a little bravado to cover what had been said, for he had believed she had been using a figure of speech. He saw a stoniness then behind her eyes, and faltered. 'I'm sorry. I didn't mean...'

He thought she might not speak to him again.

'Did I kill them? I don't know,' she said. 'Don't think I haven't asked myself. For a long time I questioned every day. But then I began to think that my mother would have died anyway, remembering the times when she had been ill before she left me. Maybe I make excuses for myself, but I cannot believe it was altogether my doing. And as for the child, I believe, oh I believe...'

But she stopped, for she had been going to say what she believed, that the child still lived on. She could see that that would not do at all, and besides, it was clear from his expression that this was something of which he was not aware.

'It is true,' she said with an effort, after more time had passed. 'I had a child. The father was gone and I was unwed. They didn't tell you that?'

His face was red. 'We don't talk about such matters. We wouldn't be told.'

'No, I can see that. Ah well, we've talked, what more do you want of me? Isn't this enough?' I will not encourage him, she was thinking, he will have to say for himself what it is that he wants.

'Shelter me for a few days.' He was urgent again, and she could see that he might be a forceful man in his prime. 'They'd never think of looking for me here. Then, in a little while, I can slip off and make my own way.'

'And then?'

'Plead my cause, make them understand that I would be more use to them as a doctor than a soldier.' He faltered. 'I'm not sure, some simply refuse to go, but I don't know whether that's what I want to do or not. Maybe I would go on a hospital ship if they'd let me, at least it would be of some use. But I need time. Just to think, to work it out in my head, you understand?'

'We'll bank the fire tonight and you can sleep by it. We'll see how things look in the morning.'

'I'll fix your roof.'

'You heard it, then?'

'Aye.'

'I said. . . we shall see.'

As she began to ascend the stairs, he called after her. 'Wasn't it enough just to punish you? Why are they still afraid of you?'

She turned and considered him. She smiled slightly but her eyes were grave. 'Because of the pleasure,' she said. 'At the time, I enjoyed my sins. You do understand, don't you?'

In the morning, while he mended the roof, she watched the paddocks with increasing anxiety. She believed it impossible for anyone to come close to the house without her knowing, so acute was her hearing and so well trained her eyesight to any movement amongst grass or trees. Still, she was uneasy.

When he came down from the roof, she said, 'I think you should stay inside a day or so. The hammering on the iron may have carried.'

'I'm sure there was nobody around, I could see clear across to the Centre and the Lion of Scotland.'

'What is the Lion of Scotland?'

'The new monument. Don't you know about that, either?'

He is just a boy really, she thought, encountering his clear gaze.

'What is it there for?' she asked.

'The migrations. The ships. McLeod.'

'Oh, so they remember a little of it?'

'Yes, of course they do.' He was half exasperated. 'But the community's changing. I told you, people think of other things too, the world beyond. Waipu's too small for all of us now.'

Or too large if it is all the world you know, Maria thought as she undid her hair in front of the mirror that night. It shone in the candle-light. She had washed it that afternoon, and afterwards she had sat in the sun with it hanging to her waist as it dried. Inside, the young man had fixed cupboards and a loose board on the stair, pretending that he was not looking at her but she knew that he was.

'What do they think of McLeod now?' Maria asked Jamie on the third night that he sat before her fireplace.

'My father speaks of him as if he were God Himself.'

'And you?'

'I think he was more like a devil.'

'A youthful view?'

'Not just the young people. You must know that. What about our grandmother, cousin? The one they called Isabella?'

'Isabella?' She was startled. '*My* grandmother. Oh well. I think maybe she had the measure of him better than most. In the end.'

'But did she like him?'

'Like? Oh I wouldn't have said that. One didn't like McLeod. No, it was my mother, your great-aunt, who was enthralled. Or so it seemed to me. Though it could be, the poor creature, that there was naught much else for her.'

He looked at her curiously. Often she appeared to talk more to herself than to him, yet he suspected there was always a point to what she said.

'We should be going up, it's late. I've made up the bed in mother's room for you.'

'You have? Why don't you sleep in there yourself?' He had observed in his explorations of the house that it was a large and much more comfortable bed than the one she slept in, with a deep feather mattress and fat plumped-up pillows. The upstairs portion of the house unnerved him, lined as it was with darkly ageing newspapers. Faded pink and blue crocheted mats hung like abandoned cobwebs on the dressers. He thought it looked like the inside of a mad castle, or Miss Haversham's house, although Maria, even in her long and unfashionable clothes, did not fit this image. He hesitated at the thought of sleeping up there, and besides, he was unsure as to whether she really wanted him to go up, or if she was merely being polite.

'It's never seemed like my bed to sleep in,' she said. And it was true. Isabella had slept there, and after her death Annie had returned to the bed she had vacated on her mother's behalf. Maria's room was screened off from the second room, small and narrow under the steep roof which had seemed large when it was built, but never quite big enough for three women living alongside of one another. When Isabella died and Annie moved back into the main bedroom, Maria felt she had made great progress in having the second room all to herself. Later, alone in the house, she dusted the larger room and polished the arched bed-ends which stood as high as her shoulder. Once a year, she turned the mattress. But when she had finished these tasks she pulled the door behind her each time with a sigh of relief. She felt like an intruder in the room and it occurred to her that while there were voices she still listened to and for, Annie's was one she did not wish to hear again. It would be bad enough

229

for her reproaches to be repeated; even worse would be the constant expressions of her love, more pathetic and misjudged than her anger. More demanding, too, of an answer, and Maria knew of no answers across the years as to why love had so failed them, why love appeared always to have failed her mother.

It was better that she did not sleep in the room.

'I'm sure my mother would have given you the best bed in the house,' Maria said. 'Come on, I've aired the blankets for you, didn't you see them on the windowsill today? It's a waste for the bed to stand empty.'

In the dark she lay awake, her eyes as dry and crisp as crackling, and through the wall she could hear him breathe, the deep even breathing of a young man sleeping. She touched herself deeply between her legs and at first was ashamed to find herself wet, and then, hearing him call out in his sleep, went to work on herself with a steady intimate hand, and when she had done, began to weep for the first time in many years.

It came to her then that she was different from the women who had gone before her. They had been made afraid, and denied choice through circumstances and violation, and what had happened to them had made them turn away from accepting themselves as they were. Nor had she ever made a choice of her own, acting always blindly and without thought. She was not certain, even now, what it was she wanted. Feeling the matter to be beyond resolution, she fell into an uneasy sleep.

At daybreak it was not the voice of her child she heard, but the young man's, as if taking up from some point where she had been in the night. She swung her feet onto the floor and sat on the edge of the bed for a moment or so. Hesitating a little longer, she unfastened the teeth from around her neck. After that, she got up and stole to the door of his room. It was ajar and she pushed it gently open.

He was still asleep. Crossing the floor on her bare feet she sat on the bed beside him, at first afraid to touch him, but then as he appeared racked by his dream she put her hand on his shoulder.

Immediately he opened his eyes and saw her on the bed. He put his arm about her and pulled her towards him, with his free hand opening her nightdress. Her breasts were large and tight, with pain around the nipples. She cried out as he fastened his mouth on her breast but as he sucked her the pain began to dissolve and she could hardly wait for him to start the other one; she wished he could have fitted them both in his mouth at once, it was so pleasurable. He is like my child after all, she thought.

But he was drawing her into the hot nest of the bed and it was clear that he was more than a child. He moved aside in the bed for her but immediately she had lain down he was untwining her knees with his own so that she was spread beneath him. She turned this way and that for a moment as if resisting.

He drew back, asking her without words what it was that she wanted and whether he was to be allowed to proceed. She touched her breast with a gesture of anguish, where his mouth had been, and then placed her fingertips on his face. I am in charge here, she thought; he is, at least, allowing me a decision. But it is hopeless, the decision is already made. I am like a ripe peach, all soft fur and ready to yield.

He moved in towards her.

Outside, the morning was alight and the room was flooded with sun. Maria was shaken by the light and the fragile sound of her own voice.

'Don't leave me,' he said every time when, of necessity, she left the bed.

They had been there for days; she felt blurred with exhaustion and at times her legs would hardly hold her up when she did walk across the room. They ate scantily of the remains of food in the house and slept fitfully. She had never slept in a bed with anyone before, except when she was a small child, with Isabella. Now she was becoming afraid of empty space beside her.

She thought of herself as a cave. There were those other caves in the history of her people, the dark caves where people had hidden, and the caves in the hills beyond Waipu where the glow-worms shone, and she thought that now she was the shining place that would provide a haven.

'What do you dream of?' he asked her one morning.

'That I am walking around the room with my head just below the ceiling. It is like flying or floating, or something of both. That is what witches do, you know, they ride the air.'

He laughed. 'It must be nice. I wish that I could do that.'

'Tell me then, what do you dream of?'

He looked sideways at her on the pillow, and his eyes clouded over. She remembered him calling out in his sleep.

'I dream that I am already dead,' he said.

Sooner or later, Maria knew that she would have to get up and go outside. If she missed collecting her groceries someone would be bound to seek her out. Besides, the fire had not been lit for several days, and the absence of smoke might invite attention from beyond.

When at last she did get up, late one afternoon, she all but crawled around in the kitchen preparing food then dressed to go out to collect firewood. She felt light-headed and giddy.

Outside, the yard was full of the navy light of evening. The paddocks lay still and dark green, and several cows had come over the hill in front of the house, grazing against the skyline. One of them shook its head, appeared to prick up its ears. Along the track a fine eddy of white dust

231

stirred and hung on the air. It is nothing, she told herself, the cow has heard the bull roar in the distance, it is the wind that throws up the dust. There is no one near. Brown ducks marched in formation towards the river, flopped over the bank, and dropped into the water. That's not unusual either, she decided, it is evening and they are going downstream to wait out the night. The river looked the same as ever.

She picked up the axe, and lifted it above her head, bringing it down over and again with strong, steady strokes, cleaving the wood. When a pile lay at her feet, she gathered it up and looked around. The hairs along her arms prickled. She put the wood down again, and took a few steps away from the house, thinking that she would walk up the hill and survey the landscape as far as she could.

She had a swift vision then, of a nameless army whose faces she could not imagine, sweeping over and down the hill towards the house to scoop up Jamie and take him away before she could save him.

So I am guarding the house, she thought, is that it? She knew it was so, and that she would not risk leaving him alone. He had committed himself to her care, and it was clear that she could not forsake him, nor turn her back upon him for a moment.

For what would become of her, if she were left on her own again?

Although she knew she would come to that. But not yet. She was not ready.

'Will you tell me about Isabella, our grandmother?' he asked.

'Why do you want to know so much?'

'She's a legend.'

'Oh, she was just an old woman,' she said quickly, wishing to change the subject. Too quickly.

'You don't want me to know about her,' he said, and for the first time there was a tension between them.

'I'm sorry.' She spoke rapidly, wishing to dispel it. 'It's true, I loved her in such a way that everyone else was excluded. Not that it mattered, because no one else could be bothered with her very much. She loved me so much, in return, as if I were a light seen after a long time of darkness. We were at each other's centre.'

She fell silent, and watching her, Jamie left her alone. For her memory was printing the words of Isabella's journal before her as surely as if the page was open in her lap.

1878

Annie is with child again and that no-good husband of hers has up and died on her, so she is moaning and carrying on that she won't manage. The truth being, I suppose, that she will not. So I am to move in with her.

Perhaps I am too hard on her. I always have been. If it is not too late, maybe this is a final chance for us to make something of each other. And I am an old woman, I might as well put what's left of my life to some useful purpose. Who knows, this child might survive and be the miracle I thought would never happen, the granddaughter I have in idle and most indulgent moments dreamed of having.

For what is there in this life, if we have no links with past or present? In this community where the ghosts of our ancestors walk with the living, I seem set to be singularly alone. For circumstance denies me connection with Hector's family, and what good would come of it anyway, knowing what I do? And remembrance of my other son desolates me, and teases me with the mysteries of his life...I have waited a long time for something that may never happen, a child who might never be born. But if it was, oh, how I should love that child.

Finally Maria broke the silence. Something inside her ached, as if her bones were betraying her. 'After my grandmother died there seemed to be nothing. People thought it was odd. She had become so ugly. And cantankerous. But never to me. They couldn't understand why I loved someone who was, in the end, so grotesque.'

'I heard she had always been bad-tempered.'

'No, that's not so. Maybe disappointed.'

'Why was that?'

'Oh, who can say? Many things. The death of Duncan Cave I suppose.'

'Who was that?'

'An uncle.'

'I never heard of him.'

'Maybe that's not surprising. I think she had conceived images of love, but they were difficult to realise.' She knew he wanted her to tell him of the mysterious uncle, but how could she do that without telling him of the journals, the secrets that rustled inside this house?

'You were certainly close to her,' he said.

'Closer than I've been to anyone,' said Maria, and saw him wince. He is so young, she thought again, wanting to have me all to himself; that is the way I was.

She put her hand on his face, leaving it to rest there. She wondered how true it was, what she had said to him. How well had she really known Isabella; how much had she been intended to know? Isabella might have said that finding out was not the same as knowing. Had she thought the secrets of her life would be useful to Maria? Perhaps she had forgotten, with age, what it was she was leaving behind. There were things which now, at this moment, Maria would have preferred not to know.

But Isabella had told her more than once to make her choices, and she has chosen to know the secrets.

'I wish I'd known her,' Jamie was saying. 'My father never spoke of her. He didn't seem to know her at all.'

'Well. She was very old,' she said by way of excuse. She saw his look. 'It was not a close family.'

'I remember you. In church,' he said. 'You were my family then.' He traced the line of her collarbone with his finger, touched it with the tip of his tongue.

'You were nothing but a baby.' Her voice was sharper than she intended.

He paused. 'Still, I remember you.'

In her mind she explored the edges of her treachery.

When Jamie had been there for more than a fortnight she saw someone passing the house. He looked like many of the local farmers, with strong, lined features and the large bony frame of some of the northernmost Highlanders. He guided his horse along the track without looking to the left or right and his hat was drawn so low that she might not have recognised him. But the shape was too familiar. It was William McIssac.

Every evening Maria and Jamie heated the copper and poured warm water over each other as they knelt in the tin tub. Tonight, when they had towelled themselves dry, she sent him ahead of her upstairs, and when he had gone she freshly ironed his clothes and took them up to the room with her, laying them beside the bed.

'Why are you doing that?' he asked.

She shrugged. 'There's a restless feeling in the air. You should be thinking of going soon.'

'You're tired of me?'

'I could never be that.'

'Are we being watched?'

'I don't know. There's nothing I can tell for sure. But when you've been watched for as long as I was, you get a feeling for it. I might be wrong. But it's an instinct I've had since you first came, and it's getting stronger.'

She touched his face. 'I've had other things on my mind since then. It's difficult to know what is happening.'

He drew her into the bed. 'We can stay together.'

'No. They wouldn't let us. And you've got your future to think of.'

'I can't see it coming to much now.'

She shook her head and drew the candle towards them, close to her own face. 'Look at me, Jamie. Soon I'll be old. I've nothing to take into the world with you. It's too late. And you, you'd fade away and die here with me. In the end. Look at you, you're fading from lack of sunlight already.'

234

'I'm not ready to go.'

This is no cave, she reflected, but a palace he has, he will never have better than this.

'I'm not going,' he said, apparently decided.

'You must. I am telling you to leave.' They stared at each other, both implacable.

'Then I must show you,' she said at last. She got out of bed and went to the dresser, pulling open the drawer which held Isabella's journals. She found the one she sought and handed it to him. 'I'm going downstairs for a while,' she said.

At the door she looked back at him. 'Forgive me,' she said.

Downstairs, she sat and dozed by the fire.

1865

Hector and Rose have had a child, a boy named William. He is my first grandchild, as was pointed out with increasing excitement as the time of Rose's confinement came closer. Naturally, when the hour arrived I was sent for, and I did help the midwife with various small services. Annie was there with sleeves rolled up, making a great show of pleasure and chattering about the fact that 'at least one member of the family was getting things right', meaning successful childbirth.

Anyway, all of our help was largely superfluous, as the child slipped into the world with very little trouble, and Rose, smiling a Madonna-like smile, held the baby up, waiting for us to praise her accomplishment. Which I duly did, in the presence of the others.

At last Rose and the boy and I were left on our own in the room. The general opinion was that I had been overcome with emotion and needed time to study the child in peace.

'He is a handsome child,' I said reiterating my applause. I paused, summoning my most dramatic effect. Then I said: 'I wonder what Francis will think of him.'

It was cruel, but then those who know me would not be surprised how irresistible I found the situation. And she has been so uppity with me, this Rose.

The colour drained out of her face. 'Who told you?' she whispered at last.

It was something of a guess but I was not really surprised that it landed on the mark. McLeod and I do not like each other much better than we ever have, but old age and mutual solitariness sometimes draw us together, and when he is out riding—which he is able to do less and less these days—he stops by my door, enquiring with civility after my health, and in return, I give him a mug of tea and a bannock cake. He is a lonely fellow since Mary died, though he won't admit it. He tells me this and that when he is passing, and sometimes offers a little information which he thinks I would be the better for hearing. The subject of Rose has come up, told to me as a pastoral matter though not pursued, for Rose is outside the old community, and Hector's problem.

Besides, it was not much McLeod told me—a whisper of yellow skirt in a barn door and Francis hurrying down the road. But I had felt in my bones that he was right.

Well, I think it is all a bit of a joke.

Towards midnight, he joined her by the fire.

'William is my brother. Or near enough.' Maria's voice was dull.

'I know.' He touched the nape of her neck. Come back upstairs,' he said. 'The fire's nearly out.' When she did not move, he took her hand, pulling her roughly to her feet. 'Come with me,' he said.

As if in a trance, she followed him up the stairs. When she was in bed, beside him again, she said, 'You will go, won't you?'

Wearily, he replied that he would.

They did not sleep for the rest of the night, but lay talking. They talked of love and kissed each other a great deal. Afterwards, she would think that there were things she could have asked him about the world beyond. When he left she would know little more than when he came, but as she lay beside him it seemed unimportant; there would never be time for this again. There would be no more lovers.

'Tell me about the old people again,' he said once during the night, thinking of what he had read.

So she lay on her back, a little apart from him, and told him of the dark abysses under the Nova Scotian ice, where a person might fall and never be seen again, especially if they ventured forth upon it when the spring thaw was coming; and about the way the moss smelled, coming up for air when the melting was finally over. She spoke of the wild strawberries that grew there in summer, and the sweet maple syrup that was collected under the trees; the way the rocks were worn smooth by the sea, and the way it was a harsh land, but beautiful too. Then she recited the names of the ships again, and the families that had travelled on them, and it was as if she had been there herself.

'It will be lost,' he said, 'in time it will all be lost,' and his voice was full of desolation.

Around four in the morning he held her closely for the last time. 'Will you be safe?' he asked.

'As safe as I've ever been.'

The last thing she asked him before he left was what he had decided to do about the war. It was a subject which had not been raised again since the beginning.

'I'm not going to war,' he said. 'They'll have to take me there by force.'

The stars going out were as she imagined snowflakes when they were falling and melting before they touched the ground.

'That is the bravest decision,' she said. 'That is what courage is about.'

Which was more than she thought she would ever regain when he slipped out of bed and pulled on his clothes. She wanted to go to the door with him, but he asked her to stay in the bed, not to leave it until he had gone. At the door, he looked at her once more. 'You must always sleep in that bed,' he said. 'It's more comfortable....Besides, you are in charge here now.'

As if he knew how the other women had occupied the shadows in the room.

When she heard the creak of the back door she got out of bed and went to the window to watch his shadow flicker against the macrocarpa tree, then dart towards the river. Long after, she would think that that was her mistake, not to have done just as he asked. For her own shadow had loomed against the window.

Now the dawn had broken and what she feared might happen to her was true. She could hear voices no longer, and calling to her daughter, there was no reply.

Outside, in the raw thin light, the grass smelled faintly astringent under the cool dew. The japonica flowers shone like blood. She stripped off all her clothes, shivering violently as she lay down on the wet grass, tearing up handfuls of it and washing her body, her breasts and between her legs.

Back inside the house, she went up the narrow stairs to the bed and lay down. She had taken her necklace from the dresser of the old room as she passed through it, but now as she clutched it she was uncertain of its power. Her belly was full of fire and pain and she knew that she was about to bleed.

For a week she lay there, barely moving, and when her foremothers spoke she did not answer them. All she heard was a new, quietly insistent voice asking her over and over again, 'What have you done to Jamie, your cousin?' And another would respond, 'What has she done to her cousin, who is also her brother's child?'

She turned her face to the wall, 'I don't want to hear you, it doesn't have to be true,' she said aloud.

And asked herself again, and a hundred times, why she had shown him the journal.

24

MARIA LAY ON THE feather mattress throughout a week of fog and indifferent weather. The mists cleared at last and the sun shone again. She got up then and cleared the room of all traces of its joint possession, making up the bed with clean sheets and putting a clean nightdress under the pillow. Outside it was truly spring. Her plum tree was flowering and the cow waited with swollen udders at the gate.

When she had fresh milk, she separated the cream to make butter, and set loaves of bread. In the evening she made up the fire and took up her knitting again, threading grey wool on her needles to knit a man's jersey.

One morning late in the summer that followed she was tying back tomatoes at the back of the house. She could not decide what to do with all the fruit; the vine was breaking with its weight and the skins splitting in the sun as they ripened before her eyes.

She did not hear William's approach. It was several months since she had last seen him and when she looked up and saw him standing beside her, the air seemed very still, only the shrill cicadas reminding her of life about them.

A ra ra te ki-te ki-te, they cried, across the hot quiet day, *a ra ra te ki-te.*

William's gaze was unfriendly, his eyes bitter and narrow as he stood beside her.

'Well?' she said. She could barely restrain her glance, raking his face for traces of Jamie. There was little she recognised, and yet there was about him what in other circumstances might have been a comfortable warmth. He was a big solid man, with creases deeply folded down his cheeks and under his chin. His hands were blunt and worn.

'His ship was sunk at sea.'

The back of her hand flew to her mouth as she stifled a small sharp cry.

'So it does move you?'

'He is lost?' Then she tried to recover herself, although on reflection she could not see that it made much difference. The whole scene had a slow inevitability about it, as if it had all been played before. 'If you mean your son, he called here once,' she said, taking up the twine again to tie up another vine.

'You sheltered him.'

'If that's what you think.'

'I know. I know what you did, Maria McClure.'

Her fingers felt numb. She pulled the knot too tight and the string bit through the stem of the vine, so that the upper half of it toppled over. Why am I doing this, she wondered. A caterpillar crawled lazily along the leaf, arching its back in ripples that reached from end to end. She flicked it to the ground with her thumb and forefinger and its green innards exploded in a small pulpy heap.

'So you sent him to war,' she said.

'Aye, we did.'

She looked him up and down then with what she hoped he would read as contempt. Yet what she saw did not really stir contempt in her, only a deep pity which for the moment must take the place of grief. A sort of cousin, a kind of brother. Who else knew? Or would she carry the secrets to her own grave? She scanned him covertly as she knelt to collect up a handful of tendrils that were escaping her trellis. His eyes were the colour of Black Doris plums with the same opaqueness extending over the pupils. A thicket of black hairs grew in his nose and ears. She might have liked this stranger. What friends they could have been! But instead, they were talking of Jamie.

She straightened up and put her scissors in her pocket. 'I might have known you would catch him. It made me ill at the time, thinking of you baiting traps, as if he was a rat instead of a man. Your own son. Dead eh? You must be proud.'

His face collapsed inwards. 'You think I wanted him dead? Listen to me, witch, the boat that he would have sailed on, except for your meddling, arrived at its destination safe and sound. You are the guilty one.'

'I see. So that is what you've really come to tell me.' She dug both hands in the pocket of her apron so that he would not see them shaking.

Above their heads swam the relentless sun, and a flock of gulls wheeling towards the sea. The centre from one of her sunflowers suddenly fell, a pile of brown seeds scattering, covering the earth below. Everything is collapsing and dying, things so ripe and pretty and deathly, she thought.

'You have other sons,' she commented, knowing this was so.

His mouth hardened so much it all but disappeared. 'They have gone to take his place. There is no one left on the farm but me,' he answered.

He took three or four steps down the path, stopped and turned back. 'My father knew you for a murdering woman. It is not true, I said to him, you are too hard on her. But he was not hard enough. They burned people like you at the stake once, and even that would be too good for you.'

She raised her eyes to his, but he shrank as if her gaze might have some evil effect. 'You've got no remorse, have you? You do not care. The third killing, Maria McClure.'

He walked away. *A ra a ra te ki-te ki-te.* The air was fretful with the

239

insects' clamour and an approaching summer storm.

My brother. More or less. She was sure it should have mattered more. After this war abroad they would never be the same. McLeod had called upon them to take care of each other, to keep out the world's madness; he could not prevent what happened inside.

I am what happens when people get lost. It seems that I cannot make new paths. I have tried that, and failed. But I am a reminder. A conscience, perhaps? What kind of fate is that?

In the morning she thinks she hears another stone. She believes it is the next morning, though suddenly, after all these years, she is really losing track of time. The night is without shape, she cannot remember what has taken place. The house is very cold, and she realises that there are holes downstairs letting in the wind. Yes, it is so very cold. Though the wind is not as high as she expected, as if the storm has veered away to the south, missing Waipu.

But the air is keen as if there is a frost outside. The bird is still on its perch, its feathers ruffled. Perhaps it has had enough too?

Painfully she gets out of bed, talking aloud to the bird. It does not budge, but opens one eye, bright still but bad-tempered.

Her voice is doubtful.

'Perhaps you should stay there after all. I don't know what to do with you. It's no good staying here.'

The sparrow does not move. She sighs.

'I'll feed you though. You know that?'

Her hands feel clumsy as she crumbles a piece of bread from the tray beside her. She throws the crumbs into the middle of the floor, half expecting the bird to refuse.

But it stretches its wings, turns its head from side to side, then flies down to the bread. It thrusts its head backwards and forwards at her with rapid darting motions, as if inviting a dispute.

'It'll do you no good,' she says. 'Sooner or later, you have to take a chance again.'

25

WHEN MARIA WAS nearly forty-three, a man arrived at her door towards dusk on a winter afternoon. It had been a bright day, cloudless and sunlit in spite of the season. The first stars were appearing like pin-points against the hollow shining sky. The grass glittered with a hint of frost.

The man was elderly, dressed in baggy trousers tied with twine at the waist and ankles. Around his shoulders he wore a cloak made of sacking.

'You must come, Miss,' he said, gesturing across the paddocks.

She shrank back into the shadow beside her door.

'Come where? I can't come anywhere.'

'You must.' Behind his stubble of beard, the man's race was indeterminate, but she could see that his features were very dark. He held his hat in his hand, turning it over anxiously. It was so threadbare and worn that the brim seemed about to part from the crown. His bald head shone like polished kauri wood. Trying to summon up some explanation for his appeal he stammered and had difficulty with his words. She saw then that he was shaking. She was not sure whether it was from fear or illness.

'Come in,' she said, opening the door wider. At least this one would not be staying a month. He took an anguished look over his shoulder, as if he were seeing the light for the last time, and stepped over her doorstep. The kettle was boiling. She emptied it into the teapot. It is my answer to everything, she thought. But at least the sight of such ordinary activity, and the offer it implied, calmed the man. He started to speak again, his teeth, where there were any, were almost worn to his shrivelled gums.

'We have the 'flu with us,' he said, and suddenly she recognised his accent.

'You are Dalmatian?'

He nodded. 'A Dally, yes.'

For an incredulous moment she looked at him, but it was not Branco. What am I thinking of, she asked herself, this is a really old man, and the man I am remembering would only be a little older than I am. She handed him a cup which he took and drank thirstily.

'We have the 'flu,' he said again.

'I don't understand.'

'The epidemic. The plague. It is here.'

She shook her head. Despite his agitation, the man appeared to believe that he had told her all that was needed.

'A sickness? Yes?'

He mustered himself with a considerable effort. Clearly he had decided she was simple, and he was no longer afraid of her. As he leaned forward, earnestly trying to make her understand, his cloak fell forward and she saw that he wore an odd little bag around his neck. She noticed a pungent odour, much more refreshing than his appearance suggested. Now he fingered the bag.

'It is the camphor bag we have been given. It is to keep away the sickness. Many people ill. The sickness, some say, come off ships, some say it is for God, for wars.'

'What do you think?'

He shook his head violently. 'I don't know, I don't know. I am Milan, very old man. I know nothing. Only that people are dying, and my son and his missus, they are dying in the cottage and no one will come to them.'

'No one? That's not like Waipu. They take care of each other.' For in spite of her circumstances, she knew this to be true. Nobody need perish untended, if they asked for help.

He shook his head again. 'Mebbe, mebbe they come, Miss. But me, Milan, I do not know who to ask. I thought, mebbe, Miss, that you come to help them.'

'I would not know what to do. I know nothing of this illness.'

'Very hot. Great fever. All over the country, people, pakehas, Maoris, my own people, they all die. There is no time to bury the dead and nobody want to bury them . . . Except . . .' He stopped, and gave her a crafty look.

'Except what?'

'Eh? Oh, I tell you, Miss,' and she knew he was changing his tack, 'the heat so great people jump into the river to cool off and then they sicker than before. My daughter by marriage is so sick and I have to hold her, stop this mad jump into the river. My son, I think he will die, and I cannot stop her jump on my own. I come here while she sleeps a little.'

Maria's head was spinning. She stood with her hand on the bannister of her steep staircase, considering what to do. She could still take flight to her room upstairs and barricade herself in until Milan went away. That was what she would like. It would be safer up there. The world could not get to her unless they came and burned down the house and smoked her out.

And why her? Did he know something about her which she imagined forgotten by now? Out there, who would still remember that the witch had once lain in the fields with a man who was not her countryman. Perhaps he knew; it was just possible.

By the fire the old man hunched himself forward. He turned his face towards her and she could see that he was ill too. So that was why he had come; the son and his wife would soon have no one to tend them at all, and he must find someone to replace him as their guardian as quickly as he could. She guessed it was already too late to protect herself from what lay outside, and that the fatal touch of illness had entered her house as quickly as she had learned of its existence. But she was reassured to know that his need was desperate and real, and not contrived around some aspect of her past.

His whole skull was shining, waxen-skinned in the light, and his eyes had receded into his head. He spoke with tremendous effort. 'What if she takes the bubba in the river with her?'

'There is a child?'

'Yes.' He looked as if he might topple forward on her hearth.

'I'll get my cloak.' She took it from its peg behind the door. 'Come now, you must tell me where I'll find these people.'

'You won't find them, it is too hard.' His breath came in short panting gasps as he staggered to his feet.

'You're too ill for this. I know these parts. It is near the river? Yes. In trees? Near the sea?'

'Not far. Among trees. Near the river.'

'I'll find it.'

'Promise you will go to them?'

'I give you my word. Now stay by the fire, keep warm.'

She was casting round in her head trying to think how to equip herself to deal with a dying family. She collected two blankets from the cupboard under the stairs and a towel, filled the billy with tea, and with a last despairing look around her, set forth towards the unknown.

When she walked out of sight of her house, little appeared to have changed. In the half-light every blade of grass and every tree, every stump from the old fires which had swept the land, every clump of toi-toi looked the same. Some things were larger, perhaps, and by the river the small wild rose was now slung in tangles over many bushes and the hawthorns loomed taller than her, spiked and glowing with berries. She came upon a lemon tree laden with winter fruit and marvelled that such bounty lay so close to her without her knowing it. From downriver the sound of bagpipes wafted but she could not see from where the sound came. Her heart turned over. She had told herself many times that the silences in her head were amply filled by birdsong and the wind in the trees, but hearing this nearly forgotten sound reminded her that she missed many things.

For a moment she was tempted to keep on walking towards the bagpipes. She could get help for the stricken family, and when she had done that she would board a coastal steamer and sail away to Auckland, just as she had once planned when she was a girl. At the time of Branco.

She shook her head to clear away this image. The old man had brought too much back in a few painful minutes. She hurried on. It was almost fully dark. The trees loomed ahead in the gloom and again she remembered them as a patch of low-growing young ground cover. Everything was still around the trees and it was only when she was nearly upon the cottage that she saw a chimney and the edge of a roof. As she approached a dog began to bark with violent, angry yaps.

There was a path leading through the trees and she followed it to a very small and almost derelict cottage. Although the building was tumbledown it was not the one she remembered, and she supposed it had been built as a temporary dwelling, as Branco's shelter had been. But the dog, a yellow and black mongrel, was springing at her, its teeth bared as it aimed at her throat. It was tied by a rope to a tree and as she stepped off the path to avoid it she tripped and fell on a branch, grazing her leg.

There was no sign of life and it occurred to her that the people inside might already be dead. Or that this was an elaborate plan to lure her into a place of punishment for all her past sins.

The dog stood across her path, barring her way back. Its territory seemed to have grown larger. She doubted that she could pass it again.

The door swung open at her touch and the stench of illness and human excrement came out to meet her in a wave. She felt as if it would drown her. Yet nothing was out of place in the room. In the open fireplace stood two polished pots. The hard-packed earth floor had been swept. She could see this by the light of a candle flickering on a table.

Maria gingerly pushed aside a curtain which hung across one side of the room. On a wooden slatted bed covered by a thin mattress lay three people. Her eyes were becoming accustomed to the gloom, and as she held the candle above the bed she was able to see that it was a man, a woman and a small girl. The woman's eyes stared back, her face ravaged and exhausted with the aftermath of high fever. The man lay on his side with his knees drawn up under his chin. In his hand he held an empty cup.

The candle guttered in its tin lid, very close to the end of its wick. Now she held it over the woman and the child. The girl stirred, stretched, and looked at her. Maria saw that she was a healthy child with normal breathing. She drew a sharp breath herself. No wonder Milan had been so desperate to find someone. He had hope for the child, left in the midst of death.

'Hullo,' said the child.

'Hullo,' said Maria, startled.

'Mummy and Daddy are sick.'

'I can see that,' said Maria, putting out her hand with care, afraid that she would frighten the girl. But she responded, accepting Maria's grip and sat up. Beside them, the woman's breathing was shallow.

'Who are you?' the woman asked in a hoarse whisper.

'Maria McClure. I live in the old house not far from here.'

The information did not seem important to the woman. Perhaps she already knew.

'I didn't expect you to speak English,' said Maria. A warning bell sounded in her head. It was a long time since she and Branco had tried to converse. Truly, another century. Maybe things had changed.

'I'm not a Dally,' said the woman. She turned her head to the wall. 'My name's Hoana.'

Maria looked round desperately for another candle. Without one, she was lost. If she was not already. She disengaged her hand from the child's and went in search. Fumbling in a rough cupboard under a stand for the water basin, her hand closed around what she was looking for. She lit one candle from the other, and pushed the fresh one down in the stub of melted wax.

With light flaring round them again she returned to the bed. Hoana said nothing, but Maria could see that she was indeed Maori, or descended from Maoris.

The woman's proximity alarmed her. She had never been so close to a Maori before. But there was no time for reflection or wonder. 'What's your name?' she asked, turning to the child.

'Christie,' said the little girl and held up her arms to Maria. Maria lifted her over the body of her father and placing her on the chair, wrapped a blanket around her.

The man had soiled himself as he died and the smell which had assailed her when she entered the cottage filled her nostrils as she pulled the blankets back. The woman looked at her impassively. Trying not to breathe in, Maria leaned over and touched her forehead. It was unexpectedly cool and dry.

In her head Maria had been wrestling with the possible illnesses which might have laid siege to the countryside in the way Milan had described. Typhoid was the only plague she knew of that moved fast and killed many people at once. But this was not typhoid and whatever it was, although the woman was very ill and weak, the worst of it had passed.

'It won't be long,' Hoana whispered.

'Nonsense,' snapped Maria, surprised at her own briskness. 'If you can get onto your feet I'll clean up here and put you back to bed. You'll get your strength back.'

'What do you know?' The woman's lips barely formed the words but there was sudden hope in her eyes. She looked towards her husband and crossed herself.

Maria shivered again. She was touching papists. There is no God, she reminded herself. But she wondered what Annie would have made of it, all the same.

Hoana was on her hands and knees on the bed, trying to raise herself. Sh slid one foot over the edge and placed it gingerly on the floor but her weight held.

'Good, good, keep the blanket over you. Now sit down. By Christie, that's right. You've got to get better. She needs someone to look after her.'

A ghost of a smile hovered on Hoana's face. 'She's a good girl, aren't you?' She put her arm around the child with the surprising and familiar name.

Maria had filled the bowl with water from the bucket. It was cold, but it would have to do. She wondered if she should have made the fire up first, but it was impossible to think of everything with the body and the smell in the room. Although Hoana was, for the moment, willing herself to survive she could sink away again. Maria believed it was possible for her to recover, but her strength was fragile. Already she was slipping sideways in the chair.

She worked with a fierce possessed energy. Her stomach kept heaving to the roof of her mouth as she cleaned the body, but it forced her to work faster, emptying the basin outside, over and over again, and refilling it with fresh water. Finally, when the body was clean she wrapped it in a blanket, rolling it from side to side, pinned the cloth with safety pins and pushed the man onto the floor. The body was very heavy, for the husband had been a well-built young man with great muscles in his shoulders. He fell with a sickening bump and Hoana winced and softly moaned.

Maria wondered what to do with him next. She could not put the body outside for fear the dog would break loose. Every now and then it howled at the butter-nut moon that shone through the window. The child was observing everything she did with solemn dark eyes; she thought, that is the child's father I am rolling around like a sack of grain on the dirt. With an effort she heaved the body over twice so that it lay against the window. She considered putting another blanket over him, but the whole bed was soiled and there were only the two blankets left that she had brought with her.

She stripped the bed down and washed all the exposed wood, then made it up with a fresh cotton sheet that Hoana had indicated in a wooden apple box. These directions were their only conversation. Maria knew that if she stopped she might not be able to do much more, for this effort of lifting the body had been greater than she realised. Her back and shoulders were stiffening painfully already.

The child appeared to have slipped into a doze against its mother. 'Get back into bed and I'll sponge you,' Maria directed Hoana. The mother nodded but did not move.

'I'll hold Christie,' said Maria. She picked up the sleeping child, cradling her in her arms. She smelt sweet and musky at the same time and her hair was silky under her hand. Like mine used to be, Maria thought with sudden wonder, except that this child's was black. Asleep, the little girl appeared to have grown flushed since Maria's arrival. Her skin, though dark, was much fairer than her mother's, and colour like that of a tea-rose had settled on her cheeks. Maria supposed that this was how children were, up one moment and down the next. She watched Hoana move back to the bed and noticed she was lame, her left foot bent slightly inwards.

When the blankets were drawn up again, Maria put Christie alongside of her mother. Hoana lay against the pillows watching as she made up the fire. There was an ample supply of firewood at the back door. Now she could warm water to bathe Hoana, and make fresh tea.

'I'll bring you soup in the morning.'

Hoana wrinkled her nose with a look of disgust.

'No, look, you must eat,' said Maria. 'In the morning, you must try something. Tonight you should drink plenty of water.'

She was sure that that was what Annie or Isabella would have said. Especially Isabella. Maria had a strange feeling that she was there in the room with her. Her strength had come from somewhere and it was easy, at this moment, to summon Isabella up before her, the downy-faced old woman with the strange, sharp eyes.

In the bed, Christie rolled over, stuffing her fist into her mouth, then pulled it out again so that she could sneeze. Hoana touched her forehead and looked at Maria.

'I think she's got it too,' she said.

Maria put her hand out to touch the child and could feel the trembling of the other woman as their hands met. The little girl's forehead flared with temperature.

'You've got a warm house?' Hoana asked.

'Yes. Warm and dry. Very comfortable.'

'Take her with you. I'm too weak to look after her.'

'But I'll stay here with you.'

'Yes, I know you would. I can see you're very kind. But I've got nothing for her here, and this place will get draughty as the night goes on. Please.'

'But what about you?'

Hoana nodded, as if convincing herself. 'I'll be all right, I'm going to get better. I'll come and get her as soon as I'm strong enough.' Her eyes pleaded. 'My husband and I thought we could look after each other but look what happened. What if I fall, or can't get to her? My feet are not strong even when I am well. Please, I don't want her to go, can't you see that? But it's best for her.'

Maria remembered how she had parted from Jamie, how setting him free had seemed the best thing to do. And how, although it had not worked out for the best, it was all she had been able to think of.

This would only be for a day or so. She supposed she must take a chance.

'I'll take her, of course, if that's what you want,' she said, 'but I don't like leaving you here alone.' She was going to say with the body, but it came to her in a flash that that was just what Hoana did want, and that she was torn between her child and what remained of her husband.

'If Christie is with me I won't be able to come back in the morning.'

'Toma's family will come in the morning. His brother lives at the Heads, but he knows we're here.'

Toma must have been the husband. Maria was ashamed that she had not asked more about him. Hoana had not mentioned Milan. Thinking of the old man, Maria guessed that she might have another body at her house.

'I'll see that someone comes to help you.' She looked down at the sleeping child. 'How old is Christie?'

'Three last April. She's small for her age, but she's forward. Go to the drawers there. You'll find her papers in the top one.'

'I don't need her papers,' Maria protested.

'You should have them. Just in case. Take them.'

Hoana seemed in an odd way to have taken charge of the situation. Maria collected the little sheaf of papers from the drawer. It was as though she was in a dream. For a moment she stood uncertainly, but Hoana's eyes were unwavering. She gathered Christie into her arms, wrapping her in a curtain she had found in the apple box. It seemed almost as if Hoana was giving her the child.

'Why did you call her Christie?' Maria asked.

'Why not?'

'It is more usually reserved for a boy.' She could hear herself sounding like a schoolmarm.

'It is Christina in full,' Hoana's voice was resentful.

Maria hurried to repair her mistake, thinking that she might not let her take Christie after all.

'It's pretty. It is just a name I am familiar with. My people often use it. I am Gaelic.'

Hoana smiled. 'We couldn't make up our minds, argued like no one's business. Dally or Maori. They reckon my grandfather was some sort of a Scotchman, or great-grandfather or something. So we settled for that. Saved any more arguments.'

'You didn't know him? Your grandfather? Or great-grandfather,' she corrected herself, as Hoana puckered her forehead.

'Nup. Nobody did. Devil probably ran off. Pakeha trick.'

Pakeha. Maria rolled the word around in her head. She knew that was what the Maoris called Europeans, but she had never heard it applied like this before.

'I'm a pakeha,' she said.

'Yep. Well. You've got to take what's going, don't you?' Again the faint smile, but Hoana was very tired. 'Take her away now. Please. Quick.'

As Maria walked out the door, she said, 'I'll come and get her. As soon as I can.' She looked at the wall, away from their departure. Outside the dog growled but lay still, smelling the familiar child.

Christie slept all the way home. Once inside the house, Maria laid her on the couch near the fire which was almost out. She banked it up and threw on wood; the reflection of flames leapt in the room and flickered on the child's pale coppery skin. On the path beyond the door her grandfather lay, not having wished to die in a strange woman's house.

Maria looked round, distracted. She had never had so much responsibility and it was hard to know what to do next. Christie's temperature was still high. She must keep her warm, but not too much; she would sponge her through the night, she decided. But how could she leave a body on her doorstep?

After a while she went upstairs and taking a pillow slip tied it to a length of kindling wood. She opened the window of her old room and put the stick out the window then jammed it back on the end as tight as she could, so that it stuck out at right angles from the house, a white flag fluttering in the night breeze.

Tomorrow, they would take Milan away.

Maria sat and watched Christie. The little girl slept deeply for the most part, half waking occasionally to snuffle and clear her nose. From time to time she stirred as if in a dream, and once she chuckled out loud without waking. Maria was entranced by the small, sculptured features. She stroked the girl's cheek with her finger, at first tentatively, then regularly and gently. When her hand appeared out of the blankets as she turned it over, Maria picked it up and the small fingers closed around hers. Christie slept on, maintaining her grasp of Maria's hand.

Then, across the paddocks, the voices came stalking her. They moved across the glittering grass and rose above the sound of the morepork.

'Go away,' said Maria, 'I've had enough of you.' But still they came, the words etched in her brain, repeating themselves.

'I take up my pen after the space of some years. It has become more and more difficult to put down things as they happen. Since the death of my son Duncan Cave at sea there have been times when there have just been great empty blanks on the page, as there have been in my life. Oh, I have gone on living my life in an even kind of way on the surface,

249

as though I had come to terms with loss as old people often will. And I am frequently amused by things in spite of myself; the absurdities and carry-ons of my surviving children cannot escape notice and so I have put it all down, a kind of record. The truth is, though, that I often think of casting myself into the sea and drifting out to some great oblivion where I need not ever think of my life and what has passed within it.

'But I am prevented by a random thought that sooner or later there will be an event which will have made it worth holding on.

'And now there is this letter from Martha McWhirtle. I have often thought of Martha, and also her mother Kate, of her many kindnesses, her faith in me, and her constancy, and then I recall the abiding love those two women had for each other. They were women of spirit, and McLeod broke their spirits. In the end, I believe I will think of him as wicked.

'But what of this letter? It bears such strange news. Martha would not lie to me. Could it be possible? Where is this other one?'

'Leave me alone,' shouted Maria, waving her arms above her head. It was round four in the morning and she was stiff and cold in her chair. She shook herself. The fire was dead. In fear she looked at Christie, reproaching herself for having gone to sleep. The child was peaceful, but her hand which had slipped out of Maria's felt cold. She gathered her up again in her arms and carried her upstairs to her bedroom where she placed her in the feather bed. She loosened her dress and crept in beside her.

Through her window a banner of clouds scudded across the waning moon so that it appeared to be rolling over. With her arms around Christie, she thought she had never known greater happiness. And she was strong enough, she was sure, to keep the voices at bay.

When next she woke it was to the voices of people outside, and banging at the door. Christie was already awake and sitting up in bed.

'Where's my mummy?' the child asked.

'She's at your house, Christie,' Maria said, feeling the child's face. Her temperature was down, and it appeared that she had little more than a childish cold. 'Your mummy is having a rest and soon she'll come for you.' Christie nodded, satisfied for the moment. The banging downstairs began again.

'I want you to stay here for now. I'll bring you your breakfast soon.'

Hastily she pushed the hair off her face and straightened her dress, glancing in the mirror as she did so. What she saw didn't please her greatly. She looked dishevelled and old, and blue shadows smudged beneath her eyes and far down her cheeks.

When she opened the door three men were standing on the pathway.

They all turned to stare, without speaking at first. One of them was William McIssac.

'Why did you call us?' asked William at last.

She looked behind them. Where she had left Milan lying on the path, covered by a blanket, there was nothing, not even an imprint to suggest that he had been there.

'There was a man here,' she whispered. 'A body.' She tried to indicate where he had lain. 'It was nothing to do with me,' she said, reading their faces. 'A man called Milan, I think he had 'flu. His son died of it last night and his daughter-in-law is still sick. She needs help.'

'Where are these people?'

'In the cottage by the river. But where is Milan? You've taken him already?'

'There wasn't a body here,' said William. He looked around the circle of faces.

One of his companions stepped forward. 'Miss McClure. Maria,' he began awkwardly. 'I'm Neil.' She tried to recall him, as she had once wrestled with William's image. Neil's hair had gone white and he was a fairer, leaner man than his brother.

'Greetings, cousin.'

'Maria, we have been to that cottage this morning. There's 'flu everywhere, and we've been checking on families in the neighbourhood, that's how we saw your flag. We thought you must be ill too and came straight away. But we didn't see a body out here.'

He looked at her more kindly than the others. 'There was no one at the cottage either. It was empty.'

'There must be.' Again she described the circumstances in which she had found the couple.

'There was no one,' William repeated.

'A dog?'

'No. There wasn't a dog.'

'I lit a fire, and left the woman in bed. She was very weak.'

'The fireplace was warm,' said the third man grudgingly. He was thin and balding and looked uneasily around him. He and William seemed to edge together uncertainly.

'Why didn't you come for help straight away if all these people were so sick?' William's face and manner were scornful.

She drew her hand across her face. Could she have dreamed it all? Had nothing happened at all in the night? They would be pleased that she was, at last, seen to be truly crazy. Then she remembered the warm child in the bed. Perhaps it would be better, easier for them all, if in fact it was a dream.

'Surely this was a desperate situation?' William persisted.

I am on trial here, she thought. Already judged; they will soon take me with them, hang me from the macrocarpa tree. She began to back away.

'Or didn't it matter much? A few more bodies makes no difference here or there, is that it? Heh? A vision in your sleep of a few more to add to your list? Well, I am sorry to disappoint you, but this time —'

'That's enough,' said Neil, cutting across his brother. 'Let her speak.'

Her throat was constricted. If William and the third man were intent on harming her, then who would look after Christie? If Christie existed. She glanced back over her shoulder. She had not been going to tell whoever came of Christie's presence in the house. She had planned, as she sat by the fire the evening before, to keep her there until Hoana came to collect her. Now it seemed there was no Hoana.

'I could not come,' she said, after a moment had passed, 'because of the child. The mother gave me her baby.'

The men looked at each other again and even Neil, who had seemed intent on defending her, was wary.

'So where is this baby now? Gone too?' asked William. Even as he spoke, his face puckered oddly.

'Maria,' said Christie behind her.

She wheeled around, almost as surprised as they were, though more because she had not expected Christie to have learned her name so quickly.

Maria opened her arms and the little girl, trailing a blanket, rushed into them, afraid of the men standing across the doorway.

'There were three people, and this child,' said Maria evenly, in command of herself again. 'I saw the father and the grandfather dead. The mother was alive and should have recovered with nursing.' She explained how Hoana and she had thought the baby might be ill too, and how she had insisted on her taking Christie.

'What can you expect, these Maoris,' the third man said. 'They run off and leave their children with anyone who'll take them.'

'That's not true,' said Maria. 'She's coming for her.'

'Did she tell you she was scarpering in the night?'

'I—I don't know about that. She said her husband's family would come. They must have taken their dead.'

'I've no idea who'll bury them,' said William morosely. 'Milan was the gravedigger.'

'Who's going to bury anyone at this rate?' said the third man. He turned to Maria. 'They're laid out in rows in the churches all over the country, waiting to be buried.'

'Shall we take the child into the centre for you?' asked Neil, meaning to the village.

'No thank you,' said Maria after a moment's hesitation. 'No, I know the mother will come. It will be all right.'

'Well...my wife could care for the little girl for a few days until the mother... until she arrives,' said Neil.

As Maria shook her head, Christie tucked her face into her neck. Oh such sweet pressure, such gentle breath against my throat, sang her heart. I must not let them take her away. I must be calm and restrained as if I am simply helping out, I should not let them see that it is of any importance. 'I can manage, I assure you. I may need some extra things sent from the store, that's all.'

'I'll see to it. Just put what you want in your list at the gate,' said Neil. He looked at the two of them holding onto each other. 'She seems to like you.'

William and the third man were already heading for their horses. When William had mounted, he looked down at Maria. His tone was still unfriendly. 'Good luck, you'll need it. She's probably half way to Auckland this morning.'

Maria's heart turned over. She hoped Hoana was well and safe. But she also hoped that as the men had predicted, she would never return.

She smiled over Christie's head at Neil. 'Thank you for your help cousin,' she said, and hoped as she closed the door that her voice had sounded suitably under control.

After a year and a half had passed Christie could talk in full sentences about a variety of subjects, count to five and draw pictures of birds and flowers.

Sometimes she called Maria by name, other times she forgot and called her Mum. She did not ask what had become of her mother and seemed content for the days to slide past, allowing things to happen without question. If she was lonely she did not show it. Soon Maria would have to think about school. She did not know how schools operated these days but she saw children walk past along the dusty red road with satchels on their backs and return in the afternoon. She assumed that was where they were going. Some of the children looked not much older than Christie. It was too young, she was sure, and dreaded the time when she would have to part with her for even a small part of each day.

At her gate a variety of goods had started arriving, some that she would not have thought to order herself. There was a doll one day and an abacus another, a tin of malt in the groceries and occasionally a bag of sweets. She sent a note back the first time or two, asking how much she owed. By return, a note said that the account was paid in full.

In the second spring four yards of gingham arrived, and three colours of ribbon. She was pleased with these items, and made the gingham into two small frocks. Christie was delighted and stood for a long time admiring herself. Maria combed out her hair which fell in long curls past her shoulders now, and tied blue ribbon in it. It is a shame that no one can see her but me, she thought. It would be more than school that she would have to consider. Soon, for the child's sake, she would have to return to the world.

This was hard to imagine after so many years of solitude. Not that the last year had felt like that. Still, she wanted to take one thing at a time. It seemed foolish to rush. She had considered going with Christie on walks away from the house, but there was plenty of space around them. It felt safer close to home. They could sit on the riverbank and watch the ducks swimming, or the eels which flicked this way and that just below the surface. There were birds to observe, which afforded Christie constant pleasure, and there was the garden to be looked after. Christie laboured behind Maria with a small wooden pail which Maria had made for her, carrying piles of dirt from one place to another or, more helpfully, collecting weeds and placing them on the pile by the fence. On wet days she stayed inside and made shapes out of dough left over from Maria's cooking. They put them in the oven with the bread, and ate them with the other food when it came out.

Christie's only difficulty was in sleeping on her own at night. It seemed to hold some special terror for her which did not arise if she shared Maria's bed. Although Maria encouraged her to sleep on her own, Christie was adamant that she could not, and secretly Maria was happy with the arrangement. The child would settle so long as she had Maria's promise that she would soon come up the stairs and get in beside her.

One evening in the high summer of that second year, as Maria was tucking the covers round Christie, she found herself saying, 'Oh my darling, I love you so much.'

The child looked at her gravely. 'I know,' she said. 'I love you so much too, Maria.'

Downstairs Maria took up some knitting. She must plan ahead for Christie's winter clothes and think about getting her shoes. The air was very still; she thought she heard children laughing. She went to the window. Without a doubt it was laughing that she could hear, and singing too. It came from behind the house and away in the direction of the sea, towards the cottage where she had found the child. She had not thought of the cottage for months.

The singing went on late into the night and she stood listening for a long time until she heard Christie calling out. She looked up and saw the child standing sound asleep at the top of the stairs.

'Stay there, Christie, don't move,' she cried. Her feet were winged. She was two steps away when Christie took the first step forward.

Lying beside her later Maria felt herself shivering. Such a close escape! The harm that might have befallen her was too terrible to contemplate.

The sound of the singing was still in her head as she went to sleep. In the middle of the night she woke, sweating and fearful.

In the morning when they were dressed she saw many people advancing over the paddock towards the house. They were dark people, and they were led by a woman who limped.

It was Hoana.

Maria stood in her garden waiting for them. Christie tugged at her skirts. 'Who are they?' she asked.

'It is your mother come for you,' said Maria.

'You are my mother.'

'For a while, my darling, I was for a little while.'

'Must I go with her?'

The people had come closer. Some of them looked at Maria with suspicion but Hoana, despite her awkward gait, walked steadily on. The garden was full of light.

'You'll be happy when you're with her,' said Maria.

'I'm happy now,' said the child.

'You'll be happy again,' said Maria.

She took Christie's hand and began walking towards Hoana. The two women stopped on either side of the gate. Hoana's friends fell in behind her. They were still, but tension rippled among them.

'I had pleurisy, they thought I might die,' said Hoana. 'I was taken away up north to my own family until I got better.'

'I understand,' said Maria. Christie's hand tightened in hers. This parting must be swift. 'I'll get Christie's things. She has some clothes and toys.'

'We'll pay for them,' said Hoana.

'Very well,' Maria answered. She could say: It is better as a business deal, that will make you feel better about taking her away. But it seemed implicit in her acceptance. Hoana counted out five battered pound notes into her hand.

'Is that enough?' Hoana asked.

'It will do,' said Maria, as if she was considering the amount. 'Christie, wait with your mother and talk to her, meet your family.'

Inside, she took an old patchwork bag that had belonged to her own mother, hoping that it would hold as she stuffed Christie's clothes into it. There did not look to be so many after all. Then she remembered that she must collect up the papers Hoana had given her at the cottage.

Suddenly her legs would not support her. She sat down on the bed and looked out the window, down to the gathering in the paddock. Christie was being passed from one person to another, and already she could see that she was laughing. Even if Maria was in a hurry, they were not.

Getting to her feet and clutching the bed-head, she made her way to the drawers at the bottom of the dresser and felt around beneath her mother's clothes. Books, the journals, letters, Christie's papers.

255

She crouched on the floor, rocking on her heels. She had never opened the papers. Once or twice she had thought that she should, and in April she nearly had, to find out the exact date of Christie's birthday. But to look at them would have been to remind herself of Christie's other life which she had not wanted to consider. Instead, she had made up a birthday for her, announcing it one morning. It had been a special day of treats.

Now her hand hesitated over the papers.

But she knew that it was not only the papers.

She knew that there were secrets which it would be easier not to know. Voices were everywhere in the room now. Squatting there, her long skirts drawn up over her knees, she felt old again, and foolish. That she could have believed the child was hers! And yet were they not tied to each other?

It seemed now as if she had all the time in the world, and might never go down the stairs to the people below. There was something she could do, something she could find out. She opened not Christie's papers first, but the letter Martha McWhirtle had written to her grandmother, Isabella.

Coromandel, March 1870

Dear Isabella,

How often I have thought of you these past few years! I have missed your company so much. You may not think so from my long silence but things have not been easy. I expect you have heard that my dear mother passed away. I longed to return to Nova Scotia to see her one more time, but it was not to be. Such journeys we have made. Sometimes I ask myself, for what. We have done well here, my husband has worked in the mines, better than he worked in the past, he was never really a farming man; we have afforded education for the children and a good roof over our heads. But to be so parted from those we love and ever held dear, well I ask myself, Isabella, if I had my time all over again, would I do the same things?

This is morbid talk, and I suppose I should tell you that I have not been so well myself. Nothing the doctor seems able to put his finger on, and at first I thought I was prone to mother's depression, but he says it is physical and the blood rather thin. I am sure I will improve but I cannot rest in my mind if I do not tell you something I have known for a long time.

When we left Waipu, you will recall that we took with us a young woman by the name of Riria whom Duncan Cave had introduced to me to help with the children. She was a fine person and I liked her very much. Shortly after we arrived in the Coromandel, I discovered she was to have a child.

At first I was very shocked but she assured me she was married to

256

the father. I asked her details of her marriage but she was very evasive. I think it was a *form* of marriage, dear Isabella, that is to say, not a Christian ritual such as you or I would have experienced, but I did not think that that was a matter which should concern me—you know how I shared your doubts about religion, indeed was an unbeliever in my youth, thanks to McLeod's treatment of my brother and the depth of hypocrisy I believed that sorry business uncovered; even now I am no better than a lukewarm Presbyterian practising for my children's sake. But a mystery remained, for Riria would not divulge the father's name to me, and gradually it dawned upon me that it might be a pakeha. I began to put two and two together. When her time was nearly due she said that her husband would come to her and I would meet him. About two months before her time, we had the news of Duncan Cave's death.

Isabella, you may wonder why I did not write to you, even then, and on reflection I think I was wrong not to have done so. At the time I did not know what to do. Riria went into a state of such profound grief and shock as I have never seen. Within a day or so she was in labour and, after a long and terrible time, when I thought we might lose her, she gave birth to a tiny boy. He was so small that I did not realise for some days that he had a deformed foot. Then I knew that what I had suspected all along was true, and you will no doubt have already deduced the same, that it was Duncan Cave's boy.

My husband took a dim view of all of this, I mean the birth and having extra mouths to feed without any work in return—you know how he is—and I was sore put to convince him that we should be patient with her. I suggested to her that her husband had been Duncan Cave and she did not answer me; she never told me yes or no. When the baby was grown, and stronger—and I must say he put on weight at a great speed, and picked up wonderfully within a month or so—she said she was making her way back to the Kaipara and her own people. I said to her, Riria, his grandmother might wish to see him. Again, she never came to the point of admitting that that was you. She said that he *was* being taken to his grandmother, meaning to her own mother.

I do not know what name he is registered under, but he was a fine child when he left here, and I thought you would wish to know what had happened. I am pleased to say that his foot was not too bad, not like his father's, and I expect it would strengthen up when he began walking. He would be twelve now, his birth date March 20, and as it has come round again, I think of him as I have done every year.

Isabella, forgive me this omission. I was afraid to meddle. Now I am afraid to die without telling you.

Yours, affectionately, Martha.

With this letter were several returned unopened from Isabella. The last was marked *deceased*.

Down below, the voices of Hoana and her family and friends were quieter, subdued as if they were waiting.

She turned over Christie's papers in her hands. It was of no consequence, whatever was there would make no difference. Or there might be no clue at all, the traces of the past having vanished already. She must go down.

But still she could not, because of the voices: her grandmother's, her mother's, the child she had had and lost. And now you are to lose this one, and you will never know if you do not take the chance to find out. She put her hands over her ears and opened the papers.

In the garden she handed over the bag to Hoana.

'There's not as much there as I thought,' she said. 'Here are some of the pounds back again.' She handed Hoana three of the notes.

Hoana looked disturbed. She understood that she would not be able to pay her dues this lightly.

'Thank you,' she said. Her voice was serious, as she put the money away in her pocket. 'You have the papers?'

Maria nodded. At that moment, Christie came bounding back to them, 'Maria, that's Nanny, and that's Auntie Ripeka, and Auntie Hine. What's an auntie, Maria?'

'You will have to ask your mother that,' said Maria. 'I think she can explain better than I can.'

'Why?'

'Because I never had an auntie,' said Maria, 'and now I think you're going to have a great many. That's something worth having. It's family, Christie.'

As she spoke, she handed Hoana the papers. Hoana flicked her eyes over them ensuring that they were all there. Nodding, she sought a pocket large enough to contain them all. Maria knew that this was the moment. If she chose, she could bind Hoana and Christie and herself forever. If she chose.

Behind Hoana, the women rustled against the grass, dark, already drawing away. She could not see them moving, but she could feel it, as if they were being sucked away in the air.

'Well, if that is all,' she said.

'We're going now, Christie,' said Hoana. 'Say goodbye.'

For a moment Christie was poised towards her, her arms outstretched. Maria leaned and kissed her dryly on the cheek.

'Be good for your mother,' she said. The child drew back, bewildered, but before she had time to think about this rebuff an aunt had gathered her up.

'Thank you, then,' said Hoana.

Under her breath, Maria said, 'She must sleep with someone. She'll be lonely otherwise.' Only she couldn't be sure whether Hoana heard. Probably they would know this anyway, it was not for her to tell them.

She went inside before they were out of sight. It felt as if she hadn't slept for weeks. In her hand were two pound notes. Such pretence. As if Hoana had not known. What would she do with the money? She had never had money of her own, more than a few coins. Not that she could remember. Or had her Uncle Hector given her a sovereign once, when she was a child? She was too tired to think, and it didn't seem important. She put the money in the fire and watched it burn.

As she might have put the handful of papers that she had clung to all these years into the flames. Only they made a kind of sense. They added up to something. When they were matched and fitted together they made a whole. Completed a pattern, like knitting. Like Christie. It had been no surprise to Maria to find on the birth certificate Hoana's maiden name, linked back to the name MacQuarrie.

For hadn't she known it, from the moment when she first saw her walk across the earthen floor of the cottage?

Blood, that's what it was.

Running together, and through them.

But not even blood could hold people. You had to wait for them to come back.

And she had come at last to the end, the final entry.

'It is time to give up thinking of this other one. I am not even sure that he existed. He may simply have been the figment of a sick woman's imagination.

'I am tired of journals. There are enough secrets here to last several lifetimes. They are not, in themselves, secrets that will change the world, but they can make a world of difference. So there is nothing more to say. The event I hoped for has occurred, and what is left of my time I will spend with this girl, Maria.'

But grandmother, what of me now, now that you have run out on me?

Oh...you will just have to wait as best you can.

Yes. Yes, that is what I thought. You and mother, you were two of a kind after all.

It has taken you a long time to find that out, hasn't it?

You mean, I couldn't have done without either of you?

Well, what do you think?

So now I wait?

If that's what you think you should do.

Until she comes back? Yes, yes, I see. That's how it is. All right, I'll wait.

26

STELLA, WIFE OF Neil McIssac, was drinking tea in Maria's front room. She wore a loose jacket over a draped skirt that came only as far as her knee. On her head she wore a cloche hat and around her neck hung a long string of pearls. Maria could not take her eyes off these clothes. They were as strange as the machines that she saw lumbering past her door these days. At the gate stood Stella's own car, a gleaming new 1928 Ford.

Stella was a bright bird-like woman, anxious to please. 'Such pretty cups,' she enthused, holding up the china to the light.

'Thank you. Father bought them for mother. After a good season, I believe.'

How polite she sounded! But she could not think what to say next, although every time there was a pause Stella filled it, as if she had rehearsed for this possibility.

This time the silence swelled around them. The other woman put her cup down carefully on the table and drew a deep breath.

'Maria, we were wondering, Neil and I, if you would care to come to dinner with us next week.'

She sat bolt upright. The visit, which had been forced upon her, was one thing. Neil had shown consideration for her when others had not and if his wife felt impelled towards a charitable gesture, she supposed she must allow it. But this was too much.

She looked down at her own clothes, her rough hands, and at Stella's clothes again. 'I think I'm a little out of touch with polite living.'

'But Maria, we can't let you stay like this forever.'

Her eyes glanced around the room. Maria was aware of its worn appearance, the frayed curtain, the peeling varnish, the patches of ancient newspaper which had even crept down to where they sat as the wind had opened up more cracks. Her supply was nearly exhausted. Soon the wind would enter, or she would have to plaster the holes with dirt. At least her brass shone brightly, and with satisfaction she noted that there was not a speck of dust in sight.

'You can't really stop me, can you?' said Maria mildly, although a small panicky voice in her head asked if the house could have been disposed of without her knowing.

'No—o,' said Stella, 'of course not.'

She sighed with relief then, almost missing Stella's next remark.

'But we do feel that perhaps you have been treated unfairly. By history.' She smiled sweetly.

'We? Who is we? You and Neil?'

'Not just us, my dear. People we speak to. They would like you to come out of here.'

'I worry people?'

'They worry about you.'

Maria almost laughed out loud. 'No Stella, no. *I worry them.* That is different.'

Her visitor looked uncomfortable.

'It's very kind of you,' said Maria, getting to her feet. 'But thank you, no. I don't want to come to dinner. I don't want to leave this place.'

'Aren't you lonely? Since the little girl left?'

Maria gripped the back of a chair. She must not show this woman how she felt. Or whether she felt at all. To show her would be to remind herself of more than she cared to remember. As with the walls, the cracks were sealed over.

And so she concentrated on remaining calm, but she felt the floor slipping away from her. Her face flushed and an intolerable wave of heat swept over her. For a moment she thought she would fall.

Stella was looking at her with lively interest. 'Oh dear, it's the change,' she said. 'Such a nuisance, isn't it? We all get through it somehow or another. Look, are you sure about dinner...?'

Maria felt herself return. 'Quite sure.'

'We do feel you should, that it would be fair to us.' She cast around for inspiration. That you owe us, she might have said. The unspoken utterance hung between them.

'Because someone pays? I thought there was provision made for me. Has it run out?'

'No. No, truly, Maria dear, that is not what I meant. That is taken care of. You are our *relative*. You hide yourself from us.'

'It is they,' Maria said, 'who owe me my privacy. Never let them stop paying.' Stella stared, blinking with incomprehension. 'You have said that history has treated me unfairly. Let them live with the history that they've made. It's true, I'm part of it. McLeod's history.'

'You're too hard on the old people.'

'No, Stella. I am not hard. They are hard on themselves. I understand courage, truthfulness to a vision, the will to survive. Uprightness, care for the weak and the sick, these I understand as well as most people. But I have never understood what it means to worship a god who dictated with absolute authority one point view and word, who dealt rough justice without consideration of the evidence, or a god who maintained the superiority of men over women.'

261

'Maria, those are dreadful things to say!'

'Why? Do you accept them?'

'I—I don't really know.' Stella touched her dress uncertainly. 'I've been more fortunate that some,' she admitted. 'In some ways, Maria. But I never had children, you know.'

Her eyes were misty blue. They watered for a moment and she blinked, then was overcome with embarrassment as she remembered Maria's circumstances.

'What of William's children?' asked Maria, both to ease the situation and because she really did want to know. Stella's eyes widened now, so that she forgot her own discomfort. Maria could still surprise her.

'You never heard? None of them came back from the war.'

Maria nodded. 'I thought as much.'

'He must have told you?'

'We hardly know each other.' Maria hesitated. 'You've been kind, Stella. But I wonder who really sent you.'

'What do you mean?'

'Perhaps it's you who hasn't been told everything.'

'I know what they say about you.'

'But you thought it might not be true? Nobody could be so monstrous, eh?'

'You're not monstrous. And we saw what you did for the child. That was very Christian.'

Maria tried not to wince and smiled instead.

'Stella. Look around you. The old community doesn't hold up. Times have changed.'

'How can you say that?' Stella cried, stung. 'When you know nothing about it?'

'Believe me, I know more than you think. They will come to look on their history with new eyes. The good and the bad. I have heard of the monument that stands in the village. I've heard pipes playing across the river, and laughter at night when the air is still. New gaiety. New purpose, perhaps. Stella, look at you. You wouldn't turn back and you'll be glad when you leave here that you are not me. But I'll tell you a secret, cousin. At last I am glad to be myself. You see, I never intend to leave here. I'll stay here till I die.'

Stella was deeply shocked. 'You can't mean that,' she murmured, but she suspected that Maria did.

'I can. That is my wish. I have thought many times of leaving but it's not important to me any more. There is no reason why it should be important to anyone else—unless, just now and then, those who look this way catch a reflection in themselves of the things they most fear.'

Flustered, Stella asked, 'Shall I call again?'

Maria paused, surprised that she had to think about it. In spite of herself, she liked the busy little woman. She might be a trifle stupid, but she appeared to be without malice and it had cost her an effort to come. Then a vision arose of successions of good women, perhaps less agreeable than this one, pouncing on her and trying to persuade her back into the fold.

'I would be grateful if you did not come again,' Maria said. 'I have a great deal more to think about, you see.'

And all eternity in which to think of it, little bird. My dreams of flight, well, there had to be an end to them sooner or later, wouldn't you say? Facing the reality. But they were so delicious while they lasted. One gains through equanimity but there is also loss; the levelling of perception is like losing a sense. Like taste, perhaps, though the appreciation of pain is not so fine. It is replaced by a dull unsatisfied ache which the dream, abandoned, cannot remedy.

Oh, it is different for you. You have the power of flight, you must fly again, you can't stay here with me, however much I should like the company. . .and I did want for company. Not Stella or her friends, but stubbornly holding out for the one who never came. . .

In a year when the grass was so dry it appeared to be white, and stood out stalk by stalk on the cracked earth, when the cows near the fenceline hung their heads with their mouths open and their purple tongues were swollen with thirst, a van pulled up outside Maria's house.

A cheerful sign painted in curling letters on the side proclaimed it the property of the W.T. Rawleigh Co Ltd.

Ben Harrison had driven past this old house several times in his four-times-a-year coverage of his territory. He knew each dwelling, the catch on each gate; come to think of it, he knew the gates themselves, whether they swung open easily at the touch or sagged in the middle, or if you had to nurse them carefully over the ground so that the broken slats did not collapse altogether. Gates were a science in themselves, part of the job. Handling a gate was half the game when it came to getting through a door; you had to enter one before you made it past the second post. But then you made every post a winning post. Ben Harrison was something of a racing man and that came in handy on the job too, pick up a tip here, give a little there, surprising what you got to hear on your rounds. He knew that once you were through that door, and you had your black sample case open with its beautiful tight compartments containing all the little phials of medicine, the bottles and the tins, the essences and the spices, the Ready Relief for colds and the liniment, the Pleasant Relief for stomach aches, and the Ru-me-xol made from hoar-hound root for comforting rheumatics, that it was simply a matter of reading form. And the message he'd got about Maria McClure was, don't bother. You'd never get anything out of the witch.

So that her gate presented something of a challenge. But nothing tried, nothing gained, Ben always said, and it hadn't been much of a day. He was so parched he was buggered if he was going any further until he had a drink in him, and maybe the old girl might come across for a bit of ointment or something. You couldn't tell him that at her age she didn't get the odd thing wrong with her. Not that he knew how old she was, but pretty old, they said. Been there forever. Well forty years maybe, since she took to living on her own. Who knew for sure? She was the witch; you didn't count witch years like other folk's.

He thought there was no one there when he tried the door. The silence was tangible when he knocked. He could hear himself breathing and was surprised the way his heart raced. He was not the kind of chap to get frightened by all the creepy stories they fed you, fairy-tale stuff.

He pushed the door and it swung open before his hand, causing him to jump back as if he'd been taken by the throat. The woman was sitting in the half-light watching the door, as if expecting someone, or something, to come through it. She was quite still and she said nothing to relieve him of his fright. Just sat looking and watching.

'I was hoping for a drink, missus,' he said. It occurred to him that he had no idea whether she had ever been a married woman or not.

'Of course,' she said, getting to her feet, her long skirt sweeping the floor. Like a bleeding duchess, as he said afterwards when he was retelling the visit. Wallis Simpson didn't have nothing on her.

When he was sitting at the board table, scrupulously clean he noted, sipping the old woman's scalding tea and wishing it were a cold pint, he opened his case. He opened it slowly and casually, as if checking it out for his own benefit. Her eyes followed his hands.

'Ever tried our famous liniment?' asked Ben Harrison.

She shook her head.

'Take half a teaspoon in a tumbler of milk, it's like a drop of whisky. I tell you, I take it myself.'

'You do?'

'Keeps me ticking over,' he said proudly. 'Look at me, I never have a day's illness.' He was a plain, sandy-coloured man, but large and well built, and there was no doubt that he looked strong. 'Man or beast, you can take our products inside and out.'

'Really?'

He guessed she was passing time, like women in these out-of-the-way places sometimes did when he called, especially if they were short of money; yet there was a breathless, fascinated air about her exclamations that made him want to boast a little more.

'I sold some of that to Mrs Munroe last time I came round. She said it done her a power of good, her nerves were shot to pieces. You know

264

Mrs Munroe?'

'I'm not sure I do. Was that the Munro that went into Parliament?'

'Eh? I don't know about that, ma'am,' he said, thinking this a more appropriate way to address her.

'There was a Munro, John his name was, he was out with McLeod you know, but he followed the Man to New Zealand in the end, and ended up famous and going into Parliament. You'd have heard about him, surely?'

Ben pushed back his hat, which he had forgotten to take off in his discomfiture at finding the old woman looking at him like that. 'I don't recall,' he said. 'No, I don't reckon it was that lot.' After some deep reflection, he added, 'There's Munros and Munroes.'

'Aye, I suppose so.' She turned the bottle of liniment over in her hand.

'Munroe with an "e",' he said helpfully, wishing he could now take his leave. The old woman kept hanging onto his liniment. She was weird but he felt sorry for her, thinking she might be lonely. He wondered about leaving the liniment with her and writing it off as a sample. Though the Depression was still close on his heels, with the thought of all those bad debts and the people who had promised to pay and had not. The firm had had to get careful with what you left with people. You only gave away goodwill when you were certain of a return, and he hadn't really got used to times being easier. It certainly didn't look as if Miss Maria McClure was going to be much of a customer, either now or in the future.

'You wouldn't think of her having nerves,' he said, floundering now. 'Mrs Munroe?'

'That's the one.' Maria put the liniment down, but she was not finished in the black case. Her hand closed round a pot of lotion. 'Sweet clover?' she said, reading the label.

'For the complexion, ma'am. Gum of the quince seed squeezed into that. Give you skin like a baby's.'

Already she was unscrewing the top and he winced as she plunged her fingers into the soft creamy mixture. She hesitated, raising the swirl of lotion to her face and inhaling deeply before applying it in even sweeps. 'Oh, it smells so beautiful,' she smiled. 'Yes. Yes, it reminds me of children, Mr Rawleigh.'

'Er, Ben Harrison's the name.'

'Mr Rawleigh, Mr Harrison, what's in a name? Do you know what they call me?'

He was silent. He had taken his hat off now and sat looking at the band of sweat that his head had left inside the crown. Maria's hand was reaching out for a box of face powder.

'And what is the trouble with Mrs Munroe's nerves?' she asked. She caught him looking at her busy fingers. 'I am going to buy this, you know.' She held up the sweet clover lotion that was standing with its lid off.

'Oh. Oh, yes, ma'am, of course. You won't regret it.' And Ben Harrison was all smiles again. 'Mrs Munroe, well it's her son. Apple of her eye, Billie was. He's gone and run off with some gal that his ma doesn't approve of. Look, there is a little powder puff for that stuff, see, you pat it on your face, like so. The rachel would be best for your colouring if I may say so, ma'am, a nice warm touch of colour would match ideally.' And with an inexpert but enthusiastic hand he was patting the powder onto her upturned face. She sat quite still, as she had when he first entered, smiling slightly and seeming hardly to dare breathe at this human contact.

He stood back to admire his handiwork, fumbling in his back pocket at the same time. That was where he kept his wallet and a greasy comb and a little slab of mirror, for he was a man who liked to check out his appearance. The customers appreciated someone tidy in their looks, and so did the girls who served him his dinners and breakfasts in the boarding houses where he stayed in tiny country towns, and told him, late at night, how they would give anything for a one-way ticket to Auckland.

He held the mirror up for her to see herself. She nodded, pleased.

'I will take some of that.'

'A good buy.' He was getting into the swing of this now, almost enjoying himself, and he could see his sales quota filled without another visit that day. 'Rouge? Just a discreet touch, perhaps?'

'What is rouge?'

He took the little penny-shaped container and opened it up. The colour glowed like a jewel. He touched her cheek. 'A spot here, and there. All right now?'

'Yes. Oh yes, please.'

As he worked on her, he felt her deep relaxed breathing.

'What is this girl like, the one that Billie Munroe has run off with?'

'Eh?' He thought she had forgotten the neighbourhood gossip. 'Oh a Maori gal he met up with.'

'I cannot see what the difficulty is,' said Maria firmly.

'Well, no, got nothing against 'em myself,' said Ben. 'But you know how it is with some people. Well, I dunno, young Billie got fed up with the farm and took off for a bit, I guess that didn't please his folks too well, and he went working down in the hotels round Rotorua, there's plenty of work down there. He wrote up home to say he'd met this young lady, and how as he'd be bringing her home. His mother said no. Prejudice, I suppose you'd call it. You're quite right, ma'am, it's not a good thing.'

He stood back again, manoeuvring the mirror so that she could see herself.

'Funny, though, this young lady's family come from up this way a long time back. Cripple gal, the mother was, with a Dally name. They don't half get mixed up these days.'

'Cripple, you say?'

Suddenly Ben Harrison noticed that the hand on his sleeve was like a claw, and was afraid. 'Lipstick?' he asked shakily.

'Eh? Oh, whatever you say,' She seemed to be groping for something.

They were both trembling as he took the top off the lipstick case and began to draw a line around her mouth. When he was half done, she plucked at his hand for him to stop.

'What is it?' he gasped, certain that he was about to be overtaken by something dreadful.

'Was her mother, this girl's mother, a widow?'

'A widder woman? I don't know, missus,' he said, reverting to his earlier address, perhaps confused by the complexities of the married state. It was a condition he had never experienced. 'Yeah, maybe, I don't know much about it.'

'And the young lady's name?'

'I don't know,' he cried wildly, for now he was looking at the lined face full of pink and orange creases, so garish and excessive that he was ashamed.

'Christie? Was the girl's first name Christie?'

'Oh aye, I reckon it was something like that.'

'But you must remember.'

'Missus, I said, yeah, I reckon. I mean people tell me things, it's not for me to pass them on. Do I look like a gossiping man? No sir, I leave that to the ladies. Now, will that be all?'

'Yes. That will be all thank you.'

The magic was over. His pencil flicked over his pad, totting up sums.

'If this war comes, it will fix things,' he said to break the tension. 'Everybody'll be off to that, and a good thing too, I reckon. We could do with a war.'

'There is to be another war?' But she was not really listening to his reply.

'Ah, who knows? That'll be fifteen shillings and sixpence.' And he stripped the paper off the pad, planting it on the table in front of her.

She stared at him, an uncomprehending expression on her face.

'The money, that's how much.'

'I have no money,' she said.

'What? Oh jeez, I don't believe it.' He looked at the opened pots in front of him.

Now she began to understand what she had done. 'I'm sorry,' she gasped, rubbing at her face, as if she could give the sticky stuff that was on it back to him. He looked menacing in the dark kitchen where the afternoon light lay dying, though it was more that he was scared of how he was going to explain away all this stuff to his employers.

'If you go to the store,' she whispered at last, 'they will give you the money.'

'The store? You're joking.'

'No I am not,' she said, with sudden resolve. 'Didn't you know that that is where I obtain my credit? I thought everyone knew that.' She was imperious now, commanding him in such a way that he began to wonder why he should ever have doubted her. In a few minutes he was backing out the door, thanking her for her custom.

When he was outside her manner softened.

'Thank you,' he heard her say. 'Thank you, Mr Harrison.'

Glancing back, it seemed to him that she was pleased with the visit, that she was happier than when he came. But he thought of himself as an ordinary person, and he could not understand why this might be so. Safe in his van he hesitated. Perhaps the heat had got to him? He turned the vehicle around and pointed it in the direction of the store.

Maria shook her head at what she saw in the mirror and would have laughed except that her head was full of what she had heard. It was something to know that Christie was alive. She supposed that as Christie had grown older she had not been told of the strange woman she had once lived with, and that gradually the girl would have forgotten that she existed.

27

S OME WOULD SAY *you're afraid to fly out the window, my feathered friend, but I know better. You will when you're ready, I know. You've been taking your time, getting your strength together. How long's it been? A week? Well, it doesn't matter. You're an easy kind of guest. Undemanding, like the better ones have been. A touch to eat, a bit of warmth up near the rafters, and a sit in the sun over there on the ledge. You know now that I'm not going to hurt you, don't you?*

I wonder, will those lads come back? Rough louts, little bird, as McLeod would say. McLeod? What do I know of McLeod, bird? Sometimes it is as if I knew them all. All the old people. It is difficult to remember which were the real ones and which were the dreams. They are all voices in my head, running into one another.

I am not afraid of the dark.

Lately she had been dreaming that McLeod still watched her. It felt as if he had always been there, as if nothing in her life was not predestined by him. He was like a watchful father who had outlived his children. She had to remind herself when she woke that he was not even of her lifetime.

Yet it was McLeod who had ordained her life. She would have liked to make a statement about it, as Isabella had done, but she supposed that her life was her own statement. She would have liked to fill in the journal where Isabella had left off, but although she could still read she doubted her ability to write intelligibly any more. She was surprised that her deliveries from the shop arrived more or less according to order. What would her life have been if she had been an educated woman?

For in her head she was telling it. She was telling it how it was.

And what did it amount to? The sum total of her mother's life, and *her* mother's before that, and so on back through time, what they had all been—was this the sum total of her own life? And what had become of her? It was because of all of them, not just herself, that she lived alone in a narrow crumbling house with a pointed roof in a sunlit landscape.

She would have liked to have known, more exactly, what it all meant, but the years had passed and there had only been one further clue. It was a badly printed snapshot which faded almost immediately to the colour of the newspapers around it when she pinned it above her bed. The photograph was of a young woman wearing a broad-brimmed hat that framed her dark face. She held the arm of a fair man wearing a good suit. A note had come with it, delivered with the groceries, for Maria had no letterbox.

The note read: 'Miss McClure, you were kind to my niece, Christie, a long time back. I thought you might like to see this wedding picture of her and Billie Munroe. I don't know that his family were too pleased but they got married anyway, and now they are off to Australia for the time being, so must hope things work out for the best. She never did settle much with her own family, for which we were sorry, nor with her father's, but that's the way things go. This war is not much good is it, hard times for all of us. I hope you are keeping well. Sincerely, from Ripeka.'

Often in her dreams she would be talking to the dark young woman. She would be sitting on Maria's doorstep and they would be shelling peas into a pot together, chatting over a cup of tea, or digging the garden. Then it would take several minutes after she woke up to convince herself that it was a dream. If it had been true she knew she could have told the dark young woman everything that was on her mind, that together they would have worked things out.

As it was, she had her blurred face on the wall. Of course she had never really lost sight of it, but this image she could really touch, like an icon.

The garden no longer existed. The weeds had taken over until it looked like part of the paddock; the japonica bush was strung with long strands of moss and parts of it had died. But then she no longer foraged for food outside. Mostly these days she ate baked beans out of tins. She had learned of baked beans when new power poles went through to North River.

Two of the men who were installing the poles turned up on her doorstep one day. They had come to dig a new pit for her dunny, they said. They laughed when she asked what a dunny was, and blushed when they had to explain. She was pleased but puzzled. The long drop from the toilet seat to the earth at the back door had been getting shorter, and she had been worrying about how she could dig a new one as deep. It would have been easier when she was younger.

'Who sent you?' she asked, when they had been working for an hour or so.

They shrugged. 'The boss told us to do it,' one said.

'Who told the boss?'

They did not reply, but kept on digging. It was easier to accept than to pursue the matter. It was the same with wood which arrived unannounced in piles at her gate. She was grateful for that too, for it became harder to find any as the paddocks were cleared right back leaving shining grass where once there had been branches and the remains of the bush.

At lunchtime the man asked if they could heat their beans. She offered to make scones which they accepted but they still wanted their beans, would be grateful if she could do it for them, in fact. When they found her deciphering the instructions on the can they became nervous, as if she might cast a spell on them. One got a tin opener from his truck and showed her how to use it. When they had gone she scraped a tentative finger around the empty tin and licked it; the taste was delicious.

They hurried through their work and finished that afternoon. Although they waved when they were working at the roadside on other days, they did not come back to the house. One day, seeing a ball of fire rising skywards in the direction of the village, she hurried down to the road to ask them if the burn-offs were beginning again. They looked at each other and studied the blaze.

'Looks like someone's place might have gone up,' one of them said.

They threw their shovels on the back of their truck and left with a great flourish of tyres. They did not return until the next morning, when one of them called out to her as she stood outside shaking mats.

'It was the house that that old fellow McLeod used to live in,' he said. 'Went up like tinder. Nobody in it.'

'McLeod's? What about his things? His furniture?'

'Ah, gone long ago. Nothing there, just junk, paper, that kinda stuff. Place was falling down, it's better gone.' He picked up his shovel, spat on his hands and rubbed them together, and began to dig.

Once Maria walked towards the sea by the old route past where Hoana and Toma's cottage had stood. It was gone now, and there were definite changes in the landscape. The paddocks were much smoother, so neatly tailored, so sewn up with fences that she felt disorientated and hurried home.

More cars passed, machines flew overhead, women changed in their appearance several times over, men began wearing uniforms soon after the letter from Ripeka had arrived, and then they stopped wearing them altogether.

When she estimated that a little more than half the century had passed there was a large gathering in the village. So many cars passed, raising such clouds of dust, and the sound of the pipes was so insistent, that she went up to the hillock, supporting herself on a stick which had belonged to Isabella, and looked out towards the village centre. It was difficult to see much, but it appeared that there was a great celebration in progress amongst a field of tartan.

She thought back with care and reopened Isabella's journal that night. It was as she had remembered. The community had been there for a hundred years. A century had passed since the first of the six ships sailed from Nova Scotia to New Zealand, and land had been taken up at Waipu. It must be 1952 or thereabouts. She sat and poked pine cones onto the fire. It spluttered and hissed, flared up, illuminating the dark room. She did not need an open fire, for the evening was warm. But lately she had been feeling the cold. And it was company. Now who ever would have thought of her needing company?

'I am made of sterner stuff,' she said aloud. A tin of beans was open and she had put bread on to toast. She stared into the fire and the toast burned. She crumbled it in her fingers. The birds would eat it. They knew a feast when they found it. They would seek her out.

The children came a second time, again towards evening. She heard their voices, the long slow chanting refrain.

Ma-*ri*-a. Ma-*ri*-a.

I will stay inside here, I will not be drawn.

Ma-*ri*-a.

Outside, the sky the colour of anemones, a great bowl of purple and pink dusk. The air so clear. You could smell the sea tonight, the tang of salt and a lone gull, out late, wheeling back towards the water that stretched from Bream Head to Bream Tail. High Brynderwyn in the distance. Beyond the hillock, the flat plains of the Braigh where the best farms lay. The confluence of the rivers racing into the valleys. You could somehow draw it together in your hand, it was all so close. The beating heart of the people. If you placed your ear to the ground you could surely hear them.

Ma-ri*a*. The changing of emphasis, more urgency in their cry. A smash, a tinkle, as if the glass were falling out of the window, piece by piece.

They will not frighten me, they are only children.

There were three of them. They were not expecting her when she appeared on her stick in the doorway. Two were half way down what remained of the path. Their faces were raised towards her upper windows, their expressions mischievous, laughing. They looked so lively and full of enjoyment she could have laughed with them for a moment, if it had not been for the thought of cold air swirling up her stairs in the night.

The third boy was beside the door.

'Go on, Ross,' cried the taller of the two in the pathway. It was clear that he was the one who had to prove himself.

He stood transfixed with the door swung open, as if his feet would not shift for him. Maria reached out and caught him by the wrist. He shrieked and struggled in her grip. The laughter of his companions ebbed away.

'C'mon, Ross, let's go. She's only an old woman, don't be a weakling.'

The two of them were running, their tanned legs twinkling in the evening light as they raced away.

Maria knew she could not hold the boy and dropped his arm, expecting him to follow. Instead, he stood looking at her. He was different from the other two. Whereas they had been sandy-haired, fair-skinned boys, Ross had a nuggety copper face and an upturned nose. His mouth was wide and full and, just discernible across the bridge of his nose was a thick row of freckles. His eyes were brown, and very large and dark at their centre.

'Well, off you go. Aren't you going with your friends?'

He took two steps away from her. 'So you're the witch?'

'Who did you think I was? Are you new around here?'

He nodded. 'Are you really a witch?'

She saw that he had wide-spaced teeth, very white in his brown face. It was difficult to tell his race.

'What do you think?' For what could she tell this strange child on her doorstep? It felt like the beginning of another story.

She put her hand to her face and touched its downiness, the hair that had grown there in the last year or so. It was too late. He was only a curious child.

'What is your name?' she asked, certain that he would disappear at any moment. He looked quickly at the broken window.

'I'll fix it up, miss. Don't tell my father.' His voice was frightened.

'Fix it? Well, that will do. I don't want to get you into trouble. What did you say your name was?'

'Ross Munroe miss. I just come here about two weeks back.' He had an odd, twanging accent.

'Munroe, eh?' For a moment it did not register, but when it did, the shock was so powerful that her heart hurt. 'Where have you come from?'

His answer was lost in the rushing sound in her ears. She thought, dimly, that he may have said Australia, but she couldn't be sure. 'What is your mother's name?' she whispered.

'Jane, miss.' He was not looking at her, stubbing his toe backwards and forwards along the path and clearly wishing that he had followed his companions. She steadied herself. 'I see. Well. You'd better go along, hadn't you.'

'Yes, miss. Miss, my dad said I wasn't to hang round here. When he come back here to live, that's what he said.'

He turned, hesitant. 'Miss, she's my stepmother. My first mum died when I was real little. I don't remember her.'

'Yes, I see. That was unfortunate. But you like your new mother?'

'She's okay.'

'That's good, then.' She would have liked to give him something, but she couldn't think of anything that a boy of twelve or so might like.

Still he hung back. 'Can I come back some other time?'

'If you like,' she said. 'But you mustn't get yourself into trouble.'

'I'll be back. Fix the window. G'bye.'

And he was away, running down the path, glancing towards the hill

273

where his friends might or not be watching. So straight, she thought, not a sign of a limp. No blemishes. It was a myth that the mark was there forever. The generations were getting stronger. This boy had to be Christie's son, and yet in an odd sort of way it hardly mattered. He didn't look especially like anyone, except for the pale touch of copper in his skin. She sensed the vitality. He was his own person. A new kind of person, without allegiance to a particular group or race. He would make new choices.

'*Beannachd*, Ross,' she said, though he couldn't hear.

It does make sense, you know, she says to the bird. It always did. How could I ever have doubted it? It's nice to be right, though. Tsst tsst, come sit on my finger, there, we are friends, aren't we? And you know bird, he is coming back.

The pain had persisted for several hours. At first she thought: I can bear this, it is part of growing old. As it grew worse it occurred to her that she had been stubborn in the past and had suffered for it. She was suffering now. And I have so much to live for yet, she told the bird when she could breath. The pain surged up again. Oh. This. This is. So hard to bear.

She heaved herself out of bed. Holding the bedpost, she took the walking stick and with trembling hands peeled the pillowslip from her pillow. It was so thin it nearly fell apart in her hands. One knot. Over another. There, that should hold.

The catch had stiffened with the years. She pushed and pushed until it gave under her hands. The stick was now poised on the edge of the sill.

I have done it.

But the bed with the feather mattress seemed a long way away.

The window is open but the bird stays until morning. There are some crumbs to find by the early light. The sky looms, so big. Another bright day. The bird cannot resist, cannot wait longer for flight.